Dear Readers,

Welcome (or welcome back) to the world of the Sazi. *Howling Moon* is not the first book of the series to reach publication. It is, however, the book that started the world. Here, in the Boulder pack, is the *original* world of the Sazi.

The love story between Cat Turner and Raphael Ramirez began the world, many years ago. It's been so much a part of our consciousness that every book has hinted at this terrific story—there have been clues about the politics, the rage, and the anguish that the attack on Catherine Turner brought to many people. The reasons why it wasn't the first to publish are varied and many, but now it's time for this book to take center stage. The story is ready to be told.

But it wasn't easy! The Sazi world originally envisioned has changed quite a bit in the decade since the first idea formed. The time line, too, was difficult to manage. For regular readers, please note that the events in *Howling Moon* begin before *Hunter's Moon* (book one) and end after the events in *Moon's Web* (book two). It's our longest book to date, timewise—but we had to be certain the events (including the moon cycles) fit seamlessly.

We think our effort has paid off, and we know you'll enjoy *Howling Moon* as much as all of the other Sazi novels. Welcome (again) to the beginning of our world!

—Cathy Clamp & C. T. Adams
www.ciecatrunpubs.com

D0018165

HUNTER'S MOON

"I read the book in one sitting. A world this enjoyable deserves more than one visit. This book has some new twists in the were-wolf's tail that are very cool." —Laurell K. Hamilton

"This unusual, artfully constructed, and enticing blend of horror and romance will have wide appeal with its male point of view, intensely sexy love story, and caperlike action."
—*Booklist*

"This incredible novel is inventive, totally riveting, as well as surprisingly tender in spots. Adams and Clamp are a powerhouse team that has opened the door to an amazing new world."
—*Romantic Times BookReviews*
(Top Pick, 4½ stars)

"Filled with an abrasive charm, intriguing characters, and a dry wit, *Hunter's Moon* is a must read for the fall season."
—*Romance Reviews Today*

MOON'S WEB
Romantic Times BookReviews
Magazine's Best Werewolf Romance

"Adams and Clamp are adept at writing intensely sensuous, hot lovemaking scenes, but where they really shine is in the creation of an unforgettable world where secret shapeshifters live, love, and scheme. Laurell K. Hamilton readers will enjoy this edgy world." —*Booklist*

"It's only taken two books for the dynamic duo of Adams and Clamp to cement their position as premier authors of paranormal fiction. Gritty and unique, with amazingly Byzantine character development, this inside look at the unconventional world of shapeshifters is a page-turner in the truest sense."
—*Romantic Times BookReviews*
(4½ stars, Gold Medal Top Pick)

"It's rare when a second book surpasses the first, but *Moon's Web* explodes onto the scene, earning a Perfect 10. If you're a fan of Laurell K. Hamilton or Kelley Armstrong, *Moon's Web* is definitely a book for you!"   —*Romance Reviews Today*

"C. T. Adams and Cathy Clamp have outdone the wonderful job they did with *Hunter's Moon*! The action begins on the very first page and doesn't let up throughout the story."
                              —*Paranormal Romance Reviews*

PRAISE FOR THE WORLD OF THE THRALL

TOUCH OF EVIL

"Unveiling a new paranormal series, the brilliant team of Adams and Clamp crafts an exceedingly intriguing heroine trying to survive a dangerous and complex world. This is an unbeatably good paranormal!"
                              —*Romantic Times BookReviews*
                              ˙ (4 ½ stars, Top Pick)

"Adams and Clamp are adept at incorporating riveting plot twists into this fully imagined world, and they don't stint on the romance."   —*Booklist* (starred review)

"*Touch of Evil* receives *The Road to Romance* Reviewers' Choice Award for the great writing of the author duo, C. T. Adams and Cathy Clamp. This book has it all and more."
                              —*The Road to Romance*

"If readers are looking for a completely different kind of vampire story, then *Touch of Evil* by C. T. Adams and Cathy Clamp will more than satisfy the craving. What's even better? There are obviously many stories yet to be told about Katie and company."   —*Loves Romances*

Howling Moon

Howling Moon

**CATHY CLAMP
& C. T. ADAMS**

tor paranormal romance

A TOM DOHERTY ASSOCIATES BOOK
NEW YORK

This is a work of fiction. All the characters and events portrayed in this novel are either fictitious or are used fictitiously.

Copyright © 2007 by Cathy Clamp and C. T. Adams

HOWLING MOON

Edited by Anna Genoese

A Tor Book
Published by Tom Doherty Associates, LLC
175 Fifth Avenue
New York, NY 10010

www.tor.com

Tor® is a registered trademark of Tom Doherty Associates, LLC.

ISBN-13: 978-0-765-35402-0
ISBN-10: 0-765-35402-0

First Edition: January 2007

Printed in the United States of America

0 9 8 7 6 5 4 3 2 1

Dedication and Acknowledgments

As with all of our books we would like to dedicate this work first to James Adams and Don Clamp, along with the rest of our family and friends who have offered patience, kindness, and unswerving support throughout the years.

Any book is a group effort, and we want to take the time to specifically thank our wonderful agents, Merrilee Heifetz and Claire Reilly-Shapiro, who have helped us so much and so often. Thanks to our terrific editor, Anna Genoese, at Tor.

We would also like to take this opportunity to thank Yolanda Sfetsos for her help with all things Aussie, Jim and all the others, too many to name, who've answered questions or shown their support in so many ways.

Howling Moon

Chapter One

RAPHAEL'S HAND SLAPPED against his clock radio several times before he realized it was the phone ringing and not the alarm.

"Hullo?" The word into the receiver was muffled by warm pillow. He turned his face a bit and cracked open his eyes.

"Raphael, it's Charles."

Throwing off the sheets, he sat bolt upright in bed, trying desperately to jump-start his sleep-fogged brain into coherence. "Mr. Chief Justice!" Morning was *so* not his time of day and it was only, he glanced at the red numbers of the digital clock, 5:00 A.M.

Shit. The sun's not even up yet.

"I need a favor."

The head of all shapeshifters was asking *him* for a favor? Granted, they were shirttail relatives of a sort, but it wasn't a relationship either of them had ever presumed upon. Charles Wingate was not a casual man. If he said he needed a favor, he *needed* it.

Heart beating frantically, Raphael fought to keep his voice steady. "Of course, sir. What can I do for you?"

Running his left hand through his bed-mussed tangle of curls, Raphael swung his legs off of the bed and onto the carpeted floor so that he was at least *technically* up.

There was a long, awkward silence. "I'm not sure where to start."

That did not sound like the Chief Justice. There were so many nuances to his voice—anger, sadness, and the one emotion Raphael would never have expected: fear.

"Sir?"

The old man sighed deeply. "Someone has been trying to block my gift."

"Is that possible?" There was shock in his voice. Charles was the Sazi's best foresight seer. *Nobody* should be able to block his ability to see the future.

"Oh, it's possible. It isn't *easy*, but it is definitely possible." There was a heat to the words. Raphael almost felt sorry for whoever had done it, because sure as hell they were gonna pay, and pay dearly.

"Jack Simpson has done it again," continued Charles. "He attacked a woman and killed her parents." There was a pregnant pause. "The woman's name is Catherine Turner. She's my goddaughter."

Oh, fuck!

"The full moon is tonight." Raphael tried to keep his voice neutral. He failed. It was a little higher and breathier than usual. On the plus side, he wasn't groggy anymore.

"Yes, it is. And Catherine will be facing her first change."

"What do you need from me, sir?" Raphael was wary. He could guess where the conversation was leading, and it was nowhere he wanted to go.

"I just learned that Catherine is staying with her aunt, Violet Wildethorne, in Boulder."

"Right on our doorstep. I'll contact Lucas." Raphael began weighing options on the proper procedures to deal with the situation.

"No!" Charles said firmly, then he backpedaled a bit. "Please don't."

Blinking with shock and the sudden derailing of his thought process, the obvious question popped from his mouth. "Why not . . . sir?" The last word was an afterthought.

There was a long silence on the other end of the line. "Lucas would simply murder the woman." The Chief Justice's voice softened. "I'd rather avoid that if I can. She—" There was a catch in his voice when he continued. "She means a great deal to me."

"Sir." Raphael chose his words very carefully. "There's a good chance she won't survive. But if she does—"

A slight rustling over the phone said Charles was nodding. "She may go feral. And *if* she is feral, she will need to be put down. I understand that. But I don't believe she will be. Catherine has always been an exceptional woman." He sighed. "And there's something else you should know. Things could get complicated. I don't *think* the press have traced her to Boulder, but there is always the possibility they might have. You'll need to be careful how this is handled."

"The *press*?" Horror fought with anger in Raphael's mind. What in the hell was Charles trying to do, kill them all? Secrecy was the single greatest rule in the Sazi culture. Humans weren't aware of their existence only because they didn't allow the press to get wind of the reality of shapeshifters.

"Unfortunately so. Catherine was somewhat of a local celebrity in California in her twenties because her father was a leading computer hardware designer in Silicon Valley and she was a bit, well . . . *wild*. Things settled down while she was away at university. But when she became engaged after graduate school, there was a scandal involving her mother that got them interested in her again. Of course, when her parents were killed and she was mauled . . . well, I'm sure you can guess the rest. But Violet has always kept a low profile, so we might get lucky. She's a romance author who writes under a pen name, and nobody in California ever connected the two families. I realize this complicates things, but if at all possible, we need for Catherine to come through this alive."

Raphael took a deep breath. Wow. "Of course, sir. But I can't make any guarantees. Um . . . not to question your authority or your absolute right to send me on any mission you choose, sir, but are you certain that I'm the best person for this job? It's been a lot of years since I've taken on a case like this."

"I know, I know. Yes, you're the person best suited to this task. Trust me." Charles sounded tired, defeated. But beneath it all simmered rage. Raphael was very glad that he was in Boulder and the Chief Justice was wherever the hell he was. "Get a pen. I'll give you the information."

It took a minute of rummaging in the drawer of the nightstand

and tossing dried up pens and broken-tipped pencils against the wall to find one that still worked. It wasn't often he needed to take notes while still in bed. He started writing, pen flying across the notepad as the older man dictated details. The reality of the situation sunk in with the weight of lead in his stomach as the Chief Justice spoke. An attack victim—a jaguar, one of the large cats—in *Boulder.* Possibly feral, definitely turned by a homicidal madman. She might inherit Jack's insanity, or his infamous temper, or both. It was a recipe for disaster. At least the address was on the outskirts of town, near one of the big parks. But a cat that size could cover ground very quickly, and jaguars tended to roam. He would need his weapons—and plenty of silver ammo. He hoped there'd be enough in the safe. He'd have to check. He hadn't needed any in years, not since he was in Wolven, the Sazi police force. At least he went to the range often, as much for entertainment as to keep up his skill. But this was the kind of thing Wolven sent teams of two or three agents to handle. There was nothing more dangerous than a feral were-animal.

Charles had finished speaking and was waiting for his reply. He needed to say something, but *what*? A woman the old bear loved like a daughter was facing death tonight—and there was a good chance that Raphael would be the one to dispense it.

"I'm going to need help, sir."

The reply was a warning rumble. "I told you—"

Raphael shook his head, even though it couldn't be seen. Charles *had* to know what he was asking with the request. He was being asked to risk his life and his pack status. He would be violating pack law by not informing Lucas or Tatya about an attack victim that could endanger the pack and breaking at least a dozen Wolven regulations as well. Yes, to an extent, Charles's word was law, beyond the reach of the council, but this whole situation went beyond foolhardy, straight into suicidal.

Putting aside any fear of reprisal, he summoned all his courage and spoke to the head of the shifters as though he *were* still on the Wolven force. He made sure to keep any annoyance and condescension from his voice—but it remained firm, commanding. "I need information. I'm not in the loop anymore. At the very least, I need photos, vehicle descriptions, license plate numbers. Is there *anyone* I can call? If I have to step outside our law, then I want to have a marginal chance at succeeding. My son, maybe?"

There was a long pause and Raphael was afraid he was going to turn down the request. But his son, Raven Ramirez, was second in command of Wolven. He could get the information without anyone asking questions—even if he was on mandatory health leave. And, he held confidences like no other man Raphael had ever known. If Charles could trust anyone, it would be Raven.

Finally, the old man sighed. "Call Raven. Find out what you can. I could tell you myself, but I'm afraid that I . . ." He took another deep breath. "I trust your judgment. It's why I called."

In the end, too many lives were at stake. Raphael knew it and so did Charles. Neither of them would—*could*—risk all of the Sazi for one woman.

"I'll do my best, sir. I swear it."

"Thank you." There was undisguised gratitude in his voice. "I appreciate that more than you know. Call me tomorrow on my private line. I'll be waiting for your report." Charles dictated the number where he could be reached, and when he finished, he hung up without bothering to say good-bye.

Raphael leaned back against the headboard once more and stared into space, desperately trying to think how to convince his son to ignore all protocol, disobey every rule that he lived by, to give him classified information. If Jack Simpson had attacked someone in Lucas's territory, it was a sure bet that Wolven knew all about it already. Would he have to find a way to the woman *around* the agents who would be arriving tonight?

The coffee was finished brewing by the time he decided how to approach the situation. If he called in a Beta Six alert, then *perhaps* Raven would get to a secure phone line to return a call without telling the higher-ups in the agency. But Beta Six was not only a seldom-used code, it might well be so old that Raven wouldn't even recognize it.

Raphael stirred sugar into his coffee and took a sip, trying to clear the remaining fog from his thoughts. A rooster crowed in the distance. It was incredibly loud to his ears, reminding him all the more strongly that the full moon was just behind the rising sun, waiting to pull the animal out from inside him—and from inside *her*.

There was no time to lose. He had to find her and isolate her from the humans before the moon rose and pulled the beast from her body.

He glanced at his watch as he reached for the portable phone next to his coffee mug. The sultry scent of the dark roast helped him relax and think in *cop* mode again.

The phone rang twice before he heard his son's familiar voice "Ramirez."

"Raven. It's me."

"Oh, hi, Dad! It's good—"

"Raven. Beta Six." Raphael disconnected the phone and set it down, feeling his heart pounding and adrenaline racing for the first time in a very long while. He tried to imagine what his son would do next. Beta Six was an internal agent code that was the equivalent of *trust no one*. If Raven understood the code, he should know not to contact anyone in charge—there was a breach of security, and everyone was suspect. Even his own father.

Raphael didn't wait for the phone to ring again. Even understanding the code, it would take awhile for Raven to verify that his father had indeed called him on his own cell phone. He would probably also check to see that the triangulation of the signal was Boulder, Colorado, and that he had not left the area by any traceable transportation before the call was placed.

There was plenty of time to get started on gathering what was needed to track a rogue feral.

Raphael was still a very young shifter, by Sazi standards, but since leaving Wolven, he'd been feeling old, out of shape. As an alpha male, he would probably live until he was two or three hundred, but there was no substitute for daily training and regular field work, and he'd had neither of those things.

When his handguns were scattered across his desk, the sets of chairs, and rags spread out over the floor, he stopped to take stock. A rifle would be better, or even a shotgun, but all of his long guns were in the safe at his pack office at the school. If he went to get them someone was bound to see and ask the questions Raphael wouldn't be able to answer. Besides, handgun fire was much easier to muffle or "bend" using his magic so humans didn't notice it.

Checking his ammo cans determined his choice of weapons. He only had silver ammunition for the Ruger Blackhawk and the 9 mm Colt. There was more ammo for the Ruger, so that would be his first choice. But the Colt would be handy to have along, too—just in case.

He checked the fit of the Kevlar vest. He'd bought it on impulse over the Internet. Tonight he wouldn't be facing gunfire, but the Kevlar *might* stop jaguar claws briefly, if he was lucky. He was making adjustments for comfort when the phone rang.

It rang a second time before he made it back to the kitchen. "Ramirez."

"Okay, Dad. What in the hell was so important that you had to use a thirty-year-old code to drag me out of the office? I had to buy a brand-new phone to call you!"

"What do you know so far?"

Raven sighed. "I know I had to dig through piles of paperwork before I could even *find* what Beta Six meant. Then I checked your position, and the phone's position, and did a satellite track. Then I made an excuse to leave the office, bought a phone, and called Granddad."

Raphael cursed under his breath. He should have expected that—he would have done the same damn thing. "He told you what the situation is?"

"He didn't tell me a frigging thing. He just said, 'Yes, your father called. Call him back,' and hung up. Big help there."

Raphael nodded even though he knew Raven couldn't see it. "I need whatever information you have on Jack's latest get. Background, aunt's address, the car she drives, license plate—everything." A long pause made him ask, "Raven? Did you get that?"

His son's voice sounded strange when he responded. "Yeah, I got it. But Jack's last confirmed attack was nearly a decade ago. Why would you need it?"

Raphael nearly dropped the phone. How could Wolven *not* know about this? They checked into every animal attack in the world, regardless of what the papers reported. Was that why

Charles had called him? Didn't he want the rest of the council to know? If not, *why* not?

"Dad? Talk to me. What's going on over there?"

"*Shit.*" He ran his fingers through his hair again. "Are you *sure* you're on a secure line?"

A pause. "As secure as I can make it in the middle of Paris."

He blew out a slow breath and sat down. Then he proceeded to tell Raven about the call from Charles and what he had been asked to do. He concluded with, "So, do you have any information, or can you *get* any information?"

"Jesus, Dad! Just drop a nuclear bomb in my lap. This is the absolute *first* I've ever heard this. I know about the Turner woman, but no hint of Jack's involvement ever reached Wolven. There were multiple witnesses to the event. Her parents were killed by a wild animal, all right. But all parties agreed that it was a *cougar* attack. Hell, someone got a *photo* as it was running off, according to what I heard! Councilman Monier personally checked with all of the cougar shifters and verified their whereabouts, so it was shunted into the wild animal files. Are you *certain* our spotted friend was involved?"

Raphael took another sip of his now-cold coffee. Bright sunshine was bouncing off the copper bottoms of the pans over the stove. He had to shift his chair to turn his sensitive eyes away. "I'm not sure of a damned thing right now. I can't imagine why Charles would lie. He seemed *shaken* when we talked—almost afraid. He said that someone had been blocking his ability to see the future, so he hadn't been able to stop the attack."

"Good God! If you're right about this . . . but why wouldn't Charles tell Lucas, Fiona, or one of the council? Why *you*?"

"He asked for a personal favor. I'm hardly in a position to refuse. After all, it's only thanks to him that I'm still *alive* right now." Raphael's chuckle had bitter overtones. This situation meant he was going to have to once again face the very thing that had nearly caused his death; the very same mistake that had made Jack Simpson his mortal enemy years ago.

"Right." Raven paused. "So, what do you need me to do?"

Chapter Two

CATHERINE SHUT DOWN the laptop she'd borrowed from her aunt and slid it back into the leather carrying case. She'd finally managed to fall asleep at 4:00 A.M., only to sit bolt upright, heart pounding in terror, less than an hour later from a nightmare reenactment of the animal attack that had killed her parents. So she'd tried to distract herself with business. It had worked. It was now 9:00 A.M. and she was wide awake. Unfortunately, she also had a whole laundry list of problems that needed to be taken care of.

She stood and stretched until she heard the soft pop of vertebrae sliding into place, then bent to touch her palms to the floor. Stretching out always seemed to ease the muscles stiffened by sitting too long in one position at the computer keyboard. Funny how things changed: when she'd been in her late teens and early twenties the last thing she would've imagined herself doing was working with computers. That was her father's bailiwick. He'd earned his fortune the hard way, coming up from nothing to become the "Bill Gates of computer hardware." She'd simply enjoyed the fruits of his wealth and status as a local celebrity. She'd become a notorious "party girl."

But while her former friends never seemed to tire of the party circuit, she'd grown bored. She had gone away to college without regret, worked hard for her degrees, and settled down. When Brad had proposed after graduate school, she'd gladly accepted.

Cat winced. Thinking about Brad would tense back up the muscles she'd just loosened. There had been e-mails from him today, the first in a very long while. Probably condolences, but she'd deliberately skipped over them. What would it prove, or solve? He'd been horrified to find out from the local press that his future mother-in-law was *not* a well-heeled, southern socialite, but rather a former high-end call girl. He'd dumped Cat before the ink was even dry on the newspapers.

"Asshole." She said it to her reflection in the vanity mirror and fought down a wave of anger and pain. She'd loved him so damned much and *thought* he loved her. Maybe he even had. More likely, he'd loved the notion of being married to a beautiful blonde who just happened to be the only heir to the Turner Computer Industries fortune.

Was everyone this cynical when they closed in on their thirtieth birthday? She hoped not.

"Aunt Violet, can I borrow the car?" Cat called downstairs to her aunt. She had deliberately waited until Violet had been happily writing for an hour or so before she interrupted to ask the favor—time enough for Violet to get over her irritation of yesterday.

Cat sighed. She hadn't meant to cause a problem. But yesterday morning she'd woken up craving meat. So she'd *borrowed* her aunt's car before Violet awoke, and escaped the stifling confines of the organic, vegan household her aunt maintained. She'd found herself at Jake's Burger Joint, a local restaurant just a few miles down the road. The infusion of steak, eggs, bacon, and strong black coffee had been a welcome relief from oatmeal and herbal tea. Cat had enjoyed the lively discussion about video games she'd gotten into with Holly Sanchez, her waitress, almost as much as the food itself. She'd like nothing more than to go back, but she was a guest in her aunt's home and didn't want to risk a repeat of the argument she'd had with Violet on her return.

Cat would love to go again today and continue her debate with Holly Sanchez, the friendly waitress she'd met, about the relative merits of different video games. But she was a guest in her aunt's home and didn't want to upset her.

Fortunately, Violet was always happiest when in the throes of writing one of her romance novels, her imagination taking her away from the humdrum of daily existence. She loved her career, and it showed in the framed copies of book covers on the wall, each bearing her aunt's name in bold pink letters. Two hours was probably adequate time for Violet's normal good humor to re-assert itself.

"Why? What did you have in mind?" Violet shouted back. Her voice was warm and anticipatory. Cat felt a pang of guilt. She didn't like deceiving her aunt, but Violet would bristle at the notion of eating out.

"I need to do some shopping." It was the absolute truth, as far as it went.

"Really?" Violet sounded surprised, and more than a little pleased. Cat supposed it was natural. After all, her first week at Violet's house had been spent alternately sleeping or crying in her bed, and the second week she wandered around like a zombie. Today was the first time she'd felt close to normal since her parents died.

They were dead. She was beginning to accept that fact. It seemed like forever, and at the same time as if it had just been yesterday. It made it worse that Violet wanted to talk endlessly about them. Cat just *couldn't*.

Therapy would probably help. But therapy was a long-term process, and she didn't want to stay in Boulder long-term. No, this was a stopgap, a short respite before she resumed her real life. Colorado wasn't home for her. But there was no fiancé, no job, no *life* for her back in California, either. She couldn't imagine going home to her parents' house without them being there. Yet, it would be a good placc to lose herself in business for a while. She *knew* she could run her father's company given the chance. Unfortunately, none of the board members believed it.

She'd followed her father's advice and started a small game design company. The plan had been to show her business savvy by running a small enterprise before he moved her in to take over for him. They'd assumed it would be years before he decided to step down and retire. There was supposed to be plenty of time. Plenty of time to learn his business, and teach him hers.

"Cat?" She blinked and realized that Violet had been speaking to her. Her aunt wore a hopeful smile. "I was wondering if you'd like a bit of company. We can make a regular day of it." She looked her niece up and down critically. "You could use a few new things. Why don't you change while I finish this chapter?" Catherine hid her disappointment well, agreeing to Violet's plan with fake enthusiasm. *So much for a meaty breakfast.*

Finishing a chapter always took longer than Violet thought it would, so Cat decided to take a quick shower and pull on some decent clothes.

She walked into the bathroom, marveling at the fact that she'd lost even the last traces of a limp. There was no explanation for it. The doctors said she'd never walk properly again. The wild animal that had mauled her took most of the long muscle out of her thigh. It had been replaced with some muscle from her calf.

In the shower, Cat rubbed her thigh. The stitches had fallen out that morning—small bits of black covering her foot and the floor like tiny spiders. The skin was pink and shiny and new, soft to the touch. There was no pain when she pushed on the muscle.

Cat was thrilled, but also frightened. There was no reason for her to be healing this quickly. It wasn't normal. She couldn't find any information on the Internet about rapid healing in humans—except, of course, on comic book Web sites about mutants. And Cat wasn't a mutant, or a comic book heroine.

So how was she almost entirely healed from the attack by a vicious cat that had left her parents dead?

After her shower, she opened the dresser drawers and began rummaging irritably through the contents searching for something to wear. Nothing appealed to her. The garments all seemed so *bland,* and they positively reeked of fabric softener.

The logical part of her realized her reaction made no sense. Just yesterday she'd been perfectly happy to wear anything in the drawers. Not today. Today they felt all wrong.

Finally, at the bottom of her underwear drawer she found what she was looking for, a sleek black bodysuit she'd used in a dance class years ago. She pulled it on, then went to the closet. Near the back she found a blood-red silk blouse that had belonged to her mother but had somehow ended up among Cat's things. Although Janet and Cat had been blessed with the same cool blonde looks and dancer's figures, they'd had wildly different tastes in clothing. Janet had preferred silk and rich, jewel tones, while her daughter dressed almost exclusively in pastels and denim. Still, the red seemed just right for today. She pulled it on, leaving it unbuttoned to fall around her hips. Black flats and a bit of makeup almost completed the look.

Cat examined her reflection in the mirror. It needed something. Maybe jewelry. She reached into her jewelry box to retrieve her silver earrings and bracelets, only to hiss in pain and drop the hoops on the floor. Her fingers turned red and puffy with what looked like burn blisters—but they disappeared as she watched, healing as fast as they'd appeared.

Rich, rolling laughter filled her ears, and she looked around frantically for the source, even knowing nobody would be there. No *physical* body, that is.

Really, kitten, you know better! *Silver?* Besides, gold is better for your coloring. But yes, I like the outfit . . . quite a lot. Very, very nice. You have a magnificent figure. You should definitely show it off.

"Shut up!" Cat slammed her hands against her ears and then down on the bureau top. She struggled to get back control of her mind from the dark voice—and prayed that Violet hadn't heard.

"Catherine, what was that noise? Are you ready to go?"

Taking a deep breath, she felt the voice recede with a final, creepy chuckle.

"I'll be right down," she called to Violet, and then slumped against the wall. A few deep breaths cleared her head.

Why should she know better? Why did the silver burn her fingers? There was no time to dwell on it, and she definitely didn't want her aunt to come upstairs. So she grabbed a pair of gold hoops from the jewelry case, careful to avoid the tangle of silver jewelry, and slid them into her ears.

She pounded down the stairs to join Violet at the front door, forgetting to hide her lack of a limp. There was no way to hide the fact that her leg wasn't bandaged, either—the body stocking showed every muscle and curve.

It almost amused Cat to see her aunt take a long look at her appearance and swallow, hard. "But . . . you're *not even limping!* *How . . . when*—" She stopped speaking and just stared for a long moment. "I think we should call the doctor."

"No." Cat realized her voice sounded cold, and she didn't know why. Nor did she care. "I do *not* want to be poked and prodded like some damned lab rat. We're calling it a miracle and leaving it at that."

She watched her aunt absorb the words. For a moment, it looked like Violet would argue, but apparently she thought the better of it. *Good,* thought Cat, *because I'm not giving in on this.* She decided to change the subject: "I'm ready to go now."

Another long stare, this time at her clothes. "That's a *different* look for you."

"Yes. It is." She waited for her aunt to pass judgment, but the older woman swallowed audibly and held her tongue. Instead, she smiled with false brightness and said, "So, would you rather go to the factory shops or to Cherry Creek?"

Cat raised an eyebrow at the offer. Violet didn't leave Boulder very often to drive down either to Denver or to the Silverthorne outlet stores. Apparently her aunt really did intend to make a day of it. The Cherry Creek Shopping Center in Denver was situated in an enclave surrounded by elegant and expensive little shops, while the mall itself had a number of the larger high-fashion chains and jewelry stores.

"You pick." She was fairly certain she knew what her aunt's choice would be. Along with all the boutiques, there was a major independent bookstore across from the mall in Denver. Violet could never resist a bookstore. She might be loathe to admit it, but she always made a point of checking with the manager to see how well her books were selling, and offering to sign some of the stock. Business, after all, was business. And business was obviously booming.

"THANK GOD," RAPHAEL muttered as his quarry slipped into one of the better mall restaurants. It was a steak place, which meant he would actually get the chance to eat some meat. A good thing, too; he could feel the pull of the moon, and it was making him antsy and irritable.

All morning he'd been keeping an eye on the pair of them, watching as Catherine Turner shopped with an abandon he'd never seen before. And oh, how she looked like Fiona—the hair, the figure, the sparkling blue-green eyes—which was, no doubt, why Jack had chosen her for his victim.

It was in the lingerie store that he'd caught the first good whiff of the woman's scent. She'd be a jaguar all right, if she survived. Right now the scent was still mostly human—but it had the unmistakably musky undertones of a large cat. There was no more doubt. She would shift tonight, or die in the attempt. Raphael didn't dare lose track of her. He had to stay close.

Raphael waited a few moments, giving the woman and her aunt time to get settled in at a table.

He ran a quick comb through his dark brown curls and tucked the white dress shirt more firmly into the waistband of his best black jeans and waited until their backs were turned before walking through the door of the restaurant.

He stopped in the cool, dim entry and scanned the patrons until he found the cat. She chose that moment to look up. Their eyes locked across the room, and he gave her his best dimpled smile.

"OH!" CAT HADN'T meant to say it out loud. Her aunt, however, turned to see what her niece was looking at.

"Now *that*," Violet said with an exhaled breath that wasn't quite a whistle, "is a man."

Cat couldn't help but agree. The man who stood in the restaurant entrance looked to be in his mid- to late twenties, but he moved with the confidence of a much older man. If she had to guess, Cat would have put his height right at six feet, but with a wonderful build: slender hips, broad shoulders. His hair was a little long, falling in curls that just begged to be touched. And that wicked grin of his was enough to make her knees weak.

His slow, thorough examination of her brought a flush to her cheeks and made her pulse race just a bit faster. It was a real struggle not to stare when the maître d' seated him right in her line of sight. Never mind polite luncheon conversation with Violet. Cat simply couldn't concentrate. She was just too aware of him. In fact, she was so distracted, it didn't even occur to her that she'd ordered a rare steak until she heard Violet's hiss of dismay.

"I'm sorry." Cat tore her gaze away from the stranger.

"No." Violet waved the protest away. "No, you've every right to eat what you like. I'd just *hoped* . . ." Violet's voice trailed off.

Cat felt a pang of sympathy for her aunt. Violet was so incredibly earnest. But Catherine was simply not cut out to be a vegan. She *liked* meat. She ate plenty of vegetables, but meat and dairy products were staples of her preferred diet.

And if Violet hadn't wanted her to order steak, why had Violet chosen a steak restaurant?

"I really am sorry," Cat apologized again, reaching across the table to take her aunt's hand. "I know it means a lot to you. But—"

"But it isn't going to happen." Violet sighed and patted her niece's hand. "Ned and your father are the same way, dear. They both *must* have their steak and potatoes. I understand."

Cat felt a stab of unexpected grief. It was like that sometimes. They'd be talking or doing something, and for just that one moment she or Violet would forget, and talk about her parents as if they were still alive. Just a half hour ago, when Violet had been picking up the ring she'd ordered for Ned, Cat had spotted a necklace in the shop window and called out to Violet, "Oh look! I've got to show this to Dad. Mom would love it for her birthday."

"Oh, dear!" Violet's distress was obvious to Cat the moment she realized she'd talked about her brother as though he were still alive. Her eyes widened, and her hand flew to cover her mouth, as though to stop more hurtful words from escaping.

"It's all right." Cat blinked back tears. "I do the same thing all the time. It just doesn't seem *real* somehow."

"No . . . It really doesn't." Violet sighed as the waiter brought their salads. Cat stuffed a bite of crisp lettuce into her mouth so she wouldn't have to keep talking—but, truthfully, she wasn't hungry anymore.

Chapter Three

RAPHAEL HAD DONE a lot of thinking as he sat confined in the sleek red sports car parked in the shadows down the street from Violet's house. After watching the girl for an entire day he understood a little better why Charles was so fond of her—she had attitude, verve. But that didn't make the situation any less dangerous. She was young, obviously athletic and strong. She might actually survive the change.

Which meant there was a very good chance he'd be dealing with a two-hundred-pound feral feline when the moon rose.

But she may not go feral.

At the sound of a light tap on the window Raphael reached over to unlock the car door so that the woman waiting outside could get in. He'd weighed his options and decided that he would need help tonight if he had any hope of accomplishing the task Charles had set him. If he succeeded, there was a good chance that the Chief Justice would understand and overlook the indiscretion. If hc failed, he'd be dead and beyond anything the old bear could do to him.

So he had used his cell phone to place a call to Dr. Betty Perdue. As the pack psychiatrist and backup physician she should be able to help tonight, even if it was only to patch him up after the fact.

Only rarely did an attack victim maintain any sense of humanity or sanity. But occasionally, when the person attacked had a particularly strong mind and will, she sometimes held onto enough awareness to prevent herself from getting lost in her animal and going into insane blood lust.

Betty lowered herself primly onto the passenger seat. She was a large brunette woman, and more than a little homely, but there was warmth and intelligence in her gaze, and she was an exceptional healer. She was subtle with her magic, but there was power there if they needed it. Tonight, they just might.

Raphael turned in the leather seat to face his passenger. "What do you know about attack victims? Not family members who get brought over accidentally. Real human attack victims."

"I've seen one change that went badly, and dealt with one survivor." Betty was utterly calm, both her scent and expression still and serene. She had to be wondering about the circumstances of this meeting, but she was able to control her curiosity. "Tony Giodone—"

Raphael nodded. He recognized the name—almost everyone knew about Tony Giodone and his human mate, Sue. "Yes, but Mr. Giodone had been a wolf for several months before we knew about him."

"Well, from what I understand, non-family member attack victims are pretty rare."

"Not as rare as you think." Raphael cast a glance out the rear window of the car. The sun was sinking rapidly over the mountains. He could feel the pull of the moon against his magic, feel his aura flaring with the additional power. He hated wasting time on explanations, but Betty needed to know what they were dealing with so she could help as much as possible.

He hadn't talked to her on the phone when he called her at pack headquarters because he could hear Tatya lecturing Michael in the background. The last thing they needed was to have Lucas's wife learn what was going on. She was even more territorial and bloodthirsty than her husband. She'd come in to kill the cat, and damn the consequences.

"Tell me," prompted Betty gently.

"All right. A human gets attacked and isn't wearing silver. First full moon one of several things is going to happen."

"His body tries to change and tears itself apart." Betty spoke softly. Raphael saw the flicker of emotion in her eyes. Apparently she remembered the sight as well as he did.

"Usually, but not always. Of the victims whose bodies manage to change, most go feral. They kill anything and everything in sight until they're brought down. And of the few who do survive their first full moon, most go crazy and try to commit suicide."

When Betty spoke again, Raphael could hear the tension she was fighting to hide, smelled a hint of fear rising off of her in a soft mist. "Raphael, why are you telling me this?"

"Jack Simpson has been a very bad boy."

Betty's eyes widened until he could see the whites around her iris. The ammonia scent of her fear flooded the car.

She clearly understood the implications, but he needed to say the words anyway. "While not as big as lions, jaguars are among the great cats. Fearfully powerful physically, a lone jaguar could take out a number of our lesser wolves before being brought down. But, as you know, magic makes it worse. Magic is always the wild card. Attack victims get half of their magical abilities from their own genetics, the other half comes straight from their sire. If this woman is *anything* like Jack Simpson, we are in for serious trouble."

"One of Jack's victims lived?" Betty whispered. "Why didn't you call Lucas and Tatya? They need to know this!"

Raphael hit the button to roll down the driver's-side window. The scent of Betty's fear, combined with the bags of meat he'd stuck in the backseat, was making it hard for him to concentrate, hard for him to hold on to his human form. Magic surged through his veins with an almost painful ecstasy. He dampened the magic by force of will, turning his attention back to the woman sitting beside him.

"I can't do that."

"Why ever not?"

"The Chief Justice asked me not to."

Silence filled the car as the implications of that hit home. When Betty finally spoke again, her voice was soft, tentative. Her fingernails, however, were digging deep into the leather of the arm rest, and she couldn't hide the tension in her scent.

"What exactly is it you want me to do?"

"If everything goes well, nothing. If the woman's feral—"

Betty interrupted him with equal parts horror and disbelief in her voice. "You want me to help you bring down a *jaguar*? I'm good, but I'm not that good."

Raphael gave a harsh laugh. "No. I want you to stay the hell out of the way. I'll put her down." Betty gave him such an unbelieving look that he was a little insulted. "I am not a lesser anything, Betty. I'm Second for a *reason*. All I want is for you to piece me back together again afterward."

She took a deep breath. He watched her take in the scent of his feelings, catalogue them, and back down. "So what's the plan?"

"First step is to seal the perimeter with magic. You're better at that sort of thing than I am. We're going to need to muffle as much sound as possible when the woman changes. I don't want cops coming to investigate barking dogs—and there will be a lot of them—or gunshots."

"You do realize that a shield that tight is going to interfere with our noses. We won't be able to scent anything worth a damn."

Raphael gave a nod of acknowledgment. He wasn't any more happy about that development than she was, but they didn't really have a choice. Keeping the humans from suspecting anything was the top priority.

"Fine." Betty agreed. "I'll take care of the shielding. But how will you get close to . . . *her*?"

Raphael pointed between the leather seats to the large black duffel. "I've got two of those bags with about fifty pounds of meat each. I'm hoping it'll distract her."

"Hoping?"

"If you've got a better idea I'd love to hear it."

Betty was saved from making a response by the buzz of his cell phone. Raphael pulled the instrument from his pocket and flipped it open.

"Ramirez."

"Raphael, it's Charles."

Raphael saw Betty's eyes widen, and he couldn't blame her. But at least she knew now that he was telling the truth. While it was difficult for alphas to lie to each other, it was *possible*.

Raphael didn't want to get into a discussion about how to do his job with Charles, so he kept his voice polite, and kept the conversation short and to the point. "Sir?"

"Catherine's in the park. She went through the window in back while you were getting the meat." Raphael swore under his breath. He'd been afraid something like that might happen, and wished that occasionally Charles's gift for foresight wasn't so damned close to the actual event. Five minutes of warning and he could have been waiting at that window—twenty and he wouldn't have stopped for the meat. But, no, obtaining raw beef had been a necessary evil if he was to have any hope at all of controlling the woman and not having to put her down. So he'd taken the chance. Now it appeared he shouldn't have.

Charles gave him concise directions. His voice was clipped, precise, and absolutely controlled. There was no sign of the emotions he'd shown in his earlier call. Then again, this call had a witness, and no doubt Charles knew it.

"Raphael."

"Yes, sir?"

"Leave Betty inside the house. We need Violet alive." Charles hung up before Raphael could ask any questions.

Raphael flipped the cell phone closed. Betty stared at him, her eyes still a little too wide. "I'm supposed to wait in the house? At the request of the Chief Justice?"

"Yup." Raphael rubbed the bridge of his nose with the thumb and index finger of his right hand. He was getting a headache. He hadn't had a headache in . . . decades. It was remarkable, really. As an alpha Sazi with healing abilities, he generally healed too fast. But the tension in his muscles wasn't going away, so the process was continuous. "You heard what he said."

"Yes, but—" Betty started to protest, but Raphael held up his hand.

"We don't have time for this," Raphael snarled. "You heard your orders. Go protect the aunt."

"Right." Betty flung open the car door and climbed out. It was obvious she wasn't happy from the way she slammed it closed again. But Raphael knew her well enough to know she'd obey the orders. No one who couldn't obey orders got to stay with the pack.

"Wait!"

She froze in midstep two steps from the car. "You're not going anywhere unarmed."

She smiled, and it was a baring of teeth. "An alpha is never unarmed."

"Yeah, well it never hurts to have a distance weapon. I assume you know how to use a handgun?" Raphael reached between the bucket seats. The Colt was in his inner-pants holster, but he had that Ruger and the box of silver-plated ammo behind the passenger seat. He pulled the semiauto from its holster. It was a sweet weapon. He checked, making sure the gun was loaded, and the safety on before passing it butt-first through the window of the passenger door.

Betty looked at the weapon dubiously. "I hope I don't need to use it. I'm not a great shot."

Raphael handed over the weapon. "If we both make it through tonight I'll start taking you with me to the range."

"Right." She took a deep breath. "Good luck."

"You, too."

His eyes followed her as she hurried toward the house. Small, solar-powered lanterns lined the long brick walk that led to a front porch framed by a pair of rose trellises that were heavy with vines and fading pink blooms. The porch light was unlit, not that it mattered. Both werewolves had excellent night vision. Even from this distance Raphael could see that while the screen door was closed, the main front door stood wide open, despite the cold November evening.

"Betty," he called softly.

Betty turned, one hand on the screen door handle. "Go deal with the victim. I'll take care of this. She won't remember a thing if I do it right." She paused, emotions chasing across her rough features. "Be careful."

The scent of worry drifted across the distance that separated them. But she went through the front door before he could comment. As she disappeared from sight he felt the shifting of energies around the house. He concentrated, calling his second sight. It wasn't often useful, but tonight he'd need it. He watched until the net of shimmering power fell into place around the building. Few shifters could see the colored auras that every living thing had. Raphael could—and it had taken years before he could turn *off* the glow that permeated the world. But after a lot of training, he now had a powerful tool.

Raphael dropped his cell phone into the glove box of the car. He'd need it later to make his report, and didn't want it to get lost or ruined should he have to change forms. He grabbed his bomber jacket from beneath the second bag on the backseat—it would hide the gun. He just hoped he would be able to control himself with the moon out, that he wouldn't wind up having to shift forms and lose them both.

There was no more time to waste. Raphael was as ready as he'd ever be. It was time to go. He grabbed the bag, slung it over his shoulder, and slammed the car door shut.

He didn't run. That would be too obvious. But he moved at a walk that ate the distance without drawing undue attention. From what Charles had said earlier, the park wasn't far from the house. That was a good thing, because the moon had risen.

His heart pounded with a heady combination of fear and excitement. God how he'd missed this—the rush of adrenaline before the chase. Boulder pack life wasn't for him, with its backstabbing and petty jealousies. And the *other* duties of a Second that so many envied . . . cold comfort indeed. Anonymous and near-anonymous sex for the sole purpose of breeding babies was hardly what he'd wanted for his life. Oh, he didn't *mind,* and he certainly wouldn't argue—but he had reached a point where he needed to *do* something. Get back into law enforcement. Find someone to settle down with. Build a *life.*

But he'd burned too many bridges trying to bring down Jack to do either—at least within the packs.

Damn Jack Simpson! God, how Raphael hated that man! How many murders was the old cat responsible for? How many more lives had he ruined? He was a serial killer and they all knew it, but it didn't matter.

Someday Jack would go too far, and, file or no file, the death warrant would be issued. Until then, Raphael had to live with the fact that the council considered the senator too powerful and too dangerous to cross.

A low inhuman growl escaped Raphael's throat. He had to fight to remain in control. The moon called to him. Magic screamed through his veins until each sense was heightened to a fever pitch.

Raphael caught her scent at the edge of the park. Musky, female, and unmistakably feline. The scent was fresh. She had passed this point moments before. Raphael slowed his pace, scenting the breeze. He sent out his magic, watching with his second sight as it spread like a mist through the area. It was nothing complicated, just an aversion, something to send any humans in the area away from the park.

Though he had little hope she'd answer or understand, he called out the woman's name. "Catherine? Catherine Turner, are you here?"

He moved slowly, using his second sight to scan the area, first on the ground, then in the trees above. It was her first night. She might glow. She might not. But he was going to use every tool in his arsenal to find her.

He heard something. Not an answer, but a sound that wasn't *right,* wasn't one of the normal night sounds. He wasn't certain what it was, or the exact location, so he stopped. He tilted his head back, scenting the breeze. He could smell her, but couldn't pinpoint exactly where—she must, he figured, be upwind.

With a shrug of his shoulder he allowed the meat-filled duffel to fall to the ground. Reaching for his gun, he stepped away from the package to get a little farther from the overpowering scent of raw meat. "Catherine. I know you're here. You *need* to answer me." Gun in hand, he turned in a slow circle, dark eyes scanning both the ground and the trees, looking everywhere for the tawny, spotted form of a jaguar.

She struck when his back was to her: a dark blur of motion, too fast for a human eye to follow. She knocked him to the ground, sending his gun skittering across the leaf-strewn earth, before she grabbed the bag of meat in her teeth and leapt into the branches of an ancient elm. Nylon screamed as she shredded the bag and began devouring its contents. He'd been watching for a spotted cat, but she wasn't.

She was the smooth, solid black of a panther.

Raphael stood, his movements deliberate and very, very careful. She could have killed him in that one leap. Normally, it took a bullet to *both* the head and the heart to kill an alpha—unless, of course the head was torn off the body, in which case all bets were off. Raphael had seen that happen.

Looking up at those bloodstained teeth and vicious claws he knew she could do it. Hell, he'd seen Fiona do as much, and

Catherine was at least fifty pounds heavier—and impossibly fast. She was definitely Jack's get, despite her coloring.

The jaguar looked down on him with slitted green eyes and snorted with amusement.

Stupid dog.

Raphael heard the thought in his head. His eyes widened. Could she have gained Jack's talent of telepathy so quickly?

The cat stared at him another long moment then corrected herself.

Not dog. Man.

He watched as she gave a long sniff of her blood-soaked muzzle.

Smells like a dog. A wet, stinky *dog.*

He took a slow step toward the tree. She growled low in her throat, warning him away. He actually felt the effort as the cat fought to force a human word, more snarl than speech, past her teeth.

"Mine."

Raphael edged farther forward. The cat laid her ears back against her broad skull. Her eyes narrowed and she gave an eerie high-pitched growl. Her lips pulled back, baring long, curved fangs.

"Catherine?" He made it a question, his head tilted slightly to one side as he stared up at her.

"*My* kill." She spoke the words out loud as well as in his skull.

"Fine." Raphael answered, holding his hands away from his body in a placating gesture. "*Your* kill." He took a step back. The great cat's body relaxed fractionally. She kept her eyes fixed on him as she ravaged the meat. When she'd eaten it all she began licking the nylon fabric to get every spot of blood.

"Satisfied?" Raphael asked.

"Hungry," she growled. He knew that talking was difficult for new turns, but it would get easier. Harder than forming the words would be finding them. The thoughts of cats were all of images, emotion, and instinct, none of which translated into human speech easily. Still, he could sense that she was trying, using the same part of her brain that had kept her from biting through his neck when she had had the chance.

"You want more?"

"More," she agreed, her ears coming forward a fraction.

"Den," he said. He hoped she would understand and translate the word to *home*—or at least, her aunt's house.

The cat shook her head, looking disgusted.

"Den," Raphael repeated sternly. He was getting through to her, but he had to keep the concepts simple, the simpler the better.

"No!" The cat lashed her tail. She glared down at him, her ears flattening against her skull. She turned, looking away, distracted by a car passing by on the nearby road. When she turned back the man had moved over to retrieve his gun. She growled.

"More meat at den." Raphael used his most soothing voice, but didn't return the gun to its holster. Not yet. She wasn't feral, not exactly, but she was still a two-hundred-pound, supremely hungry, very unhappy pussycat. He might need the weapon if she decided not to cooperate.

"Not!" she argued, backing farther up on the branch and farther out of his reach. *"Lie."* She obviously didn't want to hurt him, but there was no trust. She wouldn't want to be touched.

"More meat at *den,*" Raphael assured her, projecting the truth of his statement forceably. There *was* meat, plenty more. No lie was necessary.

She answered, clearly struggling to form the words. "Vi . . . let . . . no . . . meat."

Raphael was getting frustrated and impatient, and he could feel the moon tearing at him through his skin. Damn it. *He* would need to change, and soon. Yes, he could hold it off, but the longer he held back, the more it drained him. He had no doubt his eyes were already glowing, so he sent out a light wave of magic to make sure that no humans ventured close enough to see. If he could just get her *moving*. The aunt's house was so *close*. They could cut—

He stopped in midthought, feeling like a complete idiot as he realized what she'd just said.

It didn't seem possible, a cat in her first change shouldn't be able to think beyond food, let alone follow complex concepts, but he remembered a single line from the file that Raven had faxed him, about a local organization the aunt had founded and was still an officer in.

"Your aunt's a *vegetarian?*"

"Vegan." One word, enunciated perfectly. Raphael blinked stupidly up at her. She'd turned on the branch to focus her attention down the trail, ignoring him as she waited for prey.

"Well, shit!" Raphael was stunned. Her first change and she was not only *not* feral, she was smarter than most of his pack members on their best day. This was one *hell* of a woman. Charles hadn't missed the mark when he'd called her exceptional.

"All right," he said, no longer concerned that she wouldn't understand normal speech. "I have meat in my car and my car is at your den."

The cat turned her head slowly, her entire attention focused on him. Her eyes narrowed with suspicion. Her claws dug furrows into the tree bark, and powerful muscles tensed beneath her glossy ebony fur that was now starting to glow with a faint, pale light. It was so pale it was nearly white. "Liar."

"Smell my scent. You'll know I'm not lying if you let yourself trust your own nose." He felt like an idiot standing here, and his neck was getting a crick in it from staring up into the tree. Thank God the spell was holding and nobody was around to see him. Fiona, Raven—hell, *Lucas*—would *never* let him hear the end of it if any of them ever learned he was having this conversation. But from that tiny telepathic touch he'd gotten from her, he knew that ordering her not only would be stupid, but would probably piss her off enough that she would hurt him badly.

So far he'd managed this without so much as a scratch. He'd like to keep it that way if he could.

"Look." He decided to try reasoning with her. "I brought *this* meat didn't I? What makes you think I don't have more?"

He waited, watching for the tiny clues in her body language that would indicate trust. Normally her scent would have told him as much or more than her posture, but the scents of blood and raw meat were overpowering everything else.

"If you come with me back to my car with me there's a second bag and you can have it all."

The scent of suspicion flowed off of her in waves, and her body language wasn't happy. But after a long moment of consideration, she dropped the shredded duffel to the ground and jumped down beside him in a fluid leap. Raphael forced himself not to flinch. She was being *nice*. This whole situation was going better than he'd dared hope. Still, he couldn't help noticing just how *big* she was. His guess of two hundred pounds might have been a little low. Standing next to him he could see she was at least nine feet long from nose to tail, all gleaming black fur and solid muscle. Her shoulder came to his waist.

When he didn't start moving immediately, she head-butted him hard. Her glow flared a bit with her annoyance.

"Give me a minute," Raphael snapped. "We can't just leave the bag here. People would ask questions. You need to learn caution about this new part of your life."

She gave him a *look*. Now he could scent her impatience over her musk.

He didn't make her wait long. Her claws and teeth had been *very* thorough. Raphael gathered the few remaining ribbons of nylon into a tight package and forced the edge of it into the rear pocket of his jeans. He'd come back tomorrow during daylight disguised as park maintenance to make sure there was no other trace of what had happened here, but for now this was the best he could do.

Raphael turned to face the cat. She had settled comfortably onto the leaf-strewn ground and was using her paws to wash the last of the blood from her muzzle. "I have to touch you," Raphael warned.

She hissed at him, laid her ears back against her skull, and glared at him with narrowed eyes. I don't think so. The thought came directly into his mind with perfect clarity and the utter disdain only a cat can convey.

"I *have* to," he repeated firmly, reaching out with his left hand. "It's necessary for the magic to work. Trust me." He spoke softly, putting both magic and feeling into the words as he tried to insert the words in her mind. Raphael wasn't much of a telepath, but he was *very* good at magical persuasion. Wolven had helped him train that talent into a tool.

She rose, backing away a half step, but her ears rose up a bit. She was trying to trust, compelled to do so, but he knew it was hard for her.

"Trust me." Raphael repeated in nearly a whisper, letting his magic settle over her until he saw her shiver and felt her muscles start to relax. He reached ever so slowly toward her with his empty left hand. He needed to touch her, needed to project a nice, safe, unremarkable image around the two of them. Let the humans see something ordinary and unnoticeable. "Please?"

The cat snarled lightly, but allowed him to rest his hand on her shoulder. She wasn't happy. Neither was he. They had no choice. Raphael couldn't risk anyone seeing her as a jaguar, and he had to be touching her for his illusion to work. He closed his eyes and took a deep, slow breath, visualizing the ordinary image he wanted to project: a man walking his Great Dane. It should have been easy, but the moon was dragging at him. He hadn't eaten, not *real* food, and the erratic mental images he was getting from the cat were intruding on his concentration.

Slowly, he felt the warm golden glow of magic spread over them. The illusion settled into place with an almost audible snap. As long as they acted reasonably in character, anyone walking by would see, hear, even *smell* what Raphael wanted them to. But at a cost. When this was over he'd be exhausted, damned near useless. But it was worth it—he didn't have to kill her.

He would have. It wouldn't have even been the first time. But this wasn't her fault. She didn't ask for this. And Raphael wouldn't have relished having to tell Charles afterward.

Catherine nearly knocked him off his feet with another headbutt. *HUNGRY!*

He glared down at her. Not that it did any good. *Damned cat. Stupid dog.*

Raphael berated himself for his inability to focus. He hadn't had this much trouble controlling his magic or the moon in decades. What the hell was going on? He needed to get a grip before he got himself, or someone else, killed.

Adrenaline flooded into his veins at the thought of not only the danger he was in, but the danger the cat beside him posed. The Sazi couldn't afford exposure. Catherine Turner might have been an innocent victim, but Raphael's people couldn't afford to let her run wild. She'd conform, or she'd die.

"Come on." Raphael's voice was gruff. "We'd better get moving."

Raphael let Catherine lead him across the grass to the nearest sidewalk. Only then did he try to guide her along the concrete path. The cat's instinct would place her on the quickest route to the den, but Raphael needed the two of them to act normally. People walking their dogs do not cut straight across their neighbor's property. If the two of them acted too far out of character of the illusion they *would* be noticed.

The cat accepted his guidance wordlessly and stuck to the sidewalks. He let her lead. Casting the illusion was getting easier. Raphael knew there was something wrong with that, but his mind kept wandering. He couldn't focus long enough to really be concerned. The silvered moonlight cast blue and white shadows across the jet black of the cat's fur. Each movement had a fluid beauty that was captivating, mesmerizing.

The cat used her paw, claws only slightly masked, to push him away from the curb just in time to keep him from stepping out in front of a speeding car. He hadn't seen it. Hadn't heard it coming. "What in the *hell*!"

"Stupid dog," the cat muttered out loud, giving him a look of utter disdain.

"Not dog. *Wolf*."

There was a long pause, during which she didn't take her gaze from him. Jade-green eyes stared without so much as blinking. "Fine. Stupid *wolf*."

Raphael didn't argue. He couldn't. His heart was pounding too hard with belated panic. Something was very, very wrong. He told himself to calm down, take things one step at a time. He just needed hold the illusion, get to the house, change, and eat. Simple. But it didn't feel simple. Tomorrow he was going to the doctor. Betty or Tatya were sure to know what was wrong with him. They would fix it—whatever *it* was.

Raphael took a deep breath. Everything was going to be fine. It was important not to fear. The cat was seriously underfed. Having her smell his panic could be a very bad thing. He watched her carefully, checking for any signs that she might turn on him. There were none. She looked impatient and more than a little bit bored. She gave him a look that said, as clearly as words, *Can we go now?*

"I'm fine." Raphael growled in his throat. "Since you're so obviously worried about me."

The cat snorted in derision, checked *pointedly* for traffic by looking one way and then the other, and crossed the road.

Raphael fought down an irritated growl. The last thing he needed was a smart-ass cat. He shook his head and followed a step or two behind. They were in a residential area now. The din was excruciating. Raphael could hear every television, and all the area dogs were barking their heads off. It hadn't occurred to him to use magic to mask their scent from *animals*.

Raphael's head started throbbing in time with his heartbeat. The cat, too, was irritated, her tail slashing through the air, the muscles of her back tightening into knots. "Two more blocks," Raphael whispered, trying to sound reassuring. "Just two more blocks."

The cat stopped abruptly. She tilted her head sideways, snuffling. A low growl rumbled through her massive chest. Raphael tightened his illusion as he raised his head to scent the breeze. He caught the scent.

Jack.

That instant the night was cut by the howl of a wolf, ending in a woman's scream that cut off abruptly. Dear God! What had he sent Betty into?

Before he could react, even think, the cat reared her head back and *roared*. The sound hit his magic like a sledgehammer blow, driving him to his knees with bruising force. The cat disappeared in a blur of speed, leaping over an eight-foot privacy fence almost too fast for his eyes to follow.

Raphael stumbled to his feet and took off at a run. He couldn't change, not here where the combined light of the moon and streetlamps made it all too likely someone would see. Only when he reached the fenced backyard of the Wildethorne house could Raphael let loose the power he'd been fighting since sundown. He felt the glory of power surging over him as the heat of his magic disintegrated most of his clothing. He felt muscles and bones shift and reform; felt the thick black fur sprout from his skin. The gun thudded to the ground. When Raphael leapt through the shattered remains of the French doors he was fully a wolf.

The kitchen was a big room, taking up most of the back of the house. But it was not big enough for the fight that raged inside. It was a scene from hell, or a slasher movie. Blood, and worse, was everywhere, pooling on the floor, splattered over the daisy-print wallpaper, running down the sides of the center island.

Raphael stood, transfixed, watching the jaguars fight. Catherine had locked her jaws into the thick band of muscles across Jack's neck and shoulders, wicked claws knifing through his mottled fur as she tried to slice into his delicate underbelly, break his neck, or both. Jack roared with pain and rage, pouring blinding purple magic into the woman in waves, trying to force her back into human form while at the same time he slammed her body against the walls of the kitchen trying to break her hold.

The woman was doing fine. Hell, she was doing better than fine. If Raphael tried to join the fight at this point he'd just hinder her. There was no maneuvering room as it was. The two large cats were taking up virtually all of the available space.

Raphael shifted his attention to an inert figure curled in the far corner. A pool of blood spread from Betty's body across the white tiled floor. He could see her breathing. She was alive. Betty was alphic, and a powerful healer. Even so, Raphael wasn't sure she would make it. Not without help. The shimmer of her aura was dim and weak—she was fading.

The fight shifted. For just a moment the path was clear. Raphael darted in, moving to aid his pack mate and gave an involuntary gasp at the extent of Betty's wounds. Jack had eviscerated her. Through the gaping hole in her abdomen Raphael could see her lungs move. Blood spurted in rhythm with her heartbeat. Raphael forced himself to ignore the sweet metallic smell of blood, forced down his beast, the hunger, and the rage. He concentrated, willing himself to human form. He had a small healing talent that he'd trained himself to use, but he needed his human hands to help her. The cats would live or die, but Betty was *pack*.

He closed his eyes, struggling to concentrate. It was hard. The cats fighting was a distraction, and part of his magic and energy was already going to mask the sounds coming from the house. Betty's help with the shields had fallen when she had. He didn't dare let the neighbors hear what was going on. The Sazi secret would be kept, even if it cost all of their lives.

Raphael felt weakness coming over him in waves. The hands he used to press Betty's intestines inside her body were trembling with the strain. He pulled power from within the depths of his being, shoving pure, untrained magic into Betty's body, forcing her, *willing her,* to heal. He was able to stem the blood loss, close the wound, but that was all, and it might well not be enough.

Raphael's eyes dimmed, his breath coming in gasps. He'd pushed himself this hard before, but he'd never in his life felt so weak. He forced his head to turn, to see what was happening with the cats. Jack had managed to throw the woman off, but at a cost. His neck and throat were a red ruin where large chunks of flesh had been ripped away. Blood poured from the wicked wounds Catherine had inflicted on his sides and belly. He stood just inside the swinging doors that led to the rest of the house, staring at the feline lying in a stunned heap a few feet away. His gaze turned to Raphael, green eyes narrowing as he bared his bloody fangs. Jack's muscles bunched; he lowered his body moving slowly forward, stalking the other man.

Raphael took the gun from Betty's limp hand, aiming it steadily. He prayed there were still bullets, that the clip was not empty.

"Ramirez—" Jack's voice was a rumbling growl.

Raphael didn't know what he would have said, for they were interrupted by the sound of footsteps and the click of claws on concrete just outside the kitchen door.

Jack hissed, moving quickly away. His eyes remained locked on Raphael. Raw hatred burned in Jack's glance, the scent of it pouring from him in waves that filled the room. As much as Raphael wanted Jack's death, the jaguar probably wanted his more.

Slowly, deliberately, he stalked forward.

Raphael pulled the trigger. The cat's speed faltered with each shot, but momentum carried him forward. Blood poured from scorched wounds and dripped from Jacks fangs, but still he came forward. The hatred in his eyes was a living, breathing thing. *"I will kill you."* The words echoed both inside Raphael's head and through the kitchen.

"No." A familiar feminine voice answered from the back

door. "You won't." Tatiana Santiago stood limned in moonlight, dressed to the nines in a designer suit, high-heeled pumps, and holding a high-powered rifle. Next to her stood a wolf the size of a small pony—her son, Michael.

Adrenaline rushed through Raphael's veins as he heard the bolt of a rifle slide home. "Tatya, *no!*"

"Listen to the nice man, Tatya. There's not enough magic left in the shield to silence a rifle shot." Jack glared malevolently from one to the other of his three opponents.

"Maybe I'm willing to take my chances," she answered coolly.

Feet slipping in the pooled blood on the floor, Raphael grabbed the countertop and hauled himself upward. Pain stole the breath from his lungs as he strained to make torn and battered muscles work. "You can't."

She stood framed in the doorway, feet shoulder width apart, rifle raised and aimed.

"He needs to die."

"Yes. But we can't kill him." The bitterness in Raphael's voice was palpable.

Jack laughed, then coughed. Bloody bubbles appeared at his lips. The silver bullets hadn't killed him, but combined with the injuries Catherine had given him, he wasn't in good shape. Far too injured to risk going against the three wolves.

"I won't let him kill you." Tatya held the gun with a cold confidence that made it clear she meant every word. Michael, meanwhile, began edging away from his mother, moving slowly to the right, his muscles bunched and teeth bared for an attack.

Jack's eyes narrowed. "Another time, Ramirez." With a blur of speed that should *not* have been possible for anyone so badly injured, he was gone.

Tonight was a night for impossible things to happen. Raphael relaxed and groaned.

Tatya set the rifle on the kitchen counter and bent down to check on the wounded. She gave a soft gasp of dismay at the extent of Betty's injuries. Still, the Second Female was a tough customer. Raphael could hear her weak pulse and reedy breathing. He felt a surge of power, saw Tatya's pale green aura begin glowing more brightly. He watched, fascinated, as her magic flowed in a steady stream over Betty's wounds, stabilizing and even reversing the damage. When he was sure Betty was safe, he called out to the alpha female.

"Tatya—"

She crossed the kitchen to where the woman lay. The cat had reverted to human form when Jack knocked her unconscious. She lay sprawled where he'd left her, blood pouring from open wounds, arm splayed at an unnatural angle. Even so she was beautiful. Sun streaked golden hair, creamy skin—and a heart-shaped face that was a near perfect image of Fiona Monier when she'd left Jack for Raphael.

Michael stood over her protectively.

"Mike, step away so your mom can treat her." The wolf took two steps back, but he continued to eye Raphael balefully. He didn't quite growl, but he stood his ground between him and the woman. That was surprising, considering how low in the pack Mike was, and how much weaker in power.

Mike was a lesser alpha. There really wasn't much human left in him when the full moon called his beast, but his attention and reaction to the Turner woman was odd, and a little concerning. It was a complication Raphael didn't need. But there was a worse one coming: sirens, distant, but approaching fast.

Raphael forced himself to stand. "Mike, find the front door and stand guard. If you hear anyone coming, bark like hell. It may buy us some time." Raphael put every bit of his authority into the words until finally, reluctantly, Mike did as he was bid and pushed through the swinging doors.

Raphael checked the aunt. She was unconscious, but otherwise seemed unharmed.

Catherine was not so lucky. Her pulse was steady, as was her breathing, but blood matted in her hair where her head had impacted against the corner of the kitchen island.

"We should probably get the three of them upstairs and to bed," Tatya suggested.

"Is it all right to move her?"

He felt, rather than saw, her glare. It had been a stupid question. She was a physician as well as one of the most powerful healers in the Sazi world and knew her job. He should've known better than to ask, but her hostility to the question seemed out of character. He shook his head and held out his hands in apology, then set the gun on the kitchen counter. Bending down, he gently lifted the woman from the floor.

Tatya stepped over to the French doors and pulled the curtains closed. "Can you cast a solid illusion of glass? We want things to look as normal as possible if the police come around back, and I have to concentrate on their wounds."

"I can try." The effort it took was phenomenal. Sweat poured down his face. But he managed.

Tatya lifted Betty gently in her arms. The two of them walked with their burdens through the darkened living room and up the staircase. He'd never been in this particular house, but the floor plan was a common one in the city. Chances were good that the bedrooms would be upstairs.

The staircase turned sharply, opened into a narrow hall. There were doors on either side, and a third door at the far end of the hallway, just beyond a second staircase. Raphael followed his nose, carrying Catherine into the bedroom that bore her scent. Tatya carried Betty through the opposite door.

Raphael kicked aside a tall pile of packages from the afternoon's shopping trip that littered the floor between the door and the unmade bed. Gently, he set Catherine's body down and fought the urge to lie down beside her. He was so *damned* tired. But it was more than that. He wanted to hold her naked body next to his—just to be near her. He felt almost drugged by her scent, and being so close to her made the effects worse.

He reached down, gently brushing a strand of her golden hair away from her face.

The sound of voices beneath the window, and Michael's frenzied barking brought him abruptly back to the present.

Raphael rushed into the bathroom. There was no time to spare, but he had to rinse Catherine's blood from his body before talking to the police. He only took a minute, but by the time he was done, there was the sound of a heavy fist pounding on the front door.

"I've got it!" he called, making sure his voice was loud enough to carry through the open window. He grabbed the first thing that came to hand from the white wicker laundry hamper—a pair of lavender sweatpants. He pulled them on awkwardly as he hurried to the bedroom window.

"Who is it?" he asked. He already knew the answer. A police

cruiser was parked in front of the house, and he could smell fresh gun oil even over the scent of the roses planted beneath the window.

"Police. Open up!"

"I'll be right down!"

Raphael hustled down the staircase into the living room.

"Guard the back door," he whispered to Michael. The wolf padded quickly through the swinging doors. As soon as he was out of sight, Raphael opened the front door.

There were three figures standing in the circle of light from the porch lamp. Two wore crisp dark uniforms and serious expressions. The third, a woman of late middle age, wore a hot-pink pantsuit that was stretched taut across an ample frame.

"Who are you! Where's Violet? Where's Catherine?" She spat the words at him, dark eyes blazing with suspicion.

The police officer moved her back and to the side. "Please, ma'am. We'll handle this."

Raphael chose to ignore her and her questions. He was much more concerned with the police.

"Sorry it took so long. I had to put my dog in the kitchen."

"Your neighbor has reported a disturbance," said the female officer. She was obviously the senior of the pair. Her dark hair was silvered, and she had the flat, emotionless eyes of a veteran who'd seen it all. Raphael recognized the look. Her partner was still new enough to be wet behind the ears. A good-sized man, he was taller than Raphael, with the build of an athlete. He didn't have the obvious bulk of a football or hockey player. Muscular, but lanky: basketball, maybe swimming. He had an all-American look to him, but tough.

"*This* man isn't my neighbor," the older woman said aggressively. Each word was punctuated by an aggressive yip from the lap dog under her arm. "He's lying! Where is Violet?"

"We were watching a movie—" Raphael began.

"I know what I heard! I heard *screaming* coming from *this house*!" The neighbor's jaw thrust forward aggressively.

The female officer rolled her eyes and stepped forward a pace, putting the neighbor behind her. "If you don't mind, sir, we'd like to speak with either Violet Wildethorne or Catherine Turner."

Raphael opened his mouth to respond, but Tatya's voice from upstairs beat him to it.

"Raphael, whatever is going *on* down there?" Her voice held just the perfect trace of exasperation. Somehow the tone of just those few words hinted at sexual escapades being rudely interrupted. It was a masterful performance.

"The police are here. Apparently the TV was too loud and we disturbed the neighbors."

"That is *not* Catherine's voice!"

"Of course not." Raphael agreed. "Sweetheart, they want to see Catherine."

"Oh, for the love of God! Give us a second to pull on some clothes!"

Out of the corner of his eye Raphael could see the male officer's mouth twitch as he tried to stifle a grin, his eyes shining with suppressed mirth. The female officer was more suspicious and much less amused.

A moment later the two women appeared at the top of the stairs, Tatya's arm protectively around Catherine's waist. The two of them were quite a sight. Tatya, a petite silver blonde with a spectacular figure, was wearing only a powder-blue teddy. The color was perfect for her silver-blue eyes and milk-white skin. Catherine wore a burgundy satin floor-length robe that had been tied tightly enough around her to hide the worst of her injuries, but gaped enough when she moved to show there was nothing underneath it.

Catherine struggled to focus, her eyes lighting on the neighbor. "Oh, Mrs. Zabatos—"

"Oh my *God*!" The scent of disgusted disapproval poured off of the older woman in waves.

"Is that Catherine?" The older officer directed her question to the neighbor.

"Yes." Mrs. Zabatos, turned her back to the scene, her voice outraged.

"Ms. Turner, are you all right?" She turned her attention sharply to the woman on the steps.

Catherine looked down at her body, her expression confused. She looked up again, her eyes locking with Raphael's. "I . . . I'm fine." She sounded surprised.

Raphael let out the breath he had been holding. It wasn't a ringing endorsement, but, combined with the little push of magical persuasion he was using, it would probably be enough.

"Is there anything else we can do for you officers?" Raphael asked.

"Just keep the noise down," the older officer answered. She was shaking her head as though annoyed by a buzzing insect in her ear. That happened sometimes with strong-willed humans, so Raphael pulled back his magic a little bit. It seemed to calm her. He could tell she wasn't happy with the situation, but she wasn't going to pursue it. Her partner couldn't—he was too busy fighting a losing battle with his amusement. He waited until both Mrs. Zabatos and his partner were out of earshot. Taking a long, appreciative look at the women on the staircase, he turned to Raphael. "You are one *lucky* bastard."

"You have no idea." Raphael grinned and elbowed the officer, who grinned back, and pulled the door closed behind him when he left. Raphael was so relieved his knees felt weak.

"Come to bed, Catherine." Tatya ordered, her arm still around the younger woman's waist. Raphael could feel the surge of power as Tatya exerted her magic to influence Catherine.

"No." Catherine pulled away, shaking her head, almost stumbling on the hem of the long robe. She never took her eyes off of Raphael. "I remember you." She spoke slowly, and with great care. Her expression was confused, and he could scent worry. He didn't blame her. The images she was probably remembering wouldn't make any sense to a human who knew nothing of the Sazi.

"I'm not surprised." Raphael answered, raising a hand to signal Tatya to silence. "But *I* still need to change, and eat. You *do* need to go to bed. I'll explain everything in the morning."

"Promise?" Her plea was almost childlike.

"I promise."

She allowed Tatya to lead her upstairs then. Raphael, gratefully, pulled off the sweatpants and let the moon take him.

Chapter Four

THE BLOOD WAS pooling in the dips of the metal floor of the rental van. Thick and almost impossibly red, the smell of it filled the small space. Jack lay still, breath wheezing in and out of his injured lungs. The silver bullets had done their work, and Ramirez was as good a shot as ever.

"I still don't understand why you insisted on coming here." There was tension in the woman's voice, and veiled anger. Veiled, because Jack did not tolerate insubordination from anyone, no matter how useful she might be. And she was, admittedly, useful.

"*You* wouldn't understand. All you have to know is that I wanted to." Jack didn't say anything further. It hurt to talk. Nor was he willing to let anyone know the full extent of his plans. The female wolf, Betty, had been an unexpected complication. Worse, it had all nearly been ruined when he'd come face to face with Ramirez. The temptation to end it, then and there, in the Wildethorne kitchen had nearly been too much to resist. But no, it was better to wait. He could afford to be patient, to let things develop naturally. In the end his revenge would be complete and utterly satisfying.

He hissed as she laid dark hands on the torn and bloodied fur, but didn't lash out. The pain was phenomenal. He couldn't remember the last time he'd been hurt this badly. Maybe that time in Madrid. At least this time there was a healer nearby. Closing his eyes against the blinding glow of her aura, he let the heat of the magic wash over him as she began her work.

* * *

"Eat," Tatya ordered.

They were in the living room of the house. It was a pretty room, done in soft blues and grays. The furniture looked comfortable—lived in, but not shabby. The drapes were drawn. The thick navy panels blocked out the moonlight he knew was gleaming brightly beyond the glass.

Raphael forced himself to take a bite. Tatya had gone out to the car for the second bag of hamburger and steaks, and a fair-sized stack of meat was bleeding onto the beautiful china platter she'd set on the carpet in front of him. The smell was heavenly, but he barely had enough energy to chew. He felt as though he'd been pounded—which made no sense whatsoever since neither Jack nor the woman had laid a claw on him and he should already have recovered from expending so much magical energy.

"How's Betty?"

"She's healing. She'll be fine in a couple of days." Raphael heard, rather than saw, Tatya fling herself onto the floral couch on the opposite side of the room. She kicked off her heels. Each landed on the thick carpeting with a muffled thump.

"She came to for a bit," Tatya continued, "just long enough to tell me to thank you—and let me know where the meat was."

"*Thank* me? After I almost got her killed?"

"You couldn't have known Jack would be here," Tatya pointed out.

Raphael grimaced. "I guessed it might be a possibility when Charles said we needed to protect the aunt."

"*Charles* said?" Tatya glared at Raphael. "Is *Charles* the one responsible for you keeping information from Lucas and me?"

Raphael considered his next response very carefully. Tatya might not be able to fight with him about what was *truly* bothering her, but that wouldn't keep her from starting an argument. For all he knew, she hadn't had time to change yet, and that was enough to make anybody cranky. Still, he needed to remind her that she wasn't in charge here.

"When Lucas is out of town, *I* rule, Tatya—not you. It was my decision to make."

She growled a little, but not as though she truly meant it. "In other words, yes, Charles said jump, but you would've done it anyway. Damn it, Raphael, we're pack! Packs work *together*."

Under most circumstances, that would be true. But Raphael wouldn't have wanted to bet his life, or Catherine's, on it. Saying that, however, was out of the question. Raphael considered his next question very carefully. His first thought was that Charles had called her, had seen that Jack was here. But if not, then . . . who?

"Don't take this wrong. I'm grateful as hell you showed up, but how did *you* know?"

"Lucas called me." That stopped him cold. Raven never would have talked, and Charles was adamant that Lucas not know. How in the hell—

"Charles called him in Paris and told him to send me. "I would've been here sooner," Tatya continued, "but I was already halfway up the mountain. Then I couldn't find the damned address!" Silence fell between them, the only sound the cracking of Raphael's teeth against a steak bone while he considered his options.

When Tatya spoke again, her voice was as thick with emotion, and the cold rain smell of her hurt filled the room. "You could have been killed!" She whispered the words, afraid her son might hear from the other room. Michael might know the story of his mother's past with Raphael, but that was abstract. The pain in her eyes and voice wasn't, not at all. She didn't voice the accusation but it hung in the air between them: *Why didn't you call me?*

Raphael didn't answer. There was nothing to say. Lucas was mated to Tatya. They were married, and had been for many years. It didn't matter that Tatya was mated to Raphael and would give her life to protect him. Wolves mated for life, and Lucas had known the situation when he'd married her—which meant the three of them had danced a very delicate measure for the past few decades. One wrong word, one wrong step, and they'd all be dragged down in ruin.

Raphael was determined that *he* would not be the one to make that misstep. *Not this time.*

"I sent for more meat." Tatya's voice was taut, but controlled as she struggled past the fact that Raphael wouldn't answer her—wouldn't look at her. She paused for a second, but continued. "And for a cleanup team. The aunt is fine. She's sleeping on the bedroom floor—I figured Betty needed the bed more than she did. I want her to rest a couple of hours to build up her strength before we move her to the pack hospital. The *girl* will be fine." Her tone said it all, told him more than an outright statement ever could. Tatya considered Catherine a threat, both to the pack and to her feelings for Raphael. But for the life of him, he couldn't figure out what might have caused her attitude.

She took a deep breath. Her next words were even more tightly controlled than the last. "Lucas called me to send me here and to tell me that *we* have been instructed to raise and train the new kitten. Charles somehow managed to get a council directive."

Raphael's eyes widened in shock. How could Charles possibly have managed to get a council quorum in the space of a few hours? Then the reality sunk home. Monitoring her first change was one thing. *Training* the woman was at least a six-month commitment. Cats and wolves didn't get along at the best of times. The tensions within the pack would be enormous.

Raphael stared at her, opened his mouth, but couldn't find the right words to say.

"Don't look at me like that!" she snapped. "It certainly wasn't *my* idea."

Chapter Five

CAT GLANCED AT the clock on the bedside table. Twelve thirty. Afternoon sunlight poured through the bedroom windows. There was no hint of a breeze. The furnace clicked on, and the warmth of the central air felt surprisingly good.

She started to stretch, stopping abruptly. She hurt *everywhere*. Her entire body ached.

She lifted the sheet and looking at herself. She was naked. Her body was marked with livid bruises in black, red, and purple. Red cuts traced her torso, hardly scabbed over. The shape of the cuts was familiar. She'd had similar marks after the attack—claw marks. Cat's heart raced with panic. What had happened last night? She remembered a gorgeous Latino man with a gentle voice and a duffel bag of . . . of . . . *raw meat*. And she'd eaten it, and it tasted good.

Well, *that* part at least had to have been a dream, because, well . . . *eww*.

But the bruises weren't a dream. They were real. Where had they come from?

"Violet?" Cat called. Her voice held an edge of panic. She rolled out of bed. There was no answer from her aunt, but Cat could hear movement and muted voices coming from the kitchen. Cat took a deep breath and sneezed. The air was heavy with the scent of pine cleaner combined with the aroma of cooking meat and coffee.

That did it. Something was *definitely* wrong. There was no way Violet Wildethorne would allow meat or coffee in her kitchen, let alone both!

Cat grabbed the burgundy robe draped across the top of the dresser. Touching the satin fabric brought to mind something . . . an image of Mrs. Zabatos and the police. It was gone as quickly as it came. Cat shook her head, and instantly regretted it. *"Ow,"* she moaned. She slid into the robe before tentatively running her fingers over a large lump on the side of her head.

Cat's throat tightened, her stomach fluttering with nerves. She tied the robe's belt around her waist as she padded down the carpeted hallway. The sounds were coming up the back stairwell from the kitchen. Cat paused on the top step, listening. Both voices, male and female, sounded vaguely familiar. She didn't hear Violet.

She sniffed the air, searching for her aunt's signature perfume. She smelled it all right, coming faintly from Violet's bedroom. She tapped lightly on the door and listened. She could hear her aunt's soft snores, but there was a second set of breaths as well. Catherine opened the door. There was Violet, curled up on the navy bedroom carpet, a comforter tucked around her. She looked fine.

A woman Catherine didn't recognize lay on her aunt's bed. She was pale, her skin nearly as white as the cotton sheet that covered her up to her chest. It obviously wasn't a natural pallor. Her skin was almost gray, as were her lips. She lay very still. The only clue that she even lived was the slight rise and fall of her chest beneath the sheet and the soft whistle of breath through her slightly parted lips.

Cat stood next to the bed for a long moment. Something . . . something about the woman was familiar, but she couldn't quite pinpoint it. She struggled, trying to grab onto the wisp of memory, but it was frustratingly elusive.

"Good morning, Catherine."

She turned toward the voice coming from the doorway. Her breath caught in her throat. It was him: the man from the restaurant, and from last night's dream.

This morning he wore a pair of faded and worn blue jeans with a hole torn through one knee and no shirt. He looked perfectly comfortable, and breathtakingly gorgeous. There was not an ounce of extra flesh on that perfectly muscled body, and his skin was a warm brown. Dark stubble traced the outline of his jaw, not quite hiding the cleft of his chin.

"Who are you and what are you doing here?" Cat pulled the robe more tightly around her body and lowered her head a fraction. The words were hostile, suspicious.

He didn't act angry at her tone. "My name is Raphael Ramirez. Your godfather sent me here to help you and your aunt."

Cat wanted to believe him. It sounded like Uncle Chuck. Somehow he always seemed to know just the right thing to do and the perfect time to do it.

"How much of last night do you remember?" the man asked softly—his gaze was intense.

She hesitated, unsure what to do. He wasn't acting threatening. But there was no proof that he really was sent here by Uncle Chuck, and nothing made *sense*.

"Tell me the *name* of the person who sent you!"

"Charles Wingate. You can call him to confirm, if you think it's necessary. But I don't think you do. I think you know what happened last night. I know it might be frightening to remember, but that's okay. We met the *second* time in the park, if you remember. You could see me from above. I was carrying a—"

His voice trailed off and he raised his brows, encouraging her to continue the story. Cat struggled to put the fragmented pieces of her memory into a coherent whole. She remembered shopping and lunch with Violet, with this man smiling across the room at her. The drive home had been fine. Violet had gone into the study to write. Cat had gone upstairs. She must have fallen asleep, because she'd had the weirdest dreams: dreams of moving like a shadow through the night, every sight and scent intense. Dreams of the man in front of her, speaking softly and caressing her shoulder gently. There was blood and violence as well, and she fought the cat that had attacked and killed her parents. But she hadn't been human. In the dreams she, too, had been a cat: a huge black panther. She'd fought, struggling to kill the larger male, taking bruising blows and slices from vicious claws.

Cat shuddered, feeling the pull of the marks on her body. *Claw* marks. Cat pulled the lapel of her robe open slightly, just enough to catch a glimpse of a nasty-looking cut, right where the panther had received a blow.

"It isn't possible." She whispered the words softly. Then, louder, with a barely controlled edge of hysteria. "It isn't *possible*!"

He looked at her with sympathy, as though he wished somehow things were different. "Why don't you come down and have some breakfast? We need to talk. After all, I *did* promise you an explanation."

Cat started at his words, and a scene opened in front of her eyes, on top of what she could see in the here and now. He was standing at the doorway, looking up. She was wearing this same robe and another woman, a blonde woman, was supporting her. He promised to explain and she'd trusted him. She felt her hand go to her mouth in near-terror and Raphael looked stricken at her reaction. He started to walk toward her, but then stopped and waited. But she wanted him to move closer. She wanted—

No! She *didn't* know him. She *couldn't* know him. There was no reason to trust him. But a deep instinctive part of her *did*. In the dreams of last night he had been the one constant.

That first scene triggered a memory, then another, and another. The events of the night before unwound in her mind like a ball of twine. She remembered it all, and the shock of it made her sway, nearly faint. He cleared the distance between them in an instant, supporting her weight. He helped her sit on the edge of Violet's bed, careful not to jostle either her or the other woman on the bed. "Put your head between your knees."

"I don't believe it," Cat whispered. "It isn't *possible*."

"Easy now." Raphael crouched down in front of her. He whispered, stroking her back in gentle circles. She felt warmth flow from his fingertips as though he were creating his own heat. "Take it easy. It's going to be all right."

She looked up then, glaring at him in utter disbelief. "It was a *dream*. It *had* to be."

"I'm afraid not." A woman appeared in the doorway—the blonde woman from her dream. Her voice was a sultry alto that was nearly as beautiful as her looks. She was exquisite. Even Violet's ill-fitting navy-blue sweat suit didn't conceal the perfect curves of her body, and hair that was the natural silver-blonde screen sirens try unsuccessfully to imitate. Her clothes smelled of Violet's lilac perfume.

She smelled like a dog. No, Catherine corrected herself. She smelled like a . . . *wolf*.

Catherine's eyes were drawn back to the man kneeling in front of her. She swallowed hard, forcing herself to appear calm. It wasn't easy. Her pulse was pounding in her ears, and she couldn't seem to get a deep breath.

"Who are you? *What* are you?"

"*We*, Catherine." The woman corrected her. "What are *we*. We are shapeshifters, and you're one of us now."

"*I* am not an animal! There are no such things as shape-shifters!" Catherine protested. It wasn't true, and somehow she knew it. She began to tremble. Raphael reached for her and she let him. As he drew her close she began to cry, deep, wracking sobs that tore at her body. She cried—partly for the loss of her parents, but mostly for the loss of *herself*.

"I'M SO SORRY." Raphael tightened his hold, pressing her against his chest as she wept. "I'm so very, very sorry." He murmured the words gently into her thick, golden hair.

A sudden burst of jealousy scent poured across the room. It was thick enough to walk on and he knew the source. Burned metal and roasted pepper oil was an unforgettable combination that always made his eyes burn and water. Raphael turned his head and gave Tatya a look of utter weariness. She had no *right* to be jealous. He was just comforting a woman whose entire life had been shaken to its foundations. Besides which, Tatya had chosen *Lucas*. Being Alpha Female had been more important to her than her love for Raphael, more important than her mating bond. He let all of that show in his angry gaze, sparing her nothing.

Their eyes locked over Catherine's bent head. A dark flush crept up Tatya's neck. Her jaw thrust forward as she fought to control an unreasoning rage. Whether it was at him, herself, the woman, or the world in general, Raphael neither knew nor cared. He simply stayed as he was, holding the woman, waiting for Boulder's alpha female to get a grip on herself.

"Why don't I go tell Holly to bring the cat some breakfast?" Tatya said bitterly. She turned on her heel and left. Raphael

heard her stomp into the kitchen, heard the few terse words of
her orders, followed by the slamming of the kitchen door and
the sound of glass breaking.

She'd left.

It was probably better that she had, considering her emotional state. But Betty still needed to be taken to the pack hospital, and someone needed to give the woman breakfast and her
initial orientation lecture.

"Why is she so angry?" Catherine asked with a soft sniffle.

"Long story. It has nothing to do with you." Raphael answered. He reached into the pocket of his jeans and withdrew a
clean handkerchief, which she gratefully accepted. "But you
need breakfast. After that, there are important things we need to
discuss."

Chapter Six

CAT SAT ON the couch. Someone had closed the living room drapes. The room was dim and shadowed, despite the bright sunshine she could glimpse streaming into the kitchen over the top of the swinging doors. Raphael sat down beside her, close enough that the length of his thigh pressed against hers. Her throat went dry; Cat swallowed convulsively. It wasn't that she was afraid of him. Common sense said she should be, but she just wasn't. No, this was a deeper, and much more primal reaction.

He raised his hand to cup her cheek. With gentle pressure, he turned her face until her eyes locked with his. As she watched they changed subtly, the color shifting from a hazel-brown to intense gold. She felt the power building between them. The hairs on her body raised in reaction. It didn't hurt, but it felt strange. The temperature in the room rose as well.

When he spoke, his voice was deeper, rougher than it had been with the edge of a growl. "Since the dark beginnings when man and animal began roaming the earth there have been stories—tales of blood and magic that spoke of those who could shift their skins and become their totem animals. Some were worshiped as gods. Your godfather was one of them. He is the most powerful Sazi of us all. For years beyond count we have coexisted with the wandering tribes of humans."

She opened her mouth to speak, but the power pressed against her like a living thing, cutting off her ability to utter so much as a sound. Uncle Chuck was one of them? The *leader*? How could she have never guessed?

Raphael's harsh voice brought her back to listen. "But humans fear that which they can't understand. And they kill what they fear."

The living room where they sat vanished in a rush of power. Catherine blinked, gasping in shock and fear.

She was a small, brown-skinned girl of nine or so, her black hair pulled back in a tight braid. She ran desperately across uneven desert ground, cactus thorns and sharp rocks tearing at her bare feet and legs as she fled the screams of the dying.

She heard the thunder of footsteps, felt the ground shudder beneath her feet. She risked a glance back, and saw her mother's brother drawing ever closer, a club drawn back to swing.

She felt the club strike home, hard enough to lift her small body from the ground before slamming face forward into the sand.

He ran on, leaving her for dead. She very nearly was. But slowly, she began to heal, enough to move her head, to see the fate of her kind.

Scenes of blood and violence assaulted her senses as the killers moved like a scythe through the village, slaughtering anyone, even pregnant women, they suspected might carry the contamination.

The adults they beheaded, to make sure there would be no return, no magical healing.

Then, suddenly, it was over. There were no more screams. A familiar voice barked orders, and the attackers disappeared, back to the neighboring village from whence they came.

She lay, listening, hoping to hear the sound of some other survivor. But the silence was only broken by the harsh caws of the carrion birds, eager to feast.

One or two of the birds were bold enough to try to attack her, but they'd waited too long. She'd regained enough strength to change forms and fight them off. And when the moon rose, and it was cool enough to travel, she began the painful journey to see if any others had survived.

The images faded and Catherine was once again in her own body. Raphael's hand was still on her cheek, wet now with her tears. She heard his voice inside her head.

Only a tattered remnant of the Sazi escaped to start over, hiding who and what they were until all that was left was the rumor of skinwalkers, evil witches who could take the form of animals. Eventually even that faded to the point of myth, becoming the fodder of B movies. The Sazi survive by hiding in the shadows. We live among the humans, but apart, with our own laws, our own customs. But the first and greatest law is *always* to keep the secret.

She heard Raphael's voice come to her as though from a distance. "We lost 90 percent of our people in six days of systematic slaughter. Men, women, children . . . even infants at the breast. The Ravaging wiped out entire bloodlines."

"But, this was before mass communication . . . *how*?"

Raphael's expression was grim. "We don't know. But they did."

"I understand." And she did. She remembered Uncle Chuck talking to her father about prejudice once. She always seemed to think that there was something in her godfather's past . . . someone he'd lost. But if Uncle Chuck was like Raphael, like the little girl in the vision, then he'd lost more than she could grasp.

Raphael's voice brought her back to the comfortable living room. His voice was flat, without emotion, but she could tell that there was something deadly serious about his words. "Do you? Do you really? Can you even imagine how desperate our people are *never* to risk another Ravaging?"

He spoke the word *Ravaging* in the same tone that Cat had heard Jewish survivors spoke the word *Holocaust*. Horror, mixed with rage and sorrow.

"If you give me your word right now and pledge your *life* to keep our secret, I will help you adjust to the changes you face. I'll teach you our ways, our history. But I have to make sure you can be trusted to keep our secret. The humans are not as powerful as we are . . . *individually*. But collectively, they could destroy us. They outnumber us by the billions. Secrecy keeps us alive, keeps us safe."

"And if I don't agree? What will you do?"

He looked at her, and his eyes were filled with sorrow, but determination. "I think you know the answer to that. And if I refuse, then another will take my place, and your godfather will have *me* put down alongside you."

Somehow she had known the answer, and that she should be afraid. But she wasn't. "I know. I promise." She said it softly.

He stared at her for a long, silent moment. His eyes shifted back to their normal color, the heat in the room faded. But the electric sensation against her skin didn't diminish. When he spoke his voice was normal, human, with none of the animal undertone it had carried before.

"We call ourselves the Sazi, the cave dwellers. We're *not* all evil—any more than any human is. But we're not all good, either. We have our criminals and killers, and, like the humans, we have law enforcement. Wolven is the name of our police force. But the agents cannot always be everywhere they are needed. They were not there for your parents, Violet, or you. For that I am sorry."

"Violet?" Catherine stared at Raphael in horror and her hand clutched around his arm, fingernails digging in with panic.

He smiled and shook his head. But she noticed he didn't remove her hand from his skin. "She wasn't hurt, thanks to Betty."

"Betty?"

"The woman on the bed. The one Jack gutted in the kitchen."

Catherine felt dizzy, faint, and a little nauseous. "You're telling me—"

"The jaguar who attacked you and killed your parents was one of us. He is a serial killer named Jack Simpson."

"You used his name." She could barely get the words out. "You *know* him."

Raphael nodded, and fury filled his gaze. "I do."

Catherine pulled her hand from his arm. Her green eyes narrowed, and a low growl crawled from between her lips as she glared at him. "Why haven't you done something? Why is he still on the loose?"

Raphael's gaze never wavered, but Catherine saw the tightening of his jaw muscles, heard the controlled anger that belied his calm words. "Jack has protected himself from our laws very carefully. He's placed himself in a political position—he's a U.S. senator, protected by the Secret Service. If he dies under even *remotely* suspicious circumstances, his attorneys have been instructed to release a file to the press that contains not only absolute scientific proof of our existence, but a list of names, addresses, and identifying information about virtually every powerful Sazi in existence. He was one of our leaders once. He knows ways of determining who is and isn't of our blood and how to kill us. In other words, he has set in place the threat of a second Ravaging."

She watched him take a deep breath and swallow back what seemed to be a violent curse. "The leaders of our people are not willing to risk releasing that information and the total annihilation of our kind in order to bring Jack to the justice he deserves."

Catherine's rage was overwhelming. Her body quivered with the need to *do* something. She wanted him dead, wanted to kill him, but the images of the vision she'd had, the moments she'd lived with the little dark-haired girl, would not be denied.

Raphael spoke slowly, choosing each word with utmost care. "Anyone who wants to take down Jack Simpson will have to neutralize that file first. Otherwise they'd be assassinated without so much as a second's hesitation before they could get anywhere near him."

"And if someone *were* to neutralize the file?" Catherine's eyes burned with inhuman intensity. The heat in the room increased enough that the air conditioner whooshed to life.

Raphael's smile was a baring of sharp teeth. "Manage that, and, baby, it's huntin' season."

RAPHAEL PADDED BAREFOOT across the front lawn to where he'd parked the Mitsubishi. He needed to retrieve his cell phone and have a cigarette, and have just a few minutes away from the cat to think and relax. By now Charles was probably frantic. Or not. Last night his gifts must have come back online long enough to track the cat to the park. Maybe Charles knew everything that was happening. Maybe he'd *always* known. But why would he caution Raphael *not* to tell Lucas, and then tell him himself just a few hours later? It made no sense as far as Raphael could see. Then again, Raphael had never figured out how the seer gifts worked. Hell, he wasn't even sure *they* knew. He was just damned glad that neither fore- nor hindsight were among his talents. He liked living in the present, thank you very much.

He hit the speed dial for Charles, who picked up on the first ring and snapped, "Report."

"She survived, and you were right. She wasn't even close to feral." Raphael took a long drag on his cigarette.

He heard an audible sigh and a cough that might have covered emotions much deeper. After a few moments of silence, Charles asked, "Did you explain the facts of life to her?"

"I gave her the first lecture." Raphael searched for the right words. "Actually, she didn't strike me as the type to *listen,* so I decided to try what Nana did for me when I was a child."

"I didn't realize you were a strong enough telepath to do that sort of thing," Charles said. Raphael flattered himself to think there might have been a bit of amazement in his voice of his leader.

"I don't think *I* am," Raphael admitted. "She seems to have inherited a few gifts from her sire. But it was worth a try. After all, worst case I'd just wind up telling her after all."

"It worked? No problems?"

"It worked."

His voice was satisfied, as though a question had been answered that had never been asked. "So she probably does have some talent. Good. She'll need it."

Raphael shuddered. Goose flesh climbed up his bare arms. The woman had talent all right. She'd dragged him so deep into the vision that he'd seen, felt, even *smelled* the blood and gore, everything, as if he were living it in truth for the first time. "Definitely."

"And the aunt? How's Violet doing?"

Raphael hadn't been looking forward to this. Which was why he told the Chief Justice the good news first. "She wasn't *injured.*"

Charles's slow growl sounded like a burst of static over the wire. But Raphael knew better. "But—"

He inhaled deeply on his cigarette and then let out the smoke slowly. "She apparently saw Jack change before she fainted.

And when she came to and saw the blood and damage to the kitchen—" He let the sentence trail off.

"I see. How bad is she?"

"Bad." In fact, it had been all he could do to keep a shield up so that the neighbors wouldn't hear her shrieking. "Tatya put her under for a bit. But I'm concerned about how she's going to do when she finally wakes up."

"Call Ned Thornton," Raphael's eyebrows rose at the suggestion. Ned's family had once been prominent in the shapeshifting community, but the magic seemed to have left their bloodline. There hadn't been a wolf in their family for a couple of generations. Still, he knew the Sazi secret, and was a respected family member. The suggestion was a good one.

"Ned and Violet have been dating for most of a year. He'll be able to help her cope and explain things to her. Have him meet you at the pack hospital.

"Sir—"

"We need Violet alive, Raphael. I would never have risked you, Betty, or Tatya otherwise."

Raphael leaned against the passenger door and tapped one finger on the windshield for a moment, letting the long line of ashes from his cigarette fall to the sidewalk. "Speaking of Tatya—"

Charles sighed. It was obvious he had anticipated Raphael's objections, had even been waiting for the younger man to voice them, but Raphael plowed on.

"Sir," Raphael struggled for the right words. Diplomacy had never been one of his best skills. "Having the cat stay here—" He dropped the cigarette butt and ground it out with the toe of his boot. "I'm not sure—"

Charles spoke gently, but firmly. As usual for him, he chose to approach the problem from an oblique angle. "Raphael, I know it's always bothered you that your major talent, the one you're best known for, is a destructive one."

He flinched. Charles wasn't saying anything other than the absolute truth, but that didn't mean Raphael had to like it.

"But your *other* talents, your training, and even your *disposition*—they all make you uniquely suited for dealing with an angry and confused new turn. That was why I insisted Raven live with you after his first change, and is why Catherine will be staying in Boulder and training with you for the next few months. Not with the pack, as Tatya believes, but with *you*."

He felt cool air on his tongue as his jaw dropped in surprise. He'd never trained a female new turn, and barely knew anything at all about training cats. "But . . ."

"No buts, Raphael. This is a direct order from the Chief Justice and a directive from the council. If Mrs. Santiago doesn't like it she can take it up with me."

Raphael didn't say a word, but it wouldn't surprise him if she did.

He reached into his pocket and retrieved the last cigarette from the pack. He couldn't remember the last time he'd smoked so many in a row so quickly.

"I'll be checking in periodically to see how Catherine's doing." The tone in Charles's voice said that it would be soon, and that there had better be *progress* in her training.

He cleared his throat. "Yes. Of course, sir."

"Let me know if there's anything I can do to help."

"Yes, sir."

Raphael slid the cell phone into his back pocket and pulled out his lighter. Once he'd lit up, he walked back over to the Wildethorne house, ignoring the nasty look Mrs. Zabatos was giving him as she used a hose to water the pots of geraniums that lined her front steps. She'd need to move them inside if she wanted them to survive the winter. Then again, she did seem the type.

When he reached the front door he hesitated. He could hear Holly and Catherine talking in the living room. It had been a shock to find out that they'd known each other, even if only slightly. Apparently the Turner woman had been stopping in at the Joint for breakfast periodically over the past couple of weeks.

He tried to convince himself he didn't want to interrupt them, but the truth was something else entirely. The cat was a living, breathing distraction for him. It wasn't what she did—it was who she was. She had the whole package: looks, brains, and a sense of humor. Her scent almost made him high. The power of the magic that had flared between them when he'd touched her to share the vision had been absolutely incredible. Combined with the visceral attraction he had for beautiful women, and his natural preference for cats, *and* his animal's reaction to her being near heat—God, just being in the same building with her was damned near overpowering. And Charles wanted him to train her.

Raphael fought down a thrill of nerves as he stepped away from the front door and followed the sidewalk to the back of the house. A part of him didn't want the responsibility of training the cat. But a bigger part of him did. And that was *such* a bad idea, for *so* many reasons.

But Lucas was going to be out of town most of the time dealing with Wolven. There really wasn't anybody else powerful enough in the territory to deal with the woman if things went wrong. And Charles had made himself *very* clear. Raphael didn't dare refuse or fail on this assignment.

The good news was that Jack had been injured—badly enough that he probably wouldn't be able to come after the woman until he'd had time to go off and lick his wounds. But she was his chosen prey. He *would* be back.

Raphael just hoped the woman would be capable of defending herself when the time came. Catherine had done surprisingly well in the battle last night. A good bit of that had been due to the advantage of surprise. Next time, Jack would be expecting her to put up a good fight.

Raphael sighed heavily. He'd do his best. But frankly they were hog-tied. He couldn't let her kill Jack—even in self-defense. Not until the Sazi were safe from the contents of that file.

And Raphael would lay odds that Catherine could come up with a plan to do it. He didn't know why, considering how many had tried and failed. But he just knew she could.

Raphael allowed himself to revel in the possibility. A world without Jack: where he could go through life without constantly looking over his shoulder, without worrying how many more young woman would die while he stood helplessly by.

He sighed, the illusion shattering. It was much more likely that, sooner or later, Catherine Turner would die when Jack came back to finish the job.

In the end that was the reason Raphael planned to never pursue the attraction he felt for her. Because if Jack even suspected there was something between the two of them, he would make the woman suffer in more and worse ways than Raphael could even imagine. She'd beg for death before he gave it to her.

Raphael would just have to ignore the attraction he felt for her, keep his trousers zipped and take very cold showers.

Raphael stepped off of the concrete into the lush grass of the backyard. The ground felt cool beneath his feet, blades of grass tickling his toes as he searched to find what was left of the things he'd been wearing before his change last night. The clothes were toast. The leather jacket hadn't disintegrated, but neither had it been heavy enough to withstand the magic. His boots were still in one piece, but badly scorched. That pissed him off. It was always hard to get a pair of boots broken in, and this had been his favorite pair. *Damn it!*

But the loss of his favorite boots didn't bother him nearly as much as the next bit of bad news. Despite searching carefully, inch by inch, he could *not* find his gun. Which meant that unless Tatya had the presence of mind to pick it up, Jack probably had it—just because he'd gone through the window in cat form didn't mean he'd *stayed* in cat form, and nothing would amuse him more than to shoot Raphael with his own weapon.

Raphael clenched his jaw hard enough his teeth made a grinding noise. Just his luck—his worst enemy had his gun *and* silver ammo, too. He swore vigorously under his breath. There was no help for it, but that didn't make him any less angry.

The sound of a familiar van pulling into the driveway distracted him. Mike had left earlier, taking Tatya's vehicle to go for the cleanup crew. As usual, Holly'd been the first to arrive with breakfast. But now the boys were here. Mike, his best friend, Peter Black, and another one of the boys they hung out with had come with the replacement kitchen furniture Tatya had requested. What was that boy's name? John something? It didn't matter really, but it bothered Raphael that the pack had gotten big enough that he didn't automatically know everyone by name and scent anymore. He was supposed to be their leader, damn it. They were his people.

He shook his head. The name was just gone—if he'd ever

known it at all. But he resolved to do better at getting to know *all* of the pack members over the next few weeks while he was serving as alpha.

Right now there were other things to worry about. They needed to get the house back in shape without setting off the neighborhood snoop. Sometime later today a glazier would arrive to fix the French doors and the back door window. With the new furniture and some curtains, everything should look fine. He hoped.

Raphael motioned for Pete to come over. The other boys began carrying a pair of kitchen chairs into the house through the back door.

Pete was a good-looking kid. He was a little bit larger than Raphael as a human, standing a solid six foot two. He was built big, and all of it was solid muscle. He wore his sun-streaked blond hair just a little long and was constantly brushing it away from eyes the blue of a summer sky. He was alphic, but not particularly aggressive—smart, but not intellectual. Somehow he had managed to be everybody's buddy and still advance within the pack until he was fourth among the men, after Lucas, Raphael, and his own father, Martin Black.

He kept his gaze down as was proper. "Alpha, we came as fast as we could."

"I know. I appreciate it." Raphael gave the boy a reassuring smile. His eyes went over to the van and he got an idea. "Pete, the Second Female and another woman are asleep upstairs. Dr. Santiago put them under to rest. I need to get them to the pack hospital *discreetly*." He nodded toward the blue paneled van. "Think you could help me out?"

The boy didn't hesitate. "Of course, sir."

"Thanks. You and Mike load 'em up. I'll ride in the back just in case. There shouldn't be any problems, but neither of you have much healing ability."

"No problem." Pete gave the appropriate nod of respect and went back into the house calling Michael's name.

Raphael watched him go, wondering for the thousandth time how in the hell Daphne and Martin had managed to raise a *nice* kid. Must have been the triumph of nature over nurture—it was the only possible explanation.

Raphael gathered up the remnants of his jacket and boots and dumped them in the trash can leaning against the wall of the double garage.

He needed to report to Wolven, and sooner rather than later. But he didn't relish dealing with Lucas. *That* promised to be an uncomfortable conversation. Raphael practiced what he would say in his head for a few seconds before pulling the phone from his pocket. But before he could even hit the first number he heard shouting inside the house, and Holly's panicked voice calling his name.

Raphael sprinted through the back door, ignoring the shards of glass that dug into the bottoms of his bare feet. They'd heal. He dashed through the kitchen, diving through the swinging glass doors into the living room, and into the middle of an ugly confrontation.

"Who the hell are you, and what do you think you're doing with my aunt?"

Peter was on the bottom step, Violet draped across his arms. Michael stood two steps up above him, carrying Betty. Catherine stood in front of them, blocking the way with her body.

"Get the fuck out of the way!" The third boy, John, stepped forward, intending to shove her away bodily.

She moved into a traditional defensive martial arts posture that Raphael immediately recognized. It should have looked ridiculous, since she wore nothing but a robe. It didn't.

In fact, she practically glowed with power, and Raphael could feel the heat of her magic beating at him from across the room.

The boy's lips pulled back, and a low growl rumbled from his throat. His handsome features hardened, becoming bestial. He was almost exactly Cat's height. But while she appeared slender, he was squat and heavily muscled. It didn't matter. Cat's eyes narrowed. She began shifting her weight subtly.

"Catherine, no! They're just trying to help," Holly pleaded.

"That is enough!" Raphael commanded and his words took on the rolling rumble of his wolf. "Everybody stand down!"

Peter froze and stayed utterly motionless. If Violet's weight was a burden, it didn't show. Then again, most Sazi had extraordinary strength, and Violet wasn't a large woman. Mike was out of the way. Holly wasn't a problem. But neither Catherine nor the other boy showed any sign of backing away from each other.

"What is the problem?" Raphael asked.

"We were following your orders to take them to the hospital," Pete spoke carefully. "But she," he nodded toward Catherine, "got in the way. She said her aunt wasn't going anywhere."

Raphael grimaced. It had been stupid of him not to let Cat know what they were doing. There was no reason for her to trust any of them.

"All right. This is my fault." All three of the boys looked shocked at the admission. He stepped toward Catherine. "I'm very sorry, Catherine. I should've told you what I had planned."

"My aunt is not going anywhere with a bunch of strangers." Cat's voice was cold and hard.

"Look, I've got my cell phone." He showed her the cell phone in his hand. "You can call Ned, ask him if it's all right for Violet to go with us. If he vouches for us, you stand down. If he doesn't, we'll put Violet right back up in her bed. Fair enough?"

"*Ned* knows you, too? Why in the hell have I never heard of *any* of this before now?" She reached out her hand for the phone without ever taking her eyes off of the man who had threatened her. In fact, she'd positioned herself in a way that all of them were within line of sight. No one would be sneaking up behind her. Whoever had trained her had done a fine job, and she'd obviously paid attention to the lessons.

It was easy to hear the beep of the cell phone buttons in the thick silence of the room. Ned's voice, too, came through loud and clear.

"Hello?"

"Ned, it's Catherine."

He paused. "Catherine, you sound odd. Is something wrong?"

"There's a man here who says his name is Raphael Ramirez. Do you know him?"

"Yes," Ned said cautiously. "Will you put him on the line?"

Raphael took the phone from Catherine's hand. "Ned."

"What the hell's going on, Ramirez?"

Raphael looked at Catherine, who was watching him through narrowed eyes. He knew she could hear every word Ned was saying. "The cat that attacked Catherine and her family was one of ours."

Ned started swearing loudly. Raphael let him rant for a minute or two before cutting in. "Violet wasn't hurt *physically,* but she saw some things last night that upset her. We want to take her to the pack hospital for counseling."

"Counseling?"

Raphael flinched at the disbelief in the other man's tone. Problem was, he could hardly argue. Most of the Sazi would just kill her to keep the secret, and not even feel particularly bad about it. "The Chief Justice himself has ordered that she's to get the best possible care."

"Charles? He knows?"

He locked eyes with Cat over the bulk of Peter's body. "As you might guess, Catherine doesn't trust us."

Ned gave a harsh, bitter laugh. "Smart woman."

"Ned—" Raphael wasn't amused and let it play through his voice. This was no time for old arguments.

The other man backed down and sighed. "Fine, put her on. But know this, Ramirez, if anything happens to Violet, anything at all, I've got a rifle and I can make silver ammo."

Raphael wasn't sure how he'd have answered that, had he been given the chance. He wasn't. Two things happened simultaneously. Catherine grabbed the phone and John decided to prove his dominance.

The blow was meant to hit her in the jaw. A fast right jab, designed to knock Catherine on her ass without really harming her. But she was too quick. The swing missed entirely. She countered with a rapid kick to the side of his knee that dropped him to the ground. She bounced backward on the balls of her feet so that she was just out of reach. Raphael felt a surge of magic as the boy prepared to shift.

"I *said* stand *down.*" Raphael slammed his power in place around the boy, catching him in midkick, and preventing him from changing. It hurt, and John gasped in pain. Raphael didn't care. The entire situation was balanced on a knife's edge. He was not about to let things go to hell because one stupid teenager didn't know how to obey an order.

"What's going on?" Raphael heard Ned's voice coming from

the phone clutched in Catherine's hand. "Catherine, are you all right?"

"I'm fine," she answered. But she stayed out of Raphael's reach, and he could see that she was tensed for action. "But are you *sure* I can trust these people?"

"You can trust Ramirez to keep his word. If he says he'll keep Violet safe, he will. I'm going to hang up so I can get down there and meet you at the hospital. I've been there a few times. It's not far up the mountain from you."

"All right. I'll see you there."

"Be careful," Ned ordered.

"Oh, I will. Don't worry about that at all." Catherine shut off the phone and tossed it back to Raphael, still staying just out of his reach. He caught it with his left hand and slid it into his pocket before he began issuing orders.

"Now." Raphael pointed his right index finger at Peter first and then Michael. "You, and you are going to *discreetly* load those women into the van." He turned to Catherine. "You go get dressed. I *assume* you'll want to stay at the hospital with your aunt until Ned arrives. Holly, you can bring her." Raphael kicked John lightly with the toe of his boot as he hovered in space. "*You* are going to stay here and let the glazier in to fix the windows. Maybe your knee will have healed by the time they're done. If not, swing by the clinic and have Dr. Santiago take a look at it."

Everybody was standing still, watching each other warily. "*Move*, people."

Chapter Seven

CAT TURNED IN her seat so she could face Holly. They'd been driving for several minutes now and the silence in the car had gone well beyond awkward. The little blue Geo should have been intimate and cozy. It wasn't. After two or three miles, Cat couldn't stand the silence.

"What was I supposed to do? Let him hit me?"

Holly's fingers drummed nervously against the steering wheel as she waited for the traffic light to change. The light rain that was beginning to fall wasn't quite hard enough to turn on the wipers, but to Cat, the skies looked like they were ready to open up.

"No. But . . . well . . . *no* . . ." She turned with a somewhat desperate look. Cat could hear her heart racing. She could actually *see* the scents rising off of Holly's body. It was too odd— Cat turned away, choosing to watch the passing scenery instead.

"You're not making a lot of sense." Cat muttered irritably.

Holly took a deep breath. "Only because you don't know the pack like I do." She slowed to a stop at a red light. "John was trying to prove dominance . . . that he was bigger, stronger—"

"I know what dominance means."

"Right, but within the pack it's a big deal. As one of the males—"

"Please don't tell me that this is sexist bullshit," Catherine snarled. It wasn't raining yet, but the wind had picked up, and heavy gray clouds were blowing in over the mountains.

"Yes and no," Holly replied earnestly. "You're new. Everybody's going to try to find out where you fit in. And you're a cat, which is a wolf's natural adversary. And yes, it's sexist, but most of the males *are* bigger and stronger. They just *are*. For you to take down an alpha male so easily . . . it's a little scary, and it's going to cause problems." The light turned green, so Holly started the little car moving again.

"He'll hold a grudge?"

"Oh, hell yeah." Holly turned onto a narrow side road that ran east-west. They were reaching the far outskirts of a section of town Cat had never seen. Nothing was familiar. "John's an ass that way." She paused, thinking about it. "Actually, John's just an ass."

Cat gave a sour laugh. "No kidding! So, what *should* I have done?"

Holly started tapping her fingers again. Apparently it was a nervous gesture. "I don't know. There really *isn't* a good answer. If you don't act dominant, they walk all over you. If you do, they keep trying to fight to prove they're better than you." She shook her head sadly. "You might ask Peter. He's the only person who seems to have a really good handle on how it works."

"Peter?"

"The big blond who was carrying your aunt."

"I doubt I made a good enough impression for him to talk to me." Cat sighed. She didn't think she'd been wrong—either in confronting them about moving Violet or in taking down John. But she wasn't stupid enough to think it wouldn't cause problems. Apparently there was a hierarchy, and she'd blown right through it.

"Hopefully Raphael will be able to explain it all when he trains me."

"What?" Holly pulled the car to the curb abruptly. "Who said he was going to train you?"

Cat thought about it for a minute. She couldn't really remember. She didn't think Raphael had actually told her, but she'd heard it somehow. "I think I must have overheard him talking on the phone. Why?"

The finger tapping had increased in speed. "Well, mostly because you're a cat. Cats and wolves *so* don't get along." She gave a rueful grin, "Well, *mostly* they don't get along. My uncle seems to have a serious weakness for felines. But he's the only wolf I know who can even stand them. The longer you stay here, the more trouble there will be, and it takes months to train a new turn."

She sounded so panicked that Cat shifted in her seat to get a better look at her while they talked. She'd learned a long time ago that body language said almost as much as a person's words if you paid attention. "You mean everyone who . . . *turns*—it's always because of attacks like mine?"

"Oh, God! No! Most of the people who shift inherit the condition. But not every family member turns full Sazi. And they don't really tell you most of the rules and stuff until you turn. I'm human, so I don't know some of what they'll be teaching, but I watched four of my sisters go through training, and Jasmine just *loved* rubbing my nose in it. So I know it takes a long time to train a new turn. They want to make *absolutely* sure that you aren't going to screw up in public or do anything that might give us away."

Cat shook her head. There was an intense sadness in Holly's eyes. It was as though the other woman wanted to be able to turn . . . desperately wanted this whole life that had been thrust upon Cat unwilling. That was just so *weird*. Why would *anyone* want to turn into an animal and kill things? It made no *sense*.

Now don't be that way. You know as well as I do that there are wonderful benefits as well. The magic, the longevity . . . the *sex*.

"Catherine, are you all right?" Holly's face was scrunched up with worry.

"Holly, please—call me Cat. And I'm fine," she lied. She wasn't fine. Not at all. And what? Why did she ask Holly to call her Cat? She'd never been called that in her life—she'd never been one for *any* nicknames, not even Cathy.

"You seem pretty lost in thought." Holly said as she hit the turn signal and steered the car back onto the road.

"I guess I'm kind of tired." Cat sighed. "It's been a tough couple of days."

"No kidding?" Holly laughed wryly at the understatement, but she was serious when she added. "It will get better. Really it will."

Cat's laugh was instinctive, but she didn't feel very humorous. "It can't get much worse, can it?"

Chapter Eight

RAPHAEL PULLED A set of four battered old paperbacks from the built-in bookshelves and tossed them one at a time onto the mess of papers that covered his desk. He needed to spend some time cleaning this place out. He had both a home office and an office at the towing company, so he didn't really use this space much. There was dust everywhere, and the backlogged paperwork was inches deep. Someone had stacked almost a dozen white banker's boxes of closed files along the wall, using the room for temporary storage—although maybe not so temporary judging from the amount of dust on top of them.

Raphael knew he needed to get in there more and keep on top of everything, but the trick was always finding the time to do everything he needed to.

There was no time today, either. He'd run up here after getting Violet and Betty settled in their hospital rooms, intending to grab training books and call a few old friends to gather whatever other training materials he could beg or borrow from the archives at Wolven.

He glanced down at the books. The covers were hopelessly old-fashioned by current standards, but the text wouldn't have changed any over the years. They'd still tell the cat all of the basics about Sazi culture. *If* she'd read them. Neither he nor Raven had been particularly good about that in their day. Raphael tried to excuse himself by saying he was only four when he'd turned, and the books were too advanced. It wasn't true. He'd been reading quite well by the time he was four—in both English and Spanish. In fact, he'd been the bane of his grade school teachers' existence. Nothing worse than a bored smart-ass. No, he hadn't skipped the books because they were too hard. He'd been bored to tears by the damned things, as had his son.

But they'd both had the advantage of being raised around the Sazi. It was easy to pick up a lot of the culture by osmosis, as with *any* culture. Catherine was coming into it totally cold—she needed the information provided by the novels.

The laptop he'd set up on the small conference table in the corner by the window beeped to let him know he had an incoming message. If he was lucky, it would be either Raven with the crib notes on magical training, or Charles with background on the woman. If he was really lucky, it would be both.

Raphael crossed the room in three quick strides and brought up the e-mail program.

There were three messages. Two were ones he'd expected. The third message was from Fiona Monier. He read it first, because it was by far the most unexpected.

Raphael, I know it's been a long time. But I understand that you've been temporarily reactivated because Jack has brought over someone, and that you will be training her. I pulled the attached from Jack's old personnel file. They may or may not be useful. Let me know if you need anything else. I may be on medical leave, but I'm not helpless. Don't worry. I have faith in you. You were always good on the mats.

F

Raphael clicked on the first attachment. The document had obviously been scanned into the computer after having been typed on an old-fashioned typewriter. He guessed from the formal language that the typed document was probably transcribed from something handwritten. It was a recommendation letter. It waxed poetic about Jack as the perfect replacement as head of Wolven because of his unique talents and abilities.

While he had outstanding healing ability, the talent that was most important was his ability as a telepath. According to the letter, Jack Simpson could slide in and out of most people's thoughts at will, and could occasionally actually watch events through their eyes. This made him invaluable as an interrogator since he could enter the mind of a detainee during questioning and know the truth. It also meant that there would be no problems with faulty communication between Jack and the agents as he could pass and receive information mind-to-mind.

Catherine had inherited Jack's telepathy. Raphael knew that from their earlier encounter. Whether she'd become strong enough to do the things the letter claimed her sire could was a question for a later date. It wouldn't surprise him. Raphael decided to be very careful what he thought about her—and to work on his shielding. Until she learned to control her powers, she would probably pick up on things at random, without meaning to.

He also decided he'd have to remember to add a long conversation about ethics and eavesdropping into her Sazi training.

Raphael closed the document and moved on to the next attachments. There were no surprises, and nothing that seemed applicable to the new kitten. Still, it had been good of Fiona to send the information. Raphael wondered if she'd done it out of guilt. Did the burden of blame that they shared bother her as much as it did him? He didn't know. If it did, she'd never let on.

Raphael shook his head, moving on to the next e-mail. It was from Charles. It thanked him for everything he'd done so far, and had several attachments included with the main e-mail that would be useful background information on Catherine and her family. It was all stuff he needed to know, but it could wait until later.

As usual, his son, Raven, had come through in spades. Attached to his e-mail was a list of reference books and videos about jaguars, training information from Antoine Monier on dealing with large cats and their fighting and hunting techniques, and a note letting him know that he should expect a FedEx package at the house by 3:00 P.M. Monday. He was actually surprised that Antoine hadn't offered to train the new turn himself. He was always on the lookout for new talent.

In the distance Raphael heard the slam of car doors. He turned, watching through the rain-spotted window as Catherine and Holly ran from the car up the stairs and into the main entrance of the clinic. They'd barely gotten inside before Ned arrived as well, speeding into the lot and parking his truck carelessly at an angle across three different parking spaces before sprinting to the hospital building.

Raphael stood for a long moment, staring down at the parking lot and grounds that divided the three buildings comprising the pack complex. He needed to get moving. It was already midafternoon. With the late fall days as short as they were, the moon would be coming up soon. The cat may or may not need to change, but she'd be irritable and restless, and no fit company for the humans. He'd give her an hour with Ned and Violet before he interrupted her for their first lesson.

In the meantime, he had a couple of errands to run, pack business to take care of. Not everyone would need to hunt on all three nights of the moon, but there were a few. With Tatya missing and Betty injured, somebody would have to lead the hunt. Martin would jump at the opportunity to do it—he was always chomping to show his authority. In fact, Raphael kept waiting for the other man to challenge him, try to take the position of second, but Martin always backed away just short of an actual challenge.

Then again, Raphael had always figured Martin for more of a shiv-in-the-back kind of guy—which was why Raphael never turned his back on Martin. Ever.

CAT TURNED AT the sound of a light tap on the door. Instinctively, she sniffed the air as the door swung open. It was Raphael.

"Catherine, can I speak to you a minute?"

She glanced over to Ned. He looked like hell. Never a handsome man, his weathered features were drawn with worry, his broad shoulders hunched with an exhaustion that came more from fear than from actual weariness. He gave her a resigned nod.

"Sure." She rose, setting her purse onto the floor beside her chair. "I'll be right back."

"No problem." Ned answered.

Raphael held open the door open for her, closing it firmly as soon as they were both through the door.

They walked a short distance down a long wide hallway, painted a pale peach with white trim. The gleaming white linoleum was speckled with dark gray flecks. Medical equipment was tucked away in various corners, and everything smelled faintly of antiseptic despite the hum of an air purifier that ran continuously.

There was a large nurse's station in the center of the hall, but it was empty. The nurse who had been behind the counter when Cat arrived had apparently disappeared on some errand or other.

"First—" Cat felt the words come out before she could stop them. "Call me Cat. Please."

Raphael nodded coolly, not even asking about the change—of course, how would he know that she'd spent her life up until now trying to convince people *not* to call her by nicknames?

"So—what?" She tried to keep the irritation from her voice. She was worried about Violet, about Ned . . . hell, about everything. Part of it was the waiting. She felt so *helpless* just sitting there, wondering when, or if, her aunt was going to wake. And she was hungry. She hadn't had anything to eat since . . . Cat shied away from the thought of last night. It was just too weird thinking about it. She really did feel like she was losing her grip on reality.

Raphael stood across from her looking utterly calm, a rock in the midst of the storm. "We need to talk about your training."

"My *training*?" So, it was true then. She *had* heard something. She still had no idea where she'd heard it. But he obviously took her question the wrong way from his response.

"Cat, this was your first change. Over the next few months, as your talents manifest, we'll discover how powerful you're going to be physically and magically. Some of your talents are innate—based on who you are and things you've done as a human. Some of them will be 'inherited' from the Sazi who sired you." He sighed. "It's my job to see to it that you learn how to control your magic, your beast, and help you integrate into our culture."

Well, that didn't sound good! "And if I don't *want* to 'integrate?' " Her eyes sparkled darkly.

"That's not really an option."

She felt her brows raise, and crossed her arms over her chest. He might be gorgeous, but she didn't like bullies. "I see. And when is this *training* supposed to start?"

"Did you have something else planned for the rest of this afternoon?"

Cat cast a quick glance down the long hall to the door of Violet's room. There was nothing she could do for Violet, but it felt wrong leaving her. Still, she wasn't alone. Ned was in there, and Cat knew that nothing would harm her aunt while he stood guard.

"Your aunt will be out for another hour or two," Raphael assured her. "The magical sleep will end of its own accord when she's healed."

"You're sure of that?" She met his gaze evenly.

"Absolutely." He slid a yellow plastic bag off his wrist and tossed it in her direction. "We'll be back before she even knows you're gone."

Cat caught the bag on the fly and flipped it open. Inside were a cheap set of gray sweatpants and a matching gray sports bra, along with a set of battered fantasy novels. She gave him an inquiring look.

"We'll go down to the school gym. It's Saturday, and the kids have an away game. We'll warm up inside, go over the basics. Then I'll take you into the grounds behind the clinic and we'll see about catching ourselves a snack." He smiled. "Why don't you slip into the restroom and change clothes? I'll tell Ned where we're off to."

Cat shot another guilty look in the direction of Violet's room before making up her mind. "If you're *sure* she won't wake up."

"Positive. Now . . . shoo." The picture of him making a shooing gesture with his hands made her laugh. It had been a very long time since she'd done that.

"Fine, I'm going."

"I'll meet you right here in five minutes."

Cat watched as he walked back to the room. She couldn't help herself. There was just something about the way he moved that invited a woman's gaze. Oh, and the way those jeans fit was practically sinful. It was enough to make her drool. Under different circumstances . . .

Raphael stopped with his hand on the doorknob, giving Cat a look that all but said, *I know what you're thinking.*

Blushing, she turned and hurried in the direction of the women's bathroom where she ducked into the first stall and started to strip. She liked him—what she'd seen of him. And she liked Holly.

It didn't make sense, really. She didn't know them! But she liked them, instinctively.

Cat tore the tags from the clothing he'd bought her and pulled everything on. The sweatpants were a little big, but there was a drawstring, so she was able to adjust them at the waist, and the larger size would give her more freedom of movement. The sports bra, on the other hand, was tight enough to be just a little bit uncomfortable. Still, it would give her enough support for a workout *and* she wasn't likely to fall out of it.

She carefully folded the clothes she had been wearing and slipped them with her thongs into the bag with the books.

Raphael was waiting outside the door when she emerged. With a sweeping gesture he directed her to the staircase at the far end of the hallway. He walked just fast enough to get to the door before she did, and held it open for her to pass.

It was still raining. As she passed through the metal exit doors Cat listened to the drumming of rain against concrete, reveled in the feel of a cool mist against her skin. She inhaled deeply, relishing in the ozone-laced scent that makes the air feel as if the world is fresh-scrubbed and clean.

For no reason she could name, the rain gave her hope. Cat tilted her head upward, laughing as she dashed barefoot across the puddle-strewn parking lot shared by the private hospital/clinic, the pack administration building, and a large blocky redbrick building that could never be mistaken for anything other than a school.

Raphael took off after her. She heard him swear as his slick-soled shoes slid on the wet pavement. It was ridiculous. She laughed again as she waited under the awning that guarded the door.

He struggled to dig a large ring of keys from the front pants pocket of his soaked jeans. He had to fiddle with the lock for a bit before the door would open. Once again he held the door, letting her lead the way.

Cat glanced around, getting her bearings. She'd never been here before, but the setting was familiar. It was just like every school she'd ever attended. The walls of the entry way were filled with glass trophy cases and bulletin boards with construction papered notices. Farther down, the halls between the classroom doors were lined with tan metal lockers, each with its own padlock.

Just beyond a group of glass-fronted trophy cases were the three sets of recessed metal doors. "Do those lead to the gym?"

"Yup."

The two of them passed through the hall, the sound of their wet footfalls echoing through the empty building. Cat paused to snicker at the huge sign painted above the doorway that read "Go Timberwolves!"

"The *Timberwolves*?"

Raphael grinned, obviously pleased that she got the joke. "It seemed appropriate."

"What's the name of the school?"

"St. Francis Private Academy." He turned the key in the lock and pushed the nearest door open for her.

"Cute."

"I thought so." He remarked. "Tatya . . . not so much. But Lucas liked it, so it's what we went with."

Cat thought about that for a minute. The complex was obviously not new. All three buildings looked as though they had been built at the same time, planned as a unit. They shared the same architecture, the same red brick. Both the clinic/hospital building and the school appeared to be immaculately tended, but there were still signs of long use. If Raphael had been here at the naming of the school he was definitely older than he looked.

Raphael walked across the gym to where the tumbling mats hung on the wall beneath the nearest basketball goal. "Here, help me with these."

The navy blue vinyl mats weren't heavy, just awkward, but they got them down and laid them out without any problem. Cat immediately began doing stretches. It felt good to do something physical. The gym wasn't *cold,* but it was chilly. The vinyl of the mats *was* cold beneath her damp feet.

"You handled yourself well back at the house," Raphael observed as he slid off his wet dress shoes. "I take it you've had some martial arts training?"

"Some." Actually, she'd had quite a lot of training in self-defense, martial arts, evasive driving, even some work with guns: all of it at her parents' insistence. When she'd been ten years old, one of the vice presidents of her father's company had taken his family to Mexico on vacation. Their son had been kidnapped. Despite every effort, including paying a ransom that crippled the family financially, they found the boy dead a week later. His parents never got over it. *Hers* never forgot it.

It was partially that training that had helped Cat to survive the jaguar attack that killed her mother and father. One of her favorite teachers used to say, "Used correctly *anything* can be a weapon. Always stay alert to the possibilities." She had, and was still alive because of it.

But her parents were dead.

"Cat?"

Cat shook her head and forced a smile. "Sorry, just thinking."

Raphael gave her a long look, but didn't probe further. Instead, he changed the subject by asking, "What would you like to cover first, physical training or magical?"

"Magical?" She didn't bother to hide her skepticism.

"After everything that's happened, don't tell me you don't believe in magic." Raphael's tone was so scathing she immediately felt her temper starting to rise.

Asshole.

It's not nice to call your teacher names, Catherine, even if it is inside your head.

Her eyes widened at the sound of his voice *inside her skull.* That shouldn't be possible.

Actually, it is. Your strongest gift will be telepathy, as it's also a talent Jack has. Once you're properly trained, talking mind to mind will be as simple for you as talking to someone on the telephone. You just need to think of him . . .

Cat felt herself swaying on her feet. She felt unaccountably hot, at the same time it was hard to breathe. Her stomach knotted. *Just like picking up the telephone . . . all you have to do is think of them . . . The voice in your head—*

Her stomach roiled and she tried to run for the doors. She didn't make it. She tripped over her own feet, dropped to her hands and knees, and retched.

She heard Raphael moving around, heard a door opening in the background, and the sound of water running. She couldn't turn her head to look, though; she was simply too sick to do anything.

The man who murdered her parents, who *ate* them in front of her, had been strolling in and out of her mind at will.

Cat closed her eyes. She wanted to scream, but she was afraid that if she started she might never stop. It was just too much. It was just too fucking much!

Warm hands lay a cool wet towel across the back of her neck. She opened her eyes to see Raphael cleaning the mess with silent efficiency.

"I'm sorry." It was a croak.

"It's all right." He seemed sincere, and she appreciated that.

She expected him to ask why. Instead, he simply waited in silence with the uncanny patience she'd only seen before when watching animals hunt.

She shuddered as another spasm grabbed her stomach.

Eventually it was over. She was quivering and weak, but everything that was going to come up had. She shifted her weight, pulling her body away from the mess to sit cross-legged on the floor by the free-throw line.

"There's been a voice talking to me in my head. A man's voice. I thought I was going crazy."

"Well, you're not." Raphael narrowed his eyes and lowered himself into a squat next to her, his weight balanced on the balls of his feet. "What has he been saying?"

Cat looked up, meeting that intense hazel gaze. She watched as her next question hit him like a blow, rocking him backward onto his heels. "Little things, like suggestions as to what I should wear, not to buy silver jewelry. But *why* is he doing this? Why is he stalking me?"

* * *

RAPHAEL LOWERED HIMSELF carefully onto the gym floor. Now *he* felt sick. If Jack was maintaining contact, that meant—

He shuddered at the thought of Jack sharing the thoughts of the woman he was stalking.

Cat's eyes staring at him burned with a need for answers. And while he'd rather do almost anything else in the world than tell this story to *this* woman, he began to speak.

"Fiona Monier is a were-cougar."

Cat furrowed her brow and opened her mouth to speak, but he raised a hand to stop her question. "Bear with me here. This takes a little bit of background to understand. Fiona and her family are among the most powerful of our kind. Because of that, she was recruited into Wolven when she was still very young."

Cat was watching him avidly. He knew she could sense his reluctance to reveal this. But she didn't make another sound.

"She had an affair with the head of the agency."

Understanding flowed into her face. "Jack?"

"Yes." Raphael watched her absorb the information, saw her pondering the implications. When he thought she was ready, he continued.

"Fiona is brilliant, beautiful, ruthless," He paused, took a deep breath through his nose to calm himself down. "At the time, she was completely disinclined to limit herself to a single man."

"I'm guessing Jack didn't take that well."

Raphael leaned back, planting his palms on the floor behind him. He looked up at the ceiling, trying to organize his thoughts. "Actually, for the most part, he was okay with it. He loved her, and was mated to her, but most of all he understood her. He knew she loved him. She'd have her fling, but then she'd come back."

Cat looked confused. "So, what happened?"

"She met *her* mate and left Jack for good."

"Mate?" She tilted her head slightly, her voice and expression making the word a question.

Raphael sighed. "You've heard people talk about soul mates?" She nodded. "Well, with the Sazi it actually happens. It's both a physical and a magical bond. Sometimes, as with Jack and

Fiona, it's one-sided. One person is tied but the other can walk away at any time. If things have gone too far, and the bond is too tight, when they do walk away, the mated person's mind can break under the strain. But a mated male literally *can't* physically injure the woman he's bound to."

"So Jack is obsessed with Fiona. What has that got to do with me?"

"He can't harm her. Not ever. But he hates her so much it's driven him quite literally insane. So, he punishes women who look just like her."

Her breath stilled. But it made such ridiculously simple sense. "Me."

Raphael nodded sadly. "The resemblance is uncanny."

The two of them sat in silence for a long time. When Cat finally spoke, her voice was soft, but firm. There was no hint of hysteria. And though Raphael could smell her fear, overlaying it was the scent of absolute determination.

"He won't be giving up. He'll keep coming at me until one or the other of us is dead. He's sane enough to want to come back and get me." She stood in one graceful movement and held out a hand to help him up.

"You're right. He won't give up. I know."

"Then I have a lot of work to do before he comes back. Let's get training."

Chapter Nine

JACK PREPARED TO give the woman's thoughts a gentle nudge, just enough to move her to wakefulness. He only had a few minutes free before his next meeting to take care of this little charade. Still, there was enough time to do a little poking around. He wanted to see what was on her mind, find out if things were going according to plan.

It was surprisingly difficult. Ms. Turner was a strong-willed woman, even asleep. He slid past her thoughts of her parents, her determination to take over her father's company, even her anger and loathing of him. None of that mattered to him. When he found what he was looking for he wanted to crow with delight. The seer had been right.

Jack took a second to write a note on the pad of his desk to give to his admin assistant. Roses perhaps, or some jewelry. Laura was always good at finding just the right gift for the occasion, and this deserved something special.

Now, it was time to up the stakes a little. *Good morning, kitten.*

CAT STIFFENED AT the sound of the voice in her head. It was morning. She had just opened her eyes and been debating whether or not to climb out of the nice, comfy bed. It was *cold*, and damp, the kind of weather that made her bones ache, made her want to stay under the covers and do nothing all day. But the voice changed all that. She wanted to move, not to stay in one place too long.

My name is Cat, asshole. She sat up straight and threw off the blanket. I know who you are now. I also know what you want, but you're not going to get it. You're not going to kill me like the others. I'm going to kill you instead.

She could hear his laughter in her head, warm and rich and rolling. *So they've told you about me. Good. Have they by chance mentioned my 'insurance policy'?*

The file with proof of the Sazi existence? Oh, yeah. They told me about it. Said that if you die of anything other than natural causes, the proof gets released to the press and the humans start a witch hunt. Must really be something to have them so scared.

Cat closed her eyes, shutting out all the external stimuli. Raphael had told her that if she eliminated distractions and concentrated, she might be able to break Jack's hold on her. At the very least, she'd be able to glimpse further into his mind. Like she'd want to.

Still, she focused her thoughts, concentrating hard. If she wanted to bring Jack down, she needed to know more about him. Yes, she'd be spending tonight on the Internet, but that would only teach her about his human side. His Sazi side wouldn't be in the computer records. To know her enemy she needed to get inside his head—literally.

I'd love to see it. Because, frankly, I don't buy it. Cat tried to keep him thinking about the file, keep him distracted.

You don't need to. They do. His voice in her head was smug.

He had a point. Frankly, it was a smart move on his part, playing on the Sazi paranoia. They believed they would be hunted down and destroyed; believed it enough that Raphael had bound Cat with magic to make *sure* she couldn't betray them.

Charles wants you to be fully trained before you leave Boulder. Conveniently enough, so do I.

You do?

Oh, yes. You wouldn't be much of a challenge otherwise. As it is . . . well, I'm all aflutter with anticipation. You're doing quite well. A little clumsy, but definitely not bad for a first attempt at distracting me.

Oh, goody.

He laughed again. *You're almost as sarcastic as I am. How absolutely delightful. You have no idea how much I'm looking forward to our next meeting, kitten. It might interest you to know* that I'm already healed from our last encounter. I took a shower at my club this morning, and nobody saw a single bruise. Think about that . . . in the meantime, work hard, and learn fast. My patience isn't endless. He paused and his voice deepened, as though angry. And find a different teacher. I don't *like* Ramirez. I don't trust him.

He cut the connection easily, before she had the chance to tell him where to go and how to get there. Cat swore. He'd seen right through her. Damn it! Last night Raphael had promised that someday soon, if she practiced the exercises he'd given her, she'd be able to do just as well. She certainly hoped so.

Looking down at the angry red marks that still remained on her legs and stomach made her shiver. Jack was already *healed*? Once she started to remember the night she fought, she remembered it all, and she'd hurt him badly. On top of that, Raphael said he'd shot him several times with silver.

Damn! How powerful did that make him?

She tried to think about something, anything, else. But, it was hard going. The knowledge that Jack Simpson was out there, watching and waiting . . . she shuddered at the thought, her stomach roiling. But Raphael was teaching her, and she was determined to keep on training with him, *especially* since Jack didn't like him.

As always, she took refuge in work. Barefoot, she padded downstairs to Violet's office. Originally intended as the master bedroom, it was huge. The walls were painted a pale lilac that exactly matched the lilacs in the pattern of the ruffled curtains that framed wide, multipaned windows. The carpet was a vivid royal purple, as were the throw pillows on the loveseat that took up one corner of the room. Next to it stood a tall set of bookshelves that was filled with hardback books Violet used for research and dozens of romance novels, many of their colorful spines bearing her aunt's name in the large, hot-pink lettering that was her aunt's trademark. Cat walked over to the computer desk and hit the switch to turn on Violet's computer. She was careful not to disturb so much as a single Post-it note or sheet of paper that was strewn over the desktop. The "novels" she was supposed to study from were stacked neatly on the end table next to the loveseat.

She shuddered. Normally she liked fantasy novels. She had entire shelves filled with them in her bedroom in California. These books, however, did not make the grade. If the writer hadn't had the Sazi as a captive audience, the books would have died an ignominious death due to lifeless characters and clunky dialogue. And the attitudes were archaic—honor, challenges, and the rule that a man couldn't stay with a woman more powerful than himself.

The sad part was that she more than suspected those were the rules of the culture she was being dropped into. If that was true she was so screwed.

Cat clicked the mouse on the icon to take her to the Internet. She needed to check her e-mails, check in with the one part of her life that still made sense. It took awhile for the program to upload. Violet's computer was old and slow enough to drive Cat to distraction. When it finally finished, she stared at a screen that told her she had *ninety-three* new messages. *Jeez.*

Some of it was spam. She got rid of those with a couple of quick clicks of the mouse. Condolence messages got a quick reply. There were several messages from the attorneys handling her parents' estate. Those got forwarded to the executor—and the head of the Sazi, Cat reminded herself—Uncle Chuck.

The next message was actually from him. She opened it quickly.

Catherine, these are difficult times for you, I know. But I also know that you're strong and resilient enough to cope with what's happening. Know that despite what you've lost, you're *not* alone.

Trust Raphael. He's a good man. He can help you get a grip on what is going on in your life. He'll help you and answer all your questions honestly, without any hidden agenda.

Call me if you need *anything.*

I love you.
Charles

Cat read and reread the message. He knew. He understood what was going on. She thought for a long moment, deciding how best to phrase what she wanted to say. She needed to be vague enough that anybody reading the message wouldn't learn about something he shouldn't—but she needed to still get her point across.

```
Dear Uncle Chuck:
  You're right. Things are very hard. I feel
like my life's turned upside down.
  I'm hoping you can help me with something.
I understand that you have a copy of the in-
surance file. Is there any chance I could
get a look at it and that we can sit down
and talk? I have an idea as to a solution to
the problem. Let me know as soon as you can.
                              Catherine.
```

She hit the send button, and moved on to the messages from her friends. There were notes about concerts, babies, gossip about Brad and the office. One of her best friends from the office would be leaving for a new job at Microsoft at the end of the week.

She laughed. It had been bound to happen sooner or later. Ron's e-mail sounded so surprised. He had a minor conviction for computer hacking in his background and had thought it would keep him from getting the job. Cat knew better. It hadn't bothered her father one damned bit. Some of the best software programmers in the world former hackers. That was just a fact.

Cat glanced at the clock readout on the computer and swore under her breath. She needed to get moving if she wanted to get a run in before work.

In fact, she was dreading the day ahead of her. While she *did* trust Raphael as a person, she didn't necessarily agree with his judgment. She was almost thirty! Far too old to be working at a burger joint! And while she would never insult Holly by saying so, it was such a step down from what she was used to. Still, Raphael had insisted, saying things like, "You need to get to know the pack members, see how other Sazi behave." And, "You're too new to this to be trusted out among the humans without supervision."

As if the job weren't enough, starting Monday Cat had been ordered to attend "puppy school" for training with the newly turned wolves. The idea had sounded iffy enough—and that was *before* she'd found out Tatya was the teacher.

Tatiana Santiago, the one and same woman who'd stormed off yesterday morning for no reason anyone cared to explain.

Immersion her ass! The idea was for her to spend every waking minute in the company of Sazi so that she could get a better grip on the culture. Unfortunately, the last thing Cat wanted to do was spend her time stuck in a classroom with a bunch of preteen kids during the day and working at a burger joint at night. Especially not if John was a typical example of how pack members behaved.

Raphael had listened attentively to everything she'd said. It hadn't made one damned bit of difference. He'd made up his mind and nothing was going to change it. The best she could manage was to wring the concession from him that if she gave it her best shot and it still didn't work, they'd figure out something else.

What made Raphael think that a cat could get along with a bunch of wolves, Cat wasn't sure.

It was hours later when Cat tapped lightly on the door to Violet's hospital room. "Hello?" She stuck her head in, just in time to see Ned pull hastily back into his seat as Violet wiped quickly at her reddened eyes.

Violet looked like hell. Her skin was drawn, her color had a grayish tinge. But far worse to Cat's mind was the fine, nervous trembling that shook her aunt's body.

"Good morning, Catherine." Ned's voice held a false heartiness that cut Cat to the quick. Violet said nothing, didn't smile, and couldn't even bring herself to look at Cat. Instead, she clung to Ned's hand like a lifeline.

"So, how're you doing this morning?" Cat walked over to the chair by the window and took a seat. Emotions boiled over the top of each other as she saw Violet, looking pale and frail. She wanted to run over and hug her, but something stopped her. Instead, she struggled to appear casual, like nothing was wrong. It was a lie, and they both knew it, but it was all she could think to do.

"Oh, I think she's doing a little better. Aren't you, Vi?" Ned gave her hand a little squeeze.

Violet turned her head very slowly to where her niece sat. Her eyes were haunted and shadowed. Cat could see the effort it cost her aunt to face her fear and her heart broke from the realization that *she* was what Violet was terrified of.

Tears filled Cat's eyes, running unchecked down her cheeks.

Violet's eyes filled again, too. With a voice that was hoarse from crying, barely louder than a whisper she began saying over and over, "I'm so sorry. I can't do this. I'm so sorry."

Ned moved to the side of the bed, taking Violet's shaking form into his arms, holding her as she wept, his huge hands patting her back gently as he murmured soft words into her frizzy hair.

Cat sat there for a long moment, tears streaming down her face. The two of them were oblivious to her. It was almost as if she were invisible. In that instant she felt more alone than she had ever felt before in her life. In the past, whatever happened, she knew her parents were there for her. But they were dead. Brad was gone. Now Violet was lost to her as well.

Cat could barely see to fumble her way out of the room. She stumbled into the hallway, and ran right into a very large, solid chest.

"Are you all right?"

Cat looked up into a pair of wide chocolate brown eyes. "Do I look all right?" The sarcasm was completely spoiled by the fact that the words came out as a sob.

"Here." The boy who had been carrying the other Sazi woman from Violet's house steered her gently to the nurse's station, where he snagged a box of tissues from behind the counter and handed them to her before leading her to a set of chairs in the small waiting area near the elevators.

Cat lowered herself into a chair, dried her eyes, and blew her nose noisily a few times.

He smiled the tiniest bit, looking hopeful. "Feeling better?"

"A little."

"Good." He reached down, grabbing the small wastebasket from underneath the lamp stand. He held it out so that she could toss the used tissues inside. "You want to talk about it?"

Cat thought about it for a moment, but decided against it. While he seemed a nice enough kid, she really wasn't comfortable with the idea of baring her soul to a stranger. Besides, if she tried to talk about it now, she'd probably end up crying again. Her self-control was tenuous right now.

"No." She shook her head. "No, thank you."

"All right." He set the waste can back where it belonged, then leaned forward, putting his elbows on his knees. "We'll talk about something else." He smiled, showing straight white teeth and deep dimples. "My name is Mike Santiago, I'm the youngest son of the Alpha pair for Boulder, I'm a sophomore at CU with an undeclared major that my mother's been giving me no end of crap about. I don't have a job right now because my parents want me to concentrate on bringing my grades up." His expression grew rueful. "It hasn't been working." He smiled again, and it was like the clouds rolling away from the sun. The whole room seemed to brighten. "Your turn."

"Cat Turner." She stopped, wondering what to say.

"What're you doing in Boulder?"

"I'm staying with my aunt to avoid the press. I was on a camping trip with my family when a jaguar attacked us. My parents were killed."

"I'm sorry." Mike took her hand in his.

"Thanks." She took a deep breath, determined that she was *not* going to start crying again.

"So, where do you normally go to school? What's your major?"

Actually, I graduated a few years back. I've got my Ph.D. in applied computer science with a background in business."

"You do?"

He sounded so disbelieving her back stiffened with anger. Apparently he scented it, because he held his hands palm outward in a placating gesture. "Don't be mad." His voice took on a pleading tone. "It's just, I thought—well, you look—Oh hell. I thought you were my age."

Chapter Ten

CAT REACHED ACROSS the rumpled bedclothes to shut off the offending blare of the alarm clock. She groaned, not wanting to get out of bed, but knowing she probably should. She shook her head in amazement. It was Friday already. The week had flown by! Violet was released from the hospital, but instead of coming back to the house, she moved in with Ned, only coming down for daily therapy appointments with the newly recovered Dr. Perdue. Cat knew Violet was trying very hard to get over her fears, but the efforts didn't seem to be bearing any fruit. The best she could manage right now was daily phone calls. On the phone she could almost pretend that things were all right between the two of them. Cat had rented a car for herself, and offered to move to a hotel or apartment so that Violet could come home, but her aunt had declined.

"I won't *be* coming back to that house, Catherine. Not after what . . . happened in the kitchen. As soon as I'm feeling a little stronger, I'm going to put it on the market. In the meantime, I'd appreciate it if you would stay. I don't want it just sitting vacant. It'd be an invitation to burglars."

So she stayed, but it felt a little weird. And despite Mike's best efforts to take advantage of that big, empty house, she hadn't bedded him. Nor had she accepted any of his invitations to do things with "the crew." They all joked constantly about being "party animals." Cat wasn't interested. As she told Holly, "Been there, done that, bought the T-shirt." Mike was nice, and had been trying very hard to cheer her up, but she couldn't get the thought out of her mind that he was a . . . well, a *kid*. More to the point, he just wasn't Raphael.

And few of Mike's crowd liked Raphael.

Her relationship—acquaintanceship . . . *association*—with Raphael was just another reason for none of the wolves to like Cat. Cat was almost as frustrated with "the pack" as they were with her. Puppy school was a disaster of the first order. It was impossible to learn anything with Tatiana's sniping and the whispering and giggling of the youngsters—at Cat's expense.

She would've liked to discuss it with Raphael, but the usual Alpha Male for the pack had gotten called out of town on business, and Raphael was apparently up to his ass in alligators and sinking fast. She didn't want to make things worse for him, so she kept her mouth shut and tried to make the most of what she was learning in the few lessons he'd managed to give her.

The first night, after she'd gotten over her hysterics, he'd given her exercises regarding the telepathy: exercises that required a second person's participation. After all, you have to talk *to* someone, and confirm that he heard you. There was the same problem with listening. Raphael had just assumed she'd have somebody to work with. Well, she hadn't at first. Because while she had no doubt that Michael would be more than happy to help, she didn't particularly *want* to slip in and out of his head. Besides, she knew exactly what he was thinking. His wandering hands made *that* clear enough.

Finding a partner for her exercises had been a real problem, until Holly had stepped up to the plate.

Cat smiled at the thought of Holly. The seeds of friendship from their first meeting at the restaurant had begun to grow and blossom. It was kind of surprising how well they got along; after all, they came from such different backgrounds. Cat had grown up the only child with wealth and privilege. Holly was the youngest of a large brood, all female. Cat had earned her Ph.D. At twenty-six Holly had finally managed to save enough money to start college. She might not have had the opportunity to go for her undergrad degree yet, but she was smart and funny. And one thing she understood better than anyone was the loss of a parent. Her mother had died when she was very small, leaving her to be raised by a grief-stricken father and her older sisters.

Despite her background, Holly didn't show even a hint of bitterness. But her sense of humor was black, dry, and Cat found it utterly hysterical. Oh, the snarky things she thought at her friend during work hours! Jake and the other wolves had begun looking at the two of them very strangely because often, suddenly, for no apparent reason, one or the other would just start snickering or burst out laughing.

Mike had tried to steer Cat away from Holly, saying she wasn't their "kind." It had backfired badly. Given a choice between her new friend and a guy she wasn't all that interested in, Cat was going to choose her friend. When he'd realized that he'd backed down. But a part of him was still seething about it, she could tell.

She'd talked about it in her solo therapy session with Dr. Perdue just the day before. The good doctor made all the right neutral noises, and gave not a single constructive suggestion. Typical therapist bullshit. Still, Cat was always calmer after each appointment, so she kept her them without arguing.

The phone rang. Cat threw off the covers and padded over to where she'd left the handset on the dresser. She shivered a little. The black satin and lace nightgown she'd worn to bed last night was beautiful, but not terribly practical.

"Hello?" Cat wandered over to the window. Looking out she saw a light dusting of snow sprinkled unevenly over the dead Kentucky bluegrass of the front lawn. Where the sun's rays hit the ground the snow had already melted. It only lingered in the shadows. Not a single cloud was visible. Which meant there was a good chance for another day of unseasonably warm weather.

"Catherine, it's Ned."

"Oh, hi, Ned! What's up?"

"Violet's scheduled to be in therapy this afternoon. Is there any chance you could come up and talk?"

"Sounds serious. Am I in trouble?" She teased.

"No. Of course not." She could tell he was smiling. "But it *is* serious. There's something I want to talk to you about, but I'd rather Violet didn't hear us discussing it."

"Okaaay—" Cat dragged the word out slowly. Her aunt might not exactly be her usual self right now, but she would absolutely hate it if she thought they were keeping secrets from her.

"Don't worry." Ned answered the worry that had crept into her voice. "I'm not planning on keeping anything from her. I just wanted to get your opinion on something before I bring it up to her." He paused. "To be honest, I'm a little nervous about it."

Cat smiled. *Now* she understood. In fact, if she was the betting woman her mother had been, she'd lay heavy odds that a proposal was in the immediate offering. "What time do you want me up there?"

"Can you be here at four o'clock?"

Cat thought about it for a second. It was Friday, so she had no therapy, and there would be individual lessons with Raphael in the morning, instead of puppy school. Since she wasn't scheduled to work the Joint, her schedule was completely free after noon.

"No problem. Let me run downstairs and get a pen and paper; you can give me directions."

"Nah, just meet me at the pack complex. I'll meet you there and show you the way up."

"See you then." Cat cut the connection with a smile. If she was right about what Ned was planning, Violet would be ecstatic. She was the ultimate romantic, and she and Ned adored each other.

Humming under her breath she padded downstairs to the office to turn on the computer. She had enough time to check her e-mails before taking a shower and heading over to St. Francis for a run at the school track.

She plopped down in Violet's office chair making herself comfortable as she waited for the blasted machine to boot. It really took way too long—Cat pondered whether or not Violet's computer was full of spyware slowing everything down. She didn't have the most updated virus protection, and she did a lot of Internet research. What her aunt needed was a new computer—maybe even a laptop, especially because that way she wouldn't be off schedule now, without her computer with her at Ned's house.

It was while she was debating whether or not she should

download virus-scan updates when the first kernel of an idea struck her. She needed to know who Jack's lawyers were. If she used spyware to track all of the action on the computers at his various offices . . . There'd be a ton of data to wade through . . . Then again . . . what if . . . oh, now that was an idea.

What if she let Jack "overhear" her thinking about hiring an investigator to find the file? He would contact the right firm almost immediately, which would mean less data for her to sort through, and a faster resolution to her problems. And if it didn't work . . . well, what harm could it do?

Of course, most spyware was illegal, which meant there would be hell to pay—*if* she got caught. She pulled her legs up under her, rocking back in the chair.

She'd just have to make sure she didn't get caught.

Cat put one foot on the floor so she could scoot the chair across the room and pulled a hardback book from the shelves and a pen and blank paper from the table that held Violet's combined copier and printer. Soon she was immersed, sitting cross-legged in the chair, using the hardback as an improvised desk, alternately tapping the eraser of the pencil against her front teeth and scribbling notes. In the process she lost all track of time.

Cat? Where the hell are you?

Raphael's voice in her head caused Cat sat up in her seat so abruptly that the pen and several loose sheets of paper slid to the floor. Oh crap! What time is it? She jumped up from her seat, and wound up hopping over to the computer as her left foot was completely asleep from having been pinned under her body for so long.

It's ten thirty. Raphael's voice confirmed what she read on the screen.

Cat swore under her breath.

I take it you overslept? There was a hint of amusement in his mental voice.

No. I was working on a problem and lost track of time. I haven't even dressed, let alone had breakfast. Crap! Cat squatted down to gather up her scattered notes from the floor. She was seriously annoyed with herself. Of all the stupid things to do!

Tell you what, Raphael offered. *I'll get some food and come pick you up. I'd planned on taking you up into the woods anyway.*

Up in the woods?

Tracking and hunting. You need to know how to catch your own food on the moon. I'll be there in twenty minutes. Don't keep me waiting!

Right! Cat stacked the book, pen, and papers on top of Violet's desk and took off at a sprint up the staircase.

RAPHAEL PULLED HIS Jeep into the parking lot at the restaurant. He'd brought the more rugged vehicle to use on the steep graveled roads in the area he planned to have the two of them hunt. He was glad Cat was all right, but he did have to wonder what she'd been working on that was so engrossing she'd forgotten their lesson. He'd only known her for a week, but she'd shown no sign of being anything other than dependable and mature. Much as he hated to admit it, he'd been surprised. So much of the background information Raven had dug up on her depicted her as a wild, hard-partying airhead. But even his stepbrother Jake, who was *not* the cat's biggest fan by any stretch, had to admit she was a hard worker who showed up on time for every shift.

He was surprised Jake didn't like Cat—she was nicer to him, and to Holly, than practically anybody outside of the family.

Raphael crossed the half-empty parking lot to the glass entryway. He and Jake were close, but they'd always had their problems. Part of it was jealousy. Raphael was Second, while Jake was the lowest wolf in the pack, the Omega. But there was one thing Jake had earned for himself that Raphael had always envied: his family. Maria had been fully human, and the two of them'd had half a dozen beautiful daughters before she died. Four of them were Sazi. Bright, beautiful, and ambitious, they moved up within the Boulder pack, or moved on to other places. Rose was fully human, but she had married and relocated cross-country, coming back for the holidays. Which left Holly, the baby, and the last one living at home. She was in her twenties. She should have gone to college, been dating humans, moving on with her life. Instead she was still behind the counter at Jake's and living at home. Raphael suspected that if his brother had his way, she always would be.

And Raphael couldn't say a word about it—if he did, Jack would accuse him of being jealous. Which wasn't necessarily untrue.

But Raphael did have Raven.

Raphael pulled open the door at the Joint, the scents of humans and Sazi, fresh coffee and cooking food enveloping him. He smiled and nodded at a few of the patrons before walking up to the counter where Holly was waiting to take his order. She greeted him with a professional smile, but she reeked of anger. Jake did, too, although he was venting his rage by slamming things around in the kitchen.

"Good morning, Holly. What's going on?"

"Nothing important." Her smile grew warmer, her wide brown eyes showing a little of the affection she held for him. "Just an argument. We'll get over it. What can I get you?"

Raphael leaned onto the counter palms down and looked up at the menu. What would Cat like? He supposed he could ask her, but he'd be risking interrupting her shower. Raphael tried to force himself to think about something else—but it was nearly impossible. Every time he thought about Cat, the link between them tried to spring to life, and his body reacted. Right now his jeans were binding uncomfortably and he was damned glad it was a tall counter.

Bedding her might ease the sexual tension between the two of them. Then again, it might just make things worse. The sensible part of him thought it would cause nothing but trouble. But there was a deeper part that ached to do it anyway, and damn the consequences.

"I figured I'd bring breakfast to Cat over at the house," Raphael told Holly. In the background, the slamming grew louder and was accompanied by a few choice mumbled curses. "Any idea what she'd like?"

"Steak, eggs, hashed browns, and the biggest mug of black coffee you can find," Holly answered promptly.

Raphael laughed. "A woman after my own heart."

"Yeah," Holly agreed. "Except *she* doesn't smother perfectly good meat in hot sauce and green chile."

"I *like* hot food!" Raphael protested.

"Whatever!" Holly rolled her eyes.

Raphael laughed again. "All right, give me two orders to go and put a cup of jalapeños on the side."

She rang up his order and took the money, sliding his change across the counter to him. She got him a tall paper cup and filled it with coffee fresh and hot enough to scald his tongue. He sipped it with a smile, moving out of the way and leaning his back against the counter to survey the restaurant while he waited.

Midmorning on a weekday, he would have expected the restaurant to be nearly empty, but it was doing a fair amount of business, though most of the customers were older family members. They'd retired from their jobs and spent mornings at the café playing checkers and arguing politics over the morning paper.

Mike sat in the corner, poking savagely at the food on his plate with a sour expression. There was a ring of empty space around him. The humans were giving him wide berth. Raphael couldn't actually blame them. The scents pouring off of the boy were just nasty: anger, jealousy, frustration, and hopelessness were all mixed together at levels that were enough to make Raphael's eyes water.

On impulse, he decided to walk over and talk to the boy. Maybe he just needed an adult who wasn't a parental figure to talk to—Raphael certainly remembered himself at that age. He definitely didn't want to talk to a parent, or any authority figures from his own life. But Raphael wasn't technically an authority figure in Mike's life—except for Raphael's position as Second Alpha, which, for some wolves, was akin to Charles's position as Chief Justice. Far removed from the realities of their day-to-day lives.

As he approached the table he noticed that Mike wasn't wearing his usual Levi's and bomber jacket. Instead, he had on a worn and faded black sweatshirt with the CU buffalo on it, and baggy black sweatpants.

"Going for a run?" Raphael asked as he pulled up a chair to join him.

"I *thought* so, but apparently not," Mike answered. A fresh wave of bitterness and anger burst forth from him. Raphael buried his nose in his coffee to clear away the scent.

A woman, it had to be. There was no way he'd be this upset

if one of the guys hadn't made it. Raphael tried to guess who it might be, to remember if he'd heard any rumors, but he was drawing a blank. Then again, he'd been buried up to his eyeballs in paperwork and training Cat this past week. He hadn't been around to hear the rumors. "Why don't you give her a call?" Raphael suggested.

"She's not answering the phone." He snarled. "If she'd been practicing with *me* instead of Holly I *might* be able to just talk to her mind to mind. But *no*. That would be too *intimate*." Michael snarled again. It was an ugly sound, and several of the humans shifted in their seats, looking over at him nervously. The scent of their fear swirled in the air.

Mike's still after Cat? Raphael managed not to choke on his coffee and then berated himself for missing the obvious. He'd underestimated the boy, assumed that Mike would drop Cat when he saw the pack's negative reaction to her. Then there was the difference in their ages. Raphael felt a stab of what could only be jealousy. It surprised him. He'd known he was attracted to the woman—hell, who wouldn't be? But jealousy? Jealousy hinted at feelings a lot more serious than lust, or even the admiration he'd admitted to himself.

The big question, of course, was: what was Cat feeling? Raphael didn't *think* she would go for Mike. He was too immature, impulsive, and controlling. She'd hate that in no time. But he was good looking and attentive. Then again, those two words, *too intimate,* used with such venom, hinted that he wasn't getting anywhere with her.

Raphael couldn't suppress a surge of hope. The reaction frightened him. Logically he knew he should leave her alone, not give in. But his emotions were ready to send logic straight to hell.

"Food's up." Holly called.

"Right." Raphael turned to Mike. "Gotta go."

"Have fun with your *training session*." Mike didn't bother to hide the bitterness in his voice. Raphael knew he probably should punish him for the affront, but he really couldn't blame the kid.

He settled for a verbal warning. "Watch your mouth, kiddo." He pointed his index finger at Mike but didn't back it up with any power or threat. Turning, he went up to the counter and grabbed the to-go bag from Holly along with a huge thermal mug of coffee, easily the largest he'd seen.

"For Cat." The surprise must have showed on his face because Holly explained: "She doesn't do mornings well without coffee."

"Apparently a *lot* of coffee."

"Oh, yeah," Holly agreed. "Trust me on this."

"Thanks." He called to his brother through the kitchen pass through. "Later, Jake." He gave a quick wave and left.

The scent of the food filled the Jeep in a matter of seconds and had his stomach growling audibly by the time he pulled into Violet's driveway. He climbed out of the car, giving a cheery wave to Mrs. Zabatos, who was taking her pet for a walk. The little dust mop of a dog strained at its leash, barking hysterically as it bounced up and down.

Raphael stood at the door, one hand hidden behind his back, laughing at the fact that Mrs. Zabatos's dog actually considered itself dominant to him. He was still laughing when Cat answered the door.

She was lovely, as always. Her hair was damp from the shower, and the sweet vanilla scent of her went well with the citrus of the shampoo she'd used. Raphael had to fight the urge to pull her into his arms and kiss her breathless before peeling off those low-slung blue jeans and taking off that little blue sweater one button at a time and kissing his way down her body.

Raphael tore his mind forcibly from the image. "Breakfast." He sounded gruff. He hadn't meant to. But just thinking about her made him hard. Seeing her, having her within touching distance, it was damned near torture.

"I don't suppose you brought coffee?"

Raphael grinned, and showed her the mug he'd been hiding behind his back.

"You wonderful, wonderful man!" Cat stepped forward. Throwing her arms around his neck, she kissed him.

It started as just a quick brush of her lips against his, but it was enough to set his body alight. Warm electric energy flowed between the two of them everywhere their skin touched, through her arms on his neck, between their lips—building until she gasped from it, her mouth opening for his.

He couldn't fight it anymore. His tongue danced with hers, his body hardening at the feel of her body pressed the length of his. Both hands were full, but he wrapped his arms around her, pulling her tighter against him.

She tasted of cinnamon toothpaste. She smelled of need. She pulled back a fraction just enough to be able to speak. "We should go inside."

"Right." It was harder than it should have been to move his arms to let her go. The wolf in him fought against it, neither knowing nor caring about propriety. She was his to take—all he needed to do was reach out and claim her.

Cat untangled her arms from around his neck, letting her hands slide slowly down his chest. There was a darkness in her eyes, an acknowledgment of mutual need. But it was a need that he couldn't satisfy, as much as it was killing him.

CAT STARED OUT the Jeep window. Rugged cliffs of tan and rust stone rose sharply above the edge of the highway and the occasional boulder embedded in the pavement at the side of the road bore witness to the truth of the yellow "Falling Rock" warning signs she saw posted every few miles.

The shadows raced across the rocky surfaces mirroring the clouds that scurried in front of the bitter wind.

"Where are we going?"

"I thought we'd head up toward St. Mary's glacier in the national forest. That part of the forest isn't busy this time of year. We should have the place to ourselves."

Raphael had been quiet for most of the trip. Cat wondered if he was angry with her for not following through on the promise of that kiss, but truthfully, she hadn't intended for things to get quite that *intense*. She barely knew him. And yes, he was sexy as hell, smart, funny—but he was also a whole lot older than her. And he clearly had a whole life in Boulder, with the wolf pack. Whereas Cat didn't fit in, and didn't think she ever would—but did she fit anywhere?

California, her old life there, was just gone. Violet had offered her shelter in Boulder, time away from the press and the constant demands. Her aunt had assumed that after a month or two things would settle down and Cat would be better able to face her grief and a future without her parents. It had only been a few weeks, but Cat didn't have any more idea of what to do than she had the day she arrived.

"You're thinking awfully hard about something over there." Raphael observed. "Anything you want to talk about?"

Cat turned in her seat to take a good look at him. She needed somebody to bounce ideas off of, to help her think. Because while there was a good chance that she wouldn't live to take Jack down—or *through* taking Jack down—she needed to believe that it would happen, and that there would be a life for her afterward.

"I don't know what to do," she said, her voice soft. She waited for his reaction, but other than a slight nod to acknowledge her words, he said nothing. "Everything's changed—and I'm not just talking about the whole Sazi thing." She took a deep breath, trying to organize her thoughts. "I loved my life in California. But then the local paper broke the news about my mom's past as a call girl, and Brad dumped me." Her eyes stung, but she fought back the tears. "So Dad suggested a long camping trip, so that Mom and I could work things out."

"But . . ."

"But Jack killed them." She took a ragged breath, trying to calm herself.

She felt his hand on her arm. Just a gentle touch, but it was meant to comfort, and it did. She opened her eyes, relaxed her hands. "I can't go back. I know that. But I don't know how to move forward, either. What am I supposed to do?" The last was a pained whisper.

Raphael pulled the car off onto the shoulder of the highway and put it in park. He turned to her. Cupping her face in one hand he stared into her eyes. "Give it *time*, Cat." He gave her a sad smile. "You've been through more in a couple of weeks than a lot of people endure in a lifetime. You need time to adjust." He gave her a sad, rueful smile. "And I promise. I won't rush you . . . much."

Cat laughed. She brought her hand up to lay it against his. "Thank you. You have no idea how much I appreciate that."

"You should." He teased her a little, trying to lighten the mood. "Because it *isn't* easy."

"Are you saying," Cat arched an eyebrow playing along, "that it's *hard*?"

"Just about all the time, thanks to you." he grumbled.

She dropped her hand from his, but she was smiling. "We'd better get moving if we're going to have any time for me to do my lessons before I have to meet Ned at pack headquarters."

"Right." Raphael turned in his seat and reached down to grab the gearshift. Cat tentatively reached over, placing her hand lightly on his arm.

"Raphael?"

He turned again, looking her in the eye.

"Thanks."

They drove quite a way up the mountain in companionable silence. Raphael turned off the main road onto a rough gravel track. The uneven surface made it hard to keep the Jeep steady, and Raphael had to fight to compensate as the vehicle rocked and jerked beneath him. Gravel dust rose thick enough to make it hard to see.

Cat grunted, holding on tight to the handle mounted on the vehicle frame as she was bounced roughly from side to side. "I can see why nobody much comes up here. You'd wreck an ordinary car on this. Don't the parks people maintain this road?"

"It's deliberate. This is private land, owned by a friend of mine. There's a helipad a little farther up. Keeping the road this rough discourages unwanted visitors."

"Makes sense I suppose." Cat agreed. She really hoped they wouldn't be going much farther. The jouncing was giving her a headache.

"Almost there." Raphael turned left at a fork in the road. After about a hundred yards there was a thump and they were back on smooth pavement.

The drive curved sharply beneath the fragrant overhanging branches of the Douglas firs opening up into a clearing with a parking lot large enough for four or five vehicles. An asphalt landing pad was placed twenty to thirty yards away. It seemed a little small, but then Cat supposed it didn't need to be any bigger. After all, there were all kinds of hospitals with helipads on their roofs for emergency evacuations.

"I'm surprised nobody objected to this being put in," Cat observed. "It's awfully close to the park."

"They have an agreement," Raphael answered as he pulled the Jeep into the nearest parking space. "They let him build it. He lets them use it for things like fighting wildfires. That way everybody's happy."

He threw open the car door and climbed out. Immediately he began to strip. Cat sat, transfixed, watching dry-mouthed as he unbuttoned the heavy denim shirt to reveal a well-muscled chest and washboard abs. He slung the shirt casually over the back of the driver's seat and began unfastening the leather belt that ran through the loops of his faded jeans. Yes, logically, she knew they would have to both be naked to change, or ruin their clothes, but she'd never actually watched him strip before. They had used the locker rooms at the school.

It was a few more moments before she noticed he had stopped undressing and was staring at her with amusement. "It's not that I mind you watching, but are you ever planning on getting out of the car?"

Cat felt her face heat as she blushed to the roots of her hair. Oh, Lord. She'd been drooling. And he knew it. Oh, crap. How utterly embarrassing! And to make it worse, she was going to have to get out of the car and undress, too— unless she planned to change into cat form fully clothed. Which would, of course, leave her nothing to change back into when she shifted back.

"Right. Out of the car." She unfastened the seat belt with unsteady hands, fighting *not* to look over at him as she heard the sound of his zipper sliding down. She climbed out of the Jeep, shutting the door firmly behind her. Kicking off her shoes, she began pulling off her clothing, all the while making very sure she was facing away from where Raphael stood. She had never felt more aware of a man in her life. The sexual tension between them was practically a living, breathing thing. She shivered, and it wasn't from the cold wind whipping at her exposed skin.

Gathering her clothing into an untidy bundle, she opened the Jeep door and dropped it onto the passenger seat. She slammed the door quickly shut. Then, looking around to make sure there

was no one near other than Raphael, she concentrated the way
she'd learned in class, and shifted.

RAPHAEL FORCED HIMSELF not to watch her undress. She
smelled very embarrassed—and turned on. Not that he'd
minded. In fact, he'd been pleased and more than a little flattered that the sight of him affected her as much as it did. She
wanted him, every bit as much as he wanted her.

He knew if he pursued her now, she'd say yes. But he couldn't.
Not today, nor anytime soon. She was just too fragile emotionally. Waiting would be hell. But she'd be worth the effort. So he
stood, facing east, listening as she hurriedly stripped off her
clothes and tossed them into the Jeep. He didn't turn until he
felt the warm wash of her magic flow outward as she slipped
into animal form.

Raphael called to his wolf, felt the magic flow through him as
his body shifted into a form that was so different, and yet still
so much a natural part of who he was.

"Are you ready?" He asked it softly, realizing that there
might be more than one meaning to the question.

She paused for a moment, and then her green eyes looked out
of that lovely black fur and held his gaze. "Yes."

"Then follow me." Raphael took off at a gentle lope in the direction of the distant trees.

He felt her following a few feet behind. He couldn't hear her.
That both surprised and pleased him. This was her first time
hunting. He'd expected her to be clumsy, loud. Then again, she
was a cat. Instinct would be her friend if she could manage not
to fight it.

When they reached the tree line he set his nose to the ground,
shifting through the sent of pine needles, rocks, and earth.
There was the trace of rodents, but nothing large enough to provide much of a mouthful. He moved around a little bit, keeping
his nose down. There . . . faint, but definite, the scent of a mule
deer.

Cat, come here.

She padded up beside him.

Can you smell that?

Obediently, she put her nose to the ground. She smelled dirt, pine needles, and rocks. But beneath it, ever so faintly, she smelled urine with musky overtones.

What is that?

That is the scent of a mule deer. They still have them at this altitude. Farther up, not so much. It's faint because she hasn't been here for a couple of hours. But that is the scent we're going to try to track. As we get closer, it'll get stronger. You'll also want to keep an eye out for hoof prints, either in mud, or in the snow. I want you to use your ears, too. I'll follow behind.

He watched as she did as she was told, following the scent trail along the rough ground. Raphael knew that even over the bare rocks there were clues of the doe's passage, a scratch where hoof scraped stone, small tells.

But she was growing frustrated, tired and irritable in very short order. He could feel it beat against his mind. Finally, thoroughly out of sorts, she stopped at the base of a large tree. Extending her claws she began to climb upward.

What in the hell are you doing? Raphael stopped several yards behind, and was watching her climb, his gold-flecked eyes wide with surprise.

I'm taking a look around, thank you. Your nose may be your best sense. My eyes are mine. Ah . . . there she is. Or should I say there *they* are. There are three of them. They're about three hundred yards ahead and to the right.

He laughed, but it came out as a series of short barks and no doubt his tail was wagging. He should have thought of this himself. All of the cats he knew hunted from the air. All right. How would you hunt them?

With or without your help?

He cocked his head for a moment as he thought. Both.

She paused and he could tell she was considering. With, I would suggest you circle around and drive them to me. I spring from hiding and take one of them down.

And without?

I . . . I don't know. I mean, I could try to sneak up on them, but their ears are like satellite dishes. I don't know if I could get in close enough.

Are you hungry?

Not really. Cat dropped to the ground. The thick blanket of fallen pine needles muffled the sound so that she landed with a barely audible plop on all four paws. She padded over to where Raphael lay in the deep shadow of large boulder.

Neither am I. Raphael looked up, over her shoulder, checking the angle of the sunlight that filtered through the trees and the lengthening shadows on the ground. We're running short of time anyway. *You* have a meeting to get to. So, we'll call it a lesson and you can follow *our* trail and lead me back to the car. For your homework, I want you to find video footage of large cats hunting. Start with the cougars; they'll give you the best idea of what to do in this terrain.

By the time they dressed and started back down the mountain, the shadows had lengthened to the point they had to watch closely for wildlife leaping into the roadway.

"Oh, sure!" she commented when one particularly large buck bounded out in front of them. "Now they come looking for us!"

Raphael laughed, and she joined in. He was surprised, and flattered that her laugh was a combination of warmth and delight. She really did have a terrific sense of humor, and he was constantly amazed that she was taking everything that was happening so much in stride. Yes, there were some meltdowns, but not nearly as many as he'd expected. She was handling the transition quite nicely.

Not willing to ruin the good mood, he pressed a button on the dash, heard the CD player search, and then relaxed back into his seat to the strains of the soundtrack of *Phantom of the Opera*.

"How did you know this was my favorite musical?" she asked incredulously when the opening strains filled the car.

He smiled without turning to her, keeping a close eye out for deer. "I didn't. But I'm not surprised."

NED WAS WAITING on the steps of the administration building when Raphael dropped her off.

Cat leaned over, gave Raphael a quick kiss on the cheek, and climbed out of the Jeep, slamming the door behind her.

"Sorry I'm late." She apologized as Ned made his way down the stairs.

"No problem." He smiled, and it softened the harsh lines of his face. "How'd the lesson go?"

Cat scowled. "Apparently I am not a natural tracker."

"Almost nobody is." Ned pulled the keys to his truck from the pocket of his battered fleece-lined denim jacket and gestured for Cat to precede him to the corner of the parking lot where his truck was parked next to Violet's car. "It takes practice, and patience. Some people never get the knack of it."

"That's not exactly encouraging, Ned," Cat observed wryly.

"Don't worry." He chuckled. "You'll be fine." He hit the button to unlock the truck doors before opening the passenger door for her. When she'd climbed inside and was belted in safely, he walked around the front of the vehicle and climbed inside.

"So," she asked while he slid the key in the ignition. "What's the big secret?"

The engine turned over on the first try, and Ned reached down to switch the heater onto high.

"You mean you haven't guessed?" He ran his right hand through his hair. Cat caught a glimpse of a silver and turquoise ring. She'd been with Violet when her aunt had picked it out for him a few weeks ago, and was pleased to see him wearing it.

"I have an idea." She turned to him with a smile. "But—"

Ned put the truck in gear, checking the mirrors before backing out of the parking spot. "Fine. I'll fess up. I'm thinking of proposing to your aunt."

Cat gave a huge grin and reached over to touch his arm. "That's *wonderful*. I'm so happy for you. I just know she'll say yes."

Ned's face reddened a little. "Thanks." He turned the wheel, taking the truck onto the access road that led off of pack property, but instead of turning left toward town, he turned right. "Yeah, I think she'll say yes, too. But there's a problem."

"A problem? What?"

"Your aunt has money. I don't. And while I know she'd never say anything, I think it's important that a man and a woman enter a relationship on equal footing."

Cat opened her mouth to answer, but he waved her to silence.

"So, I've been checking into selling my property up in the mountains. I hate to part with it. It's been in the family for generations. But it's a nice place, and should be worth a fair amount, prices being what they are." A new scent rose off of him, filling the truck. Angry. He smelled angry. But for the life of her Cat couldn't figure out why.

Ned turned the truck onto the ramp that joined the access road back up to the highway. When they'd merged safely into traffic he continued what he was saying.

"Anyway, it occurred to me that all things considered, you might be wanting a place of your own to hunt. So I thought that maybe I'd take you up there, let you take a look around."

He risked a glance at her that was both nervous and hopeful. "I figure, if *you* bought the place, it would still *be* in the family, so to speak. And Violet tells me you don't plan on going back to California . . ." He let the words trickle off into a nervous silence.

"Wow." Cat wasn't sure what to think or say. On the one hand, mountain real estate was obviously a good investment, and God knew she could afford it. But that comment about keeping the land "in the family" meant that resale probably wouldn't be an option unless she was ready and willing to truly piss off her aunt's husband.

But she didn't have any place else to be. It *would* be a good idea to own land to hunt on.

The thought that she'd be close to Raphael popped into her mind unbidden.

"I don't have open access to the estate for two more years, so I'd have to check with the trustee. But Uncle Chuck is a reasonable man. If you quote a fair price I'm sure he'll go along with it."

Ned smiled, and she saw some of the tension leave his shoulders. "We'll go up and give you a good look at it first. Don't want you to go into anything blind. But it's a nice place. Worth more than what I'm asking for it, too."

It was still daylight when they pulled up the gravel drive, but the sun was sinking in the west, its dying rays painting the sky vivid oranges and purples. In the east, the first stars were visible.

The automatic lights came on, illuminating a stone walkway that led up to a large A-frame house. A deck ran along three sides of the building, its weathered wood blending gently with the gray and tan stone of the huge fireplace that took up most of the north side of the building and pale gray siding. The second-floor balcony jutted out to protect the front entrance.

Ned led her up the sidewalk, but rather than take her inside, he walked along the outer deck until they stood against the deck railing facing west, overlooking a wide meadow backlit by a spectacular sunset. It was gorgeous, utterly breathtaking.

"Wow." Cat knew Ned had deliberately timed their visit so that she'd see the sunset and be sold on the place. She knew she'd been manipulated. It didn't matter. There was a wildness about the place, and at the same time a sense of *peace* that called to something deep in her soul. She took in a slow breath of cold, clean air, letting it out slowly, watching it puff like smoke in front of her mouth.

"Well?" Ned shifted his weight nervously from one foot to the other.

"It's gorgeous, but you already knew that."

"Would you be interested?"

"That," she teased gently, "will depend on the price. But I'll ask Charles to come check out the place."

"He's been here. Many times. I don't think it will be a problem. Thank you." He said the next words with difficulty and more than a hint of sadness. "I love it here."

"I know. Are you *sure* you want to sell?"

Ned nodded firmly. "I may love this place, but I love Violet more."

Chapter Eleven

RAPHAEL DIDN'T FEEL much like cooking, so he decided to make the short drive up to Wolf's Run. The bar was a pack business run by Larry Carmichael, a family member and biker, had an attitude, a sawed-off shotgun loaded with silver shot and a pair of silver knives. Raphael figured that the reason everybody was well behaved was they didn't want to get shot and/or eighty-sixed from the only Sazi bar in two states.

Tonight was far enough after the moon that most of the crowd had as much control over their beasts as they ever would. He'd stopped by to say hi to Tatya, who sat with Mike at a table near the front of the room. She'd told him that Lucas had announced he was running late but was on his way up, and offered to let Raphael join them.

"No thanks," he declined with a smile, choosing instead to take a seat at the end of the bar.

He was in the bathroom getting rid of his third and fourth beers when he thought he heard Ned's voice, and Cat's. He didn't catch exactly what they said, but he heard Tatya's response clear as a bell.

"You can't do that! The pack has the right of first refusal."

"Yes, and you refused. So I can, and will, sell my land to whomever else I damned well please."

Shit! Raphael dove out the door, zipping his trousers as he went. Someone got in his way, he didn't look to see who. He shoved him blindly aside, trying to get across the room in time. Instead, he was still on the other side of the bar when Tatya took a swing at the human, only to have Cat protect him by stepping between them.

People were moving, shoving themselves back from the table as they prepared to support their Alpha Female in battle.

"No!" Raphael shouted, throwing his power behind the word. He used his magic in a desperate attempt to freeze not only Tatya, but everyone in the room.

It worked.

Raphael stared, transfixed at the tableaux. Tatya's fist was frozen in the instant of contact with Cat's jaw, her entire body twisted into the punch, her face distorted and ugly with rage. Ned, leaned, off balance, steadying himself with one hand against the fireplace, Cat's hand still pushing at his chest. All over the room, people were utterly motionless, even their throats stilled, so that the only sounds were harsh breathing, the hissing of food on the grill in the kitchen, and the blaring of Lynyrd Skynyrd on the jukebox.

Raphael walked over to where Mike was caught half-standing, an expression of utter horror on his face. Only his eyes moved. They followed Raphael's every motion. It was a strange, disquieting thing to see, and Raphael had to suppress a shudder. It would ruin the threat to let them see how shocked he was—they might scent it, but some of them didn't have particularly good noses, and the scent of burning food covered a multitude of sins.

Raphael caught Tatya's gaze, felt the rage burning in those blue eyes shift to him. There was a silent *demand* to that look. A demand he deliberately ignored.

He kept his voice calm. He didn't want anyone here to guess that he was as surprised as they were that he'd managed this. "Mike, I'm going to let you loose. I want you to call your father. Tell him to get his ass up here, that we have a situation."

Raphael concentrated, very carefully, slowly letting the boy have his freedom. A shudder ran over Mike's body as he stared, wide-eyed, at first one person then another.

"Mike, your dad?"

"Right." He took out his cell phone and hit the speed dial. Raphael, meanwhile walked over to the bar. Reaching up, he took the shotgun from the hands of the bartender and set it gently on the bar top.

"Larry, I'm going to let you loose now. The alpha's on his way up here to deal with this. I'm going to hold everybody in place, but I don't want the bar to burn down because you can't deal with the stuff in the kitchen." He gave the other man a meaningful look. "Don't do anything stupid."

Raphael released his grip slowly, watching to make sure the other man wouldn't do anything . . . unfortunate. Larry was fully human, but that didn't mean he wasn't a threat. He was a big man, strong and rangy. His bushy mustache was iron gray as was the hair he wore pulled back into a ponytail with multiple ties in the style favored by bikers. Tattoos covered the length of his arms that wasn't covered by a skintight Harley-Davidson T-shirt. He might be human, but he was one tough mother, and everybody in the pack knew it. You did *not* give Larry Carmichael shit, and you did not cause a disturbance in his bar. Not if you wanted to stay healthy.

When he finally could move freely, he nodded in acknowledgment to Raphael. "Neat trick. Didn't know you could do that."

"Never had to before." Raphael made his tone sound more casual than he felt.

Larry nodded again and walked through the swinging doors into the kitchen. Raphael could hear him bustling around back there. When he reappeared about ten minutes later, he was carrying two large platters. Both held massive porterhouse steaks, rare enough to still be bloody. He set the first one on the bar in front of Raphael. He placed the second in front of the stool beside him.

When Raphael raised an eyebrow in silent inquiry, Larry's answer was simple. "Lucas is coming up. There's trouble. He's pissed. I'm human. I'm thinking feeding him, getting him a drink might not be such a bad thing."

Raphael snorted with appreciation. When the bartender gestured toward the shotgun, Raphael nodded, giving tacit permission for him to put it back behind the bar where it belonged. "Probably better just get him a bottle. Put it on my tab."

"You don't have a tab tonight, Ramirez."

" 'Scuse me?"

"I'm no fool. If you hadn't hauled ass and gotten out here when you did they would've trashed the place. Tonight, your drinks are on me."

"Thanks."

Both men looked up at the crunch of gravel. Lucas had arrived. Michael disappeared through the bathroom door. Larry busied himself bussing tables around the living statues that littered the bar. Raphael sipped his beer, trying not to show his nerves, or the effort he was expending to hold the entire bar motionless. When Lucas walked in, Raphael was able to meet him with calm eyes.

Lucas stopped just inside the doorway, his hazel eyes taking in everything, from Tatiana's raised fist to Cat's snarling defiance. Every person was frozen in precisely the position he'd taken when Raphael had stepped out of the bathroom. Only their eyes moved, many showing far too much white as they panicked at not being able to control their own bodies.

He walked around a woman's crouched form to make his way to the seat waiting for him at the bar. "Thank you, Larry," Lucas murmured before picking up a tumbler of neat Scotch and raising it a salute directed at Raphael. "You have no idea how much I've been needing this." He took a long pull from his drink and set about cutting into his steak.

"Uhm . . . *Lucas*?" Raphael made a vague gesture to the room.

He shrugged, as though he expected no less from Raphael. "Are you having any trouble holding them?"

"Not really," Raphael answered.

"Are you hurting them?"

"No. A couple of them are a little panicked—and you can smell that most of them are pissed. But, no, I'm not hurting them."

"Then," Lucas bared his teeth in a vicious smile and turned toward the room so that everyone could see it, "they can *damned* well *wait* till I've had my dinner."

The look Larry gave Raphael over Lucas's head spoke volumes. Raphael waited in silence. When the Alpha was ready, he spoke.

"All right. Larry, correct me if I'm wrong. Judging from the positioning, Cat and Ned walk in and are heading to the empty table in the corner, with Cat in the lead."

"Right," Larry agreed.

"My wife stops them. They argue. Ned says something and Tatya takes a swing at him."

"Right again."

"But she *doesn't* connect the punch because Cat steps in the way."

"Yes," Raphael answered this time.

"Mike said you were in the head when this all broke out. I take it that's when you got back in the room?"

"Yes, sir."

Lucas nodded. Raphael could almost see the gears turning inside the older man's head as he tried to work out how best to clean up this mess. If Tatya had landed the punch, drawn blood from a human, it would be a Wolven matter. If Ned wasn't wearing silver—she'd be put down. But she hadn't connected the punch. That meant that while it was serious, it could be handled by internal pack discipline.

"All right." Lucas spoke grimly. "Let them loose one at a time. Start with Cat and Ned. We'll take their statements and get them the hell out of here before we release anybody else."

"This could take awhile." Raphael observed.

"Is that a problem, Alpha?" Lucas's tone made it clear it had better not be.

"Alpha?"

Lucas sighed. He rubbed the bridge of his nose with his thumb and forefinger as though a headache was forming. "Raphael, I'm acting head of Wolven. I have enemies on the council and Charles is breathing down my neck about Ms. Turner. We're going to play this *exactly* by the book. We have a very serious matter that needs investigation. We'll take care of it together so that *nobody* has a chance to complain." He raised his voice until it could be heard over the jukebox. "Until you hear differently from me, Raphael, you *are* the Alpha Male of Boulder. And I want to make sure that *everyone* knows it!"

Raphael winced in sympathy. "Right. Ned first. Larry, can we use your office? We don't want the statements getting muddied by everybody listening in."

"No problem." He tossed a ring of keys from across the room. Raphael caught them one-handed before standing up and walking through the swinging doors that led to the kitchen and the office beyond. It was going to be a long night.

YOUR TURN SWEETHEART.

Cat felt the magical vise grip that had held her in place loosen. Her muscles *hurt* from being in one position for too long. She rubbed her hand under her jaw. It hurt from where the punch had begun to connect, but not nearly as bad as it would have if Raphael hadn't stepped in before Tatya could follow through completely. The smaller woman not only had kick-ass strength, but she had put everything she had behind the blow. It could have broken Ned's jaw—hell, it could have broken Ned's *neck*. Cat felt a surge of anger. A part of her really wanted to do *something* . . . but no. No. She was supposed to go back into the kitchen and talk with the nice wolves. But Tatya had better not get out of this with just a slap on the wrist! If she did, Cat was going to be seriously pissed.

Cat strode past the bartender, bustling around, taking care of business as though everything were normal, and pushed her way through the swinging doors.

The kitchen was almost blindingly bright after the dim bar area. Fluorescent lighting shone off gleaming metal pans and walls painted stark white. The floor tiles were badly worn, but immaculately clean. Cat followed the sound of muted voices to a closed door in the back corner of the room.

The door opened as she approached, and Ned stepped out looking grim and determined. His face softened when he saw Cat.

"Before you go in there, thank you. If she'd connected that punch I'd have been in a world of hurt." Ned shook his head.

"Hey, we're family now. Remember?" Cat tried to lighten the mood.

"Only if Violet says yes." Ned smiled, but there was a hint of nerves in his voice.

"Oh, I think she will. She loves you a lot, you know." Cat patted his arm reassuringly.

"Yeah, but she's pretty pissed about me keeping the whole 'Sazi thing' secret from her."

Cat gave him a quick hug. "It'll be fine. You'll see."

"Ms. Turner? If you don't mind, I'd like to keep this moving." The voice of the man that Raphael had called Lucas interrupted them from the next room. The words were courteous, but there was no mistaking the authority of the tone.

"See you later," Cat said. Ned nodded, giving her a little shove toward the door as though to let her know not to keep the big dogs waiting. He, on the other hand, hurried out the back door of the kitchen, avoiding the front of the restaurant altogether.

Cat took a deep breath, gathered her courage, and put her hand on the doorknob. She hadn't done anything wrong. Unfortunately, that didn't make her any less nervous. Squaring her shoulders, she opened the door and stepped inside.

Raphael sat next to the door, across the room from Lucas. She hadn't been able to see him clearly in the other room, so she took a moment to look over the man who was normally Alpha for this pack. He was broad-shouldered, wearing a business shirt with the sleeves rolled up. His short salt-and-pepper hair made his intense, fiercely intelligent brown eyes leap out at her. The power in those eyes told her a lot about him. He had the same penetrating gaze that her Uncle Chuck had. She wondered if they knew each other. Yes, they must.

Lucas sat, looking tense and serious, in a green vinyl office chair behind a battered metal desk. He was using a fountain pen to write notes on a lined pad. Raphael perched on the edge of the desktop, his hands gripping the lip of the surface next to his legs. Across from them, bare inches away, was an uncomfortable-looking straight-backed chair.

"Ms. Turner, have a seat." Lucas's voice was businesslike. "Please tell us what happened."

Cat perched on the edge of the chair. She glanced up at Raphael for reassurance. There was none to be had. His expression was cold, his mind shielded so tightly she couldn't guess at this thoughts.

"Start at the beginning please," Lucas ordered. "Why were you up here?"

Cat pulled her gaze away from Raphael with difficulty and tried to lighten the mood with a smile. "God! I feel like a witness in a courtroom right now."

"Excellent analogy, Ms. Turner," Lucas replied calmly, but there was no laughter in his voice. "I'm Lucas Santiago. I'm a practicing attorney here in Boulder and a former prosecutor, as well as the present head of Wolven."

"Oh." She bit her lip in embarrassment. Taking a deep breath, she started her story without any more comments. "Well, Ned called this morning and asked me to meet with him. He wanted to talk. He planned on proposing to Violet, and wants to start their life together on an even footing. He was talking about my need to hunt, and he mentioned that he was selling his property. Since the pack didn't want it, he asked if I would consider buying it."

It took far longer than she would've expected for them to take her statement. Though there was none of the good cop/bad cop she was used to seeing on television and in the movies, it was obvious that the two men were professionals who were very used to working together. Each asked very probing questions, going over the same ground again and again. Not only did they ask what she'd seen, but just as important, what had she heard and scented. They went over it repeatedly until she was so exhausted her mind and butt were both numb, and her back ached from tension and sitting for so long in such an uncomfortable chair.

She almost wanted to cheer when Lucas told her, "All right then, I think that's everything. If we come up with any more questions we know where to find you."

Cat rose. She stretched to loosen her tight muscles, inadvertently brushing against Raphael when she did. That simple touch sent an invisible crackle of magic between them. He started, and she both felt and scented a quick burst of alarm from him before his shields once again slammed into place, locking her away.

Lucas turned quickly. Eyes narrowing, he looked from one to the other. Tilting his head back, he scented the air.

Raphael gave a discreet cough behind his hand. As if it were a signal between them, Lucas's expression changed to one of amused indulgence. He shook his head and turned back to his notes.

"It'll probably take a day or two before we hear back from the Chief Justice."

She raised her brows in a question. "The Chief Justice?"

"Charles Wingate. I believe you know him." Lucas gave a wry smile, and she noticed that it softened his whole face. She remembered that Raphael had said that Uncle Chuck was the most powerful Sazi, but *Chief Justice*?

Lucas sighed, probably thinking she knew more than she did. She kept her mouth shut and let him continue. "Normally this would be a pack and Wolven matter. But I'm acting Chief of Wolven, and Raphael is acting Alpha of this pack. While we'll be running the investigation, and Raphael will be conducting the discipline within the pack, our findings will have to be reported to the Chief Justice and the Sazi Council at their meeting in December. They'll be watching us *very* closely."

Cat could hear the worry in Lucas's voice. It occurred to her the position the man was in. After all, his wife was the one who'd thrown the first punch. Lucas was managing a poker face, and she couldn't scent what he was feeling, but she knew the fear had to be there just the same.

"If you'd be so kind as to send my son in here? We'll talk to him next."

It was a relief to leave. The tension and magic in the room had been thick enough to walk on, and powerful enough to set the fluorescent overhead lights buzzing and flickering.

Cat walked through the kitchen and back out into the bar proper. She couldn't wait to get back to the house. What with everything that had happened, she was completely exhausted. All she wanted was a good meal, and a good night's sleep, in that order.

She glanced around the room and shuddered. It was quiet enough that she could hear people drawing breath, and the wet slap of the cloth Larry was using to clean the bar. People were standing or sitting, frozen in midmotion. Only their eyes moved, and those eyes blazed with hatred.

"Mike, it's your turn."

The bar stool scraped against the floor as he rose. Pulling the wallet from his back pocket he dropped enough cash onto the bar to pay for his meal and started toward the swinging doors.

"Where's Ned?"

"I told him I'd give you a ride back. He left."

"Damn it!"

"I won't be long." Michael's expression was serious. "And we need to talk."

"I don't want to talk. I want to eat and then go to bed," Cat snarled.

He had the nerve to smirk! He'd planned this! "Well, Ned left. So you're stuck waiting whether you like it or not."

His tone of voice raised Cat's hackles. He sounded smug, controlling, and more than a little condescending. If she had her purse with her she'd call a cab, and damn the expense. Unfortunately, since Ned had been driving, she hadn't bothered to bring it. She was such an idiot. She was far too old to be making that kind of a stupid mistake. Well, she might be stuck with the situation tonight, but it would never happen again.

She lowered herself onto the wooden bar stool Mike had vacated. Larry appeared in front of her. "You're hungry?"

"Yeah, but Ned was going to buy. I didn't bring my purse," she grumbled.

"S'right." Larry tossed the bar towel casually over his shoulder and gave her a smile. "Ned's a friend. He'll pay me back. What do you want on your burger?"

"Burger?"

Larry grinned, showing a chipped tooth that, oddly, made him seem more approachable. "You're not getting steak. Just in case he *doesn't* pay me back."

Cat's laugh echoed strangely through the room and the scent of frustrated fury rose from more than one of the motionless wolves. She shivered. "Make it to go, would you?"

Larry nodded, his expression sympathetic. "No problem."

"MICHAEL, THERE IS *nothing* to talk about." Cat fought to control her temper. He was being a jerk: a *major* jerk. It had started with his whining about her standing him up this morning. She hadn't stood him up. It wasn't a date. She'd never once asked him to join her on her morning runs. He'd taken that upon himself, just as he'd taken to hanging out at the Joint about the time he knew she was due to get off, or go on break. It was just one more of the million little things he'd taken to doing to force his way into her life. She'd been trying to handle the situation delicately; after all, he was the pack leaders' son, but he was getting on her last nerve!

Cat felt her muscles beginning to tense as her irritation increased. Even the temperature in the car started to rise. She tried to calm herself, control the beast within her as Raphael had been training her to do. It was damned hard work. And what pissed her off most of all was that she appeared to be one of the few bothering to do it. From what she could see of most of the pack, they didn't think they should have to bother. The animal in *their* nature was never far from the surface; casual violence the norm, rather than an oddity.

Which brought her thoughts neatly back to Ned. If she hadn't been here . . . hadn't taken the blow . . . She couldn't believe Tatya did that. The first rule is secrecy—Cat knew that much. And right behind it were the rules to protect humans. Turning a human Sazi other than in self-defense was an automatic death sentence. How could Tatya risk it, even with her family so involved in pack hierarchy—no, *especially* with her family so involved in pack hierarchy?

But her mind answered its own question. Tatya, and the rest of the pack, had come to rely on the fact that the human family members all wore silver at all times. If the humans didn't, there wouldn't be *any* affiliated with the pack anymore—they'd've all been changed.

Or died in the attempt. Raphael's voice slid smoothly into her thoughts.

What do you mean?

Human bodies aren't meant to hold magic, to change shapes. Even for family members with generations of Sazi in their bloodlines it's a terrible risk.

Cat saw the memory in Raphael's mind. A pretty blonde preteen girl, naked in a small clearing, surrounded by her parents and Raphael. The moon rose, its light silvering the frost-covered ground, casting deep shadows that brought every detail into stark relief.

She screamed in agony, again and again, as fast as she could draw breath. Her body collapsed to the ground. Cat could hear her bones snap, saw the muscles strain to re-form. Her face distorted, elongating into a muzzle with fangs. Short bristles of gray hair sprouted from her pores, then retracted again.

It wasn't enough. Cat could feel the naked fear that clawed at Raphael's stomach as he gathered his power, forcing his own magic into the fallen girl.

For a moment it looked as though it might work. He kept trying, kept straining against the inevitable, draining himself until he fell to the ground, spent, despite the part of him that knew it was a lost cause.

Thirteen years old, barely more than a child; and there was nothing he or any of the others could do but watch in nauseated horror as her body ripped itself apart.

Cat dragged herself free of the memory by force of will. Her stomach heaved and rolled. She tasted bile on the back of her tongue. She fought against the nausea, barely managing to keep down the burger she'd eaten.

She knew it could have been Ned, Holly, even her. In that moment she realized, without him saying a thing, that *that* was what he'd expected to witness that first night. She shuddered, her stomach heaving.

"Cat? Are you even listening to me?" Mike snapped.

"Not really."

Mike slammed on the brakes, causing the car to skid and swerve violently toward the side of the road. Mike steered with it, pulling over until they were in the grassy verge, with tree limbs scraping along the passenger side of the vehicle.

"Let me guess. You were *thinking* at Raphael again."

"Michael—" Cat's voice held a warning.

"Oh, so I'm supposed to pretend I don't notice? I'm just supposed to keep my mouth shut and watch while you alienate *everybody* in the entire fucking pack? Don't you get it? You *have* to fit in. You *have* to acknowledge my mom's dominance; she's the alpha female. She *is* superior to you. And, for God's sake, *don't* buy the land. It's our prime hunting ground. Ned has no business selling it to anybody!" Michael's whole body shook with rage. "You've got to conform. They'll never accept you if you don't. Never accept *us*."

"There *is* no 'us,' Michael." Cat looked him straight in the eye as she said it, and actually *saw* the words slide past him unheeded. "And I will rot in hell before I act subservient to your mother after what she almost did to Ned tonight."

"What she almost did? You mean turn him? Like that would be so terrible. Hell, she'd be doing him a favor!"

In that instant Cat forgot her breathing exercises, forgot her self-control. Cocking her arm back she punched him full-out, a powerful right hook that connected with his nose, snapping his head back.

Blood poured through the fingers of the hands he'd brought to his face. Mike's eyes were glassy, and he swayed slightly in his seat, as though she'd almost knocked him out.

Cat didn't stay to watch, or talk. She climbed out of the vehicle, slammed the door, and stormed off in the direction of the bar. She wasn't worried about Mike. She knew she didn't need to be. *He* was Sazi. He'd heal.

Chapter Twelve

LUCAS STUBBED OUT a spent cigarette with the toe of his boot. Two fifteen. The bar was closed, and the last witness interviewed. Raphael knew that the old man had quit smoking more than a decade before. That he'd bothered to bum a cigarette and light meant that he was seriously stressed. Raphael couldn't blame him. The situation was a total fucking mess, and Tatya was right, square in the middle of it.

"It could've been worse," Lucas said with a sigh. "Would've been if you hadn't been here."

"Sometimes it's better to be lucky than good." Raphael admitted.

"What the *hell* was she thinking?" Lucas growled with exasperation.

Raphael didn't answer. They both knew Tatya *hadn't* thought. She'd reacted instinctively to the threat she thought Cat posed, and the rest of the pack members had been ready to back her up. Raphael suppressed a shudder and wondered if Ned knew just how close a call he'd had. Probably. He was no fool, and he'd been around the Sazi his whole life.

"You realize she'll never forgive you for keeping her frozen in place like that while you interviewed everybody else."

"*You're* the one who held her," Lucas pointed out.

"Uh-huh. But *you* decided the order of the interviews." He gave his friend a rueful grin. "Hope you've got a comfortable couch."

Lucas grunted in acknowledgment and gestured at the cigarette pack. Raphael tapped out one for each of them before pulling out his lighter.

"Did Ned give the pack first right of refusal?" Raphael asked as he held the lighter for his pack leader. "I didn't see anything cross my desk."

"No," Lucas sighed. "It came to me. Tatya figured she'd handle it while I was out of town."

"Oh."

Raphael watched as Lucas stared up at the star-filled sky and the silver moonlight that lined the few visible clouds. The older man hadn't actually looked at him or met his eyes since they'd left the building. "She thought, if she turned him down and then waited a few weeks, she could negotiate down the price."

"Bad idea." Raphael took a long drag of nicotine. He forced himself to relax. It hadn't been a disaster. Nothing irretrievable had happened. But *damn* it had been a close call. Sometimes Tatya was so impulsive it qualified as stupidity. "Ned's real proud of that place—and mountain land's in high demand."

"Very." Lucas took a long pull on the cigarette, making the tip glow cherry red. He slowly released the smoke from his lungs and watched as it floated upward. "Now he wouldn't sell to us if we were the last people on the planet."

"Yup."

"And Cat, who would probably have been reasonable about sharing hunting rights before, is totally pissed off." Lucas leaned his back against the large black SUV he'd driven up in.

"Right again."

"Don't suppose you can talk sense to her?" Lucas shifted his body so that he was looking straight at the other man with a burning intensity.

"What makes you think I'll have any better luck than you would? And what makes it sensible to change her mind?" This time it was Raphael who looked away and tried to keep his tone casual.

Lucas gave him a long, flat look that Raphael tried unsuccessfully to ignore. Eventually Lucas took pity on him and broke the silence. "Have you talked to Betty about getting tested to see whether the mating is one sided or mutual?"

Raphael took a deep breath. He hadn't said it out loud, but he didn't need to around Lucas. He might well be the *only* person in Boulder who understood what he was going through. Mated.

And to Jack's get—after everything that had happened. He closed his eyes and let out a short, frustrated chuckle. "I scheduled an appointment for next week. Didn't tell her what it was about."

"Next *week?*"

"Yeah, next *week,* when Daphne Black is on vacation. I'd like to keep this as quiet as I can."

Lucas flinched. "I'm getting slow in my old age. You shouldn't have had to remind me of that."

"Nah, you're just tired. Too much on your plate. Go home. Get some rest. It'll look better in the morning."

"Right." Lucas dug out his keys and climbed into the SUV. "What're you going to do?"

"Long term, I haven't got a fucking clue," Raphael answered. "But right now, it's a gorgeous night, the weather's perfect. I'm going for a run. You?"

"I'm going to drive home nice and slow—and hope that by the time I get there my wife will already be in bed, asleep."

"Good luck with that."

Lucas acknowledged the joke with a soft snort of laughter before rolling up the window and driving off. Raphael watched him go. When the SUV was completely out of sight he began to undress.

It really was a perfect night for a run. Crisp and clear, with a thousand stars sparkling like diamonds in the distance. A north wind blowing just hard enough to rustle what few aspen leaves still decorated the trees. It had been a night much like this when Candy Streeter died. Raphael shook his head. He needed to stop thinking about that. He'd done his best. Not that it had mattered—in the end, she had been just as dead as if Raphael had stood by and done nothing at all, all because of a single scratch.

The Sazi code of conduct was harsh for a reason. The consequences for carelessness were just too severe.

Raphael unlocked the door to his car and set his boots and folded clothes neatly on top of the driver's-side seat. He tucked his keys under the rear floor mat and shut the car door with a brisk slam. A moment's concentration was all it took. His body transformed effortlessly into the second shape it had been born to take. Seconds later, a huge black timber wolf disappeared into the shadowed woods.

Raphael ran easily over the rough terrain, paws skimming over frosted tufts of grass. He leapt over a dry gully that waited for spring's melt to fill with pure rushing water. The scent of pine filled his nostrils as his paw crushed needles piled beneath the trees, fading as it was carried off by the breeze. Other than the rustle of the leaves and the hoot of an owl, the forest was nearly silent. The prey had all gone to ground, hoping the predator would pass them by.

In the distance he heard the thump and crunch of brush as a startled doe bolted. Instinct took over. He turned, to give chase.

He put on a burst of speed, gaining on the doe with every stride. Raphael could hear the thundering of her heart, her ragged breathing. He felt a burst of pure, unfettered joy as he leapt, his teeth closing around her throat, his weight and the power of the impact driving her to the ground.

He finished her off quickly and settled down to feast on his kill, coherent thought washed away in the salt-sweet taste of fresh meat and blood. He gorged until he was sated, then lay on his side letting the food settle. His stomach was heavy, and so were his eyes. It would be easy to sleep here. Really, there was no reason why he shouldn't. There was no one at home to miss him, nothing but an empty house with photographs of kids he never got the chance to raise and those few things Raven left behind for use on his visits. Once upon a time he'd believed in the fairy tale. That he, too, could have the kind of life Lucas had managed; the pack, the business, a beautiful wife, and a passel of kids. It had been a cruel trick that every relationship he'd invested his heart in had wound up in disaster.

Only Raven's mother, Star, was still friendly with him. Although if he was being totally honest, the fact that she *didn't*, marry him when she was pregnant with Raven still stung.

It was probably for the best, though—if they *had* gotten married, they would've ended up divorced and bitter. They were too much alike—stubborn and hardheaded, neither one ever able to compromise on anything. He did hope he'd be able to talk her into coming up for Thanksgiving. It would give him the chance to sneak in some healing before her arthritis got too bad.

Raphael found himself wondering what Cat would be doing for Thanksgiving. As if the thought summoned her, he caught her scent on the breeze, heard her soft footfalls.

"Raphael?" Cat called his name with both voice and mind.

"Over here," Raphael answered.

He heard her turn, following both his scent and the sound of his voice. Before long she appeared at the opposite side of the clearing, moonlight gleaming off the length of her hair.

She was gorgeous, breathtaking. Low-slung jeans clung to those long shapely legs, leaving just a thin band of tanned skin showing on her abdomen between them and the little blue button-up sweater he'd been admiring . . . God, was it only this morning? It felt as if it had been a year ago at least.

Her steps slowed as she neared the deer carcass. Raphael knew a battle was raging between the two parts of her nature. The cat wanted to feed. It was obvious from the way her body stiffened, her nose twitching to get a better scent of the raw meat. But *Cat* rebelled, horrified by the bloody mess of torn flesh and bones.

"You can have some if you want," Raphael offered gently.

"Thank you." Cat's voice was taut with strain. "But no."

"It's all right to want it."

"Is it? Is it really?" She didn't bother to hide her disbelief, tinged with horror. He could hear that she was very nearly hysterical. "I don't think so!"

She stalked away from the carcass, throwing herself to the ground with her back to it, so she wouldn't have to look. But tension sang through her body as her cat fought her for control.

The human won. But it wasn't easy, and it wasn't pretty. Raphael very carefully didn't express the pity he felt for her. She was a proud woman. Pity would stick in her craw, make her even angrier than the helplessness he knew she was feeling. Instead, he lay still, waiting.

"Do you have any idea how much I *hate* this?" she asked. Tears glittered in her wide green eyes.

"I know it's hard."

"Hard?" She snarled. Again, Cat fought for control. Again she mastered herself. Eventually she broke the silence. "It's like I'm not *me* anymore. You tried to warn me. But I didn't realize—"

"It'll get easier with practice," Raphael promised.

"Oh, God, I hope so!" A single tear tracked down her perfect cheek. If he hadn't been in wolf form, he'd have brushed that tear away, taken her in his arms to comfort her.

"You're actually doing very well. Much better than I expected."

She laughed, but it wasn't a happy sound. "I hit Michael a little while ago. I think I broke his nose. I did break a couple of my fingers." Her gaze locked with Raphael's, and the scent of her pain and confusion easily overpowered the smell of the deer on the ground.

He perked his ears with interest. "What happened?"

"Where do I start?" She rose to her feet in a fluid movement and began pacing. There was no mistaking her exasperation as she related her tale. Raphael found himself growing angrier and angrier on her behalf. He watched as her body vibrated with fury, and the smell of rage boiled off of her in an almost visible mist. "So then I thought about that girl in the memory you showed me—"

"And you hit him." Raphael worked very hard not to put any emotion into the words, not anger, or disapproval, or even what he actually felt: sincere appreciation. The kid was a total ass, completely unlike his father, and he'd wished he could personally deck him more than once.

"Yep." Her voice was likewise flat, but the roil of scents told an entirely different tale. Fear, anger, frustration, worry—they were all there, blended into one tiny word.

"And broke his nose?"

"I think so."

He sighed. While Lucas probably wouldn't blame her once he learned the story, it did raise a valid question. If Raphael was mated to her, what's to say Mike wasn't as well? Multiple matings to an alpha were fairly common. It was becoming pretty obvious that Cat was an alpha to be reckoned with. "Then what?"

"Then I climbed out of the car and stormed off. I heard him drive away."

"If it makes you feel any better, I'd probably have done the same thing." Raphael spoke gently.

"Ah, but *you're* his alpha. You get to. I, on the other hand, am 'the cat that's intruding on our territory' who everybody thinks should be run out on a rail if not killed outright." She shook her head; her voice was soft, almost awed when she finally spoke again. "They would've killed me tonight, if you hadn't stopped them. They would've done it. I just don't *get* it. I haven't done anything wrong!"

"It's going to be all right," he assured her, hoping she couldn't smell his own doubts.

She glared at him. "Don't lie to me, Raphael. The pack hates me, I have a madman strolling through my mind at will, oh, *and* I get to turn into a wild animal once a month and go kill things! No," she corrected herself. "*I* get to turn into a wild animal *anytime* I want. Oh, *goody*."

Raphael lay utterly still, trying to come up with the right words to comfort her. What could he say? She had every right to be angry and terrified. Her entire life had been torn away from her. It was one of the reasons so many attack victims committed suicide within the first few months. The physical stresses were phenomenal. Mentally and emotionally it was worse. But he wanted, *needed* Cat to make it. He just wasn't sure how to make it happen. The silence grew between them, but it changed subtly, becoming less angry, but more sorrowful.

Reaching over, she buried her left hand deep in his fur, scratching the perfect spot just behind his ear. Her touch was electric, her scent . . . Raphael wanted to wrap himself in the scent of her.

"I walked back to the bar. It took awhile. Nobody was there, but your car was still in the parking lot. So I decided to use some of that training you gave me this afternoon."

"And you found me." He turned his head, licking the tear from her cheek, tasting the salty sweetness of her sadness on his tongue. "I guess you were paying attention after all."

She stuck out her tongue at him. The childish gesture made him laugh. She gave him a playful shove, but winced.

Without even thinking about it, Raphael used his magic to change forms. "Let me see," he ordered. She held it out gingerly. Two of the knuckles were red and the whole hand was badly swollen.

She'd broken it all right. Based on the damage to her hand

Raphael would bet that Mike's nose was badly broken, too. Not that it mattered—he'd heal. And Tatya would make sure his nose wound up straight. But, shit, Tatya would be pissed—nobody got to mess with that woman's cubs.

Raphael took Cat's hand in his. He concentrated, focusing his power, picturing the delicate bones of her hand whole and aligned the way they should be. The power washed out of him in a gentle wave. Cat gave a soft gasp of pleasure. Raphael's body hardened in response.

Raphael started to pull back, but she was having none of that. Pulling her hand from his, she took his face between her two palms and kissed him. It was not a chaste meeting of lips, but a slow, seductive demand.

Raphael groaned as electric energy poured through his body from their mouths, every cell aching to take this woman and make her his. He pulled her close, pressing against the strong supple length of her. His hands seemed to move of their own accord, unfastening the clothing that kept her from him while her hands explored his body in a way that made coherent thought impossible.

Keep that up and this won't last long, he warned.

She didn't answer, at least not with her mind. Her hands, however, knew the perfect response, one finger tracing along the sensitive skin behind his testes, before delicately running the length of him from base to tip in a single, languid movement.

He pulled back from the kiss to look into those gorgeous green eyes.

Raphael had been with more than his share of women. As Second for a pack with a mated Alpha, he was *breeding stock*. But never in his life had a woman affected him the way Cat did now. It was more than a wanting. It was a primal need. He had to know if she felt the same. He prayed she did, because this was no mere roll in the hay for him, and while he might be able to stop physically—magically and emotionally he might very well be too far gone to turn back. Mated.

It was a terrifying and exhilarating thought.

"Raphael, what's wrong?"

Her voice was tentative. He could see the hurt and confusion in her eyes. He felt a pang of remorse. His confusion was hurting her, and she was the last person on earth he ever wanted to see hurt. In that moment he made his choice. He wanted *this* woman. Not just for tonight: for always. To hell with the pack and the future he'd planned. Without her it would mean nothing. To hell with Jack. They'd face him, fight him, together.

He reached for her. "Just admiring the view," he teased. There would be no smell of black pepper. It wasn't a lie. She was so beautiful, inviting, lying there, and her answering smile was an invitation he couldn't refuse.

He ran his hand lightly over her breast and down her abdomen, his hand teasing the blonde triangle between her legs. She was wet for him, eager, her scent heavy with musk.

Raphael lowered his mouth to her taut stomach, his tongue teasing her belly button before licking a slow line downward. She gasped, thighs spreading for him. He slid his hands beneath her, cupping her ass as he began giving slow, sensuous licks to the skin of her upper thighs: coming ever closer, but not *quite* touching the very core of her. She whimpered then, her body arching, her hands tangling in the length of his hair as her body struggled for release.

He had to fight down his own need, force himself to wait. He didn't want to rush this. There would only be one first time. He wanted it to be something to remember.

When he pulled back, she groaned in frustration, until he slid his hand between her thighs and began using his fingers to bring her to climax as his mouth covered hers. Her body arched, muscles tightening around his hand, her cries silenced by his mouth on hers. Only when the thunder of her pulse had begun to slow did he pull away, shifting position to thrust himself deep inside her.

Not only did her body respond, her magic did as well, building with each stroke until their combined power sizzled across his skin in a way that was just one hair short of painful. It was the power that pulled him over the edge, made him lose control until they both came in a single, overwhelming burst.

Chapter Thirteen

CAT OPENED ONE eye. It was raining. Soft fat drops plopped down on her skin through the canopy of tree limbs above. She shivered, snuggling farther in against Raphael. He was so *warm*. It felt wonderful being nestled in his arms, feeling his body curled protectively around her body, pulling her close. What *didn't* feel wonderful was the sharp rock digging into her left hip, or the second, third and fourth cold drops that splattered more quickly down from above.

Raphael shifted, grumbling in his sleep, pulling her more tightly against him, squeezing until it was almost painful. She took a deep breath, reveling in the scents of him: skin, fur, and, oddly—fresh baked bread.

"Raphael," Cat whispered. There was no reaction. "Raphael, it's raining."

He shifted again, making a grumbling noise. Cat shifted, and lifting his arm, she slid away from him and stood. She needed to get dressed. But first, first she needed to find a nice private spot in the woods and take care of business.

"Where are you going?" Raphael cracked open an eye to stare up at her.

"I have to pee."

"Mnnn." His other eye cracked open as fat wet drops started beating a tattoo on his body. "Hey! It's *raining*."

Cat rolled her eyes, but didn't comment. Instead, she walked into the trees. She didn't go too far, just put enough distance between them for a semblance of privacy.

She was sore, and more than a little stiff from sleeping on the bare ground, and there were other small hurts as well. Hurts of the kind that came from uninhibited sex. It had been wonderful, really amazing, and oddly she didn't feel at all awkward with him this morning. It just felt *right* waking up next to him, as if they'd been doing it all their lives. She'd never felt this comfortable with Brad, or any of the few other men she'd been with.

Of course Raphael was the first man who'd ever accepted her for exactly who she was, faults and all. In fact, he was quite possibly the first person in her life to do so. Her parents had loved her unquestioningly, but her mother had been constantly pushing her to "toughen up," while her father wanted nothing more than for her to share his interest in all things mechanical. They'd loved her, they'd even *liked* her. But she knew there were things about her they would've changed if they could. Only fair—she had her complaints about them, and hadn't appreciated them nearly enough. It made her sad, but she didn't feel the overwhelming pain she had before. She would always miss them, but today she could actually believe that eventually it was going to get better.

It's already eight o'clock, we'd probably better hurry.

I'll be right there.

When Cat returned to the spot where they'd slept she found Raphael in wolf form, curled up next to her neatly stacked clothing. When she raised an eyebrow in inquiry he gave her a wolfy grin and said, "I got cold without you. Besides, walking through the woods in human form naked is uncomfortable. Now hurry up. I want coffee, and I want breakfast."

"Fine, fine. Jeez," Cat grumbled under her breath as she pulled her clothes on. Now she was self-conscious, but it was just because of the way Raphael kept looking at her with undisguised hunger with those big gold eyes. "Will you please stop staring?"

"Then stop looking so damned appetizing."

"Appetizing?"

How he managed a salacious look on wolf features she couldn't say, but he did, and Cat caught the hint of some very naughty images in his mind. "Raphael!"

"Oh, you're no fun," he complained, laying his head on his paws with an exaggerated sigh.

"That's not what you said last night," She pointed out as she pulled on her bra and shifted it around a bit until it was comfortable. She shook her sweater, watching as dead leaves and pine needles fell to the ground. The rain was coming more steadily now. She sighed. Her clothes were going to be soaked before they got back to his car.

"No," Raphael acknowledged happily as he watched her slipping on her jeans. "That's not what I said last night."

Once she was fully dressed he quit teasing, leading her swiftly through the woods in an almost direct line down to the parking lot. She followed, trying not to make too much of a racket. But it was hard. The thick mist limited visibility and the rain made the fallen leaves slick. She lost her footing several times because the wet, uneven ground was much harder to deal with this morning than it had been last night.

Still, it didn't take long before they were back in the parking lot and she was sitting in the Jeep with the heater running full blast taking her turn leering at Raphael while *he* dressed.

He really was gorgeous. Everything about him suited her, from the tousled brown curls and warm brown skin, to the strong bones of his face, softened by those huge dimples. Even the wicked scar that ran from hip to calf on his left leg wasn't so much a flaw as an accent, although she did wonder how he'd gotten it. Holly had told her he'd been a wolf since he was a small boy. With his healing abilities she was astonished that it hadn't disappeared over the years. No—wait—those stupid books she was supposed to read talked about that sort of thing. She tried to force the memory, but the harder she tried, the farther it slipped away. Now she was going to have to reread them. She gave an involuntary shudder at the thought.

Raphael climbed into the car. Leaning over, he gave her a quick kiss before strapping on his seat belt and starting the engine. "I think I'll take us to a drive-through somewhere," he suggested. "I could use some coffee and breakfast."

"That sounds wonderful."

It was nearly 9:00 A.M. by the time Raphael dropped her off in front of Violet's house, adequately fed and fueled up on McDonald's coffee. The very first thing Cat intended to do was take a long, hot shower with lots of soap. It wasn't that she was embarrassed about what had happened with Raphael. She certainly wasn't *sorry,* but if anyone caught a whiff of her right now he'd know *precisely* what had happened. The news would spread like wildfire, and Raphael would have yet another crisis on his hands. She ran up the sidewalk, leaping over the stairs that led up onto the porch. She needed to hurry. She didn't want to be late to her ten o'clock family therapy appointment with Dr. Perdue. Betty had specifically made time on a Saturday to accommodate Cat's work schedule. It would be incredibly rude not to be on time.

She was humming to herself in the shower when Jack slipped into her thoughts.

You certainly seem to be in a good mood this morning.

Cat tried to slam down her mental shields, but it was too little too late.

One would almost think you'd spent the night entertaining. The voice was suave as ever, but there was a menacing undertone. I do hope you haven't chosen to ignore my warning about Ramirez. Studly Screwright is not the right man for you.

Studly Screwright?

The Mountie.

Cat didn't know whether to laugh or be furious. It was just so . . . ridiculous.

It's not funny, Fiona. Jack's voice was a low, menacing growl.

I'm *not* Fiona, Cat snarled back. Never met the woman. Don't *want* to. My name is Cat Turner. I wasn't even born when the love of your life cheated on you and walked out. But if you're still so damned obsessed with her, why don't you seek *her* out? Wander in and out of her thoughts for a while, and leave *me* the hell alone.

There was a long silence. Jack didn't speak, but Cat could still feel him in the back of her mind.

When he finally said something his voice was different, softer, more rational. I can't. It was a simple admission. The night she bedded Ramirez, the night she *mated* to him, something happened. I can't reach her mind anymore, can't share her thoughts . . . touch her. She's just . . . gone.

I'm sorry. Cat was surprised to realize she almost meant it.

Don't pity me. Don't you *dare* pity me!

Don't worry, she snarled. *Not* going to happen. Pity would just get in the way, make me feel bad for killing you.

You still think you can manage that? Better than you have tried. Their bleached bones decayed to dust centuries ago.

My God what a towering ego!

God is right, kitten. Jack purred. I *was* a god. I was worshiped, offered sacrifices, given the most beautiful women.

You're not a god. You're just a really old murdering nutcase who's about to reach the end of the line.

Good luck with that. The words were a venomous hiss.

You, too.

He slammed the connection closed, and Cat found herself standing in the now cold shower, the suds from her shampoo running into her burning eyes. *"Damn. Damn, damn, damn!"* She slammed her fist against the tiled wall of the shower with each word, felt the tile crack beneath her hands and the wall give, smelled her own blood over the citrus shampoo and the chlorine in the water.

Chapter Fourteen

"GOOD MORNING, SENATOR. You're looking chipper today." Laura Kendrick placed a stack of papers to be signed on Jack's desk, picked up a gold and black mug near his telephone, and then stepped across the room to refill it with his preferred dark roast coffee. "Were you able to convince Representative Davies to sign the new clean water bill?"

He chuckled as he accepted the steaming mug from his faithful assistant, a family member who would never be Sazi. While she wasn't as valuable as Muriel by any means, she kept his senate office running smoothly. "No, today's victory is far greater, and far more . . . *personal.*"

"That's good. I've been worried about you lately. You've been looking a little more stressed than usual. Especially since your last trip. I'm glad everything is working itself out." She nodded, smelling happy to have things back to normal.

He smiled, allowing her to see a touch of warmth that was entirely contrived, but useful for dealing with staff. "I appreciate your concern, Laura. You've been a trouper lately—the last-minute flights, changing my schedule to accommodate my sudden *illness,* staying late to finish up typing. Tell you what, why don't I try to pull some strings upstairs and get you some extra paid leave? I know you'd like to spend some time with the kids this summer."

The way her eyes lit up, she didn't need to respond, and she left the office with a smile. Yes, like most of the mindless human drones in Washington, a few well-placed niceties were enough to keep her suffering abuses on her time and talent. It had been the same way for centuries, and thankfully would never change.

He allowed himself a laugh of fierce joy before leaning back in his custom leather chair and turning to gaze out over the capital. He caught a glance of his own reflection in the window and noticed he *was* looking good, perhaps a bit *too* good. With a whisper of thought, his magic altered his appearance slightly, adding a bit of gray at the temples, and a few new lines at the corners of his eyes. He turned his face slightly to check the result. No sense having any of the humans asking questions beyond the standard inquiries about Botox treatments and stylist recommendations.

Still, he refused to remove all the joy from his face, because today was a red-letter day. The little cat had fallen for his sad admission and tortured past—hook, line, and sinker. Reverse psychology was such a marvelous tool and, when combined with some subtle Sazi magic . . . well, she'd believe anything he wanted her to.

Soon, very soon—his revenge would be complete at last.

CAT HAD TO go well over the speed limit to make up for the time she'd lost in her chat with Jack. Still, she managed. She was a little breathless from sprinting up the stairs to the third floor, but at 10:01 A.M. Cat stood with her hand on the knob of the group therapy room. Gathering her courage, she opened the door and walked into a room filled with tense silence. The pleasant decor did nothing to alleviate the dread Cat felt every time she came into this room. It was obvious that it, like the entire building, had been professionally decorated. The psychiatric wing had been specially designed. Everything was very intentionally chosen to be soothing, comfortable. The walls of the group therapy room had been painted a pale peach. The carpet was a textured oatmeal-colored Berber with flakes of peach and brown that had no doubt been specially chosen to coordinate with both the walls and the furniture. A comfortable dark brown upholstered loveseat and chairs were gathered in a loose conversation group, with handy oak end tables, each of which held a supply of tissues.

As Cat passed through the doorway, scents assaulted her nose faster than the air purifier could suck them to the ceiling and out of the room: rage, mouthwatering terror, and guilt rose like multicolored mists on the false breeze, individual scent drops visible and moving like dust motes in a sunbeam.

Cat knew that Violet was terrified and miserably unhappy and the therapy just didn't seem to be helping. She desperately wanted to help her aunt, but didn't have a clue what to do. So She forced herself to smile and greet Ned and Violet as if nothing were wrong. But it broke her heart seeing her aunt looking so very fragile and knowing, smelling, the terror the older woman felt every time she walked in the room.

"Good morning." Cat crossed the room taking her seat in one of the two open armchairs. "How're you doing this morning?"

"Fine." Violet's voice was still a little higher than usual, but it was actually audible. The other day she hadn't been able to bring herself to speak much at all, and what she had managed was never above a whisper. So actual words, in a normal tone of voice was improvement. Bound to be. Cat clung to that hope. She needed to believe that eventually her aunt would recover. But she wasn't sure.

She hoped Ned was smart enough to keep his mouth shut about what had happened at Wolf's Run last night. Cat knew, to the depths of her soul, that she and Ned both could have died horribly. She'd have gone down fighting, but there had been too many of the wolves lined up against them. And the wolves had all *wanted* that fight. There was so much rage, resentment, and violence buried barely under the surface. She could smell it on the nurses at the hospital and some of her coworkers at the Joint. Most of all, she could scent it from Tatya. That was *so* not a good thing. Tatya was the alpha female. Where she led, the pack followed. The only thing holding them in check was Raphael.

Ned's soft cough brought Cat back to her present surroundings. She met his eyes across the room. Did you tell her?

Hell no. Ned's words formed clearly in her mind. Not only was he good at this, he didn't even seem surprised. And don't you either!

How are you doing this?

I'm not. You are. And no, I don't know how. But settle down and listen. Violet's worked really hard on this speech.

Cat sank deep into the brown corduroy loveseat across from her aunt. It was a comfortable chair, but it was not conducive to rapid movements. It wouldn't be easy to leap out of it and storm off. Not that Cat expected to. Today, it was Violet's turn to take center stage.

Cat fought to keep her expression carefully neutral.

"Cat." Violet spoke softly, her voice was tremulous at first, but she visibly steeled herself and the words came out more firmly. "Ned has proposed, and I've accepted. I won't be going back to the house. In fact," Violet took a deep breath and looked to Ned. His strength gave her courage. "We won't be staying in Boulder at all. Ned's always wanted to travel. So have I. Now that Dr. Perdue says I'm strong enough and we don't have to worry about a relapse, we're leaving." Again, she looked at Ned for support. He nodded, so she continued. "I've contacted a Realtor about selling my house."

Violet risked a glance at Cat. At the shock she must have seen, her face fell. "I'm sorry, Cat. I really am. I'm trying my best, but I can't cope with this. I just *can't*. At least not right now." She lowered her head, staring down to where Ned's calloused hands gripped hers. "I love you, Catherine. I wish . . ." Violet's voice dropped to a barely audible whisper. "I wish I was stronger."

Cat knew she should say something. They were waiting for her to respond. It took a long moment, and a deep breath, but she gathered her strength and forced herself to smile. "Congratulations. I'm happy for you both. I know how much you love each other." She did, and she was. But it still hurt, still made her feel very, very alone.

"Is there a ring?"

Violet's eyes lit up with hope and gratitude at Cat's understanding. "Yes." She pulled her left hand from Ned's grip, extending it tentatively so she could see the diamond. "It belonged to Ned's grandmother."

Cat looked down at her aunt's delicate hand, and the thin antique golden band shaped in an intricate leaf pattern that curled around a brilliantly sparkling diamond. "It's beautiful. I've never seen another anything like it."

"My grandfather made it himself," Ned answered. "It's one of a kind. Just like Violet."

Violet looked up at him with such love that all of Cat's anger just evaporated. The two of them belonged together. Ned would keep Violet safe, take her away from the pack, away from the threat of Jack using her against Cat.

Ned cleared his throat and spoke into the deep well of silence that had fallen on the room. "We're going to go to Vegas first, then travel cross country for a bit. Depending on how things are going, we might make it back for a visit at Christmas."

"Christmas." Cat repeated the word hollowly.

"Violet tells me it's your favorite time of year," Ned said gently.

She hadn't lied. Every other year she'd start her preparations in early November. This year she didn't even want to think about it. Imagining the holidays without her folks was just too painful.

"I think it will help, maybe, if we have some time away, give Violet time to adjust." Ned offered.

Cat turned to look at the psychiatrist. Betty kept her expression studiously blank. Somehow she'd even managed to still her scent. Cat had no clue as to whether she thought Violet and Ned's plan was a good idea or a recipe for disaster.

"I understand." Cat pushed the words past the tightness in her throat, forced the smile back on her face.

"Ned said you went up with him to look at the property?" Violet made the words a question.

"It's a beautiful place. I'm going to put a call in to Uncle Chuck. He's the executor of the estate and the trustee. He'll have to agree to the purchase."

"Oh, I don't think that will be a problem." Violet's voice held forced cheer. "I understand he knows all about your needing to hunt." Her jaw thrust forward and Cat caught a quick sniff of resentment before the air purifiers whisked the scent away. "And I'm sure *he'll* be more realistic about the land's value." Violet looked up, meeting Cat's gaze for the first time that day. "That is *if* you want it? You *do* want it don't you?"

Cat heard the note of desperation in Violet's voice. She had a moment of unexpected insight. Violet understood Ned's pride. If he didn't feel he was contributing as much financially to their life together as Violet did it would come between them. Not because she cared; because *he* did. But there was more to it than that. She might not be able to cope with what was happening to Cat, but she did love her, and in her own way she was trying very hard to help.

"Of course I do."

Violet and Ned's obvious relief gave Cat some consolation. She might not be able to do much to help her aunt adjust to the bizarre turn their lives had taken, but this . . . this she could do.

The rest of the session was uneventful. Ned pointed out that the two of them would be much safer if Jack didn't know where to find them. Cat couldn't find fault with his logic, but it didn't make her any happier. When they left tomorrow morning she'd be truly alone. But she pretended it was all right for Violet's sake, and was grateful when Betty didn't ask her usual, probing questions. In fact, Betty didn't say much at all, sitting quietly in her chair, writing the occasional note in the file.

When the bell rang that signaled the end of the session it seemed all four of them were more than a little relieved. They certainly didn't waste their time bolting for the exit.

Ned reached the door first, holding it open for the ladies. Betty strode quickly from the room, her expression troubled. Cat would have followed if Violet hadn't done something so completely unexpected that it left her niece flat-footed. Despite the terror that oozed from her very pores, Violet pulled Cat into a tight hug. Standing on tiptoe, she whispered her thanks before breaking away from the embrace and scurrying from the room.

Cat was still standing there, bemused, staring at nothing in particular, when Holly's voice brought her back to reality.

"Cat . . . Cat, are you all right?"

"Oh, hi!" Cat shook her head a little, as though to clear the cobwebs. "Just thinking. What're you doing here? You're the sanest person I know."

Holly laughed, and it brought a little of the usual life back to her warm brown eyes. Cat forced herself not to stare. Holly looked *bad*. Her smile was wan. Her scent reeked of anger and depression. Even her body seemed to sag, so that the work uniform she wore hung loosely on her frame.

Cat decided to grab the bull by the horns. "Look, I know I'm probably a pariah after last night. If you don't want to talk to me I understand."

"Don't be an idiot!" Holly's voice was harsh and *loud*. Loud enough to draw the immediate attention of both Betty and the nurse who were chatting just a short distance down the hall. "I heard about what happened last night. You stood up for a family member—a *human*. And while the pack may hate it, *I* think it's wonderful. So do the rest of the family members."

"Oh." Cat was surprised, and happy. But she was a little concerned as well. Neither the nurse nor Betty seemed pleased by what they were hearing. They weren't even trying to be subtle about their eavesdropping.

"Then what's the problem?"

Holly sighed, running her hand through her short brown hair. "Alpha Santiago called me into his office to talk about something."

Cat looked more closely at her friend. She hadn't noticed earlier, because Holly'd applied her makeup very carefully in an attempt to conceal the signs. But now there was no mistaking the fact that her friend had been crying. The evidence was all there—from the red-rimmed eyes, down to the chapped nose and upper lip.

"Bad news?"

"Yeah." Holly said with a sniffle. "The worst. But, I don't want to talk about it here. Let's go somewhere and get coffee."

"Sounds like a plan to me," Cat agreed. She gestured for Holly to precede her down the hall. The two of them passed Betty and "Nurse Ratched," both of whom fell conspicuously silent until after the door to the stairwell slammed closed behind Holly and Cat.

"So, what's up with you?" Holly's footsteps echoed oddly in the stairwell, and her words sounded hollow.

"Violet and Ned are eloping to Vegas and then taking off for parts unknown. I don't think they'll be coming back."

"Oh." Holly's eyes grew wide and she paused in midstep to look back over her shoulder at her friend. "Are you okay with that?"

Cat continued down the staircase, passing Holly along the way. "Hell, I don't know. I do think it's a good idea to get her away from here. Jack killed my parents to get to me. He wouldn't hesitate to do the same to Violet." She stopped, her hand on the metal bar that would open the door on the ground floor and let them out into the parking lot. "I'm not sure what to think about any of this." Cat pressed the bar. The door opened, letting in a smattering of rain.

Holly sprinted across the parking lot to her Geo with Cat at her heels. They climbed in, slamming the doors behind them, each turning in their seat so that they faced the other.

"So," Holly asked, when they'd settled in comfortably. "If Violet and Ned are leaving, what are your plans?"

"Well, it looks like I'll be buying Ned's land up in the mountains."

Holly cringed. "Yeah, I heard about that."

"What?" Cat looked at her friend through narrowed eyes.

Holly's sigh was audible over the drum of rain against the car roof. "It's just that, the pack always thought of that land as theirs. I mean, yeah, Ned owned it, but they've hunted on it forever. The thought of somebody else, anybody else, getting it would be bad, but a cat? They are so, like, seriously pissed." The scent of Holly's worry mingled with Cat's angry frustration until, rain or no, Cat had to roll down her window a couple of inches to get a bit of fresh air.

"Do you really intend to stay in Boulder?"

"I suppose. I know Uncle Chuck wants me to stay here and get finished with my training. Whenever that will be."

"Michael will be glad to hear that," Holly teased.

Cat's growl startled them both.

Holly's eyes widened. "Uh-oh. That's not good. What's the 411 on that sitch?"

"The condensed version? We had a fight, I broke his nose." She shrugged, hoping to make that the end of it.

Holly blinked repeatedly. Finally, she managed to say, "Wow."

"Yeah." Cat stared through the open portion of the window at the raindrops dimpling the various puddles in the parking lot, realizing she wanted to tell someone about it, someone other than Raphael. She wanted, needed, a *friend* right now. "I kind of wish I hadn't done it, but he was being such an *ass*."

Maybe it was because Holly had spent so much time with Sazis, or maybe it was because she was a waitress, but Cat noticed she seemed to understand instinctively the right tone to use. "What exactly did he do?"

"You really want to know?" Cat asked. When Holly nodded yes, she launched into her version of the night's events—up to and including storming out of the car and going looking for Raphael in the woods.

"Did you find him?"

"Oh, yeah." Cat couldn't keep the smile from either her face or her voice.

Holly stared at her for a long moment before speaking. "You *didn't*!"

"Didn't what?" Cat tried to sound innocent, and failed miserably.

"Cat Turner!" Holly was aghast. She stared at the other woman as if she'd grown a second head.

"Well, yeah, but he's nice. And he's smart, and good looking—"

"But he's *old*! And he's my *uncle*. I mean . . . well, *eww*."

"Holly stop it! He's not *that* old!"

"Um . . . like, get real! Old enough to have kids older than we are! And I do mean *way* older!"

"Besides." Cat ignored that thought, tried to be reasonable. "Men his age have been dating women our age since the beginning of time." She paused, thinking about it. "Although, usually the man's the one with the money, and they *definitely* don't look like your uncle . . . but still . . ."

Holly gave her a withering look. "It's not funny."

Cat's expression grew serious. "Okay, so it's not funny. But he's hella *fine*. Besides, I *like* him. I think about him all the time. He understands what I'm feeling, and doesn't sit in judgment about it. I know you think he's ancient, but I don't care."

Holly's face took on an odd expression. "You're actually knocking boots with my uncle? That is so weird."

"I don't know. Maybe." Cat tried to sound casual, and failed miserably. "I've never felt anything like this before. I mean, Mike's a nice enough guy, but he's a *kid*. And, I mean, the guy's a complete slacker. I've been here how long, and I honestly don't think he's gone to class once. I mean, what's the point of being in school if you're not even going to show up?"

Holly didn't even try to argue. She sat very still in her seat, her expression thoughtful. "So, what's the plan then?"

"I'd *like* to lay low for a few days, give *everybody* time to calm down. But that *so* isn't happening."

"New flash! I mean, wolves and the big cats are natural enemies. The pack's bound to hate you right out of the box." Holly's expression grew serious, her eyes darkening. "You really need to be careful. You keep trying to deal with the pack like the people you grew up with. That won't work. They may *look* human—but they're *not,* not even a little. If things keep up the way they've been going, they're going to get even uglier than they already are."

"Is that even marginally possible?" Cat joked.

Holly's response was deadly serious. "Oh, yeah."

Chapter Fifteen

RAPHAEL PUNCHED THE speed dial on his cell phone. Fast Eddie picked up on the first ring. "Ramirez Towing."

"Where's Mona?"

"Morning sickness is a bitch. What's up boss?"

"You need me in there today?"

He could practically hear the gears grinding in Eddie's brain. Morning was *not* the big man's best time of day. It took a good hour and several cups of coffee before he was up to intelligent conversation. He was, however, the best damned mechanic Raphael had ever met, so he paid him well and put up with the occasional hangover or payday advance.

"You gonna be in to sign paychecks Monday?"

"Yeah."

"Then, no problem. It's kinda slow anyway. We need a good snow."

Raphael knew what he meant. First couple of snows, people always drove like lunatics: fender benders, multicar pileups. While he didn't want to see anyone injured or killed, one good snow could make him enough money to cover payroll for more than a month.

"Well, it's that time of year. Bound to happen sooner or later," Raphael said.

"True," Eddie agreed. Raphael heard the second line ringing. "Gotta get that. Later." The line went dead in Raphael's ear.

That done, Raphael turned the car around and drove home. He fully intended to go to pack headquarters and deal with the fallout from last night's disaster, but he was going to shower and shave first. He didn't want *anyone* to catch a whiff of him with Cat's scent all over him. It wasn't that he was ashamed of what he'd done. He wasn't. Nor could he make himself regret it, despite the fact that it had been a very bad idea.

He knew he shouldn't have slept with her. There were more reasons for him to avoid Cat Turner than he could count. But as soon as he looked in those eyes, caught her scent, all logic and reason fled. The only way he'd managed *not* to act on the attraction before this was to only see her for their lessons and avoid her the rest of the time. Even that wasn't perfect. Because, like it or not, he couldn't get the blasted woman out of his mind. He'd catch himself thinking about her at the oddest moments, checking to see what she was doing.

Right now, for example, she was in the shower. Raphael jerked his thoughts away from the soap running down the wet, naked curves of her body just in time to slam on the brakes before rear-ending the car in front of him.

He tried to distract himself by mentally creating a to-do list. First, he needed to schedule a meeting with Lucas. Raphael was *acting* Alpha. Fine. But just what exactly was he authorized to do? With the old man staying right here part of the time, Raphael had been reluctant to do much of anything. But if he had the authority, there were things Raphael *wanted* to take care of. For instance, he fully intended to find out just exactly what the children had been told about the accident that had claimed Candy Streeter's life. He'd bet money it wasn't the truth—or Michael wouldn't have made that remark about doing Ned a favor. Raphael had still been connected to Cat when she'd watched some of the girls picking on Holly at the restaurant, as well. He had been surprised that Cat hadn't stepped in to stop the harassment.

He intended to find out what in the hell was going on, and put a stop to it before it went too far and someone got killed. There was some sort of financial mess at Jake's to be cleared up, and Tatya's punishment. If all that wasn't enough to keep his mind off a certain leggy blonde, then the cause was truly hopeless!

A quick call got him Lucas on the line. "If you want to meet it'll have to be today."

"You're working on Saturday?"

"After last night?" Lucas asked "Hell yes, I'm working. I'm up to my eyeballs in paperwork and I'm due to fly out of town this afternoon. Can you make it to the office by ten thirty?"

Raphael checked the clock on the dashboard. Lucas was giving him just enough time to get home, clean up, and drive back to the complex, if he hurried. "No problem."

WHEN HE REACHED the door and lifted his fist to knock, the door flew open and he gasped as a cloud of jalapeño-scented fury hit him like a brick.

"Enough!" Lucas growled deep in his throat. "Raphael, come in. Tatiana, you may go."

Raphael jumped out of the way in the nick of time as the alpha female stormed past. He watched her head down the hallway, her rage a visible cloud of swirling reds and purples in the air around her.

"I *said* come in." Lucas's voice was harsh.

"Right." Raphael did as he was bid, quickly.

"Shut the door and have a seat." Lucas sat behind a large mahogany desk. While Raphael's office had been decorated in pale blue fabrics and blond oak, Lucas, in contrast had chosen dark wood and deep rich burgundy. Three wingback leather chairs sat in a semicircle facing his desk. The chairs' brass studs were echoed by the brass banker's lamp that illuminated a clean, well-organized work space. The walls were lined with bookshelves housing leather bound classics, photos of Tatiana and the family, and mementos whose meaning were known only to their owner. It was a very "lawyerly" space, but that wasn't surprising.

"Would you like some coffee?" Lucas offered, his voice as pleasant and smooth as if the conflict Raphael had witnessed had not taken place.

"Please."

Lucas hit the intercom button. "Claire, bring the Second and me some coffee, black. Knock before you come in."

Lucas leaned back in his chair, steepling his fingers in front of his nose. "So, what can I do for you?"

Raphael fought not to fidget. He was just a little bit uncomfortable. He didn't want Lucas to think he was like Martin, grasping for power, but he did need to know just what the parameters of his new position were. The last thing he needed to do was piss off Lucas. Taking a deep breath, he blurted out the question. "Just how much authority are you expecting me to exert as 'acting' Alpha?"

Before Lucas could answer there was a light tap on the door. "Come in."

Lucas's secretary entered, carrying a tray laden with a coffee service and variety of pastries. Raphael nodded good morning to her. She acknowledged his greeting, but didn't smile. He'd known her professionally for years, both as a pack member and as Lucas's assistant, but he'd never really gotten to know her personally. She was an attractive, single, middle-aged woman: efficient, intelligent, and damned near invisible. Tatya had recommended her for the position when Alice Corona had retired to Florida. She and the alpha female were best friends.

Claire's pretty face was pale, her eyes wide, but she made no comment regarding the spectacle Tatya had made in leaving, simply set the tray silently on the desk between the two men and hastened to the door.

Lucas poured, speaking as he did so. "You are in charge of the pack. You are to be *true* Alpha. You do *not* have to consult anyone regarding your decisions. I will support any choices you make." Lucas raised his voice considerably on the last sentence, making sure his secretary and his wife would hear—judging from the scents flowing through the open door, both were lingering in the hall.

"The Chief Justice has asked that we train the cat for the first six months. I *hope* you will honor that request, but again, you will be *completely in charge*." Lucas shook his head. He took a long pull of coffee from his mug before continuing. When he did, his tone was rueful. "I'm leaving you a mess. I'm sorry for that. Apparently while my attention was elsewhere, discipline around here . . . slipped."

"Nothing irretrievable has happened," Raphael reassured him.

"I'm not so sure." Lucas took another drink of coffee. "On a hunch, after hearing the witness statements last night, I called your niece in for a meeting. I wanted to find out just what the children had been told about Candy Streeter."

Raphael's eyes widened with surprise. Yet again, he and Lucas had been thinking very much alike. He probably should have expected it. After all, they'd worked together for a long time. Still, he did have to wonder why Lucas had asked Holly when he could just as easily talked to his own son. "What did you find out?"

"My wife decided that it would be 'too traumatic' to the youngsters to learn that Candy had died because her body wasn't capable of the change. She didn't want to make them afraid of what is 'essentially a perfectly natural process.'"

Raphael grimaced. He could actually feel the muscles in his shoulders and neck tightening into knots. "What *did* she tell them?"

"That Mr. Streeter got transferred in his job and the family moved to join the Alaska pack."

"So nobody—none of her friends or classmates—has a clue that Candy's dead?" Raphael leaned back, running his hands through his hair. That explained Mike's words of last night. More to the point, it explained the overall attitude of most of the pack. While losing a human to an attempted change was a tragedy, one of the few *good* things it did was reinforce *why* the rules existed, and the punishments were so severe. Tatya's decision had taken even that small consolation away, rendering Candy's death totally pointless.

"No. They don't."

Raphael reached for his cup. The first drink of coffee scalded his tongue, but it bought him time to consider how he was going to handle the situation. It needed to be dealt with. To his mind, the sooner the better, before there was another "incident." The events of last night just reinforced how far discipline had slipped. What he did might well set the tone of his rule for the duration. Raphael didn't hesitate. "That's not acceptable." He said firmly.

Lucas nodded in agreement as Raphael continued. "As head of Wolven, you should have access to the video recording from that night."

"I'm sure there's one in the file."

"I'd like to borrow a copy. I assume that the pack still has contact information on Melody and David Streeter?"

"I'll check with Claire. If it's not in the files, I can get it for you." Lucas used a fountain pen to scratch a note on the yellow legal pad on the desk in front of him, accepting Raphael's requests as though they were orders from the territory's alpha. It felt very strange to him.

"I'd appreciate it." Raphael blew on his coffee for a second, and took another long drink. Now that his tongue had healed itself, the brew tasted positively wonderful, much better than the cup he'd bought at the drive-through earlier.

"May I ask what you're planning?" Lucas raised his brows a bit, but there was only curiosity in his scent, not disapproval or anger.

He nodded. "It'll take a few days, but as soon as I can arrange it we're going to have a school assembly and full pack meeting."

"You're planning on flying the Streeters in?" Lucas didn't sound surprised. Then again, Raphael reflected, it was the kind of thing he would do. The two men were alike in many ways. They definitely shared more than a few opinions on how a pack should be ruled. It was one reason they'd made such a good team all these many years.

"I'll ask *David* if he'll come. I'm not sure Melody could handle reliving that night. She tried to commit suicide after, you know."

"No, I didn't." A puff of sorrow, and possibly guilt, wafted off Lucas, only to disappear in the discreet ventilation system. He sighed. "David will come if *you* ask." Lucas gave a sad shake of his head. "They know how hard you tried to save her. You drained yourself to the dregs that night."

"It didn't work." Raphael didn't bother to hide his bitterness. He'd done his best, exhausted himself so completely he'd been useless for days.

"No, but they know you tried. And, they know that you put in a good word for them when they applied for a foster child from the breeding program a couple of years ago."

"How'd they find *that* out?"

"You know how hard it is to keep a secret around here."

Raphael gave a snort of acknowledgment. That was the

God's honest truth. It was one of the things that annoyed him most about pack living. There was absolutely no privacy.

"This is going to take a bit of work to manage." Lucas pursed his lips in thought for a moment before he continued. "I'll tell Claire to report to you. She can make the arrangements at this end. I'll take care of things with Wolven. Still, it'll probably be a few days before you can pull it off."

Raphael nodded in acknowledgment of the timetable, but thought he'd better comment on the rest. "Are you sure? Claire's *your* secretary. I doubt she'd appreciate being handed over like part of the office furniture."

"Raphael, Claire's the *pack* secretary. If I tell her to report to you, it'll reinforce that *you* are the one in charge." He gave a rueful smile. "I'll talk to her first, of course; explain the situation. And for God's sake be nice to her. I don't want her to quit."

"I'm *always* nice, Lucas."

"*Riiiiiight.*" The amused expression on the older man's face disappeared as quickly as it came. "Have you decided what you are going to do about Tatya?"

Raphael sighed. He set his empty coffee cup back on the tray. He was starting to get a headache . . . again. "I'm not going to be able to do *anything* about the Wolven investigation, or the council. Those wheels are already in motion, and you know as well as I do that anything I said in those circles would only make things worse."

Lucas nodded his assent.

Raphael sighed again. He knew he had burned his bridges with the council decades before. Most of them delighted in holding a grudge. One or two might even happily hand Raphael's head to Jack on a platter if they thought they could get away with it. He couldn't undo the past, but it was going to make the rest of his life a lot harder than it needed to be.

"I could claim damages—have Betty give her a beating, but you and I both know that would be utterly useless. As fast as she heals it'd be over so quickly she wouldn't take time to really *think* about what she's done."

"Which leaves?"

"Humiliation," Raphael said with a sigh. "Utter, long-term

humiliation. Once she gets past her wounded pride she'll *think* about how she wound up in the situation and take responsibility for her actions."

Lucas raised eyebrows in surprise, lowered his elbows to the desk, and steepled his fingers in front of his nose. "Do you have something in mind?"

"I'll make the announcement at the pack meeting, but yes. I do." Raphael gave Lucas a long, assessing look. He wasn't sure how his friend was going to take what he was about to propose—particularly since he'd just publicly declared that he was going to back Raphael's decisions.

"I'm knocking her down to Omega. For six months she is forbidden to take part in *any* challenges of any type. For that same six months, in the evenings she will work for minimum wage for at least thirty hours per week at Jake's Burger Joint, taking orders at the front counter and doing the cleaning."

Lucas winced.

"Every time she shows up late, or misses a shift, she adds another month to the sentence."

"What about—"

"Medical emergencies?" Raphael supplied the words. "Betty is a physician, and a healer. She will be the on-call physician while Tatya's working her second job." Raphael's expression hardened as he continued. "And since it was her policy to begin with, I've decided that Tatya will be the one to inform each pack member she waits on that 'Due to consistent abuses of the system we are no longer able to offer credit here at Jake's Burger Joint.'"

"What? *Credit?* At a hamburger place?" Lucas stared at him with an open jaw, and then leaned back in his chair so far that Raphael thought he might topple over.

"You didn't know? Jake was *required* to extend credit to the pack members. He's going broke because they refuse to pay the tabs. Apparently some of our pack members owe *thousands* of dollars." Raphael smiled fiercely. "I'm swinging by Jake's this evening to get a list of who owes what. I'll be calling on the biggest accounts myself. I'm in just the mood for bill collection."

Lucas hung his head. He began rubbing his fingers on either

side of the bridge of his nose as if it was *his* turn to have a headache. "I owe you and Jake both an apology for that. I've been putting off meeting with him. He's been asking to talk to me for weeks. I should have been paying more attention to pack business."

"As I said, you've had a lot on your plate."

"Perhaps, but this is unconscionable. How has he been surviving?"

"Not well. But Lucas, it's just as much my fault as yours. I'm his brother, and your Second. I would've done something, but I only found out the night of Cat's first change." Raphael explained. "I stopped by to get meat to use as a lure for her, and found out the freezers were damned near empty—on the *full moon*!" Raphael remembered his own shock and anger, wondering what might have happened if there hadn't been *any* meat to attract Cat's attention. More, though, he was disappointed that his brother hadn't talked to him, told him that the business was in trouble.

Well, Jake hadn't asked, but now that Raphael was going to be Alpha in truth there were going to be some changes made. Getting the restaurant back on profitable footing was one of them. The biggest debtors would whine and rage, but he didn't care. The whole situation should never have come up.

Lucas gave a delicate sniff. Raphael knew the other man scented his hurt and frustration. Hell, it wasn't that different from the scent rolling off Lucas himself.

"Deal with Tatya as you see fit. I won't interfere." He gave a rueful smile. "But I'd be really grateful if you could wait to do it until after two this afternoon."

"Why after two?" Raphael was curious.

"I'll be in the air somewhere over Kansas by then," Lucas explained. "So I won't have to watch. I don't know how I'd react if I had to see her be in that much emotional pain—and you don't need the sort of trouble I might cause. Is there anything you're going to need before I go?"

Raphael opened his mouth to say no, but then a thought occurred to him. "Actually, there is." He gave Lucas a wry look. "I could really use some of the Wolven cologne."

Lucas sat back and stared at him silently for long moments.

The Wolven cologne was a valuable commodity and one of the biggest Sazi secrets. Like any cologne, it smelled good. But it had an added advantage. It worked to burn out the scenting ability of Sazi in the area, preventing them from knowing what the person wearing it was feeling. No one outside of the agency and the council was supposed to know of its existence.

Raphael waited, watching the thoughts play across his friend's face. It was a big favor, but under the circumstances, the cologne would be very useful in dealing with the pack. They would be confused by his lack of scent and, more important, *afraid*.

"I'll drop it by your office."

"I'll be there." Raphael said it with a heavy enough sigh that Lucas gave a bark of laughter.

"You act as though you're not looking forward to running things."

"Honestly? No. I've never really wanted the pack."

"Can't say I blame you." Lucas's words were rueful. "But I know you're up to it. And if you're not, the next in line's Martin Black, and he's the *last* man I'd put in charge." Lucas's eyes darkened, and his expression grew sober. "You'll want to keep an eye on him *and* his wife."

"Amen to that."

Chapter Sixteen

CAT SPENT MOST of the afternoon at the computer. First, she contacted Charles about Ned's property. Then there were literally dozens of backlogged e-mails to take care of. Two of the ones marked "urgent" were from Brad. She opened the first one and almost immediately wished she hadn't. It sounded just like the old Brad, the one she'd loved. He went on and on about what a fool he'd been, that he'd do anything to make it up to her if she just gave him a chance.

A part of her ached to believe he meant it, that she *could* go back to her old life. The ugly, cynical part wondered if maybe it had occurred to Brad (or more likely to his parents) that with Chris and Janet gone Cat would inherit everything. She didn't want to believe it, but she couldn't unthink it, particularly when there were messages from both of his parents as well.

Mrs. Jenkins invited Cat to visit them in the Hamptons for "a little getaway." Mr. Jenkins wanted to know if Cat had access to her father's laptop. He needed to get some essential information from her if she did.

Cat responded to Brad with a carefully worded e-mail thanking him for his condolences, but avoided talking about their relationship altogether. Because while she wasn't entirely sure she was over him, she was almost certain she didn't want him back.

She graciously declined Mrs. Jenkins's invitation, and sent word to Brad's father that the laptop was in storage. She'd try to get it out and locate what he was looking for within the next few days.

The rest of the time she spent productively scheming. One of the easiest ways to get the spyware into Jack's systems would be to hide it on an e-mail. When the recipient opened the message, the program would attach. The trick was to make the e-mail legitimate, something that would absolutely be opened, without question. The obvious solution was money. After all, Simpson was a politician. There was bound to be a reelection campaign somewhere looking for donations.

Cat started cruising the Internet. Sure enough, Senator Simpson had a significant Web presence, and was soliciting contributions. His voting record showed him being strong on environmental policies and well informed with regard to Western water law issues. He was vilified on more than one site for being proabortion, or "antilife" as they put it.

The streaming video on his campaign site showed him to be handsome, erudite, and extremely well spoken. He was charismatic enough that Cat might have voted for him herself!

Jack might be older than dirt, but he certainly did know how to manipulate technology and the media to his advantage. She wouldn't be able to count on him being either uninformed or hidebound. In fact, the more she looked, the more impressed she became. Not intimidated, but impressed. Judging from what she could glean, Simpson was personally brilliant, politically savvy, and had a well-earned reputation for getting things done.

Cat glanced at the computer clock and swore. She'd had no idea how much time her virtual jaunt had taken. She'd have to really rush to get ready and get to work on time.

She was sorely tempted to call in. She certainly was dreading running into the pack after last night's fiasco. But that wouldn't be fair to Jake and Holly. Just as important, she wasn't willing to show weakness to her opponents. If they "smelled blood," her enemies would just get more aggressive. So, she'd face them down—but she'd watch her back. She hurried upstairs and changed into her uniform.

When Cat arrived for her shift at Jake's that evening the place was packed with people, all of whom fell eerily silent when they saw her come through the door. There was a low growl from somewhere in the back of the room, and the scent of anger was thick enough to walk on. Holly greeted her with false good cheer.

Cat felt as though there were concentric circles painted on her back, but followed the advice her mother had given her years ago, when she'd been snubbed by the popular girls at school.

"Lofty indifference is best," her mother had told her, "if for no other reason than it annoys the hell out of them."

All day her anger built as more and more little things happened: the deliberately spilled messes she had to mop up. The orders sent back that she'd gotten "wrong." It was petty, backbiting, childish *bullshit* and while Cat told herself she was *not* going to give them the satisfaction of playing into it, it was damned hard. Eventually even Jake tired of it. When Holly was taking out the trash he told Cat to go home early.

Cat stalked through the kitchen to the tiny break room. With deft motions she twisted the dial of the combination lock on her locker. She grabbed her purse, slammed the door closed with a clang, and locked it.

A part of her wanted to throttle Raphael for putting her in this position. Not that it was really his fault. It was nature. The wolves were a pack. Packs stick together against outsiders and Cat was even more of an outsider than the human family members.

The younger wolves picked on the human siblings. That was why so many of the humans left home as teenagers, turning their back on the entire Sazi world and culture. Holly only stayed because of her father. He depended on her to help him run the restaurant. So she stayed and she put up with the torment. She'd sworn to Cat that as soon as she finished college she'd leave. Cat hoped she would. Holly was much too nice to have to put up with the constant harassment.

Cat stepped out of the building. The heavy metal door fell shut, cutting off the kitchen sounds. They were replaced with the noise of traffic and activity in the parking lot.

Hidden in the shadows between the Dumpster and the building Cat watched as a group of young women surrounded Holly and began harassing her—again. Cat felt her temper rise. She was sick of watching and ignoring. *Assholes*. Cat dropped her purse into the deep shadows and began moving forward. Just then the circle of girls tightened and someone shoved Holly against her Geo. The blow knocked the smaller woman off balance, causing her to drop the trash bag, littering the ground with garbage.

Cat stepped out of the shadows, strutting directly into the center of the action.

The wolves flowed like water, changing position, grouping themselves behind the instigator. Corrine Castillion gave Cat a hostile look. Her dark eyes shone with malice.

"This is none of your business, *feline*." Corrine spoke in a smooth musical alto, putting just enough emphasis on the last word to make it an insult.

Cat looked down her nose at the tiny brunette. She knew Corrine's reputation. A bitch in *every* sense of the word. She was powerful, beautiful, and dumb as a box of rocks. Michael had told Cat that Raphael had been ordered into Corrine's bed to breed powerful puppies for the next generation of the pack. It boggled Cat's mind that anyone would consent to be bred like a pedigreed poodle. Michael was jealous of Raphael. He'd hoped the information would make her stay away from the older man. The only reason it hadn't worked was that Holly had taken time to explain that only the top two males of any wolf pack were fertile, and how difficult it was for most of the Sazi women to carry to term.

Since wolves were family and pack oriented, it left most couples desperate for children. Adopting a human child wouldn't work—the baby would be terrified of its parents. So, while it creeped Cat out, she couldn't really hold it against Raphael for helping them.

"Holly is my friend." Cat spoke the words without emphasis, but placed herself firmly between Holly and the others.

"Cat—" Holly began. She might as well not have spoken. All eyes were locked on the growing tension between Cat and Corrine.

Cat watched as Holly turned this way and that. She probably sensed the potential disaster in the conflict but had no idea how to head it off. Holly tried to signal for Peter to come help as he walked by, but he ignored the confrontation and walked inside the restaurant.

"You think you're special?" Corrine's voice was nearly a hiss. Her wide brown eyes had narrowed to dangerous slits. It was obvious she bore a grudge against Cat. Perhaps it was the thing with Tatya this afternoon, but Cat didn't think so. It seemed much too intense, too personal for that.

Cat felt the surge of Corrine's magic; felt her own power responding strongly enough that she had to fight to keep herself in human form. That was alarming. She knew that Corrine could change her form at will, just like she could. But the first law was to *never* risk changing where an outsider could see. They were standing in the middle of a public parking lot with a busy access road within clear view!

Cat kept her cat from emerging by sheer force of will. It was not easy. Pride forbade her from letting the others see her struggle. Her face retained its calm, almost bored expression. When she spoke her voice was smooth and cutting as a razor.

"You really must not have much confidence in your abilities." She observed with saccharine sweetness. "Otherwise why would you pick on full humans? And then only when you have them outnumbered."

"You bitch," Corrine snarled. Her eyes had darkened to black, the whites diminishing. Her skin tightened against the bones of her face.

"No, dear," Cat corrected. "I'm not a canine."

"It's *lupine,* stupid." One of the women in the background spoke. She was a blonde Michael had described to Cat as having little power and even less brains.

"Really?" Cat smiled her eyes never leaving Corrine. "I couldn't tell."

Corrine arched her back, a low growl coming from lips that pulled back to reveal lengthening fangs.

The blonde, however, was not finished. She threw another verbal barb at Cat. "You think just because you're dating the pack leader's son you can do what you want? He's not even ranked."

"I'm not dating Mike." Cat didn't have to pretend indifference.

"And even if I was, I prefer to base my reputation on my own abilities—not those of a man who has been *ordered* to sleep with me."

It was more than Corrine could stand. She snarled, her power surging as she deliberately began to change. Cat was horrified. The woman was an *idiot*. Changing in public could be a death sentence. Cat reached out, grabbing the other woman's arm. She poured her own magical power into the smaller woman in an attempt to avert the disaster she herself had provoked.

Corrine's arm was a flashing blur as she slammed her fist into the side of Cat's head. It was a stunning blow, but Cat held on. Sweat poured from her body from the heat of their clashing magic and the sheer physical strain of holding onto the struggling woman.

People began pouring out of the restaurant. At the same time, Cat heard the squeal of tires and slam of a car door. She didn't look. She didn't dare take her attention from Corrine. At the moment she had the smaller woman in a headlock, but Corrine was bucking, kicking, and had raked her nails across Cat's bare arm deep enough that blood poured from the scratches.

"What in the *hell* is going on here?" The voice was not loud, but cold, cutting and heavy with power. Corrine went limp in Cat's arms so suddenly it was a struggle not to drop her dead weight.

Cat turned to face the source of those words and found herself staring in open-mouthed awe.

Raphael stood only a few steps away, in what should have been the shadow of the building. There was no shadow. He stood bathed in a bright blue light; bright enough that she could see every detail of his appearance, from the blood red of his shirt to the shining metal tips on the toes of his black leather boots. It took a moment for Cat to realize there was no outside light source. Raphael was generating it himself. It was impressive as hell, and more than a little frightening.

"Raphael." Corrine's voice was a harsh whisper as she started to raise her eyes to his. She froze in midmotion. His granite features said more clearly than words that at this moment he was not Raphael. Tonight he was the Alpha.

Cat released her hold on Corrine, taking a half-step back

until the back of her legs brushed against Holly's car. She had not dropped into submissive posture like the wolves. Instead, she very deliberately kept her body language neutral. She wanted to be sure to give no *hint* of what had happened between the two of them.

Not that it mattered. Not now. Despite the shields Raphael had locked around his mind Cat could sense his thoughts and feelings. There was no warmth—only barely controlled fury that made his power burn like heat against her skin. Still, she refused to cower. She forced her spine straight; made herself meet eyes that had gone penetrating gold from the power of his magic. Whatever punishment she was in for, she'd take it with dignity.

"So," Raphael's words fell into the well of silence that spread out from the group. "Who wants to tell me what crisis is upon us that is so dangerous, so desperate, that I find a Sazi of status within the pack would forget herself and start changing in full view of a major thoroughfare?" His voice was a lash poisoned with sarcasm and Corrine flinched as though from blows.

"Holly?"

"Alpha . . . I . . ." Holly's voice was a whisper, her eyes focused on the ground at her feet.

Cat looked at Holly and sighed. "It's my fault," she said.

"Excuse me?" Raphael's gaze locked with Cat's. It took every ounce of will she possessed not to cringe before him.

"They were picking on Holly *again*," Cat explained in a tired voice. "I stepped in."

"I see." Raphael waited for her to continue.

Cat spoke, ignoring the pleading look Holly shot her. "I said some things I shouldn't have. I provoked her."

"Provoked?" Raphael examined Corrine as though she were a bug under a microscope.

"Provoked," Cat repeated.

"And you expected?"

"I figured we'd fight, but I thought it would be as humans. When I realized—"

"She held her." Holly interrupted. She cast a defiant look at Corrine and the others, but didn't dare face Raphael directly.

"You *held* Corrine?" Raphael looked at Cat now. His expression was incredulous.

She shook her head. "I don't know what that means. I just couldn't let her change. So I didn't." Her voice faltered. Raphael's expression was too complex to read.

The silence in the parking lot deepened. Cat could hear the rustling of the leaves of nearby trees, the distant traffic. Most of all, she could hear Corrine's ragged breathing. Everyone was staring at Cat now. It made her skin crawl. She wanted to shout, *"What?"* but didn't dare. Apparently keeping Corrine from changing was significant. Why, she had no clue.

Raphael's gaze shifted back to Corrine. For just an instant Cat thought she saw a flicker of pity. It was gone before she could be sure. When he turned to Cat his expression was carefully neutral. When he spoke his voice was utterly calm. "You are not a pack member."

Cat didn't respond. It was simply the truth.

"You prevented a pack member from endangering herself, the pack, and our entire community," he continued.

She shrugged. "Yeah, well, after I provoked her in the first place, anyway."

Raphael acknowledged that with a slight nod. "There *is* no provocation significant enough to excuse breaking the first rule. Corrine," she stirred, but didn't raise her head. "Tell us the first law."

A shudder wracked her body. Her voice was choked with tears. "Even should it cost you your life, you will never change where it might be seen by outsiders."

"Very good. I'm *so* glad you've recovered your memory."

Cat flinched. She detested Corrine, but she hated to see anyone humiliated. Corrine had been stripped of her pride, and her shoulders shook with silent sobs. Raphael turned his back on her in obvious dismissal. Cat was now the focus of his attention.

"The pack owes you a debt of gratitude."

There were audible gasps throughout the parking lot.

"That's not necessary . . ." Cat began.

"Yes. It is." Raphael stated it as a simple fact. "What can we do to repay you?"

Cat fought to keep her jaw from dropping open. She'd expected to be judged and punished; to be humiliated like Corrine. But here he was offering her a reward. From the reaction of the collected werewolves Cat knew this interaction was incredibly important. Unfortunately, she had no idea what to do. She looked from face to face, seeking guidance. There was none to be had. Finally, her eyes lit on Holly. A possible solution occurred to her. "Fine. If you want to reward me, make them stop harassing Holly. She can't help what she is. It's not fair and it's not right."

Raphael stared at Cat for a long moment before he spoke. "Peter?"

The boy stepped out from the crowd. "Yes, sir?"

Raphael knew his next words were unnecessary. Hell, half of the pack was already here watching. Still, right now the formality was important. "Make sure everyone in the pack knows that henceforth to attack Holly is to attack *me*."

"Yes, Alpha." Peter answered.

"Holly," Raphael spoke gently but his voice was stern. "I want your word that you won't take advantage. I know it's tempting to get even."

Holly stood openmouthed, and it took her several tries before she could get the words out. "I won't, Alpha. I promise."

"Good." Raphael's eyes were there normal brown again. The light surrounding him had dimmed to nearly normal. "Corrine, if you had succeeded in changing what would the price have been?"

Corrine's response was a barely audible whisper. "I would've been brought before Wolven on charges."

"And?" Raphael pressed.

"I would've . . ." Her voice cracked. She couldn't, or wouldn't, continue.

"You would've been put down."

"Yes, Alpha."

"It appears you owe Ms. Turner your life. Don't you think you should thank her?" Raphael's voice was satin over steel.

Corrine raised her eyes to Cat's. There was no gratitude there. Instead, Cat saw a deep and abiding hatred. Still, Corrine forced the hated words past her gritted teeth. "Thank you."

"Good." Raphael turned to the group, his gaze moving to each of Corrine's supporters in turn. "Rachel, Melissa, Robyn—you are to report to the alpha female's office tomorrow at 8:00 A.M. sharp. Corrine, come with me."

Chapter Seventeen

CAT WOKE TO the sound of insistent pounding on the front door. It was another wet, gray morning. A combination of rain and snow spattered against the windows in delicate counterpoint to the heavy beat of a fist on solid oak. Groaning, Cat rolled over to check the time. The red numbers of the alarm clock read six fifteen. Cat growled under her breath as she rolled out of bed. She grabbed her robe from the back of the chair and pulled it on. Her reflection in the vanity mirror looked like hell, but whoever was downstairs would just have to take her as is.

Cat pulled aside the drapes and lifted the window sash, sending snow scattering. A few of the flakes landed on the sleeve of her robe, leaving small dark spots as they melted.

"Who is it?" she called. "And what do you want?"

A figure appeared beneath the window. Michael Santiago. His nose was fully healed and perfectly straight. Cat was glad. She'd been feeling very guilty about decking him.

Mike glared up at her. From the look and scent of him he was in a fine fury. "Get dressed and get your ass down here!" he ordered. "I'm taking you to apologize to my mother. Maybe she'll be able to help you fix things with the rest of the pack."

"Screw you!" Cat wasn't particularly alert first thing out of bed. Still, she was damned if she was going to be ordered around like a storm trooper, certainly not by Michael. More to the point she hadn't done anything wrong *and* she was due over at the hospital at eight to bid Ned and Violet good-bye.

"My mother is the alpha female for this territory. Everyone

listens to her. If you ever want them to accept you, you *have* to submit." Michael was no longer shouting, but the condescending hiss he was using was no improvement.

"No," Cat answered. "I won't."

"Cat!" Michael took a deep breath. He appeared to be counting to ten.

Bully for him, Cat thought. She wasn't in a particularly good mood herself. She hadn't slept well at all, her mind whirling with too many thoughts, none of them good.

"Cat." Michael's tone was condescending. "If you don't make peace with the pack they're never going to accept us."

"Michael, I told you before," Cat fought to control her temper. "There *is* no *us.*"

"Oh, that's right." Michael's face took on an ugly flush. "You're not *ready.* It's *too soon.*" He snarled up at her. "That's not the real reason though, is it?"

Cat's voice was cold and pitiless as a Siberian winter. "I don't know what you're talking about."

"Oh, really? Do you think I'm an idiot? That I didn't *notice* you coming home the other morning with *him*?"

Oh, hell. Didn't *that* just figure. Well, there was nothing she could do about it. She just *hoped* this wasn't going to cause problems for Raphael. Of course it probably would. But either way, it was none of Mike's business and she *wasn't* going to discuss it with him.

"Good-bye, Michael." She slammed the window shut and yanked the curtains closed, hands shaking with fury.

A moment later she heard a heavy bang and the tinkle of breaking glass. A car engine roared to life. By the time she'd raced downstairs and to the front door Michael had driven off. But he'd left a "calling card." The driver's side door of her rental car had been kicked in, its window shattered.

"That asshole!"

Swearing heartily, she went into the house and pulled on a coat and shoes, then went out to the garage. A half hour later she was cold, wet, and utterly furious, but had managed to improvise a covering for the window using clear plastic garbage bags and duct tape.

Shivering, she went inside, shedding her sodden clothes on

the tile floor of the entryway. She was so *cold*. What she wanted more than anything in the world right now was a mug of hot cocoa and a long, hot bath. As it was she barely had time for a quick shower. There was snow on the roads. She'd never driven in snow before. Hell, she was a California woman whose mother hated the cold. She'd never even *seen* snow until this trip.

She set the water of the shower as hot as she dared and climbed inside, letting the water wash over her until the shaking subsided. She scrubbed quickly, shampooed her hair, and was out and drying off in a few minutes.

The phone was ringing as she climbed out of the shower. Rather than run through the house naked, she let the machine get it while she dried herself off and padded naked over to the dresser that held her clothes.

Jake Sanchez's voice came across the line. He sounded gruff, as always. "Cat, considering everything that has happened the past couple of days, I think it's best that you not work at the Joint anymore. I'll have Holly cut your final check and mail it to you."

Cat heard the click as he set down the phone.

She wasn't sure whether to be grateful or angry. The only good thing about the job had been working with Holly. But Raphael was probably going to be pissed. She sighed as she pulled on her lacy undergarments and wished that just for a little while things would go the way she wanted them to. But, no, that wasn't going to happen. The pack was trying to drive her out of the territory. If anything, the tensions were likely to get worse.

Cat grabbed the warmest clothing she could find in her drawer, choosing a heavy cable-knit sweater in a vivid shade of red that put color in her cheeks and looked good with her particular shade of blonde. Black jeans were under it, and wooly socks that were covered by boots with thick fleece lining.

She brushed her teeth, blow-dried her hair, and did her makeup with brisk efficiency that left time for the drive.

Fat, heavy flakes of snow were falling in clumps from a sky that was almost a uniform shade of pewter. Thus far, they were melting when they hit the pavement, but the grass was already almost completely covered with a thick white blanket. The temperature was dropping rapidly. The cat in her sensed that the worst of the storm wouldn't hit for a couple of hours yet, giving Ned and Violet time to get well on their way.

Shivering, she climbed behind the wheel of her rental car and turned on the engine. She *wished* she had a coat and gloves, and promised herself a shopping trip to buy some later today. She was sick to death of being constantly cold!

It wasn't a long drive to pack headquarters, but it *was* nerve-wracking. People were skidding all over the place and Cat's knuckles were white where they gripped the steering wheel. She was deeply grateful to pull the car into an empty space in the pack lot and get *out* without mishap.

A short way across the parking lot Ned's Silverado was parked next to a familiar Jeep Cherokee. She heard muted voices talking. Ned was discussing the best route to take. She stopped, abruptly at the sound of Raphael's reply. *He's here.* Her stomach tightened with excitement.

The two men stepped around the front of the truck. Raphael looked up, his eyes meeting hers, and smiled at her in a way that made her heart skip at least one beat.

He looked incredible this morning. The wind was teasing his hair, and snowflakes dusted the shoulders of his black leather biker jacket. Snug black jeans fit him like a second skin, tucked into the tops of black leather work boots. He wasn't wearing gloves. In fact, he looked as though he wasn't cold at all. Cat, on the other hand, felt like she'd turn into a Popsicle every time the wind hit her.

Morning, gorgeous.

Hi, Cat suddenly felt both happy and unaccountably shy. She hadn't been sure . . . After last night, she'd been . . .

Whether Raphael scented her emotions on the breeze, or was just amazingly perceptive, she wasn't sure. But somehow, he knew. He said something to Ned that Cat couldn't hear, then walked over to join her.

"Red's a good color for you," Raphael observed. "But you should probably be wearing a coat. You look like you're freezing."

"I am." She admitted. Her teeth weren't *quite* chattering, but they would be as soon as the next breeze hit.

"Here." Raphael slid out of his coat and held it open for her to put on.

"But you—"

"I'm a wolf. I don't *get* cold. At least not until it's well below zero." His amusement was obvious. "The coat is for show."

She slid into the jacket gratefully. It was still warm from his body, and smelled of high-quality leather and the warm, musky scent of Raphael's skin. "Thanks."

"No problem." Sliding his arm around her waist, he led her across the lot to join the others. If he saw Betty's expression of shock, he chose to ignore it. "Violet's as cold-blooded as you are. She's already inside the truck with the heater cranked up full blast." When they were just outside the passenger door, Violet rolled down the window. "I'll give you two a little privacy," Raphael offered. "Besides, I have a couple of questions for Ned." He gave Cat a quick squeeze and was gone.

"Are you excited?" Cat asked her aunt.

"More nervous than anything else," Violet answered. "I *hate* driving in the snow, and it's no better being a passenger."

"I think you're going to miss the worst of it."

"I hope so!" Violet turned in her seat so she was facing Cat directly. Visibly gathering her courage, she looked her niece directly in the eye. "I'm glad to see you're getting along with him. Ned tells me that Raphael is a good man."

"Violet—"

"Let me finish, dear," Violet scolded. "I know he's quite a bit older, but it doesn't matter. You need somebody you can count on, who can understand what you're going through." She gave a deep sigh. "I want you to be happy. I know it's hard to imagine that happening right now. Your parents' deaths are too fresh, and this . . ." Violet floundered, at a loss for words.

"Situation?"

"Yes, this *situation* is going to be all-consuming for a while. But you shouldn't go through it alone. Not if there's somebody willing to help you. Promise me you won't shut everybody out and try to do this by yourself."

"Aunt Violet—"

"I mean it, Catherine. Promise me. I know you've always

been a bit of a loner even in a crowd. But this is too much for one person."

"I promise."

"Oh, and before I forget, the movers will be arriving to clear Ned's stuff out to storage on Thursday at one o'clock. Would you mind going up there and letting them in?"

"No problem."

She pulled a set of keys from her pocket and handed them to Cat through the open window. "Oh, good! Now give me a hug good-bye. We'll be back for Christmas to see what you've done with Ned's place. And don't you *dare* start crying! If you do, then I'll start. I always look like a prune when I cry."

Cat managed, barely, to hold her tears in check until after the tail lights of their truck had disappeared from view. It helped that Raphael was right there beside her, his arm around her. When they were well and truly gone he took her in his arms, holding her as she wept into his shoulder, only half listening to his gentle assurances that everything was going to be all right.

A half-hour later, Cat was sitting across from Raphael at the table of the old-fashioned diner he'd taken her to for breakfast. The entire place was lit with neon, the walls peppered with nostalgic knickknacks, vintage gold records vying for attention with autographed pictures of Elvis, Frank, and Marilyn. A full-size vintage Harley sat on a platform suspended from the ceiling. A real jukebox and working pinball machines sat like jewels in the center of the room. The waiters and waitresses wore the old-fashioned diner-style uniforms, ornamented with dozens of buttons with humorous slogans or pictures on them.

Raphael had driven them to the outskirts of Denver because, as he put it, "Most of the *family* doesn't travel outside of Boulder. We stand a good chance of actually being able to *talk* here."

They each ordered hot coffee and the breakfast special. Once the beverages were poured, the waitress made a beeline to the kitchen, leaving the two of them alone in their corner of the half-empty restaurant.

"Oh, I almost forgot." Raphael reached into the back pocket of his jeans and pulled out a small leather folder, not much bigger than a wallet. He set it on the table and pushed it across to her. "This is for you. One of the Wolven physicians came up with it at Charles's request."

"What is it?"

"Open it up and look."

Cat opened the folder. Inside were laminated cards that resembled those of a meal plan sponsored by one of the more famous fitness gurus. But almost all of the cards were for proteins and they specifically addressed game animals that she might catch on a hunt.

"There's a letter with directions on how to use them." Raphael stopped talking as the waitress once again approached to refill their coffee cups.

Out of the corner of her eye Cat saw movement in the snow outside the fogged window. It looked a little like a dog, but when she turned her head, whatever it was had gone.

"Is something wrong?"

"Nah. I'm just a little jumpy." Cat met his eyes across the table. "I heard from Mike this morning. He was there the other morning when you brought me home. Between that and Jack popping in and out of my head—"

Raphael set his cup onto the saucer so hard it broke. Scalding brown liquid spilled over the broken shards and onto the table. Cat grabbed a bunch of napkins from the dispenser as the waitress rushed over with a wet rag to help clean up the mess.

"Jack is still getting into your head?"

Cat nodded.

"Are you doing your exercises like I told you?"

"Yes, Holly's been practicing with me."

"Holly?" Raphael looked startled.

"What?"

"I'm just surprised, is all." Raphael's voice was soft enough that none of the other diners would be able to hear it over the music and noise of the restaurant. "After all, Holly's full human. She doesn't have any magic of her own."

Cat blinked a time or two, taking that in. It honestly had never occurred to her that Holly wouldn't be able to do it. "Well, apparently she can. It works."

"Have you spoken with anyone else like Holly?"

"Ned. I did it with Ned."

"All right." Raphael pursed his lips. He drummed his fingers against the tabletop. "I want you to try something." He grinned impishly. "Have you ever met Brad Pitt?"

"No."

"Good. Tell me what he's doing right now."

"Raphael!"

"I'm serious. Try." Raphael fingers tapped faster. He watched her carefully, seeing her eyes glaze over slightly as she sent her mind outward.

Cat concentrated. Nothing. Not a blessed clue. "Nothing."

"All right. What's the maid from your house in California doing?" Raphael asked earnestly. He lifted up his coffee cup.

Cat thought about it for a moment. She let out a distressed little sound. "Oh. She's crying. She got mad at one of the worst gossips in town and said something she shouldn't have. She thinks if I find out I'll fire her."

"Will you?"

"No." Cat answered. "She didn't mean to, and she really needs the job. It's one of the reasons I kept her on full time, even though I'm not there. I mean, I don't *think* I'm going back, but . . ." Cat let the sentence drag on unfinished. She couldn't tell Raphael her plans because, frankly, she didn't have any. All her focus was on taking down Jack. Truthfully, she didn't expect to survive. Hell, she wasn't entirely sure she wanted to.

She felt Raphael watching her.

"What?"

He shook his head, but she could tell there was something he wasn't saying. "Nothing. It's just important to know the limits of your gift, Catherine. Apparently you can reach out to anyone you know, whether or not he has any talent of his own—but you can't 'find' someone you haven't met."

"Oh."

"It's a very useful skill. But I'd keep quiet about it if I were you."

"It may be too late for that," Cat said with a sigh. "Mike knows, and what Mike knows, *everybody* knows. Then again, it might not have occurred to him that it was important enough to brag about."

Raphael didn't answer because the waitress appeared with a laden tray, including a new cup and saucer for Raphael. She served the food, asked if there was anything else they needed, and disappeared. When she was out of earshot again, Raphael spoke.

"So, what did *he* have to say?"

Cat knew from his tone of voice that Raphael wasn't talking about Michael anymore.

"He told me he wanted me to get well trained. That it would make me more of a challenge. But that I should study quick because he wasn't a patient man."

Raphael's expression was sour. He stirred his hash browns idly with his fork, as though his appetite had suddenly left him.

She blushed lightly and raised her coffee to take a sip. "And he told me to find another teacher, that he doesn't like you or trust you, but . . . that you were doing a good job. Apparently I'm clumsy, but talented."

Raphael began swearing under his breath. He was remarkably good at it. Cat actually hadn't heard some of those combinations before. Considering her mother's grasp of the language, that was somewhat of a surprise.

"Was there anything *else*?"

"He's very smug about that file of his."

"He should be. It's the only thing that's kept him alive for the past couple of decades."

"So I've heard." Cat took a bite of her toast, and then continued after chewing and swallowing. "I'd give quite a bit to get a good close look at that file."

"Why?"

"Just an idea I've got." She replied vaguely. She didn't look him in the eye. Somehow, when she met his gaze he always seemed to be able to overcome any misgivings she had.

"Catherine . . ."

It was the second time in a matter of minutes that he'd used her full name. She'd noticed he only did that when he was seriously annoyed. "Oh, don't take that tone. I promised I wouldn't do anything to endanger your people and I won't. But if I do this right—"

"Do *what* right?" She could tell he was worried, and more than a little insulted that she didn't trust him.

"Look, I don't have the details figured out yet. I promise, you'll be the first to know when I do. But I definitely think it's time for me to give Uncle Chuck a call."

Raphael looked at her through narrowed eyes. She could tell he wasn't happy about this development, but that he also wasn't willing to push the issue. She could almost see him make the decision to change the subject. "I don't think I'll ever get used to you calling the Chief Justice 'Uncle Chuck.' "

"That's all right. I *know* I'm never going to get used to everybody referring to him as 'Mr. Chief Justice, *sir*.' "

Raphael gave a forced laugh and at least pretended to let her joke lighten his mood. Neither of them were likely to forget that Jack had, once again, made his presence known, but they could, and did, pretend that nothing was wrong for at least as long as it took them to finish breakfast. Raphael had a long day ahead of him, and it got even longer when his cell phone rang as he was standing in line at the cash register.

"Ramirez."

Cat heard both sides of the conversation clearly, but pretended not to listen. "Raphael, it's Eddie. We've got a problem."

"What's up, Ed?"

"Mona's in the hospital. Juan's there with her. So I'm stuck in here, we're down two drivers and *it's snowing!*"

"Shit. Is she going to be all right?"

"They think so, but she may have to be on bed rest for the rest of the pregnancy."

Raphael turned to Cat. "Look, I've got an emergency at the towing company. I need to get there right away. Can you drop me off and take the Jeep back to the hospital?"

"No problem."

"Eddie, I'll be there—" he looked at the snow falling steadily outside the window and grimaced, "—in about thirty minutes."

"Right, boss."

Raphael avoided I-70. Instead, he took I-76, turning off on a secondary road to avoid traffic that had slowed almost to a standstill.

"What's the problem, anyway?"

"My weekend secretary's in the hospital and her husband's one of my best drivers. So I've got *another* one of my men stuck behind the desk answering phones and operating dispatch. With the weather like this, I can't afford to be down two drivers. Especially not after such a long dry spell."

He downshifted, taking a sharp turn with a crunch of gravel. The windshield wipers beat a steady rhythm as they cleared the heavy snowflakes from the glass as fast as they could fall. "I'm just glad it's only Sunday. I don't know what I'd do if this happened during a weekday rush hour."

"How hard is it to do the dispatch?"

"Not that hard, really. All my drivers know the area. It's not like they're going to get lost. And we can work out who's in the best position to take a call over the line. Why?"

"Well, if you show me how, maybe I can take the calls and do the radio while you and Eddie drive the trucks."

"You'd do that?" Cat could tell Raphael was floored. She really couldn't blame him. After the fuss she'd put up about working at Jake's he probably would never have expected her to volunteer. That she was willing to pitch in, and didn't consider answering phones for a towing company beneath her, seemed to be a surprise.

"Yes." She grinned. "But don't get mad if I screw it up."

"You won't screw it up," he promised. "And tell you what, as a thank-you, I'll buy you dinner."

"You just bought me breakfast."

"Yeah, well as busy as we're going to be today, you'll have earned another meal." He kept both hands on the wheel as he turned onto the access road that led to his offices. "My cell phone is in my back pocket. You'd better call Jake and let him know you won't be in to work today."

"Not an issue," Cat answered, trying to keep the hurt from her voice. But the flat tone said just about the same thing. "He fired me."

Raphael stared at her for a long enough moment that she was worried about his driving. When he finally spoke, it was softly. "I'm sorry."

"It's not your fault."

"Actually," he admitted, "it is." Cat watched as he fought to find the right words. "I'd hoped that your being around the pack would help them get used to you. It's how they handle the species thing in Wolven. You expose people to the species they don't get along with and eventually they usually can see past the prejudice and start judging the person as an individual."

"It's not working," Cat observed drily.

"No. But I wanted it to. I wanted them all to see you for the terrific woman you are."

Cat watched him for a long moment. He looked so serious, and sad, but the compliment had fluttered her heart unexpectedly. "I'm sorry."

"Don't be. It's not your fault."

"Well," she said ruefully, letting out a small laugh. "I really haven't been trying that hard to fit in."

He laughed, and the Jeep filled with the smell of citrus. "No kidding."

"I could leave." The minute she made the offer Cat realized that she didn't want to go. Yes, Mike and the pack were a pain. But there was Holly and Raphael.

"I don't want you to go."

Cat let out the breath she hadn't known she was holding. "Oh. Good."

She expected him to laugh. Instead, she watched as he pulled himself together, visibly steeling his body. "There's something I've been meaning to tell you." The burnt metal scent of determination filled the Jeep, mixed with an odd combination of sorrow and guilt. The scents were so overwhelming that Cat had to sneeze several times to clear her head.

"I told you that Jack chose you because you look just like Fiona Monier did in her twenties, and Jack lost her to another man."

"Yes."

"*I* was the other man." He sat there, stiff, jaw set, as though expecting a blow.

"Yeah. I sort of figured that out." Cat's tone was dry.

Raphael's head jerked back in surprise, but the stiffness left his body. "You did?"

Cat rolled her eyes. "It was fairly obvious from the things he's said and the way you've been acting."

"Oh."

She managed not to laugh, but it wasn't easy. "What I *haven't* figured out is why he didn't kill *you*."

Raphael stared down at his hands. "The Chief Justice and the Council wouldn't let him. The seers said I needed to live."

"I'm surprised that stopped him. He's not exactly the reasonable type."

Raphael shook his head. "They made him an offer he couldn't refuse. They couldn't threaten his life directly—he has the file, after all. So they threatened Fiona. If I die, she dies. *And* they ordered me here under Lucas's protection. Other than Charles, Lucas is the one man that Jack won't cross." Raphael couldn't keep the bitterness from his voice. He would never have risked Fiona's life for his. Charles and the council, however, were far more pragmatic. The seers had foreseen Raphael being needed in the future. Fiona, apparently, was expendable.

"Ouch. Bet that pissed him off."

"No doubt. And not just him. I understand that Fiona's brother wound up in a duel over it."

They sat in silence for a long time, each lost in their own thoughts. It was Raphael who spoke first, asking a question that he wasn't positive he wanted answered. "Are you okay with this?"

Cat considered it for a long moment. "It happened a long time ago."

He just nodded.

"You couldn't possibly have known how he'd react. I mean nobody *expects* somebody to flip out and become a serial killer. It's just not *done*."

Raphael let out a harsh bark of laughter at her choice of words. He knew she hadn't meant to, but she made it sound like Jack's insanity was the ultimate in bad manners.

"Seriously," Cat asked, "did you know that it was Fiona?"

"No. But I should've guessed. There aren't that many cougars."

"But you didn't guess, and you didn't know. Even if you did, while it would've been a stupid thing to do, you couldn't possibly have surmised that Jack would go off the deep end. You yourself said she'd played around on him before. Why would you expect things to be any different this time?"

He didn't answer. She watched him think about her words, really consider them. Cat was glad. From what she could see he'd let his guilt fester, and had blamed himself for everything Jack did. She guessed it had been killing him, a little bit at a time.

"I don't know." Raphael said the words with obvious reluctance. He wouldn't look at Cat, choosing instead to focus all of his considerable attention into pulling the Jeep absolutely straight into his labeled spot in the nearly empty parking lot.

"There you go then." She gave him an impish look. She wanted to lighten his mood. She *hoped* what she was about to say would do it. She *thought* he had enough of a sense of humor. "I've got to ask—"

"What?" He shut off the engine, glaring across at her.

"Did they *really* call you 'Studly Screwright?' "

Chapter Eighteen

RAPHAEL'S TOWING OFFICE was a small tan brick building with tinted glass doors and windows on the front. The elaborate hand-painted sign above the door was of professional quality, but the style was familiar. It reminded her forcibly of the wolf on the press box in the high school gym.

Inside were four desks with worn office chairs. Each had its own computer. All were buried under mounds of file folders and loose papers. A bank of black metal file cabinets lined one wall, under a gray metal cabinet that was currently wide open, displaying hooks with various sets of keys. Against the back wall there was a table with an elaborate radio system and large, silver microphone. Above it, a huge, detailed map of the Denver-Boulder street system.

Raphael introduced her to "Fast Eddie" Malone, his assistant manager. Ed was a huge man, standing a good six foot eight, most of it solid, tattooed muscle. There was even an ornate Oriental dragon that wound its way up through the collar of his long-sleeved Harley-Davidson sweatshirt, its head adorning his perfectly smooth scalp.

Raphael answered calls while, in a surprisingly gentle voice, Fast Eddie lived up to his name, giving Cat a lightning-quick summary of how the phones and the radio worked. Fortunately, it actually *was* a simple system. Hit the switch to turn on the mike, press down on the button to transmit, let up to receive. It would broadcast to every one of the nine trucks Raphael had in his fleet.

"Mona uses color-coded push pins to keep track of everybody, but you don't have time for that tonight. We'll just keep in touch by radio." Eddie smiled. "And by the way, thanks. I *hate* doing dispatch." He gave Cat a quick peck on the cheek, and was rewarded with her laugh and a low growl from Raphael.

Grinning, he backed away, hands held up in surrender. "Right, boss, I get it. Look but don't touch!"

"Damn straight!" Raphael was grinning, but his tone of voice left no room for doubt that the warning, at least, was serious.

"I think I'd better get out of here!" Eddie gave Cat a broad wink. "Want me to take the flatbed?"

"Nah," Raphael answered. "Take number seven."

"Aw man, the heater's out in seven."

"I *know*." Raphael walked over to the key cabinet and took down two sets of keys. He tossed the first set to Eddie, pocketing the second. He took the jacket Cat held out to him, but dropped it on the desk. Then, much to her surprise, he pulled her into his arms and kissed her completely breathless. She was still standing there, blinking somewhat stupidly, when the two men disappeared through the door.

The day went by in a blur of work. Cat found she *liked* the men Raphael worked with, their easy banter. More to the point, they liked *him*. She could tell from the way they talked to and about him on the radio. But despite the joking, there was no question who was boss. It was obvious his workers respected him.

Business was steady, with a fair mix of local and highway calls. Cat had to wonder how busy they'd be if weather like this hit on a weekday, with rush-hour traffic. Late afternoon, when the temperature dropped, the roads became slick with black ice and most people gave up on driving altogether. At that point the calls slowed to a near halt, giving Cat a breather.

She used the downtime to her advantage, exploring the office to find the supply cabinet and, more important, the restroom. She also stumbled across a box with a couple of half-stale donuts that she washed down with coffee strong enough to stand up without the cup.

She almost choked on the coffee when *she* became the topic of radio conversation.

"So, Eddie, you got to see the new girl. Is she as hot as she sounds?"

"Hotter. Definitely hotter: a natural blonde with legs up to her armpits. But you don't even wanna *think* about it, Joey. Hell, all I did was wink at her, and I thought I was gonna get the boys handed to me."

"Aw, man!"

"Now I'm freezing my ass off in number seven. Take an honest warning from an old man who should know better. You do *not* want to go there."

"Damn straight you don't." Raphael's voice was teasing and light, but it stilled the chatter.

Cat barely got the coffee she'd spilled cleaned up when the next call came in, and they were off and running again.

It was after six when the calls finally dwindled to a stop and Raphael announced over the radio that they should all head "back to the barn." He thanked everybody for the hard work. "Cat, you did a great job. Thanks again for pitching in. Oh, and if you want to be nice, you could put some coffee on to help thaw Eddie out. Don't want to send him home to his wife with frostbite. She'll kick my ass."

"Not if you tell her *why* he was in number seven," someone else joked.

"Shut up. Everybody just shut up," Eddie responded.

Laughing, Cat emptied the stale coffee and began brewing a fresh pot. By the time it was done, she heard the stamp of booted feet and male voices outside the office door. "*Damn* would you look at the size of that paw print. That must be one helluva dog."

The two man passed into the building still arguing good-naturedly as they shook the snow from their clothing. "I'm surprised anything's out in this weather. I sure don't intend to be. Soon as I get my ass home I'm *stayin'* there!"

"Oh, no you're not, Joe. It's your night to take calls," Eddie answered.

"*Shee-it.*"

Eddie pointed a meaty finger at a cell phone sitting on the main desk. "Take the cell. I'll set the phones to forward to it."

The smaller man grumbled, but did as he was told. Meanwhile several of the others had arrived and started pouring coffee and introducing themselves to Cat. A few were exchanging war stories about the big pileup they'd worked last spring, comparing it to other wrecks over the years. At some point during the confusion Raphael arrived. She didn't have to look; she caught his scent on the breeze that blew in as he opened the door, but she was glad she did.

He looked good. The wind tugged at the dark brown curls that had worked their way loose from the ponytail he'd tried to confine them in, framing a face that looked even better with just the hint of stubble. His eyes were sparkling with mischief when he walked up to her, hands behind his back. He tried hard, but unsuccessfully to keep a straight face.

"What are you up to?" She asked suspiciously, backing slowly away from him.

"What makes you think I'm up to anything?" He was all innocence, and she wasn't buying a bit of it. Conversation in the room faded out as the men watched him stalking her around the edge of the desks, a big handful of snow cupped in his left hand. Cat made a dash for the door, diving through with Raphael hot on her heels. He caught her as she paused to reach into a snowbank, shoving snow down the back of her sweater at the same time she threw a handful of the cold, white flakes directly into his face.

Laughing, he scooped her off of her feet and dumped her unceremoniously into the drift, only to have her kick his legs out from under him to join her.

He rolled over, pinning her body beneath his. In that instant the laughter left his eyes, replaced by something more serious, and far more primal. He kissed her then, heedless of their audience. His mouth claimed hers fiercely. She felt him hard and ready against her thigh and in that moment she knew nothing of the cold, or the snow, only a deep, aching need.

"Get a room!"

Cat didn't know who made the catcall, but it brought both her and Raphael back to their senses. Laughing, he rolled off of her and sprang to his feet. He held his hand out to help her up, but she forced him to wait as she did something she'd seen in movies but had never had the chance to do: make a snow angel.

Chapter Nineteen

RAPHAEL RETRIEVED HIS cell phone from the seat of the Jeep. Three missed calls. He hit the button to check the numbers. Raven's cell phone number was first on the list, then two calls from Raphael's own home phone.

Raphael felt a surge of happiness. Raven was home! While he was incredibly proud of the fact that his boy had risen to the position of second in command at Wolven, he hated that it forced them to see so little of each other. Still, his son was due to be on leave for months yet. There was a better-than-average chance he'd come up to Boulder for Thanksgiving and Christmas.

Raphael grinned. Between the two of them, by the time Star was done with her visit she'd feel like a whole new woman.

He was still smiling when he retrieved his messages. They were short and to the point. Raven was in town for a few days and had brought someone along he wanted his father to meet. He'd brought steaks and would hold dinner until whatever time his father managed to get back to the house.

"Cat, would you mind if we eat at my place instead of going out?" Raphael asked. "I've got unexpected company and there's somebody I want you to meet."

"Sure. Why not?" Cat climbed into the passenger seat and fastened her seat belt. Reaching over she turned all the heat vents to blow directly on her. "Besides, I'm curious to see where you live."

If she was disappointed that they wouldn't be alone, it didn't show. With the vents all blowing her scent away from him he couldn't tell if she'd been hoping for some intimate time together as much as he had. Ever since the other night his imagination had been giving him very specific images of what he'd like to do to and with Cat the next time he had the opportunity. Their little romp in the snow hadn't helped, either.

With the four-wheel-drive engaged, he moved easily over the unplowed side streets. The roads were nearly deserted now. Pretty much everyone was either home or wherever else he wanted to be. Only the salt trucks and snowplows were moving in force. He could hear their heavy diesel engines in the distance.

It was a short drive. Raphael's shop and house were both located on large plots of land on the far outskirts of the city. He'd planned it that way. After all, why make the commute worse than it had to be?

"It's beautiful!" Cat exclaimed softly.

The house perched atop a tall hill, surrounded by a stone wall. The lights of the city spread out below like glitter on black velvet. A heavy blanket of snow lay across the manicured lawn leading up to a ranch-style house with a comfortably wide front porch just meant for sitting and looking out at the view.

Raphael was looking at a view—just not the one she was. Every time he looked at her she was more amazing. It wasn't just her looks, or any one thing. It was everything. He was captivated by her smile, and by the dry wit that *made* her smile; her courage in dealing with the changes in her life, her intelligence, and those long, long legs. Raphael found himself grinning as he watched a playful breeze tug at the ends of her long blonde hair. Light moved against her skin in a soft caress, throwing her perfect features into stark relief.

He watched the tension slowly ease out of her body as she took deep breaths of fresh air, the sights and scents working their own type of healing magic. He loved this place, and a part of him was hugely pleased to see that she admired it.

The porch lights came on and Raven appeared at the door with a woman behind him.

" 'Bout time you got here," Raven groused good-naturedly. "Let me guess. The towing business was busier than usual?"

"Yeah, well not everybody's driving a Hummer." Raphael

nodded toward the rental vehicle that took up a fairly large section of his driveway.

"Seemed like a good choice, considering."

"Cat Turner, this is my son, Raven." Cat stepped forward to shake the hand Raven extended. He watched as in one glance she took in his appearance from head to toe, all six foot six of him, from the steel-toed work boots he wore, past the jeans and Harley-Davidson T-shirt, to the hair that hung to his waist, held back by black rubber bands.

He saw her note the ways in which Raven looked like his father, and the ways he didn't. And he could almost hear her puzzlement over the fact that standing next to each other almost anyone would have guessed Raven to be the older man.

Raphael turned to the elegant woman who stood next to his son. She wasn't pretty, but she was striking, with milk-white skin and sharp features. Her hair was prematurely white. She wore black dress slacks with a button-down blouse of royal purple silk that brought out the color of her eyes and was cut to emphasize her spectacular cleavage. "You must be Emma." He extended his hand, and she shook it. "Raven's mentioned you."

"And you." She smiled. "It's a pleasure." She stepped forward, extending her hand to Cat.

Raphael watched as Cat took a delicate sniff and tried to identify their species the way he had trained her.

So, what are they?

I *think* Emma is a bird of some sort. She's not very tall and has the long arms and overdeveloped chest you said were common among the raptors.

Overdeveloped chest?

I'm quoting *you,* Raphael.

Ahhh.

Now, Raven . . . That's easy. Despite the name, he's a wolf, just like his dad.

Very good! Right on both counts. She is a raptor, a snowy owl.

Cat shivered as a gust of wind hit her.

"You're cold," Emma observed. "Shall we go inside?"

"Please!"

Cat stopped just a few steps inside the doorway. Taking her

time, she took a good look around. A person's dwelling can say a lot about him. Raphael's home was just that, a *home*. The style was reminiscent of Frank Lloyd Wright, with lots of natural wood and stone, combining spacious rooms with remarkable details. It was immaculately clean, beautifully decorated, and undeniably masculine. It was *not* impersonal or sterile. The living room was spacious and airy, with one wall dominated by a bank of west-facing windows. The entire north wall was a natural stone fireplace, its broad mantel adorned with dozens of family photos: Raphael standing next to a tow truck with the company logo on it. School photos of Raven and other brown-eyed, dimpled children at various ages, an aged and faded black-and-white wedding picture of a couple, the man looking remarkably like an older version of her host.

She stepped over to the fire, both to warm herself and to get a better look at the painting that hung above the fireplace. It was huge, an original landscape done in oils depicting a night not so different from this one, but with a pack of wolves gliding through the shadowed winter woods. It had been framed in distressed hardwood that perfectly matched the coffee and end tables.

All of the furnishings were of southwestern style, both beautiful and functional. Exactly what she would've expected of him.

Again her eyes were drawn to the painting. It was signed and dated, but she couldn't quite make out either because of the glare on the protective glass.

"Do you like it?" Raphael appeared at her elbow.

"It's gorgeous." She couldn't keep the admiration from her voice, and didn't try. "You can practically smell the snow."

"Thank you."

It was his tone of voice that let her know. He wasn't just thanking her for complimenting her taste. At that moment she just knew. Raphael had painted not only this canvas, but the sign at the tow company and the wolf mascot on the press box. "You should paint professionally."

"No, I'll leave that to Star."

"Star?"

"Raven's mother, and Charles's granddaughter. She's brilliant, a genius really. Makes my stuff look like paint by numbers."

"I doubt that!" Cat protested, her eyes irresistibly drawn to the painting.

"Trust me," he answered wryly. "If you're a very good girl, later I'll show you a couple of the pieces she did for me back when we were together. I got them appraised recently. They're insured for more than the house."

"Hey, Dad," Raven interrupted them, calling from the kitchen over Emma's laughter. "Do you want to fire up the grill? I brought enough steaks for everybody."

"Sure. No problem." Raphael took Cat's hand in his and led her down a short hall and out a set of French doors onto a flagstone patio.

A clear glass awning had kept most of the patio clear of snow, so the two of them were able to walk hand in hand to the huge stone and iron grill without wading through drifts. The metal doors of the built-in cabinet squealed only slightly when Raphael opened them to retrieve the bag of charcoal. A little lighter fluid, a few matches, and the coals began burning merrily.

Cat waited until he'd finished putting away the coal and lighter fluid. She knew they didn't have long, maybe only a minute or two, before Raphael's guests demanded his attention. While she had the chance, she took advantage of it. Stepping forward she put both hands on his chest and kissed him.

It started out as a gentle press of lips, but that wasn't what either of them truly wanted. It grew and deepened, passion and power both flaring as Cat and Raphael each explored the other's mouth. Raphael's hands cupped her thighs. He lifted her easily, lowering her onto the edge of the stone table, spreading her legs so that he stood between them, her knees bending so that her legs wrapped around his waist. Cat couldn't think, could barely breathe, her entire body felt as though it were on fire with the need to have him inside her as her hands slid beneath his clothing in a quest to find skin.

She moaned when he moved his head to her throat, his mouth seeking the throbbing pulse at the base of her neck, his hand sliding beneath the thick fabric of her sweater to tease her nipples through her thin silk bra.

"You fucking *bastard*! *Let her go*. She belongs to me!"

Raphael pulled away so suddenly Cat nearly fell. He moved to stand protectively between Cat and the intruder.

"Michael?" Cat gasped the name. "What—"

"You can't have her," Michael growled. "She's *mine!*"

He was drunk, smelling of whiskey, beer, and who knew what else. He was enraged beyond measure. But even in his fury his Sazi magic barely raised the hair on Cat's arms. Cat moved to step forward, but Raphael continued to block her way, so that she was forced to speak her mind from behind his broad shoulders. "What in the *hell* do you think you're doing? And who do you think you are anyway? You don't own me!"

"You shut the fuck up, woman! This is between me and him."

"The hell you say!" Cat's temper ignited and her power flared with it. The snow at the edge of the patio sizzled and began to melt.

Cat, go back in the house. Now.

Cat hesitated. She didn't want to fight with Mike, but she didn't want to leave, either. She half turned toward the door and saw Raven and Emma standing in the open doorway. The expressions on their faces were serious.

"I won't let you take her from me! I challenge you!"

Furious, Cat spun back to face Michael. How *dare* he! The stupid, egotistical *idiot!* He honestly believed he *owned* her, that she was *his*? Her power built, pouring off of her in waves. She heard Emma gasp with pain. As if from a distance she heard Raphael's sharp intake of breath as she moved around him to face Mike down.

"Michael," her voice was a soft hiss. He turned, mouth open to berate her, but she continued over the top of whatever he would have said. "You can't have what you can't hold." She quoted one of the few rules she actually remembered from the training manual at him. *"Hold this!"*

In a blast of pure energy she called out her beast, transforming in a flare of power and blinding light before bounding over the grill in a single leap to disappear into the night.

IT WASN'T HARD to find her. Raphael would know her scent anywhere, and she hadn't even tried to hide her tracks. Good for his purposes, but stupid otherwise. Cat had enemies. While Jack was foremost among them, he wasn't the only one. Hell, half the wolves in the pack would attack her just to drive her out of their territory.

It would have been both simpler and faster to travel in wolf form. But as a wolf he wouldn't be able to bring a pack large enough to carry a warm set of clothes for Cat. And she'd need them. Even in animal form she was too thin-blooded for the cold. So he'd brought a backpack with her purse and the coat he'd given her. He also took the time to go to the store and pick her up a change of clothes. It took an extra half-hour, but he knew Cat would appreciate it. Without even really trying, he'd been able to pick up her thoughts. He knew that she'd spent a long, miserable night huddled in the back of a small cave. He could practically feel the ache in her bones from sleeping on unforgiving stone.

He waited until he was only a short distance from where she had spent the night before calling out to her with his thoughts.

Cat, are you awake?

Raphael? Is that you?

In the flesh. I'm about a hundred yards from you. I brought warm clothes with me. I figured you could change back and we'd walk down to the Wolf's Run for breakfast. There are things we need to talk about.

Last night. Cat's embarrassment colored her thoughts. He could actually *feel* her blushing.

"Don't be embarrassed," Raphael reassured her with both voice and mind.

He watched the rocks where he knew the entrance to the cave to be. Sure enough, she emerged, head hanging low, her entire posture announcing her misery.

"*You* didn't do anything wrong."

"Oh, no? I only screeched at Michael like a shrew, exploded half of your patio, and took off in cat form." She gave him a *look* that was no less expressive on feline features. "Perfectly acceptable behavior. *And* in front of your son and his girlfriend."

Raphael crossed the distance between them. He slid the backpack off his shoulders, letting it drop by her feet. Leaning against a boulder he pulled a pack of cigarettes and a lighter from the pocket of his denim jacket. "Under the circumstances, you were the very picture of restraint."

"Seriously?"

"Seriously." Raphael took a long draw of tobacco and exhaled it slowly. "Normally, I would've let you come down on your own. But Michael's actions last night have some serious consequences that you can't possibly be aware of. I wanted to warn you about them before—"

Raphael didn't finish the sentence, and put on a tight shield so she couldn't read his thoughts. He'd been going to say *before Tatya and Lucas try to save Michael by tricking you into agreeing to something you shouldn't.* Not a politic train of thought. Of course that didn't mean they *wouldn't* do it, if they could. The thing was, he couldn't let them. They were his Alphas. Michael was pack. Raphael *should* support them against the interloper. But he couldn't.

Cat Turner brought out every chivalrous and protective instinct he'd ever had—and he knew why. He didn't need the appointment with Betty. It was too late for testing to find out if he was mated—far too late.

She was staring at him, those penetrating green eyes making him even more nervous. "Look, why don't you take the bag in the cave and get changed."

"Sure." She grabbed one of the shoulder straps in her teeth and carried the bag back through the cave opening and out of sight.

Raphael started speaking. Surprisingly, it was easier to talk to her if he didn't have to look at her. Then again, maybe it wasn't so surprising. Every time he looked at her, in either form, he tended to get distracted by her beauty, grace. It was only a short step from there to having his sex drive kick in and shut down higher brain function.

"Has Betty or anyone else told you anything about challenges within the wolf packs?"

"No." Cat's voice was muffled. It sounded like she was pulling on the sweater. "I'm a cat. I don't think Betty figured I'd need to know." Her voice was clearer. Raphael had to fight the picture his imagination provided of her sliding black lace panties over those long, shapely legs.

Get a grip Ramirez. We've got a crisis here. The logic of that did not clear the image from his mind, or keep his jeans from binding.

"Fine." Raphael crushed the stub of his cigarette against the boulder. "There are two kinds of challenges: mating challenges and challenges for position. For the positions of Alpha male and female, a position challenge is to the death."

There was utter silence in the cave. Raphael couldn't even hear her breathing. He hadn't had to explain the implications, but that was no surprise. After a long, silent moment she asked the question he was expecting.

"And mating challenges?"

Raphael struggled to keep his voice utterly neutral. "If you publicly claim that I am your mate, Michael has the ability to challenge me. He and I fight. If I win, I *am* your mate. For *life*. Since we're both fairly powerful, life for us could be several *hundred* years." He paused, letting her digest that bit of information. It took a minute or two. "And we all know how Jack is liable to react to the news."

"He already wants me dead, Raphael."

"There are worse things than dying." And he didn't doubt for a minute that Jack would put her through every one he could think of if he ever even suspected Raphael was attached to her. And he *was*. God help him, more every day.

The scent of Cat's emotions was strong enough to drift out to him from the cave. A complex mixture of too many feelings to sort, although fear was prominent, followed closely by anger.

"Michael isn't strong enough to beat me, so I am *going* to win." Raphael plodded on.

"But that would mean—" She swallowed hard. "I mean, the other night was spectacular, but . . . I barely know you!"

"Exactly." He sighed. "Now, if you claim you're Michael's mate, he'll believe it. In his current frame of mind—"

"That's bound to cause major problems." She finished his sentence for him as she stepped out of the cave into the sunlight.

"In the long term, yes. In the short term, though, he has the *right* to challenge me because I stepped on his turf. When I beat him, I win the right to court you for six months."

"Court me?"

"Date, try to convince you to choose me, win you away from him. For that six months, no Sazi is going to approach or date you. They're honor bound to give me my chance." He gave her a crooked smile, but it wasn't happy. "The upside is that Mike will have to stay completely away from you for six months, by which time, with therapy, he *may* be able to function normally."

"The downside?"

"I was just getting to that," Raphael answered. "We already talked about Jack. If he learns of it, which is likely, I will once again be pursuing another of *his* women."

Cat shuddered. She came over and leaned up against the boulder next to him, their bodies not quite touching.

"But there are other things you need to take into consideration as well. During the six months that we're seeing each other exclusively, we can't have sex."

Her eyebrows raised. "Excuse me?"

He looked at her strongly. "If we have sex it will mean you've accepted me. *I'll* be considered mated, again, for life. No other Sazi woman will have me. Or if she does, she'll be disgraced. Although, honestly, it might not be an issue."

"Why?"

Raphael weighed his words carefully. "I'm relatively certain that I actually *am* mated to you already. If we see each other regularly, and particularly if we have sex again, I will bond to you. If that happens, losing you could literally kill me."

"Oh."

She seemed a little stunned by that. He didn't blame her. "What about me? If you die will I die, too?"

"You're a feline. They tend to react differently to the mating bond. Even if you do mate with me, you could lose me and probably be just fine."

"No." She said it softly. "I wouldn't."

Raphael looked over to where she stood, the breeze tugging at loose strands of hair that gleamed like spun gold in the morning sunlight. "Sweetheart—"

"Look," Cat interrupted him. "Are there any signs, symptoms, that let you know if you're mated?"

"Why?"

"Just answer the question . . . please." She added the last word almost as an afterthought when he started to look annoyed.

Raphael sighed. He thought for a moment, trying to go into teaching mode and treat it as if it were an academic matter rather than one of the most intensely personal issues of his life. "It's very much like being in love, only more so, almost an obsession. You actually *need* to be around the person as much as possible. You can't stop thinking about her. You don't want anybody else, hell you can't even imagine wanting anyone else. Eventually, mated males are incapable of sex with anyone other than their mate."

"Oh."

Raphael didn't look at her. Instead, he stared straight ahead. "If the mating is one-sided, the person on the receiving end can pull power from her partner. The magical link can kick in if the person she's mated to is hurt or in danger, and there's magic . . . *real* magic between them when they touch." He paused, swallowing hard. "And you *need* to touch the person; as much and as often as possible. It's almost an addiction."

"What if they're both mated to each other?"

"That's very rare," Raphael acknowledged. "There have been a few double-mated pairs, but not many. But fully mated pairs can talk mind-to-mind even without telepathy, and they share their strengths and talents without really trying."

"You mean like me being able to see that you glowed blue the night with Corrine? Isn't that one of *your* talents?" A pregnant silence stretched between them.

Raphael turned to her, his eyes wide. "Are you saying . . ." His voice was tense with excitement, his scent a combination of hope, joy, and fear.

Cat nodded. "I think so. Is there any way we can find out for sure?"

"Yes. Like I said, there are tests. I've been scheduled for mine for a few days." He smiled sadly. "I was waiting for a particular person to be on vacation. I didn't want word about my condition to get out. I would never deliberately put you in any danger."

Cat reached over, taking his hand in hers. Electric power trickled between the two of them. She saw Raphael shudder with pleasure. It felt so damned good.

"So what's the plan?" She asked. "Can it be a mating challenge if we acknowledge I've been dating you and Mike's mated to me? Or do I have to say I'm mated to one of you, or what?"

"I'm not sure." He frowned. "I was assuming it was one sided: that Mike and I were both mated to you. That's pretty common with powerful alpha females. There are lots of one-sided matings among the wolves. Under those circumstances, you claim to be interested in him, I challenge, and we date for six months without sex."

"Celibacy?" She turned to face him, giving him a disbelieving look. "I don't think either one of us is going to be too good at *that*."

"I know." He sighed, and pulled his hand from hers. He took the cigarette pack from his pocket and took a stick from the pack, but didn't light it. "Particularly if it is a mutual mating. But damn it, I don't want Jack knowing for certain about us. It's too dangerous!" Raphael ground his teeth in frustration. This *should* be the happiest moment of his life. He loved Cat. He was mated to her. She'd just acknowledged that she might be mated to him. By all rights they should be celebrating together. Instead, he was stuck trying to figure out a way to keep her safe from not only Jack, but the pack, and find a way to keep Michael alive as well. "You'd be safer if Mike was dead." Raphael hated to say it, but it was true. Mike was mated to Cat, and unstable from it. He wouldn't harm her himself, but there were others in the pack who'd be more than happy to do it for him.

"I can't do that," Cat answered simply. "I just can't. I mean he's an ass and an idiot, and I'm royally pissed—"

"But you can't let him die."

"Nope."

He turned, and she was suddenly in his arms. Before he could think, she was kissing him. It started gentle, almost chaste, a silent acknowledgment that they were in this together. But even that small touch made heat and need flare through his body like wildfire. Raphael's jaws worked, forcing her mouth to open for his, their tongues exploring. He pressed her against the boulder, bringing his knee between her thighs as his hand slid beneath the heavy knit of her sweater to cup the fullness of her breast.

She moaned into his mouth, her hand sliding down the front of his jeans along the length of his erection.

His mouth moved away from hers to nestle at the base of her neck. He could see and hear the thundering of her pulse. The scent of her need made his body ache. He'd gone so far as to open his mouth to bite down when he recognized the urge for what it was. Cat Turner *was* his mate and a primal part of him wanted to mark her as *his* so that the world would know it. Damn the consequences.

"Raphael." Cat pushed him back gently.

"Mnnn?"

"Celibacy?"

"Shit!"

Chapter Twenty

TUESDAY MORNING DAWNED cold and clear. Cat wandered downstairs to check the answering machine.

The first message was Jake's from last night. Cat fought down a wave of irritation. *Jerk.*

The next message was from Mike. Apologizing—endlessly. Or rather, it would have been endlessly if the machine hadn't cut him off. Cat had almost made her mind up to just erase the rest without listening in case they were just more from him, but she changed her mind when Holly's voice came on the line.

"Cat, are you all right? I'm so sorry! I can't believe my dad is being such a fricking ass! Anyway, I'll bring by your check tomorrow morning and we can talk. We can cruise down to Denver if you like. I've got the whole day off."

The machine beeped again.

"This is Brownstown Movers calling for Cat Turner. We understand that you're scheduled to meet with us at the property owned by Mr. Ned Thornton Thursday afternoon. We've had a change of schedule and would like to move the time up to 10:00 A.M. Tuesday. Please call and let us know if that will work for you at 303-555-4828.

Beep.

"Catherine, it's me . . . Brad. I'm . . . worried about you. You haven't returned my calls, and your e-mail was so . . . cold. I really want to see you, see if we can work things out. *Please* call me back."

Beep.

"Ms. Turner, this is Lucas Santiago. I understand that the

rental car you've been using has sustained some damage. If you'd take it to Rowan's Auto Body they'll do an excellent job on the repairs for you at no charge. Also, my wife and I would be honored if you and Raphael would join us this evening for dinner at Roberto's Restaurant in Denver. There are a number of things we'd like to discuss. Please call my secretary and let her know if you'll be available."

Cat checked the clock. It was already eight o'clock. *Damn.* She didn't know if the mover's office would be open yet, but it was worth a shot. She rushed over to the phone and dialed the number. The woman on the other end picked up the phone on the first ring.

"This is Cat Turner, you left a message on my aunt's answering machine."

"Yes, Ms. Turner. We've had a cancellation on the schedule and were hoping you might be able to meet us at the Thornton residence today rather than when it was initially scheduled. I realize it's short notice—"

"Actually, today would be fine. What time would you like me to be there?"

"Is ten too soon?"

She nodded and scribbled the time on the pad next to the phone. "Ten will be fine."

"Oh, good. I'll tell our people to expect you."

Cat hung up the phone and hurried upstairs to pull on a pair of worn jeans and a sweatshirt over thick socks and warm boots. She didn't want to wear anything good, because once the movers were done she was going to start in on cleaning the place. Yeah, she could pay a cleaning crew, but why? She was perfectly capable of scrubbing a floor and wiping down counters. God knew she'd been doing it enough at Jake's.

She'd just finished brushing her teeth and pulling her hair into a braid when she heard Holly's Geo pull into the drive. She thundered downstairs to get the door before the other woman even had a chance to knock.

"Hi." Holly stood on the front step, a dark figure limned in the almost blinding brilliance of sunlight sparkling from virgin snowdrifts.

"Hi." Cat stepped aside "Come on in."

Holly was dressed for the snow in a bright blue down jacket with a fur-trimmed hood and warm winter boots. She reached into her large black purse with one gloved hand. "Before I forget. Here's your paycheck."

"Thanks." Cat took the check from her hand. "Can I ask you a favor?"

"No problema. What's up?"

"I need to drop the rental car off for repairs, but I'm due up at Ned's to meet the movers. Think you could drive me around today? I'll pop for the gas."

"Sure." Holly agreed. "But, I thought the movers were scheduled for Thursday."

"So did I. But they had a change of schedule."

"Sure, I'd be glad to."

"Thanks!" Cat reached into the hall closet to grab her purse and jacket.

Holly's voice was light and teasing. "I see you finally got yourself a coat."

"Actually, it was a gift." Cat said a little sheepishly. While she would have loved to talk about everything that was going on, she wasn't sure it was a good idea to talk to Holly about Raphael. He was her uncle. And she had been so very shocked when she'd found out that he and Cat were an item.

"Ah. I thought it looked familiar."

"Holly—"

"Cat, it's okay." Holly took a deep breath and plowed on. "Really. I mean, I've been thinking about it a lot, and . . . I don't know. It just kind of is right. You suit each other. He actually seems *happy*. I've never seen him happy before, and he's been around our house since I was born."

"Thanks." Cat really appreciated Holly's effort to accept her relationship with Raphael. It had been a long time since Cat had something close to a best friend. In fact, she couldn't remember a really good friend—ever. The thought of losing that friendship had hurt, badly. Even so, she hadn't for an instant considered the possibility of giving up Raphael instead.

"Yeah, well, I want you to be happy. And since Mike's turned out to be such a jerk." Holly gestured through the open door at the damaged rental car.

"How'd you know?"

"Cat, *please*." Holly rolled her eyes. "Who *else* would it be?"

She had a point. Anyone else would've left the car alone, and hurt *her*. Cat pulled on her coat, checked the pocket to make sure she had her keys. "Can we stop by the ATM—oh, and a grocery? I need to get some money and pick up some cleaning supplies."

"You might pick up some gloves while you're at it," Holly suggested. "Most of the chain groceries carry them during winter."

"That would be awesome!" Cat agreed. She pulled the front door closed with a brisk slam and picked her way carefully out to the driveway. She knew she should shovel the snow from the walk, but there was no time for it now. Who knew, if she was lucky, maybe it'd be sunny enough for the snow to melt off and she wouldn't have to.

"So, where's this repair shop you're going to?" Holly's voice interrupted her thoughts.

"You ever hear of a place by the name of Rowan's?" Cat asked.

"Yeah, it's a pack business."

"Figures. Lucas Santiago wants me to take it there. The repairs have already been paid for."

"Makes sense." Holly agreed. "Since it was Mike's fault to begin with. You can follow me. It's not far."

Chapter Twenty-one

RAPHAEL CHECKED HIS watch. Cat was late for their training session. So he concentrated, using his magic to search the connection that bound them. He found her easily. She was in Holly's car, on her way to Ned's. She was happy and excited, talking with the other woman about her plans for decorating the new place once she moved in.

Cat?

Raphael? I'm sorry! I forgot to call you. The movers changed the appointment to this morning.

That's the second time you've forgotten a training session with me, young lady. He tried to sound stern, but failed miserably. Yes, the lessons were very important, but she was doing well, and he was just too damned happy to stay angry with her for long. I'm beginning to worry you aren't taking this seriously.

I'm sorry. Really. Can we reschedule, maybe for this evening?

Did you check your messages? Lucas invited us for dinner at Roberto's in Denver.

Yeah, I know. But I'm not really looking forward to dealing with the whole Michael thing.

Raphael didn't answer, letting the mental silence stretch uncomfortably.

Fine, I'll do it. Just as soon as I've finished with the movers.

I'll pick you up at Violet's at five thirty. We don't want to be late. The last thing you need is more trouble with the pack right now. We'll have a training session tomorrow morning no matter what, 7:00 A.M. sharp.

He cut the connection between them quickly. He heard

familiar footsteps in the hallway. They paused outside the door to his office. A moment later he heard Raven's knock on the office door.

"Come in."

Emma took the lead, holding the door open for Raven. It was obvious the package he carried was not only bulky, but heavy. That piqued Raphael's curiosity. Sazi had super strength, and Raven was exceptional even among their kind.

"What are you two up to?" Raphael watched as his son looked carefully around the room before choosing a spot in the corner. Sitting on the floor, the box stood chest high.

"Well, go on. I can smell that you're curious. Open it up," Raven teased.

"What is it?" Raphael looked at Emma.

"Oh, no. I'll never tell." She waved him toward the box in a shooing gesture. "Go on. Raven's been dying to see what you think of it." She grinned. "Frankly, so am I." She'd leaned her package against the wall. Raphael didn't have to guess what that one was. By it's shape it *had* to be a painting, and a large one.

"All right, all right." He laughed. Pulling a pocketknife from his pocket he went down on one knee and began slicing open the wrapping. "But why the presents?"

"Your new promotion. You are now *officially* the Alpha of the pack. Being alpha of a pack the size of Boulder is quite the honor." Emma's voice was matter-of-fact but he could smell her pride.

"It's only temporary."

"I wouldn't be too sure of that, Dad," Raven answered. "Lucas and Tatya have been here a long time. People are starting to notice that they're not aging much—"

He was right, of course. Hell, it wouldn't be much longer before Raphael had to leave as well. Right now he could still pass it off as "good genetics." Then maybe a few years of artificially aging his appearance, but it probably wouldn't be more than a decade before he had to create a new identity.

Raphael felt the knife cut into the Styrofoam beneath the cardboard. After a quick look at Raven to make sure nothing would be damaged, he grabbed the cardboard with both hands and ripped it and the Styrofoam away.

His jaw dropped.

It was exquisite: Carrara marble, lovingly sculpted into the shape of a wolf. He knew that Raven had always wanted to try his hand, but this—he'd caught the wolf leaping skyward into battle from atop a jagged boulder, fangs bared. Every detail was perfect.

Tears filled Raphael's eyes. The boy had his mother's talent. Raphael had always known that. There weren't words for what he was feeling.

"You like it?"

He turned, letting Raven see the naked expression of his face.

"How could he not?" Emma stepped forward to run a careful hand over the textured stone. "It's beautiful. He did it himself, you know." The look she gave Raven was filled with love and pride.

"Yeah," Raphael's voice was rough with emotion. "I know."

"Okay, Emma's next," Raven announced.

"Right." Raphael coughed, clearing his throat and tearing away the wrapping surrounding the oak frame. The painting showed a pack on the hunt, the wolves flowing over rocky ground under a sky leaden with snow, in the lead, a huge black male with one white paw, Raphael.

"I don't have Raven's talents," Emma said. "But when I told Star what I needed a gift for she suggested that she give the painting and I take care of the framing."

"It's perfect." Raphael turned to give Emma an impulsive hug. "Thank you." He looked up at his son. "Thank you both."

He didn't hear Raven's answer. He saw his son's lips move, knew he was speaking. It was Cat's voice he heard, tight and tense. But it wasn't in his head, like normal. It was though he was standing inside her body, watching a desperate scene unfold.

"Get in the car Holly, now!"

"Wha—?"

Raphael saw them then, four familiar furred shapes, fanning out to circle the two women. Corrine moved forward and to the right, cutting off any chance of escape to the car.

"Let Holly go. This has nothing to do with her." Cat's voice

was distorted only slightly by the shifting of her body into cat form.

"Can't do that." Another wolf spoke; Raphael recognized John's voice. "Don't want to leave any witnesses now, do we?"

The wolves circled, looking for an opening. It was Corrine who took the lead, but it wasn't Cat whose throat she leapt for.

Raphael's head snapped back from the impact of Raven's slap. He tasted blood inside his mouth.

"*Holly!*" Raphael shoved his son away from him, hard enough to make the bigger man stumble against the desk. In a flash of power he changed to wolf form and leapt through the window.

HOLLY WAS ON the ground, blood spurting from her throat. Corrine raised her bloody muzzle skyward and howled in triumph.

Cat roared with pain and rage. Her attention was distracted by a flicker of movement glimpsed from the corner of her eye. Instinctively she ducked. She felt the wind of the wolf's body as it passed over her. Baring claws, she reached up. Using the animal's own momentum, she ripped through its underbelly. Blood and vital fluids spilled in a dark rain as a woman's scream rent the air.

The others closed and the true fight began.

It was a blur of pain and fury. There were three wolves remaining. The wolf Cat had eviscerated lay in an unmoving heap below the tree that had stopped her flight.

Again and again the wolves closed, trying for a kill. Cat fought with everything she had. Her use of magic against Jack had been instinctive. Now that she'd been trained it deserted her. It required concentration to call it deliberately, and the wolves were giving her precious little time.

While Cat was struggling with the male, the brown wolf closed in a try for her unprotected throat. Cat spun, twisting her spine to wrench away from him in a move that tore meat from her shoulder but enabled her, in turn, to close her jaws over the brown wolf's neck. She locked her powerful jaws, twisting her head sharply sideways. The wolf's spine snapped with an audible crack.

Cat threw the body into Corrine, who had been edging forward on her right. The male had pulled back slightly, coordinating his attack with the remaining female.

An ear-splitting screech cut the winter air. A blur of white hit John hard and fast from above, knocking him from his feet as wicked talons tore viciously through his thick fur, leaving bloody wounds before Emma shot upward again.

Corrine looked from one to the other of her three fallen companions. She crouched, preparing to leap. Cat steadied herself to meet the attack.

"Enough!"

A huge black wolf with one white paw appeared between them as if by magic. One moment Raphael was not there. The next he was. Sunlight shone on his muzzle as he raised his massive head to give a long, mournful howl that echoed through the woods.

A second wolf, larger, and black as night, padded over to Holly. In a shimmer of power Raven shifted forms and began working to save her. A snowy owl settled onto the bloodied ground and began checking the fallen wolves.

"How's Holly?" Raphael's voice was a rumbling growl. His eyes never left Corrine.

"We were in time. She'll need blood, but she'll live."

"Silver?"

"No." Raven answered. "The attack must have torn the cross from her throat." Raphael nodded once in acknowledgment. He paced over to the female with measured steps. "Corrine Castillion, you have attacked and infected a human in an attempted murder. Your crimes are punishable by death."

Cat watched Corrine struggle against the magic Raphael used to hold her in place. Her eyes showed white all around, and her body quivered, but she could not move, could not flee.

He moved relentlessly forward until their noses were almost touching. His form shimmered, until he stood before her, naked, but not vulnerable. "Raven, Emma, as agents of Wolven, do you concur?"

"Yes." Raven's voice was completely steady. Emma didn't speak; instead, she gave a bobbing nod of her feathered head.

"As Alpha of the Boulder pack, and as an agent of Wolven,

I sentence you to death." Raphael reached out with his right hand to touch the top of her head. Cat saw, and felt . . . something. This was not the rush of heat that she normally felt when magic was called. It was cold, and quiet, a deep, irresistible *pull,* a dangerous undertow in a warm ocean. The process was slow, as though her very essence of life was being drained from her. Cat couldn't tear her eyes from the scene, both horrified and pleased as justice was issued.

Corrine shuddered, legs stiffened, and then her eyes rolled back in her head before she fell to the ground—dead.

He repeated the whole procedure twice more on the other attackers. The fourth wolf was already dead from the wounds inflicted during the fight.

"Raven, can you handle the cleanup?" Raphael didn't look at his son. He didn't seem to be looking at anything. He turned his back on everyone, walking slowly toward the end of the clearing. Cat tried to reach his mind, but he'd shut her out, hiding his thoughts behind a barrier she couldn't penetrate.

"Yes, sir."

"Good." It was the last thing he said before he shifted back to wolf form and disappeared into the woods.

CAT SAT SIDEWAYS in the passenger seat of the Geo watching Raven deal with Holly in back. Emma was driving as fast as the weather and the narrow mountain roads would allow. Raven was a healer, and he'd done what he could. But Holly needed blood, and quickly. So they were headed to the pack hospital.

"I can't believe they did that." The words were a hoarse whisper. Tears were streaming unheeded down her cheeks. "Me, I understand. But *Holly*? She's *family*."

Raven didn't answer. There was nothing to say. But the scent of his sorrow and worry became tinged with dark rage. "Tell me what happened."

"I got a message on the answering machine. They said it was the movers and they wanted to reschedule from the afternoon to this morning."

"Is it an old-fashioned machine? With a tape?" Emma asked.

"Yes."

"We'll need that tape to do voice matching, in case someone else is involved," Emma observed. Raven nodded and gestured for Cat to continue.

"They were waiting for us. I caught the scent and told her to get back in the car, but it was too late." Cat stared at her friend. Holly was breathing, but she was so very pale, almost gray, and her lips had a bluish tinge.

"It was a setup."

"Why did she have to be there? It should've just been me." Cat met Raven's gaze over the back of the car seat. "What if she dies?"

"We're here." Emma made the announcement as she braked to a skidding stop at the clinic entrance.

Cat climbed out, tilting the seat forward so that Raven could exit behind her. He pulled Holly from the backseat and carried her inside the building.

"What if she dies?" Cat turned to Emma. The other woman gave her a penetrating stare.

"Raven said she'd make it, and she will. She won't die today."

"But the change?"

Emma shrugged, meeting her gaze. "The change . . . there's no telling." She turned on her heel, striding naked into the building. Cat followed.

Betty was on duty—she and the nurse had Holly on a bed and hooked up for blood transfusions in rapid order and Cat could watch as the wounds closed under Betty's healing magic. Almost immediately her color began to improve, and her breathing, while harsh-sounding, was stronger, more even.

Cat stayed at the hospital until *she* was certain Holly would be all right. When the other woman was alert, and talking to Raven and Emma, she slipped away, going out the fire door to the parking lot. She went to Holly's Geo to get dressed. Like most Sazi and family members, Holly kept loose clothing on hand in case of an unexpected need.

Tears of helpless rage stung Cat's eyes as she buttoned up the plaid flannel shirt and green sweatpants. Holly wouldn't blame her. She knew that. But she blamed herself. She'd seen the pack in action with Ned up at Wolf's Run—knew how much they hated her and what they were capable of. She'd put her best friend at risk through sheer carelessness. It wouldn't happen again.

Cat grabbed her purse from the bloodied floorboards and pulled out her cell. The charge was dead. She looked at the building, considered going back inside to call a cab, but no. She didn't want to see Holly, Raven, hell . . . anyone. So she slammed the door of the vehicle and started on the long walk to Violet's. The raw wind cut like a knife through her borrowed clothes, but she barely noticed.

She wasn't sure how far she'd gone before she came upon the gas station. Rummaging coins from her purse she walked up to the graffiti-decorated pay phone. Her first call was to the cab company. The second call was to her godfather.

CAT CLIMBED FROM the cab, slipping the driver enough money that he was more than happy to wait for her as she changed clothes and threw a few things into her bags. She walked across the street and asked Mrs. Zabatos to keep an eye on the house for a few days. The older woman was stiffly formal at first, but her attitude softened slightly when she learned that Violet was on her honeymoon. It was no surprise that she was more than happy to hear that Cat was leaving.

She spent most of the cab ride down to Denver only half listening to the driver chatter about his views on politics, the president, and smokers. If he noticed she was only half listening, he didn't seem to mind.

Cat felt numb. She knew she should be horrified. She'd killed a woman. Yes, it was a wolf, and yes, she'd been attacked with provocation, but—it just didn't seem *real*. *Nothing* seemed real. It seemed like some horrible dream that she just couldn't manage to wake herself from, no matter how hard she tried.

She checked into a five-star hotel in downtown Denver. Elegant, expensive, it had been a favorite of her parents on the few occasions they'd found themselves in Colorado. Even without a reservation she was able to obtain a beautiful suite of rooms on the third floor, and the concierge had been more than happy to offer his assistance. Should she require anything at all, all she need do was call.

She thanked him, tipped the bellhop outrageously, and locked the door behind him. Grabbing a tumbler, and a bottle from the wet bar, she pulled a chair over by the balcony doors. She poured herself a stiff drink and curled up in the chair with her legs tucked beneath her. For the next several hours she drank and stared out at the lights of the city as night began to fall.

At ten o'clock the phone to her suite rang. She untangled her legs and crossed the room, answering it on the third ring. It was the front desk putting through a call.

"Catherine, it's Charles. I'm in the lobby. May I come up?"

She gave him her suite number and hung up the phone. She dropped the empty liquor bottle into the garbage, poured herself another drink, and turned on the lamps. By the time her godfather knocked on the door, the place looked warm and inviting. She hadn't expected Charles to show up, but she wasn't surprised, either. All her life he'd tended to appear unexpectedly in the middle of a crisis. *Like the Lone Ranger—only taller.*

Cat opened the door to greet him. As always, his bodyguard preceded him. Tonight it was Yusef. He wasn't a tall man, but he was powerfully built. His shambling gait and prominent nose instantly marked him as one of the bears—now that she knew such things were possible—as did his scent. His eyes were small and dark, under a bushy black eyebrow that slashed across his forehead in a single harsh line. Cat nodded in silent greeting as he went past. Yusef acknowledged the nod, but set about the business of checking the suite.

Cat gave her godfather a quick hug. She hadn't seen him since the funeral, and she realized how very much she'd missed the solid comfort of his presence in the background.

Charles stood a little over six foot one, not so tall by current standards, but quite a height for a man of his age, and he seemed bigger, primarily because of his bulk. He was nearly as broad as he was tall, with massive, muscular shoulders. He was an imposing man, but generally a cheerful one, at least around Cat. Tonight he looked tired, and angrier than she'd ever seen him. The small dark eyes above his large nose burned with barely controlled fury.

"Are you sure you're all right?" Charles's gaze was intent enough to make her squirm.

"Hell, no." Cat closed the door behind him and crossed over to the seating area where she curled back up on the couch, pulling the plush hotel robe tight around her body before reaching onto the end table to retrieve her glass. While Charles took a seat she took another long pull from her drink. She'd been drinking steadily in hope that the alcohol would help her break past the cold rage that threatened to envelop her. It wasn't working.

"You can't get drunk anymore," he said, and shrugged when her eyes widened. "You're too powerful. Thought you should know. They forget to mention that in early training."

She watched as Charles took stock of their surroundings. The living room area was beautifully decorated in shades of gold and green; valuable antiques and art works mixed in with more comfortable modern furniture to create a comfortable, livable space. An elaborate stereo system and flat-screen television and DVD were hidden at the moment, in a polished cherry cabinet designed to look like an antique wardrobe.

Yusef brought Charles a double Scotch on the rocks. At a nod from the older man, he left the room. Cat knew he would stand guard in the hall outside the suite until Charles was ready to leave, even if it took all night. She remembered all of the times that Uncle Chuck and her father had played chess and talked— all the while with Yusef and Ivan guarding outside the doors.

"What are your plans?" Charles waited for the door to close, then settled his bulk into an overstuffed chair.

"I'm going to avoid the pack for a bit."

"That's probably wise." He spoke softly. He swirled the contents of the crystal tumbler he held, the ice clinking softly against the glass.

"I'll have to go back for the challenge, I suppose, and Holly's first . . . *change*."

Charles looked up, his gaze intent. "That would be a very bad idea."

She met his eyes calmly. "It's something I have to do. She's my friend."

"You could let the boy die. In fact, you probably should. Going back gives your enemies a time and place where they *know* they can get you." His voice was completely bland, as though they were discussing the weather, or the Broncos' chances of making the Super Bowl. His pleasantly noncommittal attitude irked her. There were lives at stake, damn it.

"No. Not if I can save them."

His voice was mild, but a small amount of sarcasm played through it at her horrified face. "Yet, you killed a woman today. She may have been in wolf form, but she was still a woman. I don't see you weeping copious tears for *her* death."

Cat gave him a hostile look. "No. I'm not. I had to defend myself. They were going to kill me, and Holly, too." She shook her head, her anger and frustration bubbling abruptly to the surface. "Holly's like Violet, you know. A sweeter, gentler person you'd never meet. They treat her like shit, and would've killed her without a second thought." She took a deep swallow of her drink. "I know I should feel guilty—should feel *something*. But I just . . . don't." Cat knew he heard the pain in her voice, the regret. She truly *wasn't* the same woman she had been weeks ago. A part of her had died with her parents in the attack. She was harder now, colder. For better or worse, she'd changed, and a part of her grieved for it.

Cat had a flash of insight. Growing up, everyone had always commented how much she was her father's daughter. Now, she was like her mother. It made her wonder what had happened to Janet to make her so relentlessly pragmatic? She'd probably never know.

"What about Jack, Catherine?"

"Catherine's dead, Uncle Chuck. She died in the woods with her parents. I'm just *Cat* now." She paused for a moment as he nodded his head once and took another drink. "How many years has he been doing this? How many people has he killed?"

"The first we know of was in 1954. Truthfully, we don't know how many for sure."

"Give me a ballpark figure." Her voice was cold.

"At least twenty. Probably more."

"And no one tried to stop him. How . . . *charming*." Her bitterness was palpable.

"That's not entirely true," Charles corrected her. "Raphael tried. He gathered his proof, and because Jack was still in charge of the law enforcement bureau, he presented his evidence to the council."

Cat sat bolt upright, spilling her drink. She ignored the mess, staring at her godfather intently. "And?"

"Before we could act, do anything really, the file arrived."

Cat set her drink onto the table, wiping her wet hand on her robe to dry it. "Ah, yes, the infamous file."

"It's a legitimate concern, Cat. Unpalatable as it may be— the world governments would not hesitate to sacrifice the lives of every Sazi in the world to prevent widespread panic of the human populace. We had no choice."

"There's always a choice," she snapped.

"There isn't always a good one."

She couldn't argue with that, though she wanted to. Right now she wanted to rage at someone, something, and Charles was the nearest target. And yet when she looked up at him, saw the expression on his face, the anger faded to cold bitterness. "So you did nothing."

"Not 'nothing.' We have tried, over the years, to contain Jack's excesses, although with limited success."

Cat gave a very unladylike snort.

"If you've got a better idea, I'd love to hear it." Charles didn't keep the heat from his words.

"Actually, I do." Cat rose. She padded barefoot through the suite and into the bedroom area where she retrieved her notes from the case she'd packed.

She dropped them into his lap and began pacing. As he skimmed the written notes she began presenting her plan.

It was deceptively simple in theory. There were four basic steps. First, find the original file. Second, create a duplicate file that appeared identical on the surface, but instead of containing proof of the Sazi, it would be a "confessional" with proof of Jack's crimes. Third, make the switch, destroying the original. And finally, kill Jack.

Under each of the basic steps Cat had outlined, in detail, what would need to happen, the resources required, with the potential pitfalls and how best to avoid them.

As she spoke of the plan, she watched his expressions, looking for telltale clues as to his reaction. There weren't many. Somehow he'd even managed to mute his scent.

Charles sat silently, deep in thought. "I need to consider this carefully. On the surface, it looks workable, if difficult. Then again, I would've expected nothing less. You are your father's daughter."

"I would say this was more my mother's type of thing." Cat stopped next to the balcony doors.

"Oh, yes." Charles agreed. "I learned early on never to underestimate Janet. Chris could and would forgive and forget. Janet didn't." He stood, placing the papers in a neat stack on the coffee table. "I'm inclined to agree to your plan, but will take a few days to get things organized properly. Don't go back to Violet's. The hotel is much safer. Ivan's downstairs with the car. He'll stay in Denver to help with the details of getting started and security for the mountain property and your trips to visit the pack." He reached into the pocket of his suit jacket and pulled out a thin silver cell phone. "This is for you. It's one of the phones used by my personal guard. Keep it with you in case I need to get in touch with you. Don't give the number to anyone."

"And you?"

"I have some personal business to take care of."

Chapter Twenty-two

RAPHAEL WANDERED THE national forest lands in wolf form, halfheartedly chasing down a rabbit when he grew hungry. He neither knew, nor cared, how many hours passed. Most wolves craved the pack when in pain. Right now, Raphael needed solitude.

They'd betrayed him. They'd known he was training the cat, had agreed to allow her in their territory, but they'd gone against his wishes and deliberately plotted Cat's death.

They were of his pack. He'd known them for years. Two of them he'd even liked. Corrine was a bitch, of course, in every sense of the word. But she'd been beautiful, fun, and funny. It hadn't been a hardship when they'd asked him to try to get her with puppies for the breeding program. They'd gone through her pregnancy together, and he'd held her when she cried all night after having to give the twins up for adoption.

I had no choice. It was premeditated murder.

If he hadn't been tied to Cat, both she and Holly would likely be dead now, and possibly him as well. He was mated. If he'd had any doubts about it before, they were gone now. Telepathy might enable him to talk mind-to-mind, with effort. But he'd seen through her eyes, *felt* what she'd been feeling. Just by turning his thoughts to her he *knew* where she was, what she was doing, and it was taking a serious effort to keep her from doing the same.

He regretted the necessity of killing his pack mates. But he'd do it again. He'd kill anyone who threatened her. He couldn't help himself. Which made the challenge infinitely tricky. Because he knew Michael was a threat to her. The boy was unstable. Best of intentions aside, Raphael wasn't entirely sure he had enough self-control in the heat of battle *not* to slay him. It wouldn't take much. The boy was big and strong, but slow. And he was barely alphic. If he'd had more magic he wouldn't have been *able* to get drunk, and they wouldn't have had the problem on their hands in the first place.

It was a mess, personally and politically. Raphael had never had many friends. Lucas was very dear to him. He didn't want to hurt Lucas's son, let alone kill him. Could he manage enough self-control not to do the very thing he'd just done to Corrine? Charles had been right. His best skill was to kill by touch. Only a very few Sazi had such a horrific "gift," and he wasn't sure he was strong enough *not* to use it in a challenge.

Raphael looked up at the sky. The sun was well into the west. He needed to check on his niece, and call Lucas to cancel their dinner. If the old man was pissed, so be it. Raphael just wasn't up to appearing in public tonight; wasn't up to looking at Tatya across the table and wondering if she'd had a hand in the attack, if she'd known.

He was closer to home than pack headquarters at this point. He might as well head there. It would give him a chance to thank Raven and Emma, and apologize for leaving them with the mess.

It never got easier, killing with his gift. Always, it made him feel dirty. It was so much cleaner, to his mind, to just shoot someone, or kill him with teeth and claws than to simply drain away the very energy of his life, everything that made him who he was, and let it spill onto the ground until there was nothing left to animate the physical shell and his heart and brain just stopped.

He stood at the top of a rise, the chill north wind ruffling his thick black fur. Raising his muzzle, he howled long and loud—giving voice to the pain, hurt, and frustration that haunted him. The sound echoed from the rock walls of the unfeeling canyon. As the last echoes died he picked his way over the uneven ground and began the long trek home.

It was full dark by the time he padded up the front drive, his breath misting in the frigid air. The front porch lights were on, but the Hummer wasn't parked in the driveway. A gray SUV with rental plates had taken its place. The driver, oblivious to the cold, had made himself comfortable on the front porch, sitting stretched out in one of the chairs in shirt sleeves with a case of beer within comfortable reach.

Raphael felt some of his depression lift. Ivan Kruskenik was probably the last person he would have expected to see, but the Siberian bear was a most welcome guest. The big man was one of the few people Raphael considered a true friend. They'd been partnered for a while back in their Wolven days after his best friend, Greg, had died in action. It was Ivan who'd discovered and reported Jack's plans to kill Raphael. It had cost him his career. Charles had tapped him for the Chief Justice's Private Guard, but that wasn't the same thing. Not by a long shot. Still, Ivan seemed content with his choice.

"Been waiting long?" Raphael stepped up onto the porch. He slipped into his human form and took the Corona and a pair of jeans from Ivan's hand, slipped them on, and then settled himself comfortably against the nearest railing after brushing off the snow. He twisted the cap off of his beer and took a long pull, savoring the taste.

"Nyet." Ivan gave a crooked grin and lifted his own bottle. "Only about two beers' worth. It was kind of nice, really. Peaceful. Nice place. You've got a great view." He gestured at the sunset with one meaty hand.

"Thanks. To what do I owe the honor?"

"I understand that you've moved up in the world—I brought you a gift, and both an apology and a request from Charles." He grinned. "Officially, I've come to ask the alpha of the Boulder pack for permission to spend some time in his territory."

"Granted, of course."

"Aren't you going to ask why?"

"I know better." Raphael drained the bottle. Bending down, he slid it into its slot in the carton and pulled out a replacement for each of them. "You're welcome to the guest room," he suggested as he passed the bottle over.

"I appreciate the offer, but no." Ivan twisted off the lid and raised the bottle in salute. "I've a great deal to do. I'll be pressed for time as it is."

"Ah."

Ivan laughed, his eyes darkening with merriment. He ran a hand over his bare scalp. "You've grown up, wolf. There was a time when you'd have pestered me with questions."

Raphael shrugged. "Happens to all of us sooner or later." Grinning, he took a sip from the bottle. "I *do* wonder what happened to that British accent I've heard you using the past couple of years."

"That is for acquaintances and business. *Not* for friends." Ivan's smile faded, his face growing serious. He very deliberately steered the conversation back to its original course, which meant there was something important he wanted to say. "It's a hard thing to watch sometimes, the growing up." He took a long pull of beer. Raphael waited. Ivan had always been like this. He passed on information in his own way, in his own time. Perhaps all bears were the same. Raphael didn't know. He'd only ever met two of the ursines.

"I've known Catherine Turner since three days after she was born. Her father, Chris Turner, was one of the most brilliant minds of this, or any, time. The Turner computer empire was poised to take over the computing world. Socially, however, he was completely inept. Savant really. Janet, her mother, was intelligent, not in his class of course, but in her own way quite as brilliant as she was beautiful. She was also ruthless enough to put Fiona to shame."

Raphael blinked in shock. *Nobody* was more ruthless than Fiona.

"Catherine inherited more than her father's brain and her mother's looks." Raphael felt Ivan watching him as the implications of that last statement struck home.

"She has presented Charles with a workable plan for eliminating the file and taking down Jack Simpson. Charles is going to move for a warrant at the next council meeting." He took another swig from the beer bottle and leaned back far enough that the wood of his chair groaned in protest. "He's also moving for her to keep the land she purchased. It'll be fenced off so that nothing short of a raptor is going to be able to get in." Ivan sighed. "Charles told me to let you know that he realizes that this—the attack on Catherine and your niece—is not your fault, but while he can't truly protect her from Jack, he *will* see to it she's safe from the pack." He shook his massive head. "I have never seen him so angry, Ramirez. If it were anyone other than you I think he might well have revoked the charter."

Raphael cringed. Losing a charter meant that a pack was disgraced, its members forced to scatter throughout the world, wherever anyone would take them. "I'm not sure it was the entire pack."

"No." Ivan spoke with certainty. "It wasn't." He gave Raphael a long, level look. "The Chief Justice asked me to give you his most sincere apology. He realizes that you are perfectly capable of disciplining your own pack, and asks that you forgive him for usurping that authority and executing Claire Hamilton, Lucas's secretary, for her part in the plot against his goddaughter. He meant no insult. He lost his temper."

Raphael only just managed not to choke on his beer.

"I am supposed to report to you regarding everything we learned as a result of his questioning." Ivan took a pull from his beer. "Believe me, he was thorough. There is no doubt about the veracity of the information obtained."

Raphael felt the heat radiating from Ivan. The other man was wearing Wolven cologne, so there was no scent, but he couldn't keep his power from flaring with his anger.

"The plot originated with her. Betty Perdue breached medical ethics and told Tatya that you had an appointment for testing for a possible mating, but that she was already certain of the conclusion of the tests. Tatya, in turn, revealed the information to Claire. It seems," Ivan said drily, "that she was concerned you might not be able to control yourself during this 'mating challenge' with her son and the boy would be killed."

Raphael remained silent. He was mulling the implications. Mike was mated, but Cat hadn't slept with him. There was a good chance he'd survive her death. With enough counseling he might even get over her eventually. With Cat dead, there was no mating challenge. Michael's peccadillo would be moot. There was no question in his mind that the pack would consider Mike's life more valuable than Cat's, more valuable than his own if it came to it. They'd known he was mated to her. They'd known he might die. Maybe they'd believed he wouldn't. More likely they hadn't cared.

"The Chief Justice told me to tell you that in reparation to you in this, he is going to override the council's order binding you to the Boulder territory. If and when you choose to leave, you will be free to go where you will."

"Thank him for me. I wouldn't have claimed the damages, but I won't refuse the gift."

"You'd be a fool if you did. While you are many things, you are *not* a fool."

"Don't be so sure. I'm feeling pretty damned stupid right now. How could I not have seen that it was this bad?"

Ivan laughed. "Love makes fools of us all, and mating more so." He reached past Raphael to slide his newly empty beer bottle into its slot, taking a full one in its place. "May I ask what you will do about this 'challenge' of yours?" There was a hint of reproach in the bear's voice. It was obvious to Raphael that he didn't approve.

"What do you want me to say, Ivan?" Raphael looked up then, felt the heat of anger flush his cheeks. "I don't want this. I don't want any of it. But I can't just let Lucas's son die. Santiago's my friend, and God knows I don't have many."

"Maybe not so many," Ivan agreed with a shrug. "But what you lack in quantity, you make up for in quality." There was a twinkle in his eyes again. "Speaking as one of them."

"Of course."

"The Chief Justice further orders that you provide Catherine with all of the evidence you have gathered against Jack Simpson. I am also to give you a personal message from Charles, and I quote: 'Break Catherine's heart and I'll make you wish you were never born.'" Ivan leaned forward, taking a long pull from the bottle before continuing. "I do hope that your intentions were honorable?" He made it a question, giving Raphael a hopeful look.

"They are now," Raphael answered wryly.

"Oh, good." Ivan smiled. "Because Charles isn't the only one who's fond of the woman."

"I never would've guessed."

Ivan laughed again at Raphael's dry tone. "Why don't we go inside? You can finish getting dressed and fix us dinner. *I* will bring in your presents."

Chapter Twenty-three

WEDNESDAY DAWNED COLD and clear. Cat had spent the night alternately tossing in her bed and pacing the suite. Eventually she gave up on sleep altogether, watching the bustle of the city from the window seat of her hotel bedroom. She was completely exhausted, but her racing thoughts wouldn't let her rest.

She had killed a woman.

Worse, a part of her had enjoyed it.

Thinking about it was driving her mad. She needed to occupy her mind with something—anything—else. So she wrapped herself in the blankets from the bed and sat down in front of the laptop provided by the hotel and started working on some of the more mundane pieces of the puzzle: ordering the supplies she would need online, designing the Web site.

Having trouble sleeping?

Jack's urbane inquiry made her want to scream and throw something. What she wouldn't *give* to get him *out of her skull*.

You don't have to feel guilty you know. By all accounts she was a stupid little bitch at best. And it *was* self-defense.

And how would you know that?

I know *you*, Fiona. You show everyone that rock-hard exterior, but I've seen inside your mind. I know all your weaknesses. You have this absurd notion of "honor" and "fair play" that keeps you from doing what is necessary. It'll get you killed eventually if you don't get past it. They say the meek shall inherit the earth, but from what I've seen, it's the ruthless that survive. I tried to teach you that when I was training you for Wolven, but you've never been a very good listener.

I'm *not* Fiona, insisted Cat.

Of course. I keep forgetting, new identities and all that. But you'll always be Fiona to me, kitten. Oh, and before I forget, darling, your anniversary gift is down at the front desk, something to remind you of me.

Just like that, he was gone. Almost against her will she glanced over at the phone. Sure enough, the red light was blinking, telling her she had a message. He'd *been* here? Dear God! It was bad enough that he talked to her, but that he could pull information out of her head just that easily. He knew where she was staying—had known long enough to send a flipping *gift*. *Your anniversary gift is down at the front desk.*

Cat shuddered, pulling the blankets tight around her. She couldn't stop shivering. Jack was insane, completely nucking futz. And if things kept up the way they were going, she wouldn't be far behind him.

The cell phone Charles gave her rang, rattling as it vibrated atop the coffee table. Cat unwound from the blankets, walking over to take the call.

"Hello?"

"Cat, it's Raphael."

It sounded like Raphael all right. But then again, he usually just spoke to her mind to mind. It was easier.

"I know you've decided to go to ground for a while. I even think it's a good idea. But there's some pack business I need to take care of, and I want you there when I do."

"After yesterday? I don't think so!"

He sighed. "Yesterday is the biggest part of it—that, the challenge, and the incident with Ned. Please, Cat? Raven and I will be there, and Charles. We won't let anything happen to you."

I don't like this, Raphael. She thought the words directly in his mind, mostly as a test. If he answered her thoughts she'd be able to tell if it was really him. She wasn't sure why, but she just *knew* she would.

If you decide to come, Raven's agreed to drive the limo, and Ivan will act as your bodyguard. It was Raphael all right. Cat could dimly sense the thoughts and emotions behind his words. He was frustrated and angry, but beneath all that he was sad. Something about yesterday had grieved him. It wasn't just having had to kill, she could tell. But he'd shielded his thoughts too tightly for her to see what *was* wrong.

But . . .

Charles is more worried about your safety than his. Frankly so am I. I wouldn't ask this if it wasn't important.

All right. She sighed heavily. When exactly is this fiasco supposed to take place?

Tonight at seven.

What am I supposed to wear?

Not casual, but not too dressy, either. Business clothes would be best.

Right.

Raven will be in front of the hotel waiting with the limo at five thirty.

You know where I am?

When you can see my thoughts, I can see yours, too. With that rather alarming thought he cut the mental connection, leaving Cat feeling guilty and like a nosy fool.

Chapter Twenty-four

"ARE YOU CERTAIN that Ramirez is well and truly mated to her? You smelled the bond personally?"

"I'm positive, but there's a small . . . wrinkle you might not have considered . . ."

Jack paused, waiting for the lightly accented Russian voice to continue over the phone. When it didn't, he prompted with an irritable snarl. "Well, out with it! What is this *wrinkle*?"

"The woman appears to be mated to Ramirez as well. It's a double mating. How would you like me to proc—"

He hung up the phone with a whisper, while the room spun around him. Mated. She was mated. And to that . . . that son of a—"*No*. No, for this . . . she must be punished." For this disregard of his . . . desire? Wish? No, *order*, she would pay, and pay dearly. He reached across his desk and caressed the bow on the model ship that had taken hundreds of hours to create. Every scrap of wood hand carved, every line on every mast absolutely perfect. How many hours of dreaming of his revenge against Ramirez had he put into this model? He lifted it up and turned it around so the overhead lights glowed through the nearly transparent sails.

With a vicious snarl and feline hiss, he crumpled the ship into slivers and threw it against the wall hard enough to dent the plaster.

His seer was going to pay for not warning him of this possibility. Yes, dear, faithful Muriel was going to see just what happens when Jack Simpson or, more precisely, Colecos, the legendary jaguar god of Mayapan, was well and truly *angry*.

* * *

RAPHAEL SET THE phone back in its cradle. She'd come. That was a relief. He hadn't been sure she'd be willing. Nor would he have blamed her. It was a terrible risk, and he hated to ask it of her. But if there was to be any hope of them working things out with the pack so that she could be safe, her presence at tonight's meeting was necessary. Still, he hadn't been able to hide his relief when Charles had insisted on not only being there, but on having Ivan and Raven acting as security as well. Until the pack severed their ties to Lucas and acknowledged Raphael as their alpha there were limits on the amount of magical power he had at his disposal to control them.

Raphael used his thumb and forefinger to rub the bridge of his nose. He had the mother of all headaches, and his body wasn't keeping up with healing it.

It was going to be a long day. He had a lot to get done, and not a lot of help to do it. Claire was dead, as was one of the other secretaries. Sally was the only one left and she didn't know any of the passwords, or where the files were. Worse, she alternately cringed and groveled, or burst into tears, so that Raphael felt like a monster for losing patience with her.

Raphael's musings were interrupted by a tap on the door. It was Emma, dressed in a white wool coat with a red beret and matching leather gloves. Her cheeks were red from the cold, but her eyes were sparkling. "Do you have a minute?"

Raphael smiled. "For you, always."

She walked over to the guest chair and dropped the cell phone on his desk. "You forgot it at the house this morning and it's been ringing like crazy."

"Thanks for bringing it by."

"It wasn't any trouble. I wanted to speak to you anyway." She smiled. "Something's come up and I need to fly back to New England and visit with my mother for a few days."

Raphael made a protesting noise, but she waved him to silence.

"I was *hoping*," she cringed, and started again. "I know it's terribly rude of me to invite myself—but Raven seemed to think it would be all right." She took a deep breath and said the next sentence very quickly. "Could I possibly join the two of you for Thanksgiving next week?"

"Of course! I was planning on your being here."

"I don't want to impose—" She looked at him a little helplessly.

"Don't be silly." Raphael rose from his seat behind the desk and walked around so that he was standing right in front of her. He very deliberately perched on the edge of the desktop so that they were looking eye-to-eye. "You are *always* welcome here, Emma."

"Thank you. You don't know how much I appreciate you saying that."

Actually, he probably did. Until Raven had come to live with him as a teenager, most holidays for Raphael had been spent either as an awkward tag-along, or lonely. He recognized the symptoms in the way Emma held herself, her tone of voice.

"Will you be inviting Cat?"

"I don't know that she'll be available." He said it sadly. He wanted her with him, and not just for the holidays. He wanted to look into those deep green eyes every morning when he woke, and last thing every night. But even if the mating was mutual, she was a cat. She could choose to leave. Under the circumstances, he wouldn't even blame her if she did.

"Yesterday wasn't your fault! She can't possibly blame you for that."

He took a deep breath, his emotions switching quickly from sadness to anger. "They were my people. I'm responsible."

"You haven't even officially taken power yet!" Emma protested.

"And what a way to start." Raphael tried to keep the bitterness from his voice, but didn't succeed.

"I'm sorry." She reached over to cover his hand with hers.

"Don't be. Not your fault." He squeezed her hand then let it go. He stood, giving her a warm smile. "Just make sure you make it back for the holiday. I'm fixing a big meal with all the trimmings."

"I'll be there." She stood. There was an awkward moment, where neither of them knew exactly what to do. Suddenly she leaned forward to give him a fierce hug. "I'm glad I got to meet you. It explains a lot about Raven."

"Good or bad?" he teased.

"Both." She smiled when she said it, but pulled away. "I've got to go."

"Come back soon," Raphael ordered.

From the parking lot Emma waved and blew him a kiss. Raphael laughed and returned her wave. He watched her drive off, thinking that Raven was a very lucky man, and wondering if he had any idea just how much Emma loved him.

He was still staring out at the snowy landscape when the cell phone rang. Raphael hit the button and put it to his ear. "Ramirez."

"Raphael, it's David Streeter."

"David! It's good to hear from you!" After a few more pleasantries, Raphael explained what he needed from him at the meeting tonight. David was nervous, but understood the problem. They ended the call by agreeing to meet for dinner to go over any details.

Busy as Raphael was, the time flew by. The lunch hour passed unnoticed, as did the early portion of the afternoon. It seemed like only minutes had passed before it was time for him to go home and get ready for dinner and what just might be the most dangerous pack meeting of his life.

Chapter Twenty-five

CAT BERATED HERSELF, telling herself she was being an idiot. Taking a deep breath, she tried to calm her ragged nerves. It was one thing to tell Charles she was willing to deal with the pack. It was quite another to actually do it. Her stomach did a little flip-flop as she paced barefoot over the thick carpet. She tried to reassure herself that she's be fine, reminded herself that she'd been the one to insist to Charles that she go. It didn't matter.

She checked her appearance in the mirror again. Her raw silk suit was caramel colored, tailored to show every curve, its skirt long enough to be businesslike, but short enough to show off a pair of very shapely legs. Her blouse was the color of black coffee, and exactly matched the pumps and purse that lay on the bed. Even her jewelry was old-school classic: a heavy brushed gold chain with matching earrings.

The clothing was fine. She'd pulled her hair into a French braid. It looked both simple and tasteful. She'd used more makeup than usual, but her skin still looked pale. All in all she looked every inch the elegant businesswoman.

"Are you ready?" Ivan asked.

"I wish I had some of that stuff you use to mask your scent. I can manage to *look* calm, but one whiff and they're going to know I'm terrified."

Ivan gave her a long, assessing look. "*You* are not even supposed to know about such things."

Cat wasn't sure what to say. She hadn't intentionally eavesdropped on Ivan's thoughts, but he *had* been thinking how very bad it was for her to smell terrified when heading into the pack meeting, and wondering whether Charles would be angry if he sprayed her with the Wolven cologne. "I'm sorry. I didn't mean to listen in. It was an accident."

"An *accident*?"

The door to the suite opened and Raven stepped inside. "Is everybody ready to go?"

"Give us a moment," Ivan ordered. Raven nodded and stepped back into the hallway, pulling the door closed behind him.

Ivan glared at his charge. "When this is over Cat, you and I will be having a talk about ethics. You do *not* go rummaging around in people's minds. That's a sure way to get a visit from one of us that's not *social* in nature."

She swallowed hard. Even not completely knowing what he meant, she was pretty sure it was bad. "Yes, sir."

"*Don't* do it again."

Nodding, she said, "I won't."

"Good."

Cat started to step forward, but Ivan held her back with one strong arm. With his other hand he used a spray bottle to douse her liberally with cologne.

The bottle disappeared into the pocket of his jacket. "You didn't see that, and know nothing about it. Now get your shoes and purse and we'll be on our way."

"Yes, sir." Cat smiled faintly until she noticed his frown, and then hurried into the bedroom to comply.

Raven's nostrils twitched as she stepped through the door into the hall. One dark eyebrow arched upward, but he didn't say a word. Instead, he walked two steps ahead of her, looking grim and dangerous in all black, the platinum band that held his gleaming hip-length hair back the only accent. Ivan took up the rear position, and though he wore an elegantly cut gray business suit, he would never be mistaken for anything other than a bodyguard.

People stared openly as they moved through the lobby and out to the long white limousine that was waiting at the front doors of the hotel.

It was a long drive up to Boulder, but Ivan didn't seem inclined toward conversation. Instead, the three of them listened to the muted strains of Chopin's Nocturnes. The music slowly worked its magic, soothing Cat's frayed nerves, so that by the time the car pulled up to pack headquarters she was more herself.

Raven held the car door open for her. As she stepped onto the curb Cat looked around. The parking lot was packed with vehicles. Every light in the school building appeared to be on, and Peter, dressed in a navy suit, stood stationed at the door to greet them.

Peter opened the door and held it for them as they approached the building. In the distance Cat could hear the murmuring of a crowd in the background and the sound of someone running a test on a microphone and sound system. She fought down a wave of panic-induced nausea. Standing tall and proud she followed Raven through the gymnasium doors with Ivan guarding her back. They walked the length of the hardwood between bleachers filled with suddenly silent spectators to the black draped stage that had been erected at the far end of the room.

There were three separate tables ranged behind the podium at the front of the stage. Raven led Cat to the table on the left where Holly sat next to an empty chair, looking frankly terrified. He held the chair, scooting it under her as she sat before taking his own seat at the large center table with his father, Ivan, Lucas, and Charles. On the far side of the stage, at a table directly opposite Holly and Cat, sat Betty and Tatya. Both were wearing black, both were silent and grim. When everyone had taken their places, Raphael rose.

He looked good. Cat had never seen him in dress clothes before. The crisply tailored gray linen slacks and black dress shirt suited his dark good looks. His hair was freshly cut, his face shaved to perfect smoothness. He didn't look at her as he strode to the center of the stage. He spoke without using the microphone, but his voice carried clearly.

"Ladies and gentlemen, pack members and family, I have invited you here today for a number of reasons. As many of you already know, Lucas Santiago has been selected to take over the administration of Wolven." There was a smattering of applause for the honor, which Lucas acknowledged with a slight nod of his head. "He has voluntarily stepped down as Alpha of this pack. As is the case when any pack leader chooses to leave his post, the Second becomes Alpha."

All eyes followed Raphael as he stepped down from the stage and strode across the gym. When he reached the center of the floor he called out in a ringing voice that echoed through the room. "I claim the position of Alpha Male of the Boulder pack. Do any here challenge me for that right?" He turned, his gaze locking very deliberately with that of Martin Black. There was a long, breathless silence. Without bothering to look at anyone else in the room he continued. "Does *anyone* dispute my fitness to lead or question my judgments?"

A dark flush crawled up Martin's neck, and Cat could see the muscles of his jaws clench. But still he remained silent.

"Does anyone *challenge* me in my rule?"

He let the breathless silence drag on. No one moved. No one seemed to dare breathe.

"Good." He smiled. "There has been a *personal* challenge regarding mating issues. As it doesn't directly affect pack administration, we will *not* be dealing with it until the end of this meeting."

He walked back to the edge of the stage, but didn't climb up onto the dais. "Lucas Santiago has been a brilliant pack leader for decades. The pack has prospered under his leadership, and I am grateful for everything he has done for us."

Several people called out their assent to this. Raphael and Lucas both smiled.

"But every pack leader does things in his own way and makes the changes he feels are necessary and in the best interests of the pack.

"My first act as Alpha was to call for this meeting, to address discipline problems within the pack. My second, unfortunately, was to enforce the most sacred laws of our people that had been deliberately violated."

Raphael looked around the room, his eyes locking with those of many of the spectators. Always, they were the first to look away. Cat understood from her training that it was the custom among the pack members but there was more to it than that.

"I have heard that there are those who say that by 'turning' a human we would be 'doing them a favor.'" Raphael's bitterness was palpable. "Nothing could be further from the truth. Now I will show you why. For those of you who didn't know, your friend, your classmate, Candy Streeter, did *not* move away. She was murdered." He waited until the whispers and murmurs from the crowd had died down. "One tiny scratch from a friend, *doing her a favor*, and you're about to watch the result."

As he had been speaking, Peter—looking ashen and trembling—had quietly wheeled in a cart with a projector on it. He set it up while Raphael held everyone's attention. At Raphael's cue he dimmed the lights and hit the switch that lowered a large projection screen from the ceiling. Candy Streeter's first full moon came onto the screen. Her screams echoed off the cinder-block walls and lofty ceiling.

Cat sat rigidly in her seat, her back turned to the screen. She'd seen it before—lived through it in Raphael's mind. But she couldn't ignore Holly's sobs beside her.

She would *not* throw up. She *wouldn't*. But many others did, and not all of the screams and sobs were coming from the speakers or from Holly. When the tape finished and the lights came back on, not one member of the audience wasn't shaken.

Raphael climbed onto the stage. He stood, tall and commanding in front of the podium. "To change a human other than in self-defense is a capital crime. Yesterday, members of this pack deliberately attacked Cat Turner and Holly Sanchez, a human family member. Those who did it have been punished. But that does not change the fact that the next full moon may be Holly's last."

There were gasps of shock. All eyes shifted to the table where Holly and Cat sat. Under the table, Cat reached for her friend's cool, trembling hand and held it firmly. Holly was holding onto her control with teeth and toenails as she avoided the collective gaze of the pack on her. In the background Peter discreetly unplugged the AV equipment and removed the screen before wheeling the cart out of the gym.

"But the attempt they made was made possible by actions of two other, senior, pack members—both of whom should have known better." He gestured to the table where Betty and Tatya sat rigidly. "I have consulted with Wolven and the Chief Justice, and we find that Betty Perdue and Tatiana Santiago have gravely damaged Cat Turner and Holly Sanchez."

There were gasps throughout the room. Cat turned to stare at Raphael. She didn't remember much from those training books, but *that* she remembered. If you injured someone, she was entitled to claim damages commensurate with the injury—the ultimate eye for an eye. *Grave* damage meant that if she or Holly wanted it, Betty and Tatya would be killed.

"Holly Sanchez, do you wish to claim your damages from Betty Perdue and Tatiana Santiago?"

Holly's face moved from rage to pain to emotionless. But finally, after a long pause, she replied. "No."

"Cat Turner, do *you* wish to claim the damages you are due from Betty Perdue and Tatiana Santiago?"

What good would it do? Two more deaths in a string of other deaths? More people hurting as much as she did? She shook her head and closed her eyes for a moment. "No."

Cat opened her eyes and watched as Lucas let out the breath he had been holding. Betty and Tatya both sagged a little bit in their seats. It was obvious they'd believed she'd do it.

Many people would have. Charles's voice came clearly into her mind.

Raphael continued to speak. Cat could hear him in the background talking about Betty and Tatya being brought before the council on charges regarding a breach of medical ethics. But her mind was on her internal conversation with her godfather.

You sound as though you don't approve.

She could hear him sigh in her mind. It wasn't my choice to make. It was a merciful decision. I just hope you don't live to regret it.

The meeting seemed to stretch on forever. It wasn't boring. It was exhausting. Cat was completely drained in no time and her mind began to wander. She couldn't imagine how Raphael kept going.

Cat brought her wandering mind back to the present abruptly at the sound of Raphael saying her name.

"Cat Turner has purchased a section of land that has traditionally been used for pack hunting." There were audible growls at that point, and pack members began shifting restlessly in their seats. Cat could feel their hatred beating at her.

"Ms. Turner agreed to this purchase *after the pack had exercised its right of first refusal*." Raphael cast a glance at Tatya, who blushed and hung her head in obvious acknowledgment of her part in that refusal.

The crowd was still muttering, but they sounded marginally less aggressive.

Raphael turned back to the crowd and continued. "I have been informed that a petition will be made before the council for her to retain full possession of that property. In light of the attack on her, it is likely that the petition will be granted." He raised one hand to still their protests. "It is my *hope* that if this happens, Ms. Turner will negotiate with the pack regarding hunting rights."

Cat heard someone, she couldn't see who, shout out that they shouldn't *have* to negotiate. It was their land damn it! Let the cat go somewhere else. Another anonymous speaker questioned whether Raphael was *capable* of putting the pack interests before those of his *mate*.

There were more than a few gasps throughout the room at that bit of news, and Charles's expression grew murderous.

Just like that the cat—Cat snickered despite herself—was out of the bag. There was no keeping something from Jack if the whole pack knew. God alone knew what Jack would do about it. He'd do something, though. She was sure of it.

Raphael's face darkened with anger. His granite expression frightened Cat and he gestured toward the crowd. But before he could speak there was the thud of a body impacting against the gymnasium doors. The doors then slammed open with a bang. Three men stood framed in the doorway. Two wore traditional Arab garb; the third, an exquisitely tailored business suit.

Low growls erupted throughout the room, all of which were loftily ignored by the intruders, who strode arrogantly across the gymnasium, stopping only to give the briefest of bows to the Chief Justice, who stood center stage. Ivan was now a protective presence at Cat's back, and she was grateful for it. She didn't know who these intruders were, but she could sense they were dangerous.

Raphael dropped his shields. Suddenly she could hear his thoughts, sense what he was feeling. She felt both his anger at the betrayal of one of his people, and the wary mistrust he had for the intruders. *His name is Ahmad al-Narmer. He is the council representative for the snakes, a friend of Jack's, and a very old enemy of mine.*

She watched as Raphael's golden eyes scanned the crowd. Someone had betrayed him, invited his enemy to this very private meeting, and Raphael intended to find out who.

Nearly every face showed surprise and mistrust mingled with fear. Only Martin and Daphne Black appeared unmoved. They didn't even seem bothered by the fact that their son lay unconscious and very still in the gymnasium doorway.

Peter wouldn't support his father in this. He's loyal to Lucas, and to me. There was gratitude and pride in those words. Raphael knew it had to have been hard on Peter to make that choice. There was no doubt that for all their faults, he loved his parents. *Martin wanted the pack. He was trying to undercut Raphael's authority, make a move to take over the pack leadership.* Raphael could see the realization dawn in Lucas's eyes. *Ahmad would push for capital punishment for Michael's crimes. If Raphael refused he risked appearing weak before the pack. That combined with the pack's mistrust for Cat could trigger a riot or revolt.*

Cat, mind-speak to Betty. Have her go tend to Peter.

Right.

Cat did as he bid, and saw Betty discreetly leave her seat to climb down from the stage and head to the doorway.

"And to what do we owe this *honor,* Councilman?" Raphael's voice brought Cat's attention back to the main action. He didn't bother to hide his displeasure. She saw his thoughts. *This was his pack, his territory. Ahmad was a trespasser, an interloper. Councilman or no, it was for him to explain why he should not be killed outright. That he came with only two bodyguards—*

Three. Cat corrected him in his mind.

Are you sure?

He left one behind in the hall. It's in snake form. I heard him shift.

Raphael bared his teeth at the leader of the snakes. "Councilman, please bid your third guard to come join us. There's no need for him to be left out."

Ahmad's visage darkened, his eyes narrowing. After a long moment he gestured. A huge cobra slithered through the doorway, its scales making a soft hissing noise as it slid across the hardwood. Cat noticed that several people sitting on the first row of bleachers moved to higher ground as the snake passed by.

"So, Councilman. Why have you chosen to join us, and without even giving us the opportunity to prepare a suitable welcome?" Raphael was not growling. His words were perfectly polite, but there was a hint of sharpened steel beneath the velvet. "I am *surprised* you chose to omit the customary courtesies."

Ahmad tilted his head slightly. It was the traditional gesture of deference between equals, but he managed to make the movement somewhat ironic. When he spoke there was the slightest hint of amusement in his voice. "Apparently there has been a . . . *miscommunication*? My people made arrangements for this visit with your Second, Raphael. Or Lucas's Third. Under the circumstances I'm not sure how to refer to him." Ahmad turned a calm gaze to Martin, who looked as though he'd been forced to swallow something large and unpleasant. "I'm *astonished* that you weren't advised."

Even from this distance Cat smelled the black pepper of a lie, but far stronger was the orange scent of amusement. The snake was *enjoying* this.

"Martin Black," Raphael's voice rang through the clearing. "Come forth."

Cat watched as Peter's father stepped out of the crowd. He was a handsome man, tall and blond, with a square jaw and strong features. But Cat instinctively disliked him. It might be Raphael's impressions bleeding over on her, but she didn't think so. Something about the way he stood, the way his eyes were constantly scanning the crowd, made her distrust him. Everything about Peter was honest and open. His father was demonstrably not.

Raphael didn't give Martin a chance to explain. He gave him no chance at all. Before the man had even come to a stop there was a shimmer of magic. A huge black wolf leapt, attacking the other man with teeth and claws.

Blood sprayed through the air in a wide arc. Martin fell to the floor with Raphael riding him. He shifted in a shimmer of power. He was a large, traditionally marked wolf. But even though he was larger than Raphael he was struggling to fight back, to defend himself.

It was a mistake. She realized he had earned a harsh punishment for going behind the Alpha's back and for humiliating his pack leader in front of visiting dignitaries. Raphael was *expected* to do exactly what he was doing. His form began to glow blue with the power of his magic until it hurt her eyes to look at him. Cat felt a surge of heat. She and everyone else in the gymnasium watched in shocked silence as with only the power of his mind Raphael threw Martin's body more than twenty feet across the room to slam into the cinder-block wall. If he still breathed, Cat couldn't see it.

The room was utterly silent for a long moment. Then, one by one, every wolf in the building, including Raven, sank to his knees in acknowledgment of Raphael's authority until Lucas and Raphael were the only wolves still standing. Neither Ahmad nor his men had moved more than a finger's breadth, although their clothing had been liberally splattered with Martin's blood.

"MICHAEL SANTIAGO, COME forth." Raphael's voice was calm and clear. He was not the least bit winded.

Michael was still in human form. He wore faded blue jeans and a plain white T-shirt that stretched taut across his muscular chest. He belly-crawled in human form across the floor until he lay facedown at Raphael's feet.

Raphael didn't bother to look down for a long moment. Instead, his eyes were first for Ahmad, then Lucas. Cat could feel *something* pass between the eyes of the two wolves, but she couldn't comprehend it. Their communication was almost an emotional shorthand, the kind of nonverbal communication that only came from years, decades, of working closely together.

"One of the most solemn duties of the Alpha Male of a pack must enforce the laws of our people and dispense justice." Raphael gave a nod of his huge head to where Martin was just starting to stir.

He was healing. Damn.

"Michael Santiago, you broke both the human and the pack laws by drinking underage and driving drunk."

The crowd began to murmur. Tatya rose to her feet, her posture rigid with nerves.

"If you had been arrested by the human authorities, this would be a matter for Wolven. Luckily, you were not. Thus this is a matter for pack justice."

The crowd murmured more loudly. Cat saw Tatya's eyes narrow, her nostrils flaring as she tried to use her sense of smell to determine what Raphael was up to.

Michael lay utterly still, barely daring to breathe.

Raphael softened his voice, deliberately sounding less stern. "I've lost a woman I loved . . ." He gazed at Tatya for the benefit of the crowd, then nodded to Lucas, who gave his own nod in acknowledgment. "If I could have, I probably would've gotten drunk," he commented wryly.

A few members of the crowd laughed nervously.

"You do realize that what you did was incredibly stupid?"

"Yes, sir." Michael's voice was a whisper barely audible to even Sazi ears.

"And there is a price to pay. First, you *personally* will pay reparations to everyone you damaged that night. I understand from your father that it's quite an extensive list, but that you've already made a start."

All eyes went to Lucas, who nodded in acknowledgment.

"But, there are other things you've done as well—including deliberately vandalizing an automobile when you were stone cold sober." There was no warmth in Raphael's voice now. The silence was palpable, as nearly everyone in the gym held his breath.

"The cost of the damages would have moved the offense to a felony under the human laws, and the fact that you lost control to that level speaks of a serious problem. So, I offer you a choice. Once we've dispensed with the mating challenge you can either voluntarily go to an inpatient facility and undergo a minimum of six months' counseling at your or your family's expense." Raphael looked over to Ahmad whose eyebrows had risen high enough to disappear beneath his hair. Even in the open gym Raphael could scent the snake's surprise. "*Or* I will take the damages out of your hide." Raphael sighed. "Frankly, I'd rather not. I'm not sure you'd survive."

"I'll go." Michael turned his head to look at Cat. A look of intense pain crossed his face. "There's nothing here for me anymore."

Cat forced herself to keep her expression calm. Her emotions were in turmoil. She couldn't help feeling an odd combination of sympathy, regret, and frustrated anger at Michael's self-pity.

"Fine." Raphael's voice brought her back to the situation at hand. His voice was utterly unemotional as he continued. "Then all that remains is the challenge. Since we have both dated Cat, and we are both mated to her, we'll consider it mutually called. I would prefer to fight in wolf form. Do you object?"

"No."

"You may pick the format."

Michael risked a look up at Raphael. It was obvious he was surprised that Raphael was giving him the choice. "I choose a physical rather than magical, or all-out battle."

"Excellent. Change forms and we will begin."

Michael shifted without bothering to strip, leaping to the attack as his body was still reforming in hope of having the advantage of surprise.

Raphael felt a jarring impact as his body hit the polished hardwood floor. The boy was strong, heavy, and determined to do everything he could to make it a true challenge.

Raphael used his momentum to roll away from his attacker. He regained his feet in a blur of speed. He crouched, edging sideways, fangs bared as he looked for an opening in Mike's defenses. He was large and muscular, with traditional markings. His strength was obvious, but he was clumsy, and there was no subtlety to his fighting style. Every move was telegraphed in advance, giving Raphael plenty of time to move out of the way.

Raphael was not clumsy. He trained for years with Wolven to move with fluid efficiency born of experience and power. Not the slightest movement was wasted. He dashed in, ripping with his fangs, only to slide out of reach before Michael could close and use his heavier build to an advantage.

In the end there was no contest. Raphael closed the fight by grabbing Michael's neck ruff and throwing him on the ground hard enough that everyone heard his bones crack against the floor. Raphael dived forward, his jaw closing against Michael's throat too gently to draw blood, but firmly enough that the other man held utterly still.

"Do you submit?" The words were muffled by the thick fur and skin that filled Raphael's mouth.

"Yes."

Raphael loosed his grip, backing away from his fallen foe as he licked the blood from his fangs. "Michael Santiago, for your own good you have agreed to leave this territory. Arrangements have been made for you to go into intensive counseling to help you in dealing with the one-sided mating bond that you have formed. You will only be allowed to come back to Boulder for the Founder's Day celebrations and one other holiday of your choosing. Before each visit you will check with your psychiatrist and the Boulder pack administration so that appropriate arrangements can be made. Do you understand and accept these terms?"

It took three tries before Michael could roll over onto his belly and rise to his feet. His back legs were not working properly, as though sometime during the fight there'd been an injury to his spine. Even so, his voice taut with pain, he spoke clearly enough that his words carried through the crowd. "I do."

"I claim right to court Cat Turner exclusively for six months. Does anyone gainsay me?" His golden eyes locked with Ahmad's dark gaze. "Are you satisfied that justice has been served, Councilman?"

Ahmad smiled and let out a small chuckle. "I would say that you've handled it all remarkably neatly. Not a single misstep. I, and I speak personally and on behalf of the council, am *delighted* to offer congratulations to you on your triumph."

Raphael sensed the trap in the polished words. His golden eyes narrowed, and he had to fight not to snarl.

But the councilman continued, making sure that his words reached every ear in the room. "Am I to assume that in *this* at least, the customary rules will apply?"

Raphael started swearing inwardly. He could see Cat's confused expression, but he didn't dare take the time to share the information with her even mentally. His whole focus was on Ah-mad. When he spoke, his response was perfectly civil. "Of course." He gave a somewhat ironic bow to the council member and padded to the center of the gymnasium. Martin had made it to his feet with Daphne's help. Michael had dragged his injured body to stand with his parents at the edge of the stage.

"There are two more minor items that need to be dealt with." He licked some more of the blood from his lips. "First, Martin Black, while you have declined to challenge me in open court at a pack meeting as is proper, you have deliberately sought to undercut my authority, and have fostered seeds of dissension within my people. I won't tolerate it. You and your spouse have twenty-four hours to get out of my lands. Your sons can either stay or go at their pleasure. Peter Black remains welcome in this pack. But know this, if *you* ever set foot in my territory, for any reason, I will consider it a challenge to my authority and will act accordingly."

There were some gasps among the crowd, but more than a few grim nods.

Raphael continued. "Anyone——" His eyes settled on the cluster of Holly's sister, Jasmine, and her husband, Max Black, both of whom supported Martin—"who is not willing to submit to my rule, and my decisions as to what is good for this pack should join them in leaving. Because I will not allow *anyone* to put my people at risk."

He padded back to the stage and leapt up on it in a single, graceful bound. Turning, he faced the crowd. "And last, before we close, I want everyone to know that pack credit will no longer be accepted at Jake's Burger Joint. All existing accounts are to be paid *in full*, with cash or certified funds, by no later than three months from this date. Any cases of true hardship can be brought by petition to me personally, but know that they will *not* be looked on favorably." He glared at a few individuals in the crowd, who each hung his head in embarrassment.

Raphael announced that the meeting was ended. Cat waited at her seat as the spectators filed out of the gymnasium. Holly went over to join the few people who had approached the stage to offer Raphael congratulations on his promotion. Cat knew she should do the same, but she simply could not seem to gather enough energy to manage it.

"Cat." Cat turned at the sound of her name. Tatiana had left Michael's side and now stood on the opposite side of the table. She was beautiful in a black designer suit and pearls, her silver blonde hair worn loose so that it flowed across her shoulders. For the first time since Cat had met the woman she *didn't* smell of anger or jealousy. "I want to apologize to you, and thank you." She swallowed hard. "Betty made a mistake. She thought there was as signed release authorizing her to discuss the situation with me. I don't have that excuse."

Cat didn't answer. She wasn't sure what to say. She could only guess how hard it must be for this woman to swallow her pride and humiliate herself.

"I owe you my life, and the life of my son. I won't forget it." She turned and left before Cat could answer, walking over to where her husband was helping support her injured son. Cat watched her go. And when Lucas mouthed the words "Thank you" over the top of Tatya's head, Cat managed to give him a smile.

"Are you ready to go?" Ivan asked.

"God, yes. Get me out of here."

"Good. Raven is taking us out the back way. Just in case."

Chapter Twenty-six

WHEN THE HOTEL phone rang the next morning, Cat groaned and rolled over. *Go away!* Didn't whomever it was realize that she'd been up until almost two in the morning? She was *tired,* damn it!

The ringing stopped, for all of a minute. When it started up again Cat threw the covers off and, grumbling mightily, grabbed for the receiver.

"This better be good."

"And good morning to you, Cat." Ivan sounded awake, alert, and *damn it,* amused.

"Good morning is an oxymoron."

He laughed at the joke. "I have your birth certificate and the title for the automobile you requested. We will come with the limo to pick you up in a half hour."

"The movers aren't due at Ned's until one o'clock."

"If you truly *insist* on going to Boulder, it is better if we arrive early. It is always safer to do the unexpected."

"Fine, fine. I'll meet you downstairs at seven."

"Again, no. Wait in your room. Answer the door for no one but me, and use your nose. Voices can be duplicated much more easily than scents."

Cat wanted to argue, but she didn't. Ivan knew what he was doing. He'd been chief of security for Charles for as long as she could remember. Nor could she honestly claim it wasn't necessary. But she hated it. Just as she had hated the necessity of the endless self-defense classes her parents had insisted upon. She trusted his expertise. Eventually Cat would arrange it so that

Ned's property became a veritable fortress, with high, electrified fences, video and audio surveillance.

Until then, she needed to stay away from the pack as much as she could. It wouldn't be easy. There was still Holly's change and Ned's movers to deal with—and, of course, the courtship. Still, she'd do the best she could.

Truthfully, she was looking forward to starting the fake life. First thing tomorrow she was going to pack her things and get ready to leave the hotel. Once the stores opened she'd need to change her appearance and get a picture taken for Charles to give to the expert who would create her new driver's license. With a valid license she'd have everything she needed to set up a bank account and start applying for the corporate cleaning jobs. She'd need to learn how to switch the file Jack hid, as soon as she found it. Then, she needed to pick up used furniture, and set up her new apartment.

Once she had a place to work, she'd begin getting the materials to start the replacement file. In short, she had enough work to keep her busy for *days* without a single pack or romance-related crisis. The thought was positively refreshing. The bulk of today, however, would be spent up at Ned's. And while she hated to admit it, Cat was very glad that Ivan, Raphael, and Raven would all be there with her. There were too many enemies lying in wait for her. The constant, unrelenting pressure was pushing her very nearly to the limit. But she held on, stubbornly determined not to give up. Because she'd found something worth fighting for in Raphael. Between the two of them they *would* defeat Jack, *would* find a way to have a life together. She just had to be strong until then.

With that Cat got up and started the bath water running to get ready.

At exactly seven o'clock there was a knock on the door to the suite, followed by Ivan's voice saying, "It's me."

Cat started for the door and stopped just short. She called out, "Just a minute. Be right there." Then she stepped just to the side of the door and bent down to the crack, taking a deep sniff. Raphael was there, but she *heard* two people. Whoever was with him was wearing that damned cologne. There had to be a way to check the identity of the man at the door without putting her eye to the peephole and *inviting* a bullet to the brain.

Use your telepathy, Jack suggested.

She started and bumped her head against the wall. Damn it! I *really* wish you wouldn't do that.

He chuckled. Which is, in no small part, why I do. Besides, I have to see how your training is progressing. I want you to be a challenge. I *don't* want you to be *too* good.

W*hatever.*

Don't take that cavalier tone with me! I won't stand for it! Just as I won't stand for your coupling with Ramirez. I saw you last night. Saw Raphael's "challenge" with Inteque's puppy. *Believe me,* when *I* decide to fight him for you, *he* will be the one to crawl, and beg—before I kill him and feast on his entrails.

You don't want me. You want Fiona. *I am not Fiona.*

He paused and she heard his voice shift again, to the sane suaveness she'd heard on the television. No. If you were Fiona, you'd be safe from me. But *you* will never be safe, Cat. Not as long as I draw breath. Perhaps I need to remind you of that.

Jack withdrew from her thoughts then, but before he did she got an image of where he was. He had been standing on the porch of a log cabin, staring out at an expanse of desert as the sunrise painted the cloudless eastern horizon with shades of lavender and pink.

"Cat, are you all right?" Ivan's voice came through the door clearly, with just the right note of concern.

Cat sent a tendril of thought outward. Raphael and *Raven* were on the far side of the door. They'd left Ivan out at the car. Tricky. Very tricky.

I'm fine, Raven. Good morning, Raphael. Cat answered in both of their heads simultaneously. She'd never tried it before, but it seemed to work just fine. Sorry for the delay. Jack dropped by.

"What?" Raven's shout through the door was loud enough that Cat flinched in pain, since her face was still plastered against the wood.

She heard Raphael's reply to his son. "Jack's a telepath. He 'visits' Cat for fun."

She could hear Raven swearing under his breath as she grabbed her purse and the leather trench coat she'd bought to replace the ruined biker jacket. She paused briefly at the mirror. The black turtleneck and matching jeans emphasized her figure, but the color was harsh. She looked older, and more than a little strained. Then again, it'd been a rough couple of weeks. A little more makeup might help compensate, but the boys were waiting. So she opened the door and stepped out into the hallway.

This morning Raphael was dressed in faded blue jeans that clung to his legs like a second skin, the fabric worn and soft looking. He'd left the first three buttons of his blood-red cotton shirt undone, showing just a hint of tan, muscled chest. His denim jacket matched the jeans; its red plaid lining picking up the colors from the shirt as well.

She had to touch him, needed to bask in the warm scent of him, to feel the tingle of electricity between them. Last night had frightened her, more than she'd like to admit. Things could have gone so badly for him. As it was, she'd felt both his anger and his hurt at how very many of his people had no faith in him. He would fight for them, *die* for them if it came down to it. But somehow it wasn't enough. *He* wasn't enough. Raphael hid his pain well, beneath a hard exterior and jokes filled with black humor, but she'd seen what was behind the curtain. And while she'd take the hurt from him if she could, she didn't know how.

She went to him, putting her arms around his waist, laying her head on the warm skin of his exposed chest. She listened as his heart sped up, reveling in the scent of the emotions rising off of him. Yes, there was the musk of lust, but mingled with it was the scent of bread baking and cookie spices. Those were the scents of love. Even if she hadn't read about it, she would know. She needed this, needed *him*. She couldn't have stopped herself if she wanted to; and she *didn't* want to.

With that thought everything seemed to fall into place. She suddenly understood about Michael, and Fiona, and even, in some dim way, understood the root of Jack's madness. It was inexcusable, but it made *sense*.

Raven gave a discreet cough. Raphael laughed, leaning down to give her a quick kiss before saying, "We'd better get moving. Charles and the others are waiting."

Cat leaned back to look up into Raphael's eyes. "Uncle Chuck and *the others*?"

"The Chief Justice wanted to set up a secure meeting before he left town," Raven explained. "The limo is large enough, and private, and the drive should give us enough time for the discussions we need."

"Oh." Cat stepped away from Raphael, feeling the magic stretch between them, as though it was reluctant to let him go. "Wish I'd known. I'd have dressed better."

"You look fine." Raphael gave her a reassuring smile.

Raven led. Cat followed, with Raphael bringing up the rear. Both men stood guard in front of her in the elevator, causing the elderly couple who rode down with them no end of heart palpitations. Cat knew because she smelled it—*heard* it, loudly enough that it set her stomach growling, reminding her forcibly that she hadn't eaten in a *very* long time.

They passed through the lobby without event, stepping out from under the awning into the early morning sunshine. A gleaming black stretch limousine pulled to a stop in front of them. Yusef climbed from the driver's seat walking around the front of the vehicle to open the limo door as Cat stepped up to the car. She took a deep sniff and a quick look before climbing inside to join Lucas and Charles. Raphael and Raven followed her. Ivan was next. Cat was relieved when the car door slammed, because even a stretch limo could only hold so many powerful Sazi. The scents were almost overpowering, and Cat felt magical energy crawling painfully across her skin. Raphael had slid a pair of sunglasses on.

"Will Councilman al-Narmer be joining us?" Lucas asked politely.

"No." Charles didn't bother to hide his annoyance. "The councilman accomplished his mischief last night. He's on his way to stir up trouble elsewhere. Some days I truly wish he weren't such a *superb* councilman for his people."

"His people often wish the same." Lucas smiled, and Charles chuckled. Cat could see ages of history between Uncle Chuck and the Wolven chief pass in a look.

"Good morning, Cat." Charles was fully smiling now. Cat heard the motor of the car turn over, felt the vehicle shift as it started moving and Yusef pulled it into traffic.

"Cat, gentlemen, we're here regarding Jack Simpson. Jack killed Cat's family and turned her. He is insane. We all know he needs to be put down. The problem, of course, is Jack's 'insurance policy.' Cat and I have spoken at length after ensuring Jack was unable to read her thoughts I'm likewise shielding this conversation. She has convinced me that she has a workable plan for neutralizing that file."

Charles continued for some time.

Every question and comment was discussed at length. In the end, all agreed that, assuming the original file could be found, there was a good chance it would work.

"Raven, you are technically on extended leave. People would expect you to stay in Boulder because of your father. It is the perfect cover. While I dislike imposing on your rest, I see no way around it, and I expect the two of you to cooperate *completely* with each other."

Cat opened her mouth to protest. Charles silenced her with a gesture. "Cat, your life is in constant danger. I do *not* intend for this plan to fail in the event of your death. I trust my great-grandson implicitly. He is the absolute *best* we have. This mission will not, *must not* fail."

Great-grandson? But she thought that . . . "Fine," Cat agreed.

"The fewer people who know where your proof against Jack is hidden, the better," Charles continued. "But I do *insist* that you confide in at least one other person here other than Raphael. Again, in case of your death."

Other than Raphael?

I'm mated. If you die, I die. Remember?

No, she hadn't. She swallowed hard. When she answered Charles her voice sounded a little strangled. "All right."

"I have purchased an apartment complex in Denver at your request. I trust you can make a unit available for Raven's use?"

"I can."

"Very well. The two of you can get together after this meeting so that he can get the address and other information. Lucas and I will each provide Raven with our copy of the file to bring you when he moves in tomorrow. Raphael, as we discussed, I would ask that you put all of the evidence you have gathered against

Jack over the years at her disposal. Does anyone have anything else to add?"

Silence.

"Good. Ivan, would you be so kind as to pour me a drink? I'm parched."

Ivan poured drinks for everyone. As Cat sipped the burning liquor she let her mind wander, not bothering to take part in the light conversation going on around her. Everything seemed so unreal. Part of it was the lack of sleep. But more than that, she was almost shell-shocked from the repeated blows to her reality. Her mind was having trouble adjusting.

Penny for your thoughts. Raphael's voice slid gently into her mind.

Don't waste your money. I'm not sure I'm capable of coherent thought right now.

Not a morning person? he teased.

No. But it's more than that. Too much has happened in too short a time.

Life's like that. Bouts of insane activity sandwiched between long stretches of boredom. He reached across the seat to take her free hand in his. Have I mentioned I'm proud of you? I don't know anybody else who could have handled this as well as you have. I'd have gone completely insane long before now.

Are you sure I haven't? I *am* hearing voices in my head, she observed drily.

Raphael laughed, snorting his drink out his nose. He had to take a handkerchief from his pocket to wipe up the mess. He finished just as Yusef announced their arrival over the car speaker.

Cat said good-bye to her godfather, giving him a quick hug and kiss on the cheek. "Thanks for everything." I'm sorry I was such a bitch the other night.

It was nothing. Charles gave her a quick return squeeze. And I deserve every bit of it. But do me a favor. Get rid of the file so we can eliminate Jack. Then I won't have to try to justify the unconscionable.

I'll do my best, she promised mentally as she followed Ivan out of the vehicle. She closed the door and stood, watching as the limousine turned in the driveway and went back through the gate. She was sorry to see Charles go. He was one of the few remaining links she had to her past. Just knowing he was here was a comfort.

Cat's musings were cut short as Ivan took control of the situation. "Raven," the big Russian said. "You are familiar with the property?"

"Yes."

"Good. You will show me. We will plan the security. Raphael will guard the lovely Cat *inside* the cabin."

His tone brooked no argument. Not that he would've gotten any. Cat had been hoping to have a chance to talk to Raphael.

The "cabin" was actually a large A-frame house. A deck ran along three sides of the building, its weathered wood blending gently with the gray and tan stone of the huge stone fireplace that took up most of the north side of the building and pale gray siding. The second-floor balcony jutted out to protect the front entrance.

Cat reached into her purse to retrieve her key to the front door. "Have you ever been here before?"

"Nope." Raphael followed close at her back, like the trained bodyguard he was. "I've hunted on the land for years, but I never got to know Ned well enough to receive an invitation."

"It will need a little work, but it's really quite nice." She reached inside the doorway to switch on the overhead light.

RAPHAEL FOLLOWED HER inside. The entryway was relatively small, and made more crowded by a stack of half-packed boxes. There was a door to the immediate left that he assumed opened the coat closet. The staircase to the second floor was just inside the door as well.

Raphael took the three steps down to the right, walking into the great room. It was huge. The ceiling was open to the top of the peaked roof, with natural stained beams that held a pair of large wrought-iron chandeliers. The fireplace on the north wall was flanked by built-in bookshelves that rose twelve feet from the floor. The furniture was old, comfortable but battered, and the rugs that covered the slate floor were a little threadbare. But there was a solid oak entertainment center with a big-screen plasma television, and it was obvious the house itself was still solid and had an unmistakable rustic beauty.

But it was the west wall that was most spectacular. The entire rear wall of the house was made entirely of double-paned glass and offered an unobstructed view of the meadow and woods from both the living room and the kitchen. It was absolutely gorgeous, and a security nightmare. Raphael took the three steps back up and turned left. A short hallway led to a large bathroom on the left and a walk-in pantry to the right.

"*Very* nice."

"Can we go upstairs?" she asked, gesturing toward the spiral stairs.

"It's your house, sweetheart."

Cat grinned at him, showing the deep dimples he liked so much, but had so seldom seen. "It is, isn't it?" Cat almost skipped up the staircase with Raphael close behind.

"Hey, I *like* this." Raphael came up behind her in an open doorway and slid his arm around her waist, making her laugh. The master bath opened both to the upstairs hall and directly into the bedroom. A set of three steps led up to a tub built for two and air jets that made it double as a Jacuzzi. The wallpaper was a floral pattern with brightly colored butterflies. Drooping plants hung from the ceiling and the window ledge. Ned had left them without thought to their care. Cat rummaged in the cabinet under the sink until she found the watering can. Raphael watched her happily watering the plants before wandering through the door that led to the bedroom.

The master bed had been hand built of pine logs, the large dresser was of matching knotty pine. The room was a bit of a mess, but Cat didn't appear to mind. She stood in the middle of the floor, sunlight from the French doors playing with her hair. She tilted her head sideways, turning toward the windows. "I hear a car."

His light mood vanished. "Stay back." Raphael shoved Cat away from the glass opening and watched the car approach from the side. After a moment, he turned his head to where she stood. "It's okay. It's Holly. Although what the hell she's doing here I have no clue. She's supposed to be on duty at the Joint training Tatya."

"Training *Tatya*?"

Raphael sighed and unlocked the French doors. Sliding them open, he stepped onto the deck with Cat following right behind. "I demoted Tatya to omega for six months for the incident with Ned up at Wolf's Run. She's got to put in thirty hours a week at Jake's and tell every customer that there's no longer credit."

"You didn't announce *that* last night!"

"No. When Ahmad arrived I forgot all about it. But she starts today, and Holly was going to be the one to train her."

As Holly climbed from the vehicle, Cat smiled and waved happily from the deck. Raphael wondered if it was his imagination that led him to think his niece's answering smile was less enthusiastic than usual. On closer examination he noticed the sag of her shoulders and her chapped, red-rimmed eyes. He opened his mouth to say something, but Cat was quicker.

"What's wrong, Holly?" Cat asked. "What are you doing here?"

She stared up at the two of them, her expression miserable. "I didn't know where else to go."

"We'll be right down," Cat said.

The two of them hurried downstairs to open the front door. The minute she could, Cat pulled Holly into a tight hug.

Raphael could sense Cat's fury at her friend's tears. But by the time Holly was seated inside and had told them the story, Raphael had become just as *pissed*. A part of it was his own anger. A larger part was Cat's rage. It beat at him through the tightest shields he could erect. She was doing her absolute best to control her temper, and failing miserably.

"She is *not* joining you in your new life, Cat. It is too much of a risk."

Ivan had come to investigate the arrival of a visitor. He turned to address Holly. "I do not doubt your courage or your integrity. Both your cousin and your uncle have vouched for you. But each time Cat breaks cover there is more risk. You are an attack victim. You will *need* to be with your family the night of the full moon, need the strength of everyone connected to you in order to survive."

"Cat lived through her first change," Holly pointed out.

"And we have no idea *why*. I can't allow you to risk yourself so foolishly," Ivan responded.

"I'm not going back. I'm never speaking to any of them again."

"Holly!" Raphael protested.

Holly stood up, her eyes blazing, her stance more fierce than he'd ever seen it. The wolf was taking over, and she was letting it. "Goddamn it, Raphael! Dad *stole* my tuition money. He stole my *future!* He *knew* that I had to make the payment by Friday. He *could* have asked. But he didn't. His name was on the account so he just *took it* for a fucking *freezer* for the restaurant. He didn't even tell me. My *check bounced!* I could be arrested! That's a *felony,* and now that I'm Sazi, I'm subject to Wolven!"

"You are *not* going to be arrested, and you *are* going to college. I'll cover the costs." Cat's voice was cold enough to frost the windows.

"Cat!" It was Holly's turn to be shocked.

"Oh, don't look at me like that," Cat snapped. "It's not like I can't afford it."

Raven's voice was calm, but Raphael knew his son well. When he was annoyed he'd argue, even raise his voice. But it was when he grew quiet that he was at his most dangerous. "Actually, I'll be the one paying, but thank you Cat. It's very generous of you to offer. But this is a family matter. Dad doesn't dare get involved, but I can."

Raphael stood with his back to them, staring out the windows. He was only half listening to the argument. If Holly wanted to go to school, she'd go. It'd get paid for somehow. There was no question about that. And while he was furious with Jake, his heart ached for him, too. He *knew* Holly. She was just like her mother had been: gentle, quiet, patient to a fault—until you crossed that last, invisible line. Then it was over. Maria's father had crossed it when he forbade her marrying Jake. Now Jake had done it by taking the tuition money. There would be no going back. And no matter how dangerous it was for her to be with Cat, he'd rather that than have Holly out there alone. Cat was an attack victim. If Holly lived past Tuesday, Cat could help her deal with the inevitable physical and mental changes in a way no one else could.

"Raphael?" Ivan made the name a question. "It's your call."

Raphael didn't turn around. He just watched a hawk circling

above the meadow, "She can either go to school as Holly Sanchez or go undercover with Cat. Not both. It's too risky. Everyone knows they're friends. They'd just follow her back to Cat." The hawk dived, plummeting downward. When it rose again, a small furred form was clutched in its talons.

"Then I'll wait and go to school in the fall. Can you get me an identity, too?"

Ivan sighed. "I can." He shook his head, turning to Raphael. "Charles will not be pleased when he finds out."

"He's a seer." Raphael watched Ivan's movements in the reflection of the glass. "Chances are he already knows."

Ivan hung his head in defeat. Raphael could tell just how unhappy he was with this turn of events by the fact that just a trace of his original accent and speech patterns came through in his words. "Volves." He muttered. "With volves it is *always* something. Never is easy."

It was a complaint Raphael had heard from Ivan often when they'd worked together. Today, he couldn't honestly argue. This was just one more problem in an ever-growing pile.

The silence stretched on uncomfortably. Six people, and nobody was talking.

"How much longer until the movers arrive?" Holly finally asked just to break the tension.

"Four hours," Raven answered.

"So, are we supposed to pack or something?"

"Nope," Cat answered. "Ned paid the movers to do it."

"Oh. Right. Well, anybody want to watch a movie?" Holly asked.

Raphael laughed. He couldn't help it. Leave it to Holly to try to come up with a way to make them all more comfortable. He looked over at Raven, who had a wry grin on his face. The bigger man walked over to the entertainment center. "Why not?" Raven agreed. "Doesn't look like Ned's disconnected anything yet."

They argued about movies for a bit, finally settling on *Die Hard*. Raven and Holly drove down to Wolf's Run to get them all beer and food for lunch. When the movers arrived everyone was in a better mood and was milling about the house or out onto the deck to stay out of the way. Raven and Ivan were teasing

Raphael about shooting, each of the three claiming to be the best shot until they finally agreed to settle the score for certain at the shooting range, with the loser buying dinner.

Then Holly's sister Jasmine drove up her SUV raising a cloud of gravel dust as she slammed on the brakes and skidded to a stop.

"Holly Sanchez, you get in this car right now!" Jasmine shouted at her sister through the open window. "How *dare* you just walk out and leave Dad alone at the restaurant just before a full moon!"

Several of the movers had stopped and were staring. Jasmine didn't even notice.

"Jasmine." Raven stood, casting a meaningful look at the non-Sazi, which his cousin blithely ignored. The movers, however, went immediately back to work, very deliberately ignoring the brewing argument. But the antifreeze smell of their curiosity didn't dissipate.

"Get *in* the car, Holly!"

Holly rose slowly, but rather than walk to the vehicle, she followed one of the uniformed humans into the house.

"Holly Marie Sanchez!" Jasmine shrieked her sister's name at the top of her lungs, her voice shrill enough to do a raptor proud. Throwing open the SUV door she leapt out, then slammed it hard enough to rock the vehicle. She started to storm after Holly but Raphael was just, suddenly, in her path.

"Stop right there," he ordered. When she tried to brush past him, he used his magic, first to hold her in place and then, slowly, to adjust her posture to a more natural position. Her eyes blazed with fury and defiance, but she could *not* move.

"This place is crawling with humans." Raphael kept his voice pleasant and low enough that none of the "civilians" would hear. "And you have very nearly said more than you should." A flicker of fear flashed through her dark eyes. "These past few weeks should have taught you—I will not have you risking all of us with your temper. The fight between your sister and your father is *none of your business*. They'll work it out, or they won't." He loosened his control, intending to let her walk to the car. Instead, she tried to push past him, forcing him to clamp down his control again.

"I need to talk to her." Jasmine forced the words out through rigid lips.

"No," Raphael answered. "You don't." He tried a different tack. "Now's not the time. She's too angry. If you push this now, you'll just drive her further away."

He saw tears sparkle in her eyes. "But . . . Daddy was *crying*."

Raphael's heart ached for his brother, but it didn't change a thing. "Now is *not* the time," he repeated. "Don't make things worse than they already are." Once again he loosened his control. This time she didn't try anything.

"He won't tell me what happened."

"No. He wouldn't."

"You know? What was it? What did she do? It's that damned cat, isn't it!" She turned, glaring daggers at Cat. Her body tensed. This time Raphael stopped her with a hand on her sleeve.

"It has nothing to do with Cat. It's between your father and Holly, and it's none of your business."

"*You're* only saying that because you're mated to her. It's why you keep choosing her over your own people. Well, alpha or not, the pack's not going to put up with that for long. You'll have to choose. You can't have her and the pack both. They won't stand for it." Jasmine's normally pretty face was twisted and ugly with rage.

Raphael's expression hardened. "Leave. Now." He released her arm. "Before I do something we'll both regret."

"Fine," she spat the words at him. "I'll go. But I'm right about this. Just wait. You'll see."

Chapter Twenty-seven

RAPHAEL SHOOK HIS head. He'd been staring out the newly repaired window of his pack office, watching the world go by. If he lived to be as old as the chief justice he would *never* understand human nature. Tatya was a prime example. She was proud, stubborn, and frequently difficult—but when he'd stopped by the restaurant this morning for coffee she'd actually seemed to be *enjoying* working at Jake's. Of course, this was only the first day. The novelty would no doubt wear thin in a few weeks.

Then, of course, there was Cat's Aunt Violet. The movers had still been loading up furniture when Cat's cell phone had rung. It was Violet, and Ned, calling to make sure that the movers had arrived and to have Cat "witness" their wedding at the Little White Wedding Chapel in Vegas—with Elvis and Celine Dion impersonators there to sign the license as witnesses. At the end of the five-minute ceremony Elvis and Celine had, as a wedding present for the happy couple, serenaded Cat with a spirited (and off-key) rendition of "Happy Birthday" in honor of her upcoming birthday.

Raphael grinned at the memory. The incident had been completely bizarre. But, oddly, it had been the perfect antidote to Jasmine's bitchiness so that everyone in the house had spent the rest of the afternoon snickering at the odd moment. Even Holly had cheered up a little.

The grin faded abruptly. The rift between Holly and the rest of the family was a painful problem. He wished there was something he could do. There just wasn't. Given time, things might settle down. But none of Jake's older girls were known for their patience. They'd try to force the issue, and make things worse in the process.

A knock on the office door distracted him from his musings. "Come on in."

Peter appeared in the doorway. He kept his head down, his posture submissive. Raphael looked at the boy carefully. He still didn't look entirely *well*. Then again, he'd taken a fair beating along with a pair of venomous snakebites. Had it not been for Betty, he'd probably be dead, despite his own healing abilities.

"Good morning, Peter. What can I do for you?"

"I have a problem, Alpha." Peter spoke so softly it was difficult for Raphael to hear.

"Come in, have a seat. We'll talk about it." Raphael walked over to the desk, taking his seat. Peter pulled the door closed behind him. He almost collapsed into the chair across from Raphael.

"So, what's this problem, and what can I do to help?" Raphael asked the question, even though he was fairly certain he knew the answer. Martin's deadline for leaving town was fast approaching, and it left Peter with a very difficult decision to make.

Peter looked up for the first time, his eyes wide with the same surprise that rose off of him in a mist.

Raphael gave a rueful grin. "Despite my reputation to the contrary, I'm not a *total* asshole."

Peter gave a very weak version of his usual stunning smile. "It's my dad," he sighed. "After the other night, we got into a big fight. He told me I had to choose, that I couldn't be 'your man' and 'his son.' "

Raphael sighed. He had expected it, but it was still hard to hear. "I'm sorry, Peter. You shouldn't be forced to make those kinds of choices."

"It's not your fault." The boy answered sadly. "It's my dad. He's always been this way. I love him, but—"

"But you don't agree with him."

"No." He raised his chin defiantly, his jaw set in a stubborn line. When he spoke, his voice was firm. "No, I don't. So I left. He threw all my stuff out at the curb in the mud."

He shook his head, both weary and angry. There wasn't

anything to say. It was a petty, vindictive thing to do, and completely in character for Martin Black.

"The thing is, I don't have anywhere to stay. I'd go to the Santiagos', but with Mike gone . . . I don't have a job. I don't have a place. Most of my stuff is trashed." Hopelessness rose from Peter's skin in a slow mist.

"All right. This is what we're going to do," Raphael began, his tone businesslike. He reached into the desk drawer and retrieved a pen and notepad. With sure strokes he scrawled a note to Eddie Malone. Tearing the sheet from the pad, he folded it in half and handed it across the desk to Peter. "Take this to the towing company. I'm short a dispatcher for the next few months. You can fill in. If you work out, we'll move you into another position once Mona gets back from her maternity leave." Raphael pulled his checkbook from the back pocket of his jeans. "I'm going to give you an advance on your salary, so that you can get yourself a room at one of the extended-stay hotels and replace some of your stuff. You can pay me back over time."

Peter took the check Raphael extended, his eyes widening when he saw the amount.

"You'll be paying it back. Remember."

"Yes, *sir.*" Pete nodded firmly, his jaw setting stubbornly. "I will."

"Now get out of here, and get to work."

"Yes, sir."

Raphael waited until Peter had his hand on the doorknob before speaking again. "Pete."

"Yes, Alpha?"

"I appreciate your support."

Peter paused, obviously searching for the right words. When he spoke, they were carefully chosen. "When I realized I was alphic, and going to be powerful, I started watching—you, Lucas, my dad. You can be hard, and really tough on people, but you've always been fair. You've never just picked on somebody weaker because you could. Neither has Mr. Santiago. And I decided *that's* the kind of Alpha I want to be."

He ducked through the door before Raphael could respond. Just as well, because he was actually speechless. Over the years he'd tried to do his absolute best by the pack and its members, but his efforts were more often than not greeted with anger and resentment. Hearing Peter say what he had meant more to Raphael than even he would've expected.

Unfortunately, Peter appeared to be in the minority. Raphael ran a hand through his hair in a gesture of frustration. Jasmine's words yesterday had hurt him badly. Honesty compelled him to admit that he wouldn't have been nearly so bothered if, in his heart, he didn't believe it was true. Despite her best efforts, Cat *wasn't* fitting in and it was obvious that most of the wolves had no intention of accepting her on any terms.

Raphael slammed his hands palm down on the desktop. If he sat here, in this office, he was just going to brood about things he had no control over. He needed a break! Raphael reached for the intercom button. "Sally, I'm going to the pistol range. If anybody needs me urgently, they can reach me on my cell phone."

Betty appeared at the door while he was retrieving three of his guns from the hidden safe in his office. Her attire was completely businesslike, with crisp navy blue wool dress slacks and a cobalt blue silk blouse with a high, scarflike neck. Her expression ruined the effect. She seemed hopeful, and more than a little nervous. "Sally told me that you were going shooting?" The lilt in her voice made it a question. While she kept her eyes downcast as was proper, he could scent her eagerness and frustration before both scents were whisked into the ventilation system.

"Yes." He gave her a rueful grin. "I'm supposed to compete with Ivan and Raven at the range a couple of days from now, and unless I get some practice in, they'll clean my clock."

"Is there any chance you'd let me tag along?" Betty asked. "You did promise me a day at the range if we survived Cat's first change."

Raphael had forgotten all about that. Even if he'd remembered, he wouldn't have expected her to take him up on the offer. The two of them had worked together smoothly for years, but the relationship had never been close enough to qualify as a friendship. Still, there was no mistaking her earnestness now.

"I don't see why not. Do you need to borrow a weapon, or do you have one of your own?"

"Mine's at the house." She stepped into the office, walking

across the room to where he stood. She stared admiringly at the safe. "I never even knew this was here." She shook her head. "I mean, I figured it was likely, I know Lucas had one built into his office, but I couldn't figure out where you'd put it in this room. Very nice." She stepped closer, until she could see the contents. "Oh, my! I think there may be developing countries with smaller arsenals."

Raphael laughed. "It's not that bad!"

Betty arched an eyebrow. "It looks like something out of a Bond movie." She shook her head. "I'm not even sure I *want* to know what some of these are."

Raphael grinned, but didn't enlighten her. There *were* some nice weapons tucked away here. Most were from his days as an agent, and while he probably *should* have turned them over to Fiona when he'd "retired," nobody had asked him to, and he hadn't volunteered. Each piece—from the matching silver boot knives, to the sniper rifle and antique "Tommy" gun he'd inherited from his father—was in perfect working condition. There was a shelf with stacks of regular and silver ammunition as well, neatly divided by make and model. There was even a grenade launcher.

"A little something for every occasion," Raphael joked.

"And such *interesting* occasions, no doubt."

"Let's see, what would be the best fit for you?" Raphael glanced at her hands. They were surprisingly small for a woman her size, blunt fingered, with short, neatly trimmed nails. He debated with himself, trying to figure which of his guns would best fit her grip. She was strong enough that he didn't need to worry about kick or caliber.

He finally decided on the Browning. He took it and the holster down from its perch on the wall and handed it over to Betty. His eyes strayed back to the boot knives. He'd worn them every day of his life as a Wolven agent and for most of the first months thereafter. He vividly remembered hanging them up. It had felt as if a part of him died. But it was overkill to go armed in a pack where nothing ever happened that couldn't be handled by mere teeth and claws, and it made the lesser pack members nervous.

Raphael ran his finger over the nearest sheath, pulling it down from the wall to slide out the blade, checking the edge, checking for tarnish. The scent of burning flesh filled the enclosed space.

"You still miss it, don't you?" Betty spoke softly, as though she were almost afraid of how he'd react.

"Miss what?" Raphael looked over at her, his expression deliberately bland.

"The excitement, the *challenge*. It's not much of a life for you here. The pack practically runs itself most of the time."

"Not so much lately," Raphael answered drily.

"No." She agreed, giving him a sad smile. "But that's a different kind of challenge. Don't take this wrong, Raphael, but you're not exactly a born administrator."

His bark of laughter was more than a little harsh. Leave it to the good shrink to tell him an unpalatable truth. "Shows, does it?"

"Not most of the time. You hide it well, and you work hard at it, and do well enough that nobody really notices." She set a gentle hand on his right arm. "But you were forced to settle down; forced to come back here. It wasn't your choice. It's only reasonable that you'd have a certain level of resentment."

Raphael gave her a cold, hard look. "Is there a point to this, Doctor?"

"Just that I'm glad you're back."

CAT ROLLED OUT of bed at the first hint of dawn, dressing quietly so as not to wake Holly. She tiptoed into the living room area and booted up the laptop computer provided with the room. With the pressing of a few buttons she was online and down to business—sending and answering e-mails, ordering supplies, and setting up a basic Web site for the dummy corporation that would send the donation e-mail to Jack's campaign office with the attached spyware.

By eight o'clock her stomach was growling and she was desperate for coffee, so she took a break to call room service and use the bathroom. Fortified and fully caffeinated, she finished the Web site in short order. She had to admit, it looked good. And hell, there really *was* going to be a "Citizens for Wilderness" corporation. Maybe when this was all over she actually *would* fund the charity. Her father had always supported giving back to the community. Her mother would have appreciated the irony. Cat stood, stretching to untie muscles that had clenched into knots from working so long at a poorly designed workstation.

After a long hot shower, she dressed in distressed jeans and a white cotton T-shirt with the same gold jewelry she'd worn the other night. She chose a tomato-red blazer to dress the outfit up further and ward off any chill. She combed out her hair, leaving it loose. She chose understated makeup and black dress flats. She would, after all, be meeting with attorneys, and while it probably shouldn't matter how she looked, she'd learned from watching her mother that it did. If you dressed well, you got better service. It was that simple.

She was ready and waiting when Raven arrived. It was his job to bodyguard her today while she shopped and took care of all of the various errands that were needed to set the plan into motion. Ivan had told her last night that he wouldn't be able to come to the hotel until sometime late in the afternoon. He would be busy meeting with the construction manager until then.

Holly was still snoring peacefully in the other room when Raven tapped on the suite door. Cat checked mentally to be sure it was him before opening the door. She put a finger to her lips in a shushing gesture, grabbed her purse, and stepped out into the hallway. She hung the plastic "Do Not Disturb" sign on the doorknob.

Raven was wearing a navy polo shirt over khaki trousers, his long black hair pulled into a tight braid that hung down his back, almost invisible against the dark leather of the jacket he wore to hide his shoulder rig.

"Holly sleeping?" Raven asked. Cat nodded. His brown eyes darkened almost to black, and Cat could smell the muted combination of anger and determination, but he changed the subject. "So, what's on the agenda?" he asked as he pressed the button to summon the elevator. The bell rang immediately, the polished brass doors sliding open to reveal it was empty. Cat stepped inside first, pressing the button for the lobby.

"The post office, the hairdresser, several clothing stores, and a meeting with the attorney at ten thirty."

Raven's eyes widened. "You actually expect to get all of that done before noon?"

"Want to make a bet?" Cat teased.

"Fine." He agreed. "Loser buys lunch, *winner* picks where."

"Done," Cat agreed as the elevator slid to a halt, the bell chiming their arrival.

They walked through a lobby bustling with activity. Even though it was days until Thanksgiving, members of the hotel staff were busy festooning the entryway with holiday lights as Bing Crosby's "White Christmas" played from speakers discreetly hidden around the room.

Cat was familiar with the area from visits to Denver with her parents. Several of the office buildings had bank branches and amenities such as convenience stores, restaurants, and boutiques. In fact, the hair salon she planned to visit was tucked into the basement level of the Republic Plaza building, and the bank branch and the attorney had offices there as well. A shuttle stop for the Sixteenth Street pedestrian mall was located at the edge of a small plaza behind the building. The buses were free, and ran the entire length of downtown, stopping at nearly every corner. It was probably a security nightmare, but she honestly wasn't that worried. The pack was up in Boulder, and wouldn't make a move in public anyway. Jack . . . well, Jack wasn't going to be using a sniper gun; he wanted the visceral satisfaction of using teeth and claws. Abduction might be an issue—but that was what Raven was here for, and she knew for a fact that he and Ivan were the best at what they did. Charles wouldn't have left them in charge if they weren't. She squared her shoulders, her jaw thrusting stubbornly forward. Living in constant fear wasn't *living* at all to her mind. She'd be careful, but only up to a point.

As soon as she pushed her way through the revolving door of the Plaza building every sense was assaulted. The hotel might just be getting its decorations up, but it was obvious that the staff at Republic Plaza had gotten a jump on the season. Christmas was everywhere, from the pine garlands festooned with fake snow to the towering tree that soared to the top of the three-story atrium, its decorations ranging from full-sized sleds to glitter-covered ornaments the size of beach balls. Carolers dressed in Victorian costumes stood in a semicircle next to a piano, their songs echoing off the forest-green marble walls. Fake

Christmas packages stood in stacks as high as she was tall in various corners, their wrapping reflecting colors onto the white marble floor.

Cat gestured away from the bank entrance, toward the stairs leading to the basement. "The food court is downstairs; I want to pick up another cup of coffee."

"Do you *live* on that stuff?" Raven teased her as he descended, passing businessmen and women in traditional business suits, and a UPS deliveryman in his crisp brown uniform.

"Sometimes. It's been worse since Violet tried to force me to give it up." She gave him a sheepish look. "I think I'm a little contrary."

"Then you should be the perfect match for my father." Raven laughed.

Cat followed him past the lower level elevators toward the convenience store. The layout of stores had changed slightly since Cat's last visit. A new Pak-'n-Ship shop had taken over the space right by the glass doors leading to the food court.

"Oh, stop here."

He did as she bid, following her through the doorway up to the gleaming white counter. An older man in a striped uniform shirt stood behind a short counter. Behind him was a display of boxes, bubble wrap, tape dispensers, and various other sundries, with computer printed labels indicating their price. The left wall was covered with posters with shipping rates for the various carriers. The right was taken up by row after row of brushed steel post office boxes.

"Can I help you?" The man asked.

"Please." Cat smiled. "Do you have change-of-address forms? And how much do you charge for a postal box?"

"Yes, we do." He handed her a printed packet with the U.S. Postal Service emblem, and gestured to a poster that listed the various box sizes and rates.

"Good!" Cat smiled. "I'll take the largest size. Do you have a pen?"

Five minutes later she had completed the paperwork for her and Violet's mail to be delivered to the new box. She slid the key into the front pocket of her jeans along with the receipt with the address information. Thanking the man behind the counter she hurried off to the gourmet coffee shop with Raven two steps behind, shaking his head with amusement.

At eleven forty-five they were escorted to their table at Max's Steakhouse and Raven verbally conceded his defeat. "I have to admit I'm impressed. I can't even *imagine* what my father's going to say."

"It *is* a little striking, isn't it?" Cat said with a grin. She turned her head, listening to the soft tinkle of the row of golden hoops that now decorated her ear.

"That's one word for it."

"Don't be a spoilsport," she scolded him. "It changes my entire look." Cat turned to catch a glimpse of herself in the reflection of the glass of a nearby picture frame. Her long, blonde hair had been shorn until it was only a half-inch long all over her head, the top spiked with gel so that it stood up. Small glasses with thick dark frames and lightly tinted lenses perched on a nose that was pierced with a garnet stud. She'd traded her more conservative clothing for oversized black jeans with wide legs, a wide leather belt with steel spikes, and a T-shirt emblazoned with "I do what the voices in my head tell me to do." It had just been too perfect to resist. Her "biker style" leather jacket was adorned with snaps, zippers, and a pair of perfectly functional handcuffs. It was a testament to the quality of the service that no one in the restaurant had so much as blinked an eye.

"You do realize," Raven spoke softly so that his voice would only be audible to her, "that when you change there's a very good chance your appearance will revert back and you'll have to do this whole thing all over again."

"Just the hair and the piercings," Cat contradicted. "The clothing and makeup won't be affected. And you have to admit, *nobody* is going to recognize me. Cat Turner wouldn't be caught *dead* in this outfit."

The waiter reappeared, and Raven chose their wine, waiting to speak until the bread basket had been delivered and their water goblets filled.

"Most Sazi use their noses more than their eyes."

"True," she agreed, "but I don't plan to be where they'll look for me."

Raven sighed. "I wish it were that easy." He took a roll from the basket and used a knife to smear it with whipped butter from the china dish the waiter had left.

"Why *wouldn't* it be?"

"Because Councilman al-Narmer insisted on the *customary* rules of courtship."

Cat's stomach muscles clenched with nerves. Raven's tone of voice and scent were a nasty combination of both worry and anger.

"And what are the *customary* rules?"

"You and my father will have to go out together, publicly, in front of pack witnesses, at least three times per week until the courtship is over."

"I see." Cat was annoyed. *This* was a complication she didn't need. Every time she broke cover it increased her risk. She drummed her fingers irritably against the linen tablecloth. "What if I accept him?"

Raven choked on the bite of bread he'd taken. He coughed and hacked a bit before grabbing the water goblet to wash the crumbs down. "Excuse me?"

"If I accept Raphael the courtship is over right?"

"Cat—"

"Right?"

"You can't do that. If you accept him, for him it's permanent. He's trapped."

"In case you haven't noticed," Cat said bitterly, "we're already trapped. Those books you guys gave me go on and on about the wonders of 'mating.' But the fact is, it *is* permanent. If I die, he dies."

Chapter Twenty-eight

"WHAT'S THIS?" RAPHAEL gestured to the rope-handled paper bag with the logo of a large independent bookstore imprinted on it that Betty was handing over to him. At her request the two of them had stopped by her office. This was apparently why.

"It's an apology gift for Cat. I didn't get a chance to talk to her the other night, and I wouldn't blame her if she never speaks to me again." Betty shook her head sadly. Raphael scented her resigned sorrow and guilt before the smells were swept away by the ventilation system. "But I spoke with Nana, our seer, and she told me about something that they used back when she was working with Fiona's sister, Aspen Monier, to get control of her gifts."

"Didn't work very well, did it?" Raphael took the bag. He reached in, pulling out one of three books on yoga.

"Actually it *did*." Betty shrugged her shoulders. "Apparently what we've seen is the new and improved model."

Raphael shuddered. He'd always liked Aspen but he had to admit she scared him. Her gifts of foresight and hindsight were immensely powerful. Her visions were vivid enough that they frequently left her adrift, not knowing *when* she was. How often had he heard her ask, "What day is it?" then, "What year?" Still, she was one of the few people who had never once blamed him for what had happened with Fiona, even though she'd taken great pains to claim damages for her twin against their younger sibling in a manner that left permanent scars, both mentally and physically. Bobcats might be *small* animals, but you did not tangle with one lightly. "That's just terrifying."

Betty nodded her agreement. "Anyway, I wanted to make some gesture to show just how sorry I am about what happened. I'll never truly be able to make it up to the two of you. I know that. But . . ." Betty turned away, blinking. Raphael started to pretend not to see her crying since she was obviously trying not to, but then thought better of it.

"It's all right." He patted her awkwardly on the back with his free hand. "It was an honest mistake. Everyone signs the damned release. The only reason I didn't is that Tatya's only got midlevel security clearance. People were bound to find out sooner or later."

"Later would've been better." Betty reached across the desk to grab a box of tissues. Pulling one from the box, she blew her nose noisily.

"Spilt milk and broken teacups," Raphael said firmly.

"Excuse me?"

"It's what my foster mom used to say. 'No use crying over spilt milk or broken teacups. Just clean up the mess and move on.' "

"I can just hear Albina saying that! It sounds exactly like her." Betty chuckled as she patted her eyes dry with a clean tissue.

"Is this everything you needed?" Raphael changed the subject. He didn't want to think too hard about his family right now. It just reminded him of Jake and Holly. "I'd really like to get going."

At Betty's nod he turned toward the door, only to jump aside as Sally burst into the room.

"Alphas, I think we have a problem . . ."

CAT, YOU CAN'T go back to the hotel. Cat forced herself to keep a neutral expression on her face despite her shock at the sound of Raphael's voice in her head. She even managed not to drop her fork onto the plate from the surprise.

Why not?

The press have found out where you're staying. There are pictures all over the Internet. They're from the security camera at the hotel. They're in black and white, and blurry, but there's no mistaking it's you.

Hang on a sec. Cat concentrated, bringing Raven into the mix and catching him up on what Raphael had told her. He was still swearing internally when she connected the three of them in a mental conference call.

What am I wearing in the pictures?

It's the outfit from yesterday, and the date is at the bottom of the camera frame. He stared at the computer screen over Sally's shoulder. Cat knew because suddenly she was seeing the screen, too—through his eyes. It was a new experience and as unnerving as it was useful.

How are you doing that? Raven asked.

I don't know.

Doing what?

Cat's making it so we can see the screen along with you, Raven explained. I didn't know that was possible.

Neither did I.

Cat wasn't paying much attention to their conversation. She stared at the screen, lost in thought. Somebody obviously had a source at the hotel, which meant that they would find out what she was wearing this morning when she left, even trace her tracks if they tried hard enough. *That* would completely blow her new disguise. Unless . . .

I have to go back.

What? the two men chorused.

I have to let them see me now, in the same outfit I wore this morning, looking exactly like Cat Turner with a bunch of packages. That way they'll think I was just out shopping and not follow up too closely.

It's a helluva risk, Raphael grumbled.

I don't like it any better than you do. Cat's mental voice was firm, with more than a hint of annoyance. But I *don't* want them finding out about my trip to the attorney. I'll give up the disguise if I have to, but Jack and his people can't find out about the corporation I'm setting up. It'd ruin everything.

Raphael couldn't keep the excitement out of his voice. You sound like you have a plan.

Yes, I do. Raphael, do you remember the Cherry Creek Mall?

Yes.

Cat started to think fast. This could work, if she was very careful. It has a pair of attached parking garages. The one on the east side of the building has an entrance directly into Jordan's Department Store.

I know.

Can you be outside that door in a car with the engine running in an hour?

Make it two.

Fine. I'll see you there in two hours.

Cat cut the connection, finding herself abruptly back in her own body. It was almost shocking to be looking out of her own eyes into the busy restaurant. Raven had raised his hand in a signal to the waiter, who hurried over.

"We'll have our check please."

"Of course, sir."

"I'll meet you outside," Cat announced. "I need to go powder my nose."

Raven looked at her through narrowed eyes. She could tell from his expression that he was trying to speak mind-to-mind to her, but didn't have the talent. She wasn't going to help him, either. She knew she was being rude and high-handed, but she was simply too furious to be anything else. She'd been so careful, checking into the hotel under a pseudonym, explaining the need for secrecy to the manager. It hadn't done a bit of good. Like it or loathe it, the press was an issue in her life again and the timing couldn't have been worse.

Cat scooted her chair away from the table and reached down to grab the plastic bag containing her purse and the clothes she'd left the hotel in this morning. She stood, and moving swiftly she made her way through the crowded restaurant until she had reached the dimly lit hallway leading to the restrooms. She pushed the door open and found herself alone in an elegantly appointed waiting room with thick Persian rugs on the floor and comfortable chairs. An open arch led into a tiled area with the sinks and individual stalls that had walls and slatted wooden doors that reached to the floor.

Cat dropped the plastic bag onto the floor, pulling the door closed and sliding the bolt closed. With swift movements she stripped the glasses from her face and removed the various jewelry, sliding them into one of the pockets of her leather jacket and zipping it closed so they wouldn't be lost. She pulled off the jacket first, folding it neatly and placing it on the floor. The jeans, T-shirt, and shoes followed in rapid succession. Finally she removed the delicate lace undergarments she'd been wearing underneath. She took a careful step backward, getting as far from the clothing as she could. The stall was sized for the handicapped, and bigger than most, but it was still going to be very cramped in here when she changed to cat form, and she didn't want to damage or incinerate anything with her magic.

Cat concentrated, calling her beast forth. It was getting easier every time she did this, and less physically painful, but it was still disorienting. She was fairly certain she'd never really get completely used to it.

She stayed in cat form only for a moment, then shifted again, so that she stood, naked, her hair long once again. She pulled on Catherine Turner's clothes and began preparing herself mentally to *be* Catherine. Not Cat—who was Raphael's lover and Holly's friend. But Catherine Turner, computer geek, victim of the paparazzi. The change in mindset was *hard*. So much had changed in the past few weeks. *She* had changed, far more than she'd even realized. It occurred to her that *Catherine* had always been a victim in one way or another. It showed in the way she dressed, the way she moved. It was what had made her so vulnerable to peer pressure, and made Brad so very sure she'd welcome him back with open arms.

Suddenly so many things made sense—but she simply *did not* have time to think about it. Raven was waiting impatiently outside, and somebody was bound to come into the bathroom sooner or later. But it was definitely something she was going to have to think long and hard about when she had the time.

She pulled on her clothes swiftly. The blue jeans and white tee were all right, but the jacket was distinctly worse for wear, heavily wrinkled from being folded and stuffed into the bag.

There was nothing she could do about it, so she pulled it on. Next she took the heavy gold jewelry from out of the clutch she'd been carrying this morning and put it on before sliding back into her shoes. She grabbed the clothing from her disguise and stuffed it into the bag. Taking a deep, steadying breath, she slid open the lock and stepped back into her old life.

Chapter Twenty-nine

RAPHAEL CHECKED HIS watch for the twentieth time. He was in the Jeep, in a parking spot not far from the entrance where, in five minutes' time, Cat was due to come out the doors. One level down, in a spot close to the exit gate, Betty was stationed in her white Volvo. If everything went according to plan, Cat would come through the doors and jump into the Jeep. He'd drive down the ramp, honking his horn. As soon as they were past, Betty would pull out of her space, effectively blocking anyone from following.

It was as good a plan as they could come up with on short notice. Frankly, he'd been impressed with Cat's choice of venue. The mall would be crowded with early Christmas shoppers, and there were a number of exits. She *should* be able to give any paparazzi that had managed to stay on her tail from the hotel the slip. But it was nerve-wracking sitting here, waiting. Every sound echoed off the concrete walls irritatingly, and the whole place smelled of car exhaust.

He glanced at the dashboard clock. Two minutes to go. A flicker of movement behind the glass doors to the department store drew his eye. Raven was standing casually in the menswear department as Cat flipped through a rack of dress shirts, a bunch of plastic shopping bags hanging from her left wrist. They were in place.

Raphael shifted the Jeep into gear, pulling out of the parking space. He braked to a stop, leaning over to throw open the passenger-side door. She leapt inside, throwing her packages and purse into the backseat and yanking the door closed. They pulled away with a squeal of tires, leaving Raven stalwartly blocking three camera-bearing men from following.

Raphael leaned on the horn as he took the corner onto the down ramp. He heard Betty's answering honk, and hit the accelerator. As they passed, she pulled out, cutting off any possible pursuit.

Cat snapped on her seat belt, turning to glance over her shoulder. Horns were blaring in the background as they emerged into sunlight and Raphael turned off of the access road into the traffic on the main drag.

"The Volvo was a nice touch. Your idea?"

"Yup." Raphael checked his mirrors. They were clear. "It's Betty. She'll block them for a minute or two, then come out, circle the block, and go back for Raven."

"Should I *tell* him?"

"He knows." Raphael assured her as he signaled to change lanes. "I did have to brief Betty, but it's a fairly standard maneuver. We don't use it often, but occasionally people like Antoine attract more press than we're comfortable with."

"Antoine?"

Raphael looked over his shoulder to make sure there was room to merge before changing lanes. If he followed the left fork he'd wind up on Colorado Boulevard. It was a main route that he could take to the highway. "Antoine Monier, aka 'Antoine the Magnificent.' He's the council member representing the cats."

"I've heard of him! He's a *cat*?"

"Almost everyone has heard of him. He makes sure of it." Raphael forced himself to keep his tone neutral. Fiona's twin brother was powerful, charming, and blamed Raphael for everything that had gone wrong between his sisters. Cat would be *just* his type.

Raphael fought down a surge of irrational jealousy. Cat turned toward him, arching an eyebrow, her nostrils twitching slightly as she scented the air inside the car.

"What?" Raphael snapped.

"Nothing."

Raphael sighed. "I can't help it. Every time I think about you with somebody else I go nuts." He stared at the road ahead, not meeting her gaze.

Cat shook her head. "You don't need to worry, you know."

It was Raphael's turn to look shocked.

"Seriously." Cat turned in her seat so that she was facing him. "I skipped a bunch of grades in school, so I was too young for everybody I met, and my parents were seriously overprotective to boot. When I hit my rebellious stage I dated a bunch of celebrities, but not seriously. Then I dated a couple of guys from work, but they were jerks. Then, of course, there was Brad—"

"Brad?"

"I was engaged, briefly," Cat said. "It ended badly."

Raphael pulled into the left-turn lane to wait for the green arrow. His expression was serious as he turned to answer. "I'd say I'm sorry, but I'd be lying," Raphael admitted. "Because if it had worked out, you wouldn't be here with me. I'd like to know more about that part of your life."

Cat opened her mouth to speak, but he gestured her to silence. "I know it's too soon. You just lost your parents, you've got to adjust to being Sazi, there's Jack to deal with. I understand. But I can't help wanting what I want. And what I want is you, with me, always. Part of it's the mating. But mostly it's just *you.*"

Raphael didn't dare look at her right then. He'd promised himself after all the previous disastrous relationships that he'd never let himself be this vulnerable again. But in spite of his best intentions, she'd managed to slip through the walls he'd built to protect himself, and now he not only couldn't imagine being without her, he didn't *want* to.

He turned at the click of her seat belt unfastening. She moved across the seat, taking his face between her palms, and kissed him with a controlled passion that made him forget everything—until the angry honking of car horns brought them both back to their senses.

She laughed, scooting back onto the passenger side as he stomped on the gas so that the Jeep leapt into the intersection just as the light turned yellow. She pulled the seat belt back on. "So, where are we going anyway?"

"My place." He gave her a sly wink. "Right after we make a couple of stops."

* * *

THE "COUPLE OF stops" took a couple *of hours,* so that by the time they drove up Raphael's driveway, it was nearing dark.

He turned off the Jeep and opened his door. Cat started to do the same when his voice eased into her mind.

Remember, you have to get out on my side. She stopped and released the handle, having nearly forgotten the plan they'd devised. Wait until I bend down to fix my boot.

She was still having a hard time grasping that for the past several hours, anyone watching the Jeep would believe that Raphael was alone. He'd used his illusion magic to make her disappear completely, so that even if reporters had followed them from place to place, they would have no idea she was with him. But it was harder to hide a car door opening of its own accord.

He looked so absolutely natural as he got out as though she didn't exist. He glanced down at his foot and then twisted his leg as though he couldn't quite see the problem with something at his heel. When he stepped forward, out of the way of the door opening and bent down to fiddle with the boot, she slid out and stood motionless back a few paces until he shut the driver's door. She watched with unabashed admiration at the play of muscles under his white cotton shirt and jeans as he opened the rear door and removed the packages they'd purchased at several different stores. The wind toyed with his curls and brought color to his cheeks. But what made her eyes really light up was the file under his arm that he'd retrieved from a safe deposit box in town miles to the northeast of Boulder.

The file on Jack.

She was nearly salivating, wanting to look through it—and yet, was terrified to see his history of torture and murder of other women that looked like her. She remembered a television special about serial killer Ted Bundy, and when the photos of all of the dead girls had flashed on the screen, she was shocked that they all looked alike. Even the hairstyles and smiles were the same. No doubt the file in Raphael's hand would be the same—dozens of women that looked just like her. All of them dead. But it had to be done.

She walked into the house after he turned the key and kicked open the door awkwardly, appearing to juggle his packages without dropping them. He pushed the door shut with his foot as well and then proceeded to set down the packages and draw the curtains. He motioned her into the kitchen where the blinds were already down and closed, glanced at a box on the wall with a blinking red light that was making a hig-pitched buzzing noise, and then let out a slow breath.

"Okay," he said in a normal voice. "We should be fine here. The box on the wall over there is a radio frequency jammer. I asked Raven to install it the day we met, when I knew I might be going up against Jack again. Most likely, Raven included whatever new technology he could find at Wolven headquarters. I have no clue what all it does, but nobody should be able to hear a thing inside this house, regardless of what gadgets he uses. Even Sazi senses should be muddied by the buzzing."

Cat shook her head as he spoke. "I see what you mean. It's not quite an annoying sound, but I have to really focus on you to understand what you're saying."

Raphael smiled. "I can't say that I mind you'll have to focus on me all evening. Or vice-versa."

The look in his eyes made her blush. It shouldn't have. They'd already had sex, and she was hungry for his touch again. But this look was deeper, somehow different, and she couldn't help her reaction.

They stared at each other for a long moment over the center island. Raphael started toward her, but then stopped, as though changing his mind. Instead, he asked in a light tone, "How about some dinner? You had lunch with Raven, but I haven't eaten all day. We can go over the file afterward."

Cat shrugged. "Sure. I could eat. What did you have in mind?"

Raphael walked to the refrigerator and glanced inside. "Let's see. We have eggs, bread, some leftover baked potatoes, and some of my world-famous green chile." He pointed at the counter over the top of the open fridge door and Cat's gaze followed. She smiled when she noted the high-end coffeemaker. "How about you brew up some coffee and I make huevos rancheros?"

She nodded and started toward the counter, searching for where the coffee might be. He motioned to the cupboard above her with his chin, his arms loaded with supplies. She opened the cabinet door and let out a delighted squeal that nearly made him drop the egg carton.

"What's the matter?" he asked with alarm, moving quickly toward her.

She removed a box with a distinctive brown and gold logo from the lower shelf almost reverently. "You drink Gevalia Kaffe—and even Breakfast Blend! Awesome! This is my absolute *favorite* coffee! Where in the world do you buy it around here? I've looked absolutely *everywhere*!"

He chuckled at the reason for her squeal and turned back toward the island. "It's what Jake uses at the restaurant, so when he orders he makes sure he gets me a few pounds."

Cat raised her eyebrows. Even though she'd worked there, she hadn't known that. "Really? No *wonder* I like the coffee there! How can a restaurant afford such pricey ground?"

Raphael let out a little growl and his scent matched the frustrated tone. "Before the whole *credit* fiasco, the restaurant made pretty good money. Not enough to retire on, but my brother raised all five girls comfortably. I suppose Jake kept trying to convince himself that it would get better, so he never stopped his regular supply orders."

She spooned out the coffee into the filter, and tried to keep her tone light. She was curious about so *many* things about Raphael, but didn't want to seem nosy. "You say he's your brother, but you have different last names. Are you steps?"

She heard the sound of eggs cracking and turned with coffee pot in hand to fill it at the sink. "No," he replied, his scent not revealing any anger or concern. "We're not actually related. But when I got kicked out of the house by my stepfather as a kid for being too aggressive, Jake's parents took me in as a foster kid. I wasn't easy for them, but they got me turned around. After they died . . . well, Jake and the girls are the closest thing I have to family."

She finished filling the coffeemaker and turned it on, then took a seat at the table to watch him cook. "But you have kids, right? Holly said you have more than just Raven."

He glanced at her a bit nervously. "Did Holly explain the breeding program? Do you understand how that works, and what I did as Second of this pack?"

She nodded and watched as he took a casual whiff of air from her direction. She didn't mind that he was checking her reaction. It actually didn't bother her. "Yeah. I still think it's a little weird, but I guess no more than a surrogate mother is. You're just a surrogate *father*. But do you treat them like *your* kids? Do they even know who you are?"

The pan he was tending started to sizzle and he added chopped onions and peppers to the egg and potato mixture. "Oh, sure. They all know me. Their parents explain it to them when they're pretty young. I get school photos every year and Christmas cards from the parents. Sometimes I'll get the odd wedding invitation, and a few even send me birthday cards. But I only really got to *raise* Raven. Star made sure that I was involved in all the major decisions, and we did the whole visitation rights thing when he was a kid. He moved in here with me in his sophomore year. He turned really late, and it was hard for him. He's probably the one who understands most what *you're* going through. He had a life, friends, plans for his future—until he turned. He lost it all."

Cat felt her brow furrow. "Why did he lose it all just because he turned?"

Raphael glanced at her with a sad expression. "He was a football player, and a good one. All-state running back where he lived with his mom. He had his pick of colleges, even as a sophomore, and scouts for the pros were already knocking. But Sazis can't compete with humans. It's not allowed. One wrong scratch during a game—"

Cat's hand flew to her mouth. "Oh, my God! I never even thought of that! What about Holly? She was going to school to be a vet. That's still okay, isn't it?"

Raphael wouldn't meet her eyes, but his scent was worried and angry. "What's been happening when you walk through a neighborhood of pet owners, sweetheart?"

She thought about it. "Well, the dogs start to bark, and the stray cats will run away . . ." Her voice trailed off as understanding sunk home. "They'll be *afraid* of her. Dogs, cats . . . *rabbits*." She felt tears come to her eyes. "Oh, Raphael! Do you think she knows?"

"Probably. She and Raven spent a lot of time together when he was here. He confided in her a lot. If it hasn't occurred to her yet, it will. I think that maybe she's trying not to consider anything past the next full moon."

An uncomfortable silence followed, where the only sounds were the dripping coffee and frying food. She really didn't want this evening to wallow in anger and sadness, so perhaps a subject change was in order. "So . . . how 'bout them Cubbies?"

He looked at her, startled, and then burst out laughing. "Better change it to *Rockies* if you don't want to get lynched around here."

She stood up as she noticed the food was nearly ready to eat and wandered over to the cupboards again to find some plates and flatware. "What can I say? It was all I could think of. How about, 'So, what do you do for fun?' instead?"

He poured a bowlful of green . . . *goo* over the top of the egg mixture and put a lid on the top as she brought the dishes back to the table and set them in place. She went back and opened a few more cupboards until she found the cups and poured them each a cup.

"Hope you like your food hot," he said. "My green chile is four-alarm. Oh, and one spoon of sugar in my coffee, please."

She grimaced at the thought of sugar in coffee, but did as he requested. "Sugar? Ick. I've never had green chile, so I don't know how I like it. But back to *fun* . . ."

He smiled slightly and tipped the lid off the pan to check inside. The scent of the mixture was making her mouth water. He waggled his head and replaced it, being careful not to let the moisture drip onto the stove top. "Let's see—for fun? Well, I paint, as you saw. I play a little keyboard, but I'm not really very good. I read novels and listen to music—mostly rock and bluegrass—and I used to play a lot of computer games. Things have been pretty hectic lately, though, so I've fallen off on a lot of stuff. How about you?"

A small laugh escaped her. "Ditto on everything except the painting. I can't draw a straight line. But I *design* computer games, in addition to playing them. Oh, and I spend hours online in hacker chat rooms and love RPGs."

Raphael raised his brows as he turned again to the skillet. "You're a computer hacker? I thought you wrote software. By the way, I have to tell you—I was pretty damned impressed at your credentials when I saw them in the file. But I didn't picture you as a hacker, and I don't even *know* what an RPG is."

She laughed, and it was the right kind of laughter—bright and happy. It felt good. "What do you think hackers are, Raphael? They write code, the same as software designers. It just depends on who you write the code *for*. I'm not a hacker, but I know a lot of them. RPGs are role-playing games—you know, Dungeons and Dragons? But a lot of the new ones are way more intricate. I should show you some of them if you have a good connection."

"I've got DSL. I figured you'd want to go online once you've looked at the file. So, tell me about college and your family. What went sour with . . . *Brad,* was it?"

Cat took a deep breath. "God, where to start? Actually, college wasn't so bad. I got lots done because I wasn't in any clubs or cliques. It was pretty much a cakewalk. My professors all said I was a savant in computers. And, like many savants, I didn't deal well with people. Even now, it's hard for me—all this politics and stuff. But I have to admit, it is great training to hopefully take over Dad's company someday."

"Ivan mentioned your father. Said he was a brilliant computer designer, very rich and very powerful. It seems strange I never heard of him before now. Is it a big company?" Cat noticed that while Raphael tried not to appear concerned, his scent gave him away. Big company meant big investment of time and energy. She instinctively knew all of the questions it would raise in his head. Would she have to move back to run the company, or make frequent trips? Would he forever be *Mr. Turner*, like Ned was probably going to accidentally wind up *Mr. Wildethorne* when he accompanied Violet to her book signings and conferences?

She didn't want to lie to him. He could make a conscious choice, and now was a good time to discuss it. "Yeah, it's a pretty big company. I'm not surprised you haven't heard of TI— that's Turner Industries. We make the stuff you *don't* see inside a computer—the motherboards and capacitors—and do R&D on new ways to make chips faster. There's a board of directors and management who actually run the day-to-day business, but Dad was very involved in the direction of the company—the products to manufacture and marketing. Fortunately, he did most of it by e-mail, and only visited the plant about once a month. But, yeah, it is an issue in my future, *if* the board ever decides that I've grown beyond the airhead flake I was ten years ago so that I can run things."

Raphael turned to her, his expression mixed between horror and amusement. "Is that an issue? Why would they think that you hadn't? I mean, you have a *doctorate,* for God's sake!"

She raised one finger in the air with raised brows. "Ah, but degrees can be bought . . . for the right price. There was some question whether I was savant in computers, or just *rich* to have finished so quickly. Dad was trying to convince them I was talented. He helped me with some investment capital to start my own software company so I could prove . . . as he called it, my *business acumen,* before he turned over the reins. But then everything sort of blew up when the news about Mom hit, and then the rather . . . sudden end to my engagement to Brad." She couldn't help it. Tears welled in her eyes before she wiped them angrily away. The pain and outrage didn't just suddenly stop because she willed it to.

Raphael must have smelled something, even though she tried to hide it with a smile. He touched her hand lightly. "If you'd rather not talk about it—"

She waved it off. "No, it's okay. It's over. Talking about it won't stop the hurting, but it won't make it any worse, either. Okay, so Brad Jenkins was the son of my father's vice president. We sort of grew up together, ran in the same circles. But his folks decided to send him to boarding school in Europe after middle school, so we lost track of each other. I'd already gone through my period of *finding my center,* as Mom tastefully referred to it." She caught Raphael's grin out of the corner of her eye and it made her laugh lightly. "Actually, it was closer to *partying till my eyes bled.* But then I got accepted to college, and by the time Brad returned to the States after graduating from Oxford, I'd already finished grad school. We met up again at . . . oh, hell, I don't even remember which company function, and started to date. It seemed a natural progression to getting engaged." She thought back to the event and was amused by the realization. "I loved him, but there was no wild excitement when he offered the ring. It was just . . . I don't know . . . *expected.*"

Raphael turned off the stove, brought the skillet over to the table, and scooped a healthy portion onto her plate. He did the same for himself before taking the pan to the sink and filling it with water to soak. "But then something went wrong? Must have been pretty serious to break you guys up after all that history."

Cat nodded and then poked her fork into the strange colored mix of food on her plate. Tentatively, she speared a pepper along with some egg and slid it into her mouth. Wow! Tastes rolled and collided on her tongue and she eagerly followed the first bite with a second. She'd never in her life tasted anything as good as Raphael's green chile. It was thick and meaty with pork chunks and some sort of sausage, and seemed to have a variety of peppers and onions.

"Omgawd! This is *amazing*!" She swallowed quickly and tried to get her thoughts back on track. "Yeah, it was pretty serious. We announced the engagement in the paper and, of course, it was picked up by all the society pages in the city. Naturally, they did all the *proper* tie-ins—company background of both the parents, charitable donations, and the like. Dad and Mom were both on lots of committees and boards. Education, literacy, animal charities, disaster relief. All the obvious ones. But then one of the papers did some digging and broke the scandal."

She'd been diligently trying to ignore the heat that started slowly, but it sank deeper to sear through her tongue and gums. Despite her best efforts, she finally gave in and raced to the sink for water to stop the burning, much to his amusement. By the third filling of her glass he was chuckling.

"Stop laughing!" she said, trying hard not to laugh herself. "It's *hot*!"

"You'd better get used to it. This is how I eat all the time. Jalapeños are the mildest thing you'll find in my cooking. So, what was the scandal?"

The plate was nearly empty when she sat back in her chair and sighed. "I'd always grown up hearing that Mom was a debutante from one of the southern states—Daughters of the American Revolution, cotillions, all that sort of stuff. Turns out she wasn't. I guess nobody had ever asked the right questions, or they knew and never printed it because of Dad, but my mother was apparently a high-priced call girl when my father met her." That raised Raphael's eyebrows, but he didn't comment one way or the other. "Naturally, or . . . actually, not so naturally . . . Brad decided that perhaps I wasn't the best fit for his family. He used all the proper methods, said all the proper things . . . and dumped me." Tears threatened again, so she took a deep breath and smiled instead. "And that was that. Life sucks, and all that jazz. Anyway, let's not talk about that anymore. Let's talk about how great a cook you are. That was truly an incredible meal."

Raphael dipped his head in acknowledgment, stood up, and walked around the table, carrying his plate. He picked up her plate and carried them to the sink. For reasons she couldn't quite fathom, she stood and followed him the few short steps and then leaned against the counter, watching him. Her heart leapt into her throat when his nose twitched and he turned to fix her with a penetrating stare.

"I'm sorry that happened to you. You deserve better," Raphael said softly and looked down. "You missed a bite." She followed his gaze down to her plate. There were still a few bits of egg and potato buried under the thick sauce. He slowly . . . ever so slowly scraped her fork around the edges of the plate until he'd scooped it up. He raised the fork and held it out to her. She opened her mouth and let him slide the food in, all the while being transfixed by his complete focus on her and the thick scent of rising musk. She closed her mouth and chewed, this time relishing the burning that seemed to seep through her whole body, making her palms moist and her skin tingle.

She felt a tickle on her chin, and watched him reach out to wipe a dollop of chile away with his finger. She couldn't tear her eyes away as he eased it to his own mouth and licked it clean.

She'd stopped chewing, had nearly stopped *breathing,* and swallowed convulsively, nearly choking on the food in the process.

A slow, lazy smile curved his lush lips and she realized she was trembling. He reached forward again and ran the back of his fingers along her jaw lightly. "You deserve so much better." Her eyes closed, reveling in the sensation. She heard, felt—smelled him move forward and when he brushed his lips against hers, a jolt ran through her body that weakened her knees.

She became lost in the sensation of his lips coaxing her entire body to need through her mouth. He sucked lightly on her lips, one at a time, and then her tongue, as though seeking the last taste of chile. One hand cupped under her cheek while the other reached for her waist. Instead of pulling her closer, he pressed her back against the counter. She could feel him, hard and ready, against the sensitive nerves of her hip and a moan escaped her.

She reached up into his dark curls, let the soft strands slide through her fingers. The fine trembling in her fingers was growing worse, causing heat to rise to her face and making her palms sweat. He pulled back from the kiss and fire burned deep in his eyes when they met hers. The golden glow made her shiver.

"You're shaking," he whispered.

She nodded jerkily and let out a nervous chuckle. "I don't know why. We've had sex before."

He surprised her by not laughing. His face, his eyes, grew even darker and more serious. "Are you certain that's what this is?"

She felt suddenly lost in the intensity of the moment, as scents swirled in the air strong enough to make her entire body clench. "I—"

He leaned forward again and her lips opened, waiting. But he dipped lower, and she felt his breath hot on her throat. Her pulse thundered so hard that she could feel her temples throb as his teeth grazed a sharp line from her jaw to her shoulder. The growl that reached her ears was from deep in his chest and she gasped as his fingers dug into her shoulders to pull her closer. She inhaled and her nose fought to sort the scents. Sultry cologne blended with thick musk and mingled with a dizzying blend of emotions to create a combination so erotic that each breath nearly brought her to climax.

The whisper into her ear was a husky, rolling rumble that told her his wolf was close to the surface. It weakened her knees once more. "I'm pretty sure this won't just be sex, Cat." He moved back again and slid slow hands down her arms and then cupped her breasts while he stared at her. The trembling in her body became a throb that flushed her skin and made her suddenly wet. "What do you think?"

She couldn't think of what to say. Her tongue felt thick and useless. She could only nod in agreement, wondering what she'd gotten herself into. A small part of her was suddenly afraid—of the intensity, of something that was deeper inside her, bigger than she'd ever imagined. But she didn't fear Raphael, or what mating might mean. She realized that nothing he could ever do would frighten her.

"C'mon." Raphael stepped back and took her hand in his. He backed up and she followed smoothly, knowing without asking where they were going. They walked through the quiet house hand in hand. Sunlight was fading through the curtains of the bedroom as she stepped inside. He closed the door with a faint click and then once again cupped her jaw with his hands and kissed her slowly. She ran her fingers along his forearms as she met his searching lips and tongue with ever increasing need.

He ended the kiss and stepped back a pace. The husky whisper made her shiver again. "Take off my clothes, Cat. I want to feel your fingers on my body—feel your lips on my skin."

She suddenly wanted the same thing. She stepped forward and started to unbutton his shirt, placing a gentle kiss on his smooth chest each time the shirt opened wider. His breathing grew deeper and she felt his fingers slide through her hair. She let her hands wander up his ribcage and around to the strong muscles of his back and shoulders while her lips and tongue teased his nipples, each in turn. His hands began to clench knots in her hair and groans began to replace breaths as she eased the shirt off his shoulders and let it drop to the ground.

Make love to me, Cat. Raphael's voice touched her mind and a violent shudder raced through her. I want to be yours. I want to make you mine.

He reached for her, and began to remove her clothes as she removed his, bending down to tease her ear with lips and heated breath while she ran a slow tongue over his collarbone. His shoes and pants quickly followed the shirt, and her clothes joined them on the floor as both of their actions grew more frantic—hungry to touch skin to skin. The feelings he was arousing in her made her want to scream, to shout, to beg to go further, faster.

"God, Raphael! I can't stand this teasing anymore." She wanted him to possess her, take her. His erection was pressing mercilessly against her as he hooked his thumbs under the sides of her panties to pull them down. She reached her hand down, inside the elastic band of his briefs and felt his whole body clench as she wrapped her hand around his thick cock. He growled lightly and stripped off the underwear, then moved her hand back to his shoulder.

With a movement sudden enough to make her gasp, Raphael grabbed the backs of her bare thighs and lifted her until her legs were wrapped around his waist. He moved her back and forth across his stomach several times, flared his nostrils, and then smiled hungrily at her. "You're wet. I like that. Let's make you wetter."

His glowing eyes and bared teeth sent another jolt through her body. She tipped his head and desperately claimed his mouth, needing to feel his jaw working against hers.

He didn't disappoint her. The kiss was fierce, hungry—his tongue thrusting deep into her mouth as he walked forward toward the bed. He crawled up onto the comforter without ever releasing her and leaned forward until her back sank into the puffy goose down.

He began to rub himself against her slick opening, not entering her, but teasing her swollen flesh. Her breathing erupted into shallow pants as he kissed her nearly breathless. One hand moved to her breast and began to flick the hardened, sensitive nipple, while the other snaked between their bodies and began to flick between her legs with the same maddening slowness.

She squirmed under him restlessly, trying to satisfy the growing need deep inside her, but he'd managed a position that she couldn't escape from unless she wanted to end this completely—and she didn't.

He finally pulled back from the kiss, and Cat gasped for air desperately before he lowered his face to her chest. She cried out as his mouth found her breast and sucked greedily at the nipple just as his fingers slid inside her. Something deep inside her wanted, *needed*, more. She didn't know what it was, but the need pounded her heart with fear.

Raphael seemed to know and raised his head. "Let go, Cat. Just let it happen. Trust me."

She did trust him. With her life. *And with her heart.*

He bit down lightly and then growled. "You're mine now. Nobody else's." His mouth moved to the other breast, where he laved that nipple with his tongue until she whimpered.

Without warning, magical energy filled the room. She couldn't think, couldn't move. As he entered her, his power washed over her, making every hair on her body stand up. The sensations that raced through her as he thrust his powerful hips against her, as he worked her body into a frenzy, were too intense, too strong. Powerful convulsions wracked her as his mouth found her neck. She felt his teeth bite down, deep into the skin over her pulse.

Yes. *This* . . . this is what she needed. "Yes," she groaned. "I'm yours. Nobody else's."

His fingers convulsed on her hips and he thrust again—*hard*. The ripples of pleasure abruptly became crashing waves of a violent orgasm. Her breath raged in her lungs as her entire body shuddered and collapsed from sheer exhaustion. But Raphael wasn't done with her yet. He slowed his thrusts, moved his hips from side to side so that every movement touched a new part inside her.

When his face rose to hers again, she smiled lazily. "Your turn," she said and thrust her hips against him, enjoying the look on his face from desire.

"Yeah," he said with a wolfish grin. "I agree. But I think we can make you even wetter first."

He didn't lie.

Magic became a flame that touched her, filled her with fire and an aching need for release. Her skin felt swollen, engorged with blood and magic. She raised her legs even farther to take him in deeper. And then she felt the press of power from a new source. The moon had risen. It pulled at her seductively, called to the cat inside. Raphael felt it, too, and gave himself to both her and the moon. His hands dug in to her hips, and he began to thrust hard enough to leave bruises—if she were still human. But in that moment, she knew she wasn't. She was something else, something new and with conscious thought, she gave herself to this new life, gave herself to the man in her arms.

Every thrust took her higher, and his strong arms held her firmly against the heady new sensations. He pushed her further, forcing her body to release once more. "Oh, God! Raphael!" A second, mind-shattering climax ripped through her, bowing her back enough to raise him into the air. She felt his body clench as her muscles pulled at him—literally dragged the climax out of him with a harsh cry, followed by a deep moan.

"*Mine.*" He whispered the word into her ear huskily and then let himself collapse onto her.

She smiled into his sweat-soaked hair and sighed. "Yours."

Chapter Thirty

IT WAS NEARLY 2:00 A.M. when Raphael walked silently down the darkened hall that led to his home office with a coffee cup in hand. He wore only a pair of lightweight gray sweatpants held up by a drawstring. Normally he wouldn't even have bothered with that much, but Cat was still too human to be completely comfortable with casual nudity.

Raven had called a bit ago. He would be by in the morning to take pictures for Cat's and Holly's new driver's licenses and passports, and to drop off the keys to the car registered in her new name. Holly would pack up everything at the hotel and be ready for Raven to pick her up first thing in the morning.

Raphael stopped in the doorway, content to simply watch Cat huddled over the keyboard. She wore one of her new T-shirts, black with white lettering that read "I hear voices, and they don't like you." He stifled a snicker. He'd been amazed to find out just how similar their senses of humor were. He was still discovering all the amazing little things about her, like the way she tapped her lip with her index finger when she was lost in thought.

Right now she was doing exactly that as she sat with one foot curled beneath a bare thigh, the keyboard clattering with rapid staccato from her one-handed typing on the number keypad. The only light in the room was from the computer screen. It threw her face in sharp relief, giving him a clear view of the absolute intensity with which she was working.

He didn't want to interrupt her, so he blurred himself with illusion and stepped into the room, then replaced the nearly empty coffee cup with the full one in his hand and left before she could scent him.

He was nearly back to the kitchen when he heard, "Raphael? Are you up?"

"Yeah."

She laughed lightly. "Thank God! I nearly dropped the cup when I took a sip of coffee and it was *hot*!"

He chuckled, filled a cup for himself, and then joined her in the office. "Sorry about that. I was trying *not* to disturb you. What are you working on?" He leaned forward, putting one hand on the edge of the desk and the other on the back of her chair. This close the scent of her was nearly overwhelming, heavy as it was with musk from their earlier lovemaking. He took a deep breath, reveling in the heady smells, before turning his attention to the work that so absorbed her.

"Corporate records?"

"Yup." She turned her head so that he felt her warm breath on his cheek. "Bluebird Express Delivery Service was incorporated in Arizona in 1960. The corporate offices were at 2150 W. Ironhill, Suite 480, and the registered agent was one Lloyd E. Waters, Esq., of Waters, Wilson, and Jones."

"And why do I care about Bluebird and Mr. Waters?"

"Because until 1975 there was no national shipping agreement between the forty-eight contiguous states. You'd sometimes have a package go through two or three different carriers to get to its destination." Cat gestured at the pair of boxes sitting on his desk. Each had contained a copy of Jack's file; the first was from Charles, the second from Lucas. "Both of those are UPS boxes, with the old labels on them. *But* I noticed a second label on each of them with a bluebird logo. I've been spending the last several hours doing research. The *only* shipping company I can find with a bluebird trademark back then was Bluebird Express. So I went into the property tax records for Phoenix. Guess who owned several apartment buildings in the area in 1964 when these babies were shipped?"

"That doesn't prove Waters is the attorney," Raphael said.

"No. But it gives me a starting point. Because *somebody* filed the deeds on those properties, and *that* information will be right there in the records, ready to be looked up." Cat's eyes gleamed, her body was almost quivering with excited tension.

"Are the records online?"

"Nope. I tried. Too old. I'm going to have to go in person."

"Not you."

She stiffened, her jaw thrusting forward aggressively. Raphael set his hand lightly on her shoulder and squeezed gently to head off the almost inevitable argument. "The press are looking for you *and* you still haven't figured out how to keep Jack out of your thoughts. We don't want to tip our hand. No, it has to be somebody Jack won't be watching—which means I can't go, either."

She obviously didn't like it, but she was smart enough to realize the sense of his argument.

"Raven?" Cat suggested.

"Or Ivan, either one."

"Fine. I trust them." Her sigh let him know that while she saw the sense of sending someone else, she'd really rather perform the research herself. "But in the meantime I'm going to do a little cross-checking, see if Mr. Waters or any of his partners turn up on the donors lists for any of Jack's political campaigns."

Raphael grinned wickedly then leaned down to nuzzle her neck. "Can it wait a couple of hours?" The words were a warm whisper that played against her sensitive skin. "I can't even tell you how irresistibly sexy I find a woman with brains."

She swiveled the office chair so that she was facing him, and raised a single finger to trace a lazy path from the center of his chest down to the drawstring of his pants.

"Prove it."

A low, delighted chuckle escaped him then, and he claimed her lips with his. She opened her mouth to him, their tongues dancing as he moved his hands until he held her by her waist beneath the T-shirt.

He lifted her from the chair, pulling her close as she wrapped her long supple legs around his waist, one hand sliding between their bodies to tug at the drawstring of his trousers. His body throbbed with need, pressing hard and ready against the thin barrier of fabric. Power and need built between them until it was nearly painful.

Her legs and one of his hands held her as he swept files and loose papers off of the desktop with his other arm. He set down her bare ass on the very edge of the wood. He backed away from her seeking hands and sank to his knees. Her eyes widened as he used his hands to spread her thighs and slowly, gently, began kissing and licking his way from her knees inward, on first one leg, then the other, coming close, but never quite taking the invitation to put his mouth to her and taste the sweet wetness.

She whimpered and squirmed, her back arching so that her weight was on her hands. He could see the hardness of her nipples pressed against the thin cotton of the shirt, could scent the deep musk of her need. He moved in closer, her bare legs resting on his shoulders, his hands sliding along her outer thighs and up her back as he used his tongue to taste and tease. Again and again he brought her to the edge, only to pull back, leaving her gasping and moaning with need. Electric heat filled the room, raising the hair on his arms, calling to the beast within him. Raphael stood and pulled down the sweat pants so that she could see every throbbing inch of him for a long moment before he stepped forward and slid himself deep inside her.

She cried out, her body spasming as her back arched, forcing him deeper inside. A low moan escaped his lips, and he fought to maintain his control. He started a slow, deep rhythm, but she would have none of that. She ground herself against him, their flesh pounding ever faster. She came then, screaming as she did, and still he wouldn't let himself go. Instead he used his strength and the power of his thrusts to build her pleasure toward a second, deeper orgasm. He felt it coming, felt his own pleasure build in response until there was no thought, no reason—only the deep, sweet, electric sensation of claiming his *mate*.

Chapter Thirty-one

CAT TILTED HER head sideways, looking skeptically at the photograph in the book in front of her. "Wow. I'm limber, but I'm not *that* limber."

Holly peeked over Cat's shoulder at the book in her hands. "Um, I think that's one of the advanced postures. Maybe we'd better start with the easy ones?" Holly took the book from Cat's hand and flipped to one of the earlier pages until she found something that appealed to her. She showed the picture to Cat, who nodded. "That looks doable."

The two women stood in the center of the living room of a small apartment that smelled of fresh paint and sawdust and had been decorated with an eclectic mix that combined furnishings from the flea market and an inexpensive rental store and the framed posters that Violet had sent to her niece. *I Was a Teenage Werewolf* with Michael Landon had a place of honor above the entertainment center, while *An American Werewolf in London* hung above a plush tan couch, its throw pillows striped in black, tan, and cream. Inexpensive bookshelves took up a third wall, and they were already almost filled. It was an odd mix. On the top shelf there were ancient-looking hardback books that Violet and Ned had found at an antique dealer discussing shapeshifter legends, the battered copies of the training manuals. The lower shelves held several books and videotapes on both jaguars and wolves, and, of course, yoga.

Cat stood in the middle of the one truly expensive item she'd used to furnish the house, a twelve-by-twelve cream-colored rug that was thick, plush, and incredibly soft between the toes when you walked on it. She would've considered it worth it at twice the price, but had debated long and hard over the purchase.

After all, Cerise Boudreaux was a corporate cleaning woman. She did not have extra money to waste on luxuries. She would've had to save for months for a purchase like this. And if anyone asked, that's exactly what she'd say she'd done. Not that she expected anyone to inquire.

In the background, Cat and Holly could hear Ivan and Raphael discussing the best way to wire the exhaust and air filtration systems in the office where Cat would be doing most of her work. They were doing major renovations, including an overhaul of the electrical systems for the entire building to accommodate everything that would be needed. It was a nuisance, but nobody had even tried to argue the necessity of it.

"All right," Holly announced. "This is called the Eagle Pose. Stand erect. Lift the right leg and twist it over the left leg."

Cat did as she was bid.

"Now cross your elbows in front of your chest with the left arm on top and the arms pressed together."

"Huh?"

Holly stepped forward and showed her the picture. Once she could see what she was supposed to do it was simple enough. "Now reverse the position and stand on your right leg, with the left leg hooked over the left."

"I still don't see what this has to do with magical training," Cat complained.

"It strengthens the mind/body/magic connection and increases control," Raphael called from the office.

Cat made a harrumphing noise and rolled her eyes, but tried to listen carefully as Holly read the section describing the five sheaths covering the soul: the annamaya kosha, pranamaya kasha, the manomaya kosha, vijnanomaya kosha, and finally the anandamaya kosha and what each represented.

There was no point in arguing. Raphael was absolutely determined that she was going to do this as part of her training. She needed to be able to keep Jack from sifting through her thoughts and finding out the details of their plans for him. Hell, she just wanted the ability to keep him out—period.

Cat gave an involuntary shudder. Jack was never far from her thoughts, but on those rare occasions when she started to put him aside *something* always moved him back to the foreground. Last weekend was a good example. She'd been at Raphael's eating breakfast, utterly happy after a night of research and spectacular sex. Then Holly and Raven had shown up with all of the stuff from the hotel. Including, of course, Jack's anniversary present for Fiona. Cat had completely forgotten about it until she opened the card tucked inside the velvet Cartier box. "Something to remind you of me."

Cat shivered from a cold that had nothing to do with the snow outside, goose flesh crawling up her arms.

She'd recognized the jewelry the minute she'd opened the box: the collection Panthère de Cartier. An absolutely stunning heavy gold necklace and ring both perfectly depicting the head of a jaguar with emeralds for the eyes, and a diamond-encrusted clasp that connected the necklace to the gold stick chain. It was exquisite, but the mere thought of it made her nauseous, and Cat couldn't keep herself from wiping her hands against her jeans as if to rid them from some clinging filth.

"Cat, what's wrong? You smell weird."

"Nothing," Cat lied. She untangled her arms and began rubbing them briskly. "Read me that last part again. I need to get it right."

They started again from the beginning. This time Cat was able to do the exercise with relative ease. Of course it was at the worst possible moment that the phone rang. Holly dashed into the kitchen to pick it up. Cat listened to the conversation as she exhaled on the count of five and slowly straightened up.

"Cerise is tied up right now. Can I help you?"

"Oh! I'll go check. Hang on."

"Ca—Cerise," Holly corrected herself in midsyllable. "Your boss is on the phone. He wants to know if you can come in to work tonight after all. Somebody called in sick."

Cat untangled her legs with a sigh. She could hear Raphael grumbling in the background. They'd planned on going out to dinner this evening on an actual *date*. But it was important that she make a good impression on her new employer. She'd only been working for them for three days. It was absolutely typical for people to call in sick the day before a big holiday, too. Cat remembered hearing *that* complaint from her father more than once.

She walked into the kitchen, goose bumps rising on her skin in reaction to the cold of a draft coming from beneath the back door. She picked up the receiver. It was her supervisor from the cleaning company. He talked quickly, firing words off like bullets, as though he expected an argument. Then again, he probably had. After all, this was a plum night to have off—the day before a major holiday.

"No, it's fine." Cat assured him. "I understand. I'll be there at six." She started to hang up the phone, but turned at the sound of someone coming through the door behind her. It was Raphael. This morning when he'd arrived he'd looked positively scrumptious in tattered, faded jeans and a tight navy-blue T-shirt that hugged every inch of his muscular chest and washboard abs, his dark hair in loose curls that positively begged to be touched. Now a thin layer of white plaster dust was sprinkled lightly over his skin and work clothes. He still looked scrumptious—but now he was more of a powdered donut.

She snickered and set the receiver in its cradle.

"What's so funny?" Raphael stepped close, putting one hand on either side of her so that she was pinned lightly between him and the counter. He smelled of sweat, fur, and plaster dust, but beneath that, more subtly, of baking bread and cookie spices. Cat's heart caught in her chest when she remembered which emotions those scents were supposed to represent. *Love and happiness.* Not lust, not mating. Real, honest-to-God love.

Raphael gave her an inquiring look as she reached up to cup his face with her left hand. She leaned forward, kissing him with a chaste brush of lips. "I love you, Raphael Ramirez."

"I love you, too." He raised one hand to brush a stray hair from her face. Just that small touch sent tingles of electricity between them, her body tightening in response. Yes, she loved him, but lust was definitely a part of the mix.

"You still haven't told me what you were laughing about." He whispered the words as he moved his mouth to the base of her throat, nipping gently at the pulse point. There was something so primal about that particular movement that her body ached

with sudden, intense need, her breath catching in a soft gasp
that was almost a moan.

He leaned forward, and his body pressed against hers, hard
and ready. His hands moved to her hips, pulling her tight
against him so that she could feel every muscular inch of him
pressed against her as his mouth moved up to claim hers in a
kiss that was anything but chaste.

"Ahem." Ivan gave a pointed cough from the kitchen doorway.

Raphael turned his head, his grin utterly unrepentant.

"You *said* you were coming in here to get us each a beer."
The old bear complained good-naturedly. He stepped past them
to the corner where the refrigerator stood. Pulling the door
open he retrieved a bottle for each of them, plus a can of Cat's
favorite soda for her.

"I would've gotten around to it." Raphael shifted away from
Cat to take the bottles from Ivan's hand. He passed Cat's drink
to her before he twisted off the cap of his beer. He turned so
that he was leaning against the counter next to her, the length
of their bodies touching, his free arm wrapping automatically
around her waist.

"Did I hear correctly? You are working tonight?"

Cat nodded as she took a long swig of her drink.

"Are you *enjoying* your work?"

"It's not too bad." Cat set her drink down on the counter, her
expression wary. "I've only been working a couple of days, so
I'm still learning the job. *Why*?"

Cat felt the tension sing through Raphael's body. His scent
changed. He was eager. He'd known Ivan a long time, and apparently sensed that something was up.

"I just got a call on my cell phone from Raven,"

A shiver of anticipation ran through her body. "What did he
have to say?"

Ivan's smile was a beauteous thing. "The deeds were prepared by your Mr. Waters. He is not only still alive, but he
maintains his old office even though he is semiretired."

Cat held her breath. There was more. There had to be. She
could scent the joy and fierce anticipation pouring off both Ivan
and Raphael.

"The safe is an old one, and wasn't top of the line in the fifties when it was installed."

"He *saw* the safe?" Cat whispered.

"He *opened* the safe," Ivan corrected her. "He *saw* the file, and took many, many beautiful pictures so that you, and I, can make our replica *perfect*."

If Raphael hadn't been holding her she might have fallen. Her knees just gave way. They'd found the file. They'd *found the file*. And it wasn't inaccessible, in some high-security vault that would require months of work to access. Raven had gotten to it *easily*.

"Is he sure it's not a trap?" Raphael's words had raised a concern that it had been *too* easy.

He shrugged, and his scent was a mixture of worry and hope. "As sure as we *can* be."

Cat gave Raphael a fierce hug and a huge kiss before stepping out of his embrace. She then did the same thing to Ivan—just not quite the same *kind* of kiss. When she released him, she began walking out of the room.

"Where are you going?" Raphael asked.

"I have to get ready for work."

"That doesn't really seem to be necessary," Ivan pointed out.

"Maybe. Maybe not. But either way I am *not* leaving them shorthanded the night before a holiday weekend." She turned, grinning at both of them. "Anybody need in the bathroom before I get in the shower?"

Chapter Thirty-two

RAPHAEL STRETCHED. THE bones in his spine popped audibly. He'd been standing in one position for a long time now, putting the last detailed brush strokes on the canvas. He stepped back to look at it. It was good, *damned* good, even if he did say so himself. It was, without doubt, the best thing he'd ever painted. He wanted so badly to get it exactly right.

"Ivan, come in here a minute."

"In where?" The bear's voice came from the direction of the den. Raphael could hear the familiar sound of the movie *Casablanca* playing on the television. The delectable scent of buttered popcorn filled the house.

The two men had come back to Raphael's house after they dropped Cat off for work. Ivan had wanted to relax. Raphael had needed to finish a project before Cat's birthday tomorrow.

"The spare bedroom."

Ivan stepped through the doorway. He was still wearing the worn jeans and work shirt he'd had on this morning. He stopped abruptly, his eyes widening as he stared at the painting propped on an easel in the center of the room.

"Well?" Raphael turned to his friend, who stood staring in awed silence.

"It is perfect." Ivan stepped forward, but kept his hands clasped behind his back. "I don't know how you did it." He shook his head in amazement, "but you breathed life into their picture. You can see the laughter in Janet's eyes, and the love in his." Ivan leaned close to examine the details. "I know you never met them. Did you get the image from Cat's mind?"

Raphael let out a breath he hadn't realized he was holding. If Ivan thought he'd gotten the image from Cat, he'd done a very good job indeed. "Nothing that exotic. I was afraid she'd catch me." He shook his head with a laugh. "I had to stoop to having Charles send me a photo by e-mail. Think she'll like it?"

Ivan smiled gently. "She will *treasure* it, as well she should." He turned to Raphael, his expression serious. "I think I owe you an apology, my friend."

Raphael tilted his head sideways in inquiry, but didn't say anything.

"I was afraid you would toy with her, break her heart. You have, after all, always had something of a reputation."

Raphael snorted. "Don't remind me."

"Do you love her? I know you are mated, but that is not the same thing at all."

Raphael smiled ruefully. "Yup. And it scares the shit out of me. Because I can't help thinking that *that* is exactly what Jack has been counting on. It's not like him to wait like this. I don't like it."

Raphael gathered up the various brushes he'd used and dropped them into an old coffee can that he'd half filled with water. Acrylic paints cleaned up easier and dried fast, which is why he'd always preferred them. He'd never had the patience to work in oils. He used a damp cloth to wipe spots of black paint from his hands.

"Neither do I," Ivan agreed. "How is the training coming?"

Raphael wiggled his hand up and down. "Cat's got plenty of talent, but she needs to practice harder and more consistently."

"A lot has been happening to distract her."

"She can't afford to *be* distracted. When Jack comes for her, she'll need every ounce of skill and more." Raphael sighed.

"You don't think she'll be ready." It was a simple statement of fact.

"I don't know. Hell, I'm not sure I could be ready, or you, or . . . hell, Lucas if it came to that. Jack may be totally insane, but he's damned good." Raphael gathered up the paint tubes lying on the top of the dresser, checked each to make sure the lids were screwed on tight and placed them neatly in the carved wooden box he used to store them.

"So are you. Between the two of you, you and Cat will be a match for him. You'll see to it."

"That's the plan." Raphael glanced at the clock. "Why don't you go get dressed while I clean out the brushes? We can go up to the Run for dinner."

"We *could* hunt," Ivan suggested.

"I thought you didn't like hunting with wolves," Raphael joked.

"I don't like hunting with *most* wolves. You, my friend, are *not* most wolves." Raphael acknowledged the compliment, for it was meant as one. "Normally, I'd love to, but Raven's due back with his pictures."

"And *I* for one do not want to wait an extra minute to see them." Ivan's face was alight. "I cannot say how much I'm looking forward to ending this. I haven't slept well in decades."

"My fault. If you'd stayed out of it—"

"I'd have lost sleep from a guilty conscience instead," Ivan said wryly. He ran a meaty hand over his balding pate. "No. I have no regrets. Frankly, I enjoy working for the Chief Justice much more than I did being an agent. And I *like* coming to Boulder and drinking your beer." He gave Raphael's shoulder a friendly squeeze. "We'll eat at Wolf 's Run."

Raphael finished cleaning up the mess while Ivan showered and changed into clean clothes from his bag in the back of his car. In a matter of minutes they were in Raphael's Jeep on their way to the Run for dinner chatting about friends they'd known in the old days, arguing good-naturedly about who was the better shot.

It was a beautiful night: clear, with a biting wind that made Raphael want to slip into wolf form and run beneath the silvered light of the waxing moon. The parking lot was half full. Raphael recognized a number of the vehicles. Lucas's SUV was parked next to Tatya's Saab; Jasmine and Max's shining new Beemer was parked at an angle over two spaces so that there would be no chance of someone dinging its doors. The sound of the jukebox playing Bob Seeger's "Old Time Rock and Roll" carried clearly to him as he climbed out of the vehicle.

He took a deep breath of air tinged with the flavor of roasting meat and grilled onions, his mouth watering in response. "Damn that smells good!"

Ivan nodded wordlessly, crossing the parking lot in swift strides, his dress shoes crunching on bits of loose gravel. Raphael followed at a more leisurely pace, in large part because his feet hurt just a little. The old boots from his Wolven days didn't quite fit like they used to. Still, it felt good to be wearing them again, to *know* that his old knives were right back where they were supposed to be. Betty had been right. Not that it was exactly a surprise. She was, after all, a talented psychiatrist. But he'd given up a part of himself when he'd given up his weapons, and it was *very* good to be back.

He walked through the door with a smile on his face. Ivan was shoving a pair of tables together and pulling up extra chairs so that they could join Lucas and Tatya in the center of the room. They waved him over, calling a little *too* heartily for Larry to bring a round and a pair of steaks for the new arrivals.

Throughout the room conversations stopped, and re-formed. Some of his pack mates smiled and nodded their respects. Others gave the minimal acknowledgment due his status, and that only grudgingly. In the far corner Jasmine and Max were glaring daggers at him, a fact that he pointedly ignored. Yes, technically it was disrespectful. But he was not going to play into their game and get into a huge family argument in the middle of the restaurant, in front of dozens of witnesses. It was exactly the kind of thing Jasmine reveled in, and Raphael wasn't inclined to indulge her.

Lucas gestured to the chair across from him. "I'm glad you came. I was afraid I'd have to *try* to catch you at your office." His eyes were sparkling, and the scent of his amusement filled the air. Tonight, apparently, he'd chosen not to wear the Wolven cologne.

Raphael shrugged, looking a little guilty.

"Don't." Lucas shook a finger at Raphael, but he was only half joking and his voice showed it. "You don't have to justify yourself to me or anybody else. *You're* the one in charge now." He moved his elbows from the table so that the waitress could set his steak on the table in front of him. "Which leads to my first question. How do you want to handle the full moon? It'll be Holly's first change. I thought you might want to spend the first night with her. Tatya will be there, of course. If you do, I'll be happy to lead the pack for one last hunt."

"I'd appreciate it." Raphael was grateful for Lucas's understanding. "I know we need to do the severance ceremony—"

Lucas shook his head. "It can wait until the second night of the moon. Unless," again his eyes were sparkling, "*you* are in some sort of a hurry."

"No," Raphael answered drily. "I'm not."

"Have you decided how tightly you're going to bind the pack?" Lucas cut a big chunk off of his steak and began chewing it vigorously, his expression rapturous. "I'd suggest a light binding at first, it's what they're used to. You can always tighten the bond later." Across the table, Tatya smiled indulgently at her husband.

"That's what I intended. But I have to say, you two are certainly in a good mood tonight."

"We got a call from the doctors right before we came. It'll take awhile, but Mike is going to be all right!"

"Congratulations!" Ivan and Raphael chorused the word. Raphael felt as though a load lifted from his shoulders. He'd been damned worried about Mike, and had felt irrationally guilty as well. It was good to know that eventually the boy would be okay.

"Which leads me to *my* question." Tatya set her knife and fork delicately on either side of her plate. Her gaze was earnest, but she kept her eyes downcast, as was appropriate for her new status as Omega.

"Alpha, I would ask your permission to travel to visit my son for a few days over the holiday weekend, and spend the first week of December at a convention in Chicago. It's been scheduled for some time, and I would rather not miss it. If you will allow it, I will make up the time by serving at Jake's an additional two weeks."

"Granted," he agreed. "But make sure that Jake has somebody else to cover the restaurant. Now that Holly's not working there, he doesn't have anybody on hand to cover your shifts."

"Yes, sir. Of course."

Raphael fought not to show his surprise. Tatya was *never* this docile. It had to be an act, probably for the benefit of all the pack members who were pretending not to stare and listen. But even if it wasn't entirely sincere, he appreciated the gesture. Their support carried a great deal of weight within the pack, and judging from the way people were acting, he'd need every bit of it.

Raphael felt a pang of bitterness at that. To his surprise, Tatya reached across the table, setting her hand on his in a gesture of comfort. Lucas pretended not to notice, taking another bite of steak.

Raphael heard the sound of a chair scraping harshly across the wooden floor, and the rapid staccato rhythm of Jasmine's high heels as she stalked across the room to their table.

"Well," her voice was cold. "I suppose you'll be sharing Thanksgiving with your *mate* instead of your family this year."

She stood at the table, lovely face twisted with anger. She stank of rage, bitterness, and other darker emotions.

All conversation in the room stopped. Everyone was staring, just as Jasmine had planned. Raphael started to rise, but Tatya's nails dug lightly into his hand.

"Alpha," her voice was light. She was almost purring. "May I request an indulgence?"

Raphael froze, half standing. "What?" One word, but it was filled with suspicion.

"I know that you dislike disciplining family members. May I *please* be the one to punish Jasmine for her impertinence? I promise to be *very* thorough." The dark light in Tatya's eyes, and anticipation in her scent showed just how much she meant it.

Jasmine paled, and the ammonia scent of her panic filled the area near the table in an instant.

"Feel free," Raphael answered with a smile as he settled back into his seat. "But take it outside. We don't want to annoy Larry or damage the furniture."

"Of course, sir."

She put her napkin onto the table and rose. With a graceful flick of the wrist she gestured politely for Jasmine to precede her, and Raphael felt the pulse of power that forced the woman to do so.

More than a few people rose from their tables, drinks in hand, following the women outside so they could watch.

Raphael kept his seat. He was sorry for the necessity, but Jasmine really *did* need to learn how to behave. Unfortunately, she was as dense as she was proud. He doubted that one beating would do the job. Still, if anyone could manage it, it would be

Tatya. She might not choose to discipline people often, but she was exceptionally good at it.

Lucas watched the room empty, shaking his head slightly with amusement. "She's been wanting to do that for a *very* long time."

When Raphael raised his eyebrows in inquiry, Lucas answered the unspoken question. "Your niece can be *extremely* irritating."

Larry brought their food himself, carrying a large tray to the table. He set the steaks for Raphael and Ivan in front of them, adding a large bowl of fresh berries to the bear's side of the table. He set an elegant display box with a big red bow in front of the new pack leader. Raphael blinked as he read the label on the package. Herradura Selección Suprema was one of the world's finest tequilas, and not easily obtainable in the United States.

When Raphael gave him a look of inquiry, Larry smiled. "It *is* traditional to give the new pack leader a gift."

"Thank you."

"I do hope you intend to share," Lucas suggested. "I happen to love tequila, and it has the most interesting effects on my wife." His grin was lascivious enough that he didn't need to elaborate.

Raphael gestured for Larry to bring enough glasses for all of them and opened the bottle. Each man lifted his glass, but it was Ivan who proposed the toast. "To the future."

"The future."

Chapter Thirty-three

CAT TOOK A deep breath and tried to convince herself that she wasn't nervous. It wasn't working. Even though she and Raphael were lovers and had been seeing each other regularly for their training sessions, this was their first real "date." It would have been easier if they could have done some small thing off alone. But, no, the "rules" of the courtship stipulated that there had to be pack members available as witnesses. Cat still thought it would be simpler just to acknowledge that she had accepted him, but Raphael had insisted she keep quiet for now.

His reluctance made her nervous. A part of her couldn't help but wonder if he had regrets. After all, being with her was causing no end of trouble with his people.

So she worried, despite the evidence of his scent, and the words he whispered to her when they were alone. She'd been so very wrong about Brad, it was hard to trust her judgment. But her every instinct told her she *could* and should trust Raphael. She just wasn't sure she was ready to do so.

The antique clock in the sitting room chimed the quarter hour. He'd be here any minute. She checked her reflection one last time, threw up the sturdiest mental shields she could, took a deep, steadying breath, and went back into the outer rooms.

The suite was exquisite. She'd chosen a different hotel, still downtown, but farther down the mall. It was newer, part of an extensive high-end chain that was used to catering to celebrities who flocked to the area on their way up to the mountains during ski season. It was only for sentimental reasons that she hadn't chosen it in the first place.

Are you ready? Raphael's voice slid gently into her mind a moment before he knocked on the door of the suite. She knew he hadn't eavesdropped on her previous thoughts, but the when she gave her reply to him, she answered her own doubts as well.

Yes. I think I am.

THE RESTAURANT THEY chose was only two blocks from the hotel, on the Sixteenth Street Mall, a pedestrian-only thoroughfare whose only motorized vehicles were the shuttle buses that ran the length of downtown. Cat and Raphael walked hand-in-hand in the flickering shadows cast by windblown trees festooned with twinkling lights. Tonight he wore his signature black, from head to toe. His suit jacket was exquisitely cut to emphasize his broad shoulders, the silver-tipped belt his narrow waist. He'd left his hair loose, and even with the new cut, his dark curls fell softly to the neck of his collarless raw silk shirt. More than one woman was casting an envious glance.

Cat was exquisite in an emerald green sheath cut to emphasize her figure. The hem came to her calf, but a daring slit showed pale, perfect skin well up to her thigh. She wore matching pumps with just enough heel to leave her eye-to-eye with Raphael. Diamonds and emeralds glittered at her throat, ears, and wrist. She, too, wore her hair down tonight, and it flowed loose across her shoulders and down her back.

They chatted amiably. Raphael asked after Ned and Violet.

"The truck broke down in Reno, so they're staying there a few days for repairs. I would've thought they'd be upset about it, but they seem fine. Violet was going on about how Charles had gotten them front-row tickets to see Antoine the Magnificent."

Raphael grinned. "They'll like that. He puts on quite the show."

"Oh." Cat remembered Raphael's earlier comment about the councilman for the feline shifters and the surge of jealousy that had followed. While she didn't scent anything untoward coming from him, she didn't want to push the issue, so she changed the subject. "Look, a horse-drawn carriage! I've always wanted to ride in one." She pointed across the street where a gleaming white carriage was hitched to a large bay with long white hair feathering its hooves.

Raphael checked his watch. They had nearly a half hour before their reservations. *Why not?* We can try it if you like, but we'll have to shield like a sonovabitch, he warned her. Otherwise the horse will bolt.

It will?

Animals can sense the predator in us. It generally makes them very, very nervous. Still want to try?

Oh, yes! Please, if it won't make us late.

We have time. And it won't hurt anything if we're a few minutes late. Lucas and Tatya will understand.

The horse shifted nervously at their approach, snorting loudly and tossing its head. Still, the driver managed to calm it enough that Cat and Raphael were able to climb into the back of the carriage onto the crushed velvet seat. Cat curled up beneath Raphael's arm, resting her head on his shoulder, and the carriage pulled away from the curb, the clop of the horse's hooves against the gray paving stones a gentle counterpoint to the music and voices floating on the evening breeze from the various bars and restaurants lining the mall. At the far end of the mall the clock tower struck the quarter hour.

Christmas decorations and advertisements adorned the various shop windows, but Cat ignored them. She wasn't looking forward to the holidays this year, and she didn't want to spoil the mood. This was, by far, the most romantic thing any man had ever done for her, and she wanted to relish the moment.

Raphael was caught in the moment as well, reveling in the clean scent of her shampoo, the warmth of her curled up next to him. The need he felt for her was deep, and dangerously addicting. He knew the trap Ahmad had set for him, but he didn't care. Raphael *wanted* to win this woman, and not just from the mating compulsion. She was truly everything he'd ever wanted: warm, funny, intelligent, and breathtakingly beautiful. Her courage awed him, as did her determination and will. She'd shown compassion to Michael, loyalty and protectiveness to Violet, Ned, and Holly. For the first time in his long life he'd met a woman who he not only desired, but with whom he could imagine spending the rest of the long years of his life.

I love you. The words popped from his mind to hers unbidden.

It was true. He did. But he really wished he hadn't said it. *I know it's too soon. Too much has happened . . .*

Cat reached up to put a finger against his lips, though he hadn't said a word with his mouth.

I love you, too. She smiled then, and leaned toward him to take his face in her hands. She kissed him, a chaste, gentle brush of the lips. Even that small touch stirred the magic between them. She pulled away, unwilling to go too far.

Too much is happening, too fast. He could hear the regret in her mental voice. *There are things I need to do.*

Things we need to do, darling. Because from now on, we're in this together.

Raphael kissed her forehead, relishing the warm scents of love and happiness floating up from her skin. The tingle of magic racing between the two of them was electric. His body tightened in response. He suppressed a groan. Cat gave a low chuckle.

"Dessert comes *after* dinner, Raphael."

"We could stand them up," Raphael offered.

"No." Cat tried to sound stern, but there was laughter in her voice. "We can't. You'll just have to wait." She teased as she slowly traced one manicured nail across his lips. "But I'll make it worth the wait."

"I'll hold you to that!"

"You'd better."

They were laughing when they entered the restaurant and were escorted to the table where the Santiagos awaited them. After all the weeks of Tatya acting jealous and angry Cat had expected dinner to be torturous. Instead, it was a delight.

The food was delicious, the evening filled with laughter and light conversation. Cat was astonished at just how nice Tatya could be when she made the effort. It was obvious that the older woman was doing her absolute best to keep things from being awkward. Cat appreciated it. Still, she wasn't sorry when the meal ended. Ever since the carriage ride she'd wanted a chance to be alone with Raphael. The sexual tension had been building with each smile, each casual touch.

It was the same for him. She could see it in his eyes, in the way he watched her move. The two of them bade their companions good-bye at the door to the restaurant and walked back to the hotel.

The lobby was empty except for the concierge and desk clerk. Cat and Raphael walked hand in hand up the wide curved staircase, both too impatient to wait for an elevator.

Cat fumbled with the card key, her impatience making her pull the card too fast for the lock to register and unlatch. Finally, Raphael took it from her. Let me.

I'm perfectly capable . . .

Cat, if I have to wait one more minute I'll break *down* the damned door. I want you *now*.

He pushed the card in the slot, sliding it out slowly. The light flashed green and the latch clicked open. Raphael handed her the card key and opened the door.

The room was limned in the moonlight that streamed through the balcony windows. Colors faded to silvered shadows of their true shade, blackest shadows patterning the thick rugs that carpeted the floor.

Raphael closed the door, but didn't bother with the light. Cat dropped her purse on the nearest chair and turned to him, her eyes dark and eager. He closed the distance between them, taking her into his arms.

The kiss was slow, deep and fraught with hunger. Cat's body molded to his as their tongues tangled and danced. Raphael held her close with his left hand, his right sliding underneath the slit of the dress, over the thin silk of thigh high stockings to the warm smooth skin of her upper thigh.

A small, needful sound escaped her lips as he moved away from the kiss, using lips, tongue, and teeth to tease at the lobe of her ear, the curve of her jaw, slowly making his way to the base of her throat.

Her hands stripped the jacket from his back, letting it drop to the floor. Slowly, one button at a time, she began to unfasten his shirt, her tongue licking a slow wet line along the flesh that was revealed.

There was a quick sizzle, and the scent of burning flesh as she unfastened his belt. Raphael took her hands in his then, kissing away the pain, power flowing gently between them until the burned flesh was once again whole.

Her hands played along his chest, teasing at his nipples as he reached behind her to unfasten her dress. She stepped back, allowing the silk sheath to slide from her body and pool on the floor.

Raphael's breath caught in his throat, his body throbbed with an aching, desperate need as he stared at the beauty standing before him. Moonlight bleached her skin milk white, soft shadows emphasizing the curve of calf and thigh, the soft flesh of her abdomen and belly and the sweet, heavy mounds of her breasts. She stood before him wearing only her silk stockings and heels. Slowly, gracefully, she dropped to her knees. He gasped as with sure fingers she unfastened his trousers so that she could take him into her mouth.

Chapter Thirty-four

CAT WAITED AT the curb outside the office building. The city wasn't completely still. Christmas decorations sparkled, and the sound of canned Christmas carols filled the air. In the distance she could hear muted laughter and the sounds of a Salvation Army bell ringer, and of a homeless man bedding down for the night in the doorway of an abandoned shop just across the street. But the crowds were much thinner than usual, even for a week-night.

Most people were probably at home spending time with their families. Cat's eyes stung at the thought.

She missed her parents. Hell, she missed Violet and Ned. God how she'd laughed at the birthday serenade they'd arranged for her. It was so . . . them. The gifts, too, were a hoot. Violet might not be able to cope in person, but her choice of the movie posters and the books with werewolf legends showed that she was trying to adjust—and was determined not to give up on her niece.

Cat wasn't giving up, either. But tomorrow was going to be the first holiday, and her first birthday without her family, and honestly she was dreading it. Oh, Holly would be there, and Raphael. It would help. But it wouldn't be the same.

Fortunately, Holly pulled up to the curb before Cat could get any more maudlin. She was driving Cerise's "new" car, an old Honda CRX that was mostly red, although the back quarter panel was primer gray. It looked more than a little battered, but Raphael and Raven had spent a great deal of time working to make sure it ran like a champ. The engine purred like a con-tented kitten, and was more than capable of hauling ass if the need arose. Cat knew that because Raphael had taken her on a white-knuckled test drive.

"Hi." Holly climbed from the driver's side, handing Cat the keys as she walked around to get in the passenger door. "Sorry I had to come in your car. Mine wouldn't start," she explained with a sigh. "Apparently it's the starter. Raphael promised they'll fix it and give it a complete overhaul this weekend."

"No problem." Cat walked around and climbed into the driver's side of the car and strapped herself in. It still smelled strongly of cleaners and cinnamon and ever so faintly of dirty gym socks, despite the air freshener that hung with a pair of jaguar print fuzzy dice from the mirror. The former had been a necessity. The latter was a gift, from Raphael of course.

"You still miss your Geo, don't you?"

"Yeah," Holly admitted. "I miss the car, and I miss the family." Holly got a horrified look on her face when she realized that she might have been insensitive.

"It's okay, Holly," Cat assured her. "You get to. And at least there's a chance that you and your dad can patch things up eventually." Cat fought to keep the bitterness from her voice as she put the vehicle in gear and pulled away from the curb. "Are you going to call him tomorrow?"

"Maybe. I don't know."

Cat didn't push. Instead she grabbed a CD at random and slid it into the player, cranking up the volume. Punk music began blaring out of a sound system that cost nearly as much as the car itself. Cat was rewarded with her friend's smile. By the time she turned onto Colfax, she and Holly were both singing along in a rousing and slightly off-key punk rendition of the show tune "Cabaret."

Cat was grateful for the music. As much as she liked Holly, and understood that her friend needed to talk about what was going on with her family, Cat simply wasn't up to listening tonight. Yes, she sympathized. But a bitter little corner of her mind that she didn't even want to admit to kept thinking *at least you* have *family*. So she kept the music playing to keep herself from saying something she shouldn't.

"Can we stop by the grocery store on the way home?" Holly asked. "I need to pick up a few things for tomorrow."

"Sure, no problem," Cat agreed. She turned the car onto Sheridan and drove toward the big twenty-four-hour grocery store that was less than a block from the apartment complex. She was tired, but she really wasn't sleepy. Maybe doing something as boring and mundane as grocery shopping would help her wind down and get ready for bed. Besides, she kept finding things she needed around the house. She could pick them up while they were there.

She pulled the car into a parking spot near the entrance. The two of them walked in past freshly cut pine trees that would be very, very dead by the time Christmas actually arrived. Still, they smelled wonderful, and the scent lifted Cat's spirits as they stepped into the bright lights and bustle of a store crowded with last-minute Thanksgiving shoppers.

Holly grabbed one of the metal carts. Tossing her purse casually into the upper bin, she began wheeling her way methodically through the store, starting at the produce section and moving slowly through every single aisle in the store. She took her time, comparing different brands, checking prices, and riffling through an envelope from her purse that contained a thick stack of discount coupons.

Cat checked her wristwatch. It was almost midnight. The store was emptying out, and still Holly showed no sign of wrapping it up. She was beginning to regret having agreed to the whole endeavor, and was just about to say so when Holly finally steered the overflowing cart into the checkout line.

"I think you've bought half the store!" Cat tried to make the complaint good-natured, but her impatience was beginning to get the best of her.

"I wanted to stock up the pantry," Holly explained. There was a hint of amusement in her voice and she smelled anticipatory.

"Holly—"

"What?" She gave Cat a look that was all wide-eyed innocence, but there was definitely a sparkle in her big brown eyes.

"What are you up to?"

"What makes you think I'm up to anything?" Holly tried to look hurt, and failed miserably.

"Uh-huh." Cat didn't bother to keep the suspicion from her voice, but couldn't pursue it further because the cashier had told Holly the amount due and started up a conversation. Still,

Cat had every intention of finding out just what was going on the minute they were outside the store. Unfortunately, when the time came, Holly asked for a bag boy to help them load the groceries in the car.

By the time the groceries were loaded, she had the stereo playing and was strapped in and ready to go.

Cat waited until the bag boy was walking off with the cart before turning in her seat to face her friend. She reached over, switching off the music. "Holly, you're up to something. What's going on?"

"Cat, can we *please* just go home now?"

"I was ready to go home an hour ago!"

"Yeah, well, I'm sorry I took so long." She didn't sound sorry. She *did* sound nervous. "Next time I'll hurry, I promise."

Cat let out a little growl of irritation. She waited, hoping her friend would say more, but Holly was staring out the passenger-side window and wouldn't meet her eyes.

"Fine. Whatever." She grumbled as she turned back in her seat and started the engine.

It only took a minute to drive the short distance to their place. Cat pulled the car into its spot under the back carport and started to help gather the groceries, but Holly waved her away. "Can you go ahead and open up the gate for me? I've got these."

Cat shook her head, but did as she was bid, crossing the frost-covered grass. She paused to unlock the deadbolt on the wrought-iron gate to the back courtyard, then moved on to Holly's back door. The movement turned on all of the light sensors, so that the lawn was bright as day. She rifled through her keys, looking for the correct one as Holly came up the sidewalk behind her, shopping bags clutched in her hands.

She found the key, turning it to unlock first the deadbolt, then the matching lock in the knob. Reaching through the open doorway, she turned on the light.

Half a dozen familiar voices shouted *"Surprise!"* and *"Happy birthday!"* simultaneously.

Cat stared, dumbstruck, her jaw hanging wide open. Raphael stood behind a kitchen table laden with presents and a large birthday cake. Raven and Emma stood arm-in-arm in front of the kitchen counter. Ivan leaned against the refrigerator, while

Charles and a bodyguard Cat didn't know stood in the arched doorway that led to the living room.

Cat turned slowly to face Holly, who was practically dancing with glee. "Gotcha."

"Well, come inside!" Charles ordered. "You need to open your presents."

Cat stepped inside, reveling in the warmth of friends. Her eyes misted as she saw that Uncle Chuck had one of Aunt Amber's infamous carrot cakes with him. They all sang "Happy Birthday" off-key, as she blew out her candles. Then it was time to open the gifts. Raven gave her a brand-new locking briefcase—filled with the photos he'd taken of the file. Emma had framed an original movie poster of *Cat People* while Holly had found an utterly luxurious bath set with every conceivable accessory (except her uncle). Ivan's gift was a necklace that had been specially crafted by a shaman he knew. She loved the gesture, and loved the comforting weight of it between her breasts when she slid it around her neck.

Only Raphael's gift remained. It was large enough that he'd leaned it against the far wall rather than putting it on the table with the rest. She gave him a quick glance, noting how very nervous and excited he was. Still, he'd shielded his thoughts so that she couldn't get a clue as to what lay beneath the shining silver wrapping paper and big red bow. With shaking hands she grabbed the corner of the paper and pulled, ripping it away to reveal a painting. But it was not just any painting. Cat's breath caught in her throat, her eyes widened, filling with tears.

It was so amazingly lifelike. She almost expected her parents to step out of the frame. Nothing could have been more perfect. She turned to Raphael, wanting to say something, but unable to come up with the right words. "I . . . you . . ." Her mouth moved, but nothing coherent would come out. She could tell he understood, though, by the look on his face as he stepped forward to take her into his arms. As she hugged him tight she whispered, "I love you. It's amazing. Thank you."

THE PARTY HAD ended shortly before dawn with everyone agreeing to meet back here at three for a full Thanksgiving dinner with each guest providing a side dish while Raphael cooked the main course, a honey-baked ham.

It took a long time for Cat to fall asleep. It felt good to be curled up with Raphael, listening to the steady rhythm of his heart beating, basking in his scent and the warmth of his body next to hers.

She loved him. It wasn't just lust, although heaven knew that was part of it. But it was so much more: warmth, kindness, absolute acceptance, and mutual respect. Cat finally understood what her father meant when he'd said of her mother: "It was like I found a part of myself I hadn't realized was missing."

"You okay?" Raphael spoke into her hair.

"Fine." She shifted her head to look up at him. "Happy even. Now tell me about this contest you and Raven were talking about."

Raphael chuckled. "When Raven was a teenager, I was getting ready to put on some music after dinner, and he started giving me a hard time about one of the songs I like. So I threw one of the really bad ones he listened to in his face . . . and well, it just kind of moved on from there until now every year we compete to see who can come up with the best *bad* songs that have actually made it onto the radio."

"The best bad songs?"

"Oh, yeah. Just wait till you hear it. I've got some amazing stuff lined up this year."

"Oh, goody."

Raphael laughed.

They lay together in silence. Everything was all right. She wasn't even dreading the holiday dinner without her parents. Oh, nothing would keep her from missing them, but having Raphael here helped more than she would have believed possible. Eventually she dozed. For the moment at least she was happy and content.

It was the calm before the storm.

Chapter Thirty-five

RAPHAEL FELT AS though he might smother from the power that surged and flowed in a skin-crawling rush in the close confines of the car. The days between Thanksgiving and the full moon had passed in a blur. Originally Raphael and Holly had been going to go up to the mountain alone. There had been a change of plans. Now they were the ones to meet Cat at the mall. He was driving the Mitsubishi at just above the speed limit. He didn't want to get stopped by the police right now. Not with the sun lowering toward the horizon and the full moon calling for his beast to come out and play.

He was afraid. He could admit that to himself. He was afraid for Holly, afraid what losing her would do to his brother, to Raven, and to Cat. They loved her so very much. Losing Maria had nearly destroyed Jake. He'd have killed himself if he hadn't had his daughters to think of, and the restaurant business to immerse himself in. Now his daughters were grown, gone, and had lives of their own. The business was crippled with debt. Raphael wasn't sure his brother would be willing to go on if he lost youngest daughter.

He tried reassuring himself by saying that she had wolves in her ancestry for generations, and that three of the best healers in the world would be there tonight. But that didn't keep his stomach from roiling, or his gut from clenching with fear.

The power surged, biting at his skin like fire ants. Raphael pressed the gas pedal farther to the floor as they cleared the outer edge of the city and merged onto the highway leading out to the mountains.

The drive seemed to take forever, until he could pull the car to a stop at the gate to Cat's property. The sun hadn't fully set, but it was sinking toward the horizon, painting the western clouds orange and blood red.

Cat climbed from the car, pulling the keys from her pocket. She unlocked the gate, swinging it open wide enough for the car to pull through, closing and locking it behind.

Gravel crunched beneath the tires as he pulled up the curving driveway to the front of the house with Cat following on foot.

Holly climbed from the car and started toward the meadow, walking as though bemused to where three large furred shapes waited in the shadows. Raven, Betty, and Tatya had changed early, hunted, and come cross-country in wolf form. Having fed, they would all three be at full strength when the time came. And the time would be soon.

In the distance the moon rose, its magic sliding in a smooth, erotic touch over his body, calling to the animal within. Raphael shuddered in response. It felt so good, so right to be here, tonight. He turned to look at Cat. She smiled, but strain showed around her eyes and he could scent the ammonia of her fear, see the pulse pounding in that slender throat.

Why don't you go ahead and go on to the meadow. I've got to set the spell for the perimeter.

What kind of spell?

An aversion and an alarm. The aversion focuses and reflects fear. Any human or lesser Sazi who tries to come here will feel unreasoning terror to the point where he *can't* continue.

The alarm.

That gives me warning in case someone does manage to breach the perimeter, so I can head him off before he sees something he shouldn't.

Cat stepped forward, pulling him into a tight hug. He held her against him, his hand stroking her hair as he tried to comfort her, ease her trembling. "I love you, Raphael." The words were almost desperate.

"I love you, too." He put one finger underneath her chin, tilting it upward so she was forced to look him in the eye. "It will be all right." He forced confidence into the words, trying to make them both believe him.

"Of course it will." She forced herself to smile up at him. "Now go set your perimeter and get your ass out to that meadow. I don't want things to start without you."

Cat walked up to the house, letting herself in the front door. She still wasn't completely comfortable being naked in front of many people. She judged it to be much better to change here, privately, and join the others in cat form. Moving through the house by moonlight, she crossed to the French doors, sliding them open for her eventual exit. She stepped away from the windows, into the deep shadows of the living room area, and stripped. She folded the clothes, stacking them neatly on the fireplace mantel, then stepped to the center of the room and called her magic.

Always before there had been a shock of pain when she called the power to change. Tonight, it felt natural, right, and good. There was no flash, no smell of burning or ozone. One moment she was Catherine, the next, the cat.

On silent feet she padded out of the house. She moved with casual grace, leaping easily from the edge of the deck. She didn't run until she heard the first of the screams.

Cat nearly flew across long grass shadowed by the shifting clouds. She felt Raphael's spell slam into place like the closing of a vault door, felt him shift forms and run full out toward the field.

They arrived at nearly the same time from opposite directions, joining the others to form a rough circle with Holly at its center.

Holly was writhing in the tall grass, screaming as fast as she could draw breath. Her bones broke and rebroke as her body started to change, then shifted back to its familiar human shape. Thick gray fur sprouted from her skin, only to pull back and recede below the surface. She struggled onto her hands and knees, the whites of her eyes a solid red from ruptured blood vessels. Throwing back her head, she howled, her face elongating, reshaping.

Cat felt Raphael pull power, pull strength from her and throw it into his niece's body. This time when her legs broke they stayed in wolf configuration, while her upper body stubbornly remained human. He pulled again, desperately dragging every ounce of their combined energy out and throwing it into her.

Cat's eyes dimmed. She stumbled, falling gracelessly to the ground. Nor was she alone. Betty collapsed in a dead faint. Cat forced her eyes open. She watched in terror as Raven threw everything he had into his cousin, again and again, until there was nothing left for him to give and he, too, fell unconscious.

Tatya staggered, but stubbornly remained upright. Cat could feel her pulling power from somewhere beyond their circle, pulling it, and shoving it into the bloody mess in the center of the circle that was neither human nor wolf and barely breathing.

The clouds parted, the light of the full moon shining full on the thing that was Holly. She gave one last, lingering scream as the moonlight dragged the wolf from her skin. But it didn't move.

Consciousness faded to black.

Catherine had no idea how long it was before she felt Raphael's presence in her mind. Knew he was alive and moving. She hurt. The pain wasn't localized. Every cell of her body ached equally, and there were no words to express the exhaustion she felt.

Are they . . . It was hard to form a coherent thought to form the words. Speech was definitely beyond her.

We're all alive. More or less. Eventually we'll even be all right. Can you move?

Not yet.

Stay still then. Rest. You need to eat. There's a cooler in the trunk of the car with meat in it.

Just like last month. Cat closed her eyes.

Cat awoke to the smell of meat. Someone, probably Raphael, had placed a huge chunk of uncooked hamburger beneath her nose. Before she even opened her eyes she snapped up a mouthful. It tasted wondrous, and the fact that it was fully ground meant that she could swallow without the exertion of chewing. A good thing since she barely had the strength to open her jaws.

She felt Raphael's hand stroking her fur. "You're going to be all right, baby, and so are Holly, Raven, and the others."

"You?"

"I'm fine. Tired as hell. But I'm fine."

Cat forced her eyes open. The moon was still up, but it had moved well across the sky. Lucas sat not far away in human form.

A silver-gray wolf Cat assumed must be Tatya lay with her head across his lap. He stroked her fur with slow, even movements of his left hand while he fed bites of burger to her with his right.

"Lucas?"

"He knew Tatya was in trouble, so he had Peter take over the hunt and came. He wasn't the only one, either." Raphael nodded in the direction of a pair of traditionally marked gray wolves, one male, one female. "Jake forced his way through the perimeter to get here."

"But you said—"

"That lesser wolves would be overwhelmed with fear." There was pride in Raphael's voice and expression. "He was. He came anyway."

Chapter Thirty-six

IT WAS HOURS later when Raphael left to go to breakfast with Holly and Jake. Both Cat and Lucas thought it was a bad idea, but Holly and Jake were family, and they wanted him there in case things went badly. So he went. Lucas took the keys to the Mitsubishi to drive home the three healers, who barely had enough strength to walk themselves to the car. Cat was left alone in the empty house, waiting for Ivan. It gave her time to get dressed and to think.

She was running out of time. She could feel it. Jack was out there, somewhere, just waiting for her to let down her guard. And while she loved Raphael, and Holly, she'd let everything with them distract her from what needed to be done. If Jack struck now, she wasn't ready, and she needed to be.

The crunch of gravel outside let her know that Ivan had arrived. Good. That meant she could get down to business.

Cat locked up the house and joined Ivan at the limo.

"Did she survive?" Ivan asked softly as he swung open the door.

Cat nodded wearily. "Yeah, but it wasn't easy. We're all pretty wiped out." She climbed in, taking the seat nearest the cab of the vehicle.

Ivan leaned his head through the door as she settled into her seat. "Lay down, rest. It's a long drive."

It was excellent advice. So she tried. She lay down on the long bench seat and closed her eyes. Unfortunately, while her body was utterly exhausted, her mind kept racing.

She hadn't heard from Jack. That was both refreshing and oddly alarming. Yes, she had been doing her exercises religiously. And the necklace Ivan had given her seemed to help as well. Still, something was going on. Cat could *feel* it. A sense of impending doom pressed on her, making her drive herself ever harder at her lessons, and her plan.

Information was pouring in from the spyware she'd planted with the e-mail from the charity she created donating to Jack's campaign. Every night she and Raphael worked their way through it all, sorting the wheat from the chaff. By far the best information came from the computer of Jack's personal assistant. Muriel Spenser had access to *everything,* although it appeared that she was on a vacation. She hadn't logged in for a number of days, which was perfect. Cat checked, double-checked, and triple-checked every bit of information she could gather. As unlikely as it would seem, Jack apparently only used one attorney for all of his business: Waters.

The file was the key. Then again, it always had been. She'd been creating the replacement paperwork, aging paper and labels with the aid of a sunlamp. Raphael had used dots of paint on the glass of her photocopier to create spots and flaws on the copies that were identical to those of the original. It was meticulous work, but it wasn't *difficult.* Raphael's old evidence kit had provided forensic evidence and samples that could be switched out with those in Jack's files. The problem was the video. She needed to find something appropriate to switch it out with. But what?

Cat felt the jerk of the wheels as they went from gravel to the smooth pavement of the interstate. Eventually, the gentle whir of tires on asphalt and the rocking of the car lulled her to sleep.

She dreamed of her mother. A part of her knew it was a dream, and was desperately sad at the same time she grasped onto the image.

They were in the kitchen at the beach house. The thin white lace curtains were blowing in a breeze that had the tang of saltwater and seaweed. Morning sunlight gleamed off the white tile surfaces. Janet was bustling around, popping bread into the toaster and gathering up a pair of cups to pour coffee for her daughter and herself. She wore her usual weekend garb, a

*man's denim shirt tied at the waist over a tank top and matching
shorts. She was barefoot, as well.*

Mom?

*Janet turned and smiled, fine laugh lines appearing at the
corners of her wide blue eyes. She handed Cat a mug filled with
steaming coffee.*

"Sit down, darling. We need to talk."

Janet gestured to a stool at the breakfast bar.

"I—"

*"Shh. We don't have a lot of time and I've got a lot of things
to tell you." She took a quick sip from her coffee mug. "First,
quit beating yourself up about being angry with me. If I had
had any sense, I would've told you about my past myself. It was
a rotten way for you to find out, and I'm sorry."*

*Cat blinked several times. Apparently her mother was just as
blunt in dreams as she'd been in real life.*

*"And yes, we would've liked Raphael. A lot. He suits you.
Don't let people give you a hard time and tell you to wait. Life is
too short to waste time worrying about other people's opinions." Janet set her coffee mug onto the counter and walked
over to stand inches away from Cat. She took her daughter's
face in her hands. "Don't worry. You can do this. And the answer to your problem? It's in your memories of the attack. You
just have to be willing to look at it." She leaned forward to kiss
her daughter on the forehead, and was gone.*

Cat woke with tears streaming down her cheeks. She rummaged around in the back of the limo until she found a box of
tissues. She spent the rest of the drive to Denver having a really
good cry.

Ivan reached behind him to slide open the glass partition that
divided the driver and passenger areas. "Are you all right?"

"I'm fine." Cat answered. "Crying helps sometimes, and I've
been needing to for a while."

"If you say so." He sounded doubtful.

His tone of voice made her smile. "I do." She scooped up the
pile of used tissues and dumped them into the waste can.

"We're almost to the mall," Ivan announced. "And I am done
here. I would rather not go just yet, but the Chief Justice needs
me elsewhere."

"I'll be fine, Ivan. Really."

"You are sure?"

"Positive." She put a smile in her voice. "But do me a favor. Come back for Christmas?"

"I can do that." His eyes met hers in the rearview mirror, his expression serious. "Be careful, Cat. Take no unnecessary risks. And if you need help, you will call me, *right*?"

"Right."

The mall was just ahead. Ivan caught the green light. Flicking on the turn signal, he turned the car into the driveway, slowing to a stop at the main entrance. He came around the car, opening the door for her. She climbed out. Stopping beside him for a moment, she got up on tiptoe to give him a quick kiss on the cheek. "Thank you so much for everything," she whispered.

"It has been my pleasure."

Chapter Thirty-seven

RAPHAEL STRETCHED OUT on the bed. He needed to rest. It had been a long day, and it was just getting longer. It wasn't the lack of sleep. He was used to doing without sleep on the three days of the full moon. But Holly's change had been difficult, and drained them all. Then, there had been the disastrous breakfast with the family at the Run. Raphael tried not to think too hard about that. He'd hoped that when Jake fought his way to Holly's side they might have been able to patch up their differences. It might have worked, too. But Jasmine had shown up, looking much the worse for wear after her punishment from Tatya.

Raphael sighed and rolled over, punching the pillow into a more comfortable configuration. There was nothing he could do about the family mess. It would iron itself out one way or another eventually. He just wished . . . But no. Better to keep out of the middle of it, and there were more urgent matters to be dealt with.

Late this afternoon they would have the ceremony where Lucas severed his ties to the pack and Raphael took it over. It wasn't that complicated a task magically, but it required a great deal of power. Which meant he needed to be at full strength. That, in turn, required *rest*. But his mind wouldn't leave him alone. His thoughts chased each other like a pup after its own tail.

Raphael rolled over onto his back and stared up at the bedroom ceiling. He was taking over the pack. It was real. All the years of playing second in charge and working in Lucas's shadow were over. He should be happy. But the fact was, he wasn't. This wasn't *his* pack, or his people, and they'd made that abundantly clear. The pack was splitting, because of *him*. Yes, only a few of them had chosen to go with Martin and Daphne. Most hadn't wanted to give up their jobs, homes, and lives here. But that didn't mean they wouldn't cause trouble. Hell, Raphael's own niece was one of the worst. If Jasmine didn't get in line he was going to have to take steps, and that would cause no end of trouble in the family.

Which brought him right back to the mess with Holly. She wouldn't be at the meeting tonight. She'd made her fealty to him privately this afternoon so that she wouldn't have to face Jake and the others. Her first real hunt would be with Cat, not with the pack that should be her home.

Was it so unreasonable for him to want the pack to accept his mate? He didn't think so. She had a lot to offer his people, if they could open their minds just a little bit and look at her as an individual instead of dismissing her from outright prejudice. Unfortunately, they hadn't shown any inclination to do that in the time she'd been here, and it didn't look as if that situation was likely to change.

As much as he hated to admit it, Jasmine had simply said what nearly the entire pack had been thinking. He had hoped it wouldn't come to a choice between his mate and his people, but that hope was fading fast. He had a home, a business that he'd spent decades building. He didn't want to lose them. But he would set it all aside in a heartbeat. Because these past weeks with her he'd learned the difference between existing and living.

He closed his eyes and focused on his mate. Right now she stood in the middle of the living room of her apartment. The portrait he'd painted of her parents was propped against the wall in front of her. There were tears in her eyes, but they were happy tears. He could actually feel her amazement that he'd gone to so much trouble, and her joy that he'd gotten it just exactly right. She reached out, placing a gentle fingertip against the canvas.

But simmering underneath her joy at the picture, there was rage. He shared that rage, and had for decades. They had to stop Jack—had to stop him before another family was torn apart. It would happen soon. Raphael could feel it in his bones. The tension was building with each separate document they created for the dummy file, with each computer file they sorted. He and Cat probably knew more about Jack right now than any other living being. Hell, they probably knew more about him than *he* did. His schedule, his movements, every detail of his existence was all documented. Raphael and Cat went through all of it, from the scheduled lecture on water rights at UCLA this afternoon to the VIN number of his brand-new private helicopter.

Raphael opened his eyes and threw off the sheet. It was useless. He wasn't resting. He wouldn't be *able* to rest. He might as well get up and go over the ceremony details again.

You seem exhausted, kitten. I take it you poured all your strength into saving the Sanchez girl? Not wise, my dear. Not wise at all. If I came for you tonight, you wouldn't stand a chance.

Cat growled at the empty air. Go away! Leave me alone. Either come here and take your best shot, or go away. Haven't you done enough damage to me?

Oh, no. Not by—What? No, I don't want any calls, Laura. Tell whoever it is that I'm in a meeting.

This was strange. For the first time, she was intruding on Jack's thoughts—being present when he thought he was alone.

He used *what* name? From Chicago? Oh, yes. I'll be more than happy to talk to . . . *Inteque*. Put the call through. I'm just in a mood for—

There was silence for a moment, and he must have realized that Cat was still connected. He gave a low, menacing growl that made her shiver to the tips of her toes before slamming down mental shields in a way that nearly blinded her with pain. Tears streamed from her eyes as she staggered toward the bathroom in search of something, anything, to dull the agony.

Chapter Thirty-eight

CAT HAD EXPECTED to hunt by herself, but Holly was waiting on the front porch of the mountain property when she drove the fully repaired rental car up the driveway. She had very deliberately switched vehicles in a covered parking lot in downtown Denver. No one other than the current, chosen few was to find out that Cerise and Cat were the same person, and she was taking every precaution to prevent it.

Cat could tell that Holly had been crying, but her scent held more rage than sorrow.

"Don't take this the wrong way," Cat said. "But shouldn't you be with the pack tonight? What if you have a hard time shifting again?"

"I won't. It was only that first time that was dangerous. I've shifted twice already today with no problem. Apparently I'm an alpha."

Holly didn't sound happy about it. That was kind of a surprise. While Cat couldn't see what the big attraction was to being able to change forms away from the full moon she'd learned from her books and lessons that it was considered a really big deal among the Sazi, and particularly among the wolves. Cat would have expected her friend to be delighted.

"All right, what's up?"

"Nothing." Holly was obviously lying—Cat could smell it. She shifted her weight uncomfortably from foot to foot, making the floorboards creak. "It's not important."

Cat gave her a long look. Holly wouldn't meet her gaze, but she didn't answer, either. She sighed. If and when Holly was ready to talk about it, she'd be there for her. In the meantime, they had other things to deal with.

"So," Cat spoke briskly. "Do you have any idea how we go about doing this? This is only my second moon, and both times so far Raphael came riding to the rescue with meat from the butcher."

"Oh, crap. I didn't think of that." Holly's eyes went wide. "I haven't got a clue. Didn't they train you in puppy school or something?"

"I quit early, remember."

"Well, hell," Holly shook her head ruefully. "Doesn't this just suck?"

Cat walked up to the house and opened the door for them both. "We'll either figure it out, or I'll spring for steaks when we get back to town."

The two women stripped, each folding her clothing carefully and stacking it neatly. The last thing Cat removed was the necklace Ivan had given her. She set it almost reluctantly atop her piled clothing and began walking to the French doors. She had just put her hand on the handle when she felt the intrusion and let out a gasp of pain.

Jack didn't slide into her thoughts, he bulldozed through them. While a part of her knew she stood in her cabin, looking out at a meadow, she saw another scene entirely.

It was an empty warehouse, at least three stories tall, its rough wooden supports covered by corrugated metal. A skylight, several of its panes cracked and broken, let the light of the full moon pour down into the building, illuminating some areas, while casting others in deepest shadow. A man was staked, spread-eagled faceup on the floor. Cat struggled to see who it was, but the angle was wrong, and Jack refused to move closer.

"I've noticed something about you, Cat."

Cat shuddered. Jack seemed totally coherent. He knew who she was. But was that a good or a bad thing?

"You are very protective of your human pets. You'd do almost anything to keep them from harm. You fought me to keep me from hurting your Aunt Violet, you stepped between Ned and the lovely Tatiana, and you've repeatedly done everything you can to protect Holly Sanchez."

"They're not pets.*"* *Her voice was harsh in her own head.*

"Perhaps that was an unfortunate choice of words." Jack shrugged. *"I told you to stay away from Ramirez. You disobeyed me. I intend to punish you for that."*

Jack paced restlessly around the edge of the room, always staying just far enough away that Cat couldn't see who his captive was.

His tone was bitter and seethed with rage when he continued. *"My first choice, again, was your aunt. But she seems to have disappeared. Nobody has heard a thing from her other than you. And you, my dear, have developed the irritating ability to block your thoughts. You've shut me out, my dear, and I don't like it."*

So, he had been trying to intrude. Cat would've felt more like cheering if she wasn't getting a psychotic's-eye view of someone she knew tied·and struggling at his mercy.

Then there was your friend Holly. As Raphael's niece she'd be perfect. *Unfortunately she's part of the Boulder pack, and is still under Inteque's protection."*

Cat remembered the last time he'd used the name Inteque. It had been the night of the challenge. He'd referred to Michael as *"Inteque's puppy."* So Inteque was either Tatya or Lucas. From what she'd gathered, Tatya wasn't much older than Raphael, which meant Lucas was the more likely . . .

Jack's words brought her back to the present. *"So, I was forced to search a little further into your past, and I came up with—"*

Jack stepped forward with a grand sweep of his arm, giving her a clear view of his prisoner, Brad, whose terrified eyes looked into Jack's—and into her own.

Cat threw up, all over the floor inside the French doors. Again and again, her stomach heaved until there was nothing left to come up. It severed part of the connection. Cat could no longer see the inside of the warehouse. Her eyes took in Holly's fearful expression, the moonlit meadow. But she heard the roar of a jaguar, the wet rending of flesh, and every hopeless scream.

Chapter Thirty-nine

CAT PULLED THE car slowly into the parking lot of the storage business the following morning. The closer she came to the building, the more tense she became. Her stomach was still roiling from last night. She could still hear Brad's screams echoing along with Jack's laughter in her mind.

She shuddered. Closing her eyes, she fought back tears. Brad was dead. Nothing she could do would bring him back. But she could avenge him, him and all of the others. And she could make sure it never happened again. But to do that, she needed the right tools, and that included the right computer.

Inside one of those units, behind one of those bright orange doors, was the Winnebago she and her parents had been camping in when they were attacked. She would have to go in there, face it. She *had* to. Cat forced her breathing to slow. She was starting to hyperventilate. She was suddenly cold, her body trembling.

I could just buy another laptop, she thought, but she knew that nothing she could get over the counter would match the quality of the machine in storage. She'd been "making do" with the standard machines at the hotel and Raphael's, and before that with Violet's home computer. All of them were solid enough machines for everyday use. None of them had the kind of "upgrades" that had been given to her by her father, upgrades and sample programs that hadn't even made it all the way through testing, let alone hit the market.

"I can do this," she told herself as she pulled the CRX into the parking space nearest the office door. Cat closed her eyes and took slow, deep breaths. "I *will* do this."

It was hard getting out of the car. She was trembling so badly it made her clumsy. Cat dropped her purse twice before she'd even managed to push the car door closed. Still, she forced herself to begin walking toward the office. Each step was more difficult than the last. Cat swallowed rapidly, forcing bile back down her throat. She would *not* be sick. Her heart was racing so that all she could hear was the sound of her own blood pounding in her ears.

Cat forced herself to open the glass door to the office, and pushed herself inside by dint of sheer willpower.

"May I help you?" Cat dragged her attention to the man standing behind the counter. Tall, thin, probably only in his late teens, the man had spiked hair that was dyed purple and didn't seem to go with his starched striped uniform shirt and navy dress pants. His face showed concern, as if he could tell she was in bad shape.

"Hi." Cat's voice was weak. She took a deep breath, staring into his warm brown eyes. "I'm Cat Turner. My aunt rented a storage unit for me here." She put the envelope with the bill on the counter. "I need to pay the bill and get some things out of it." Her voice sounded a little breathy, and she felt unsteady on her feet, almost lightheaded. She set her purse carefully onto the countertop and rested both hands against its smooth surface to steady herself. Inside her head beat a silent mantra, *I can do this, I can do this,* over and over. She hoped it was true.

Cat pulled out her checkbook from her purse, making the payment out for the exact amount before pushing the check across the counter to him.

"I'll need to see some ID."

Cat pulled her wallet out of her purse, showing her driver's license. He looked from her to the license, checking carefully before handing the wallet back.

"Unit 45." He gave her a look that was heavy with concern. "Are you okay?"

"No." She gave him a weak smile. "I've got the flu," she lied. "I should probably be home in bed, but I *really* need my computer equipment from the closet in the Winnebago."

"Bummer."

"I don't suppose," Cat asked wistfully, "you could go get it for me?"

"I can't go into a unit without the renter," he said with regret that seemed real. "It's against the rules. I'm sorry."

"If I come to the door with you?" She wheedled. She opened the wallet, drawing out a twenty-dollar bill and setting it on the counter.

His eyebrows rose, disappearing under his bangs.

"I *really* don't feel good," Cat explained.

He looked from the twenty to her pale face. Whatever he saw there made up his mind. He shoved the twenty back across the counter. "Keep the money," he told her turning to retrieve a set of keys from the desk behind him.

He stepped out from behind the counter, then opened the glass office door and held it for her. He followed her through, stopping only long enough to lock the door behind them.

That done, he turned to Cat. "Unit 45 is just around the corner." He smiled, and it made him look both younger and more handsome. "By the way, my name is Tom." He extended his hand for her to shake.

"Catherine, but my friends call me Cat."

His smile widened, showing teeth that were white enough and straight enough to be the result of a good orthodontist. Cat forced herself to return the smile, and shook the extended hand before following him around the corner of the building.

Number 45 was the third unit. It was huge, with a rolling garage door with latches on either side. The latches were held shut with a matching pair of padlocks that seemed much too small for their duty. Cat wasn't thrilled with the security, then decided, what the hell. Did she really care if someone stole what was behind those doors? In honesty, it might actually be a relief.

Between each of the large rolling doors on this side of the building were regular, human-size doors, each with a light shining directly above it. Tom walked over to the one marked 45/46 in block black numbers, inserting a key and opening it. He held the door open for Cat who, with growing reluctance, followed him into the dim corridor. It was a cramped hallway between unpainted drywalled walls, only just large enough for two people, the water fountain, and a small wastebasket. A locked door graced each side, opening into each of the two units.

Cat's stomach roiled. She felt bile rising in the back of her throat. She sank to her knees on the cold concrete floor, her stomach heaving as she threw up into the wastebasket.

"You *really* must need this stuff," Tom observed.

"You have no idea," Cat gasped, not bothering to look up.

Still shaking his head, he opened the door. He used his foot to flip the doorstop in place, keeping the door propped open. Cat heard the click as he switched the overhead lights on inside the unit.

"Where did you say this stuff was?" Tom called, his voice echoing in the large open space.

"In the closet of the kitchen," Cat called back. She didn't go to the door of the unit. She couldn't. It was all she could do to kneel here, hugging the waste can, within sight of the doorway. It shamed her, but she couldn't help it.

She heard the sound of his work boots climbing the metal steps of the motor home, heard the creak of the door opening.

Tom's voice was faint, but clear. "There's a ton of stuff in here," he called. "What all do you need?"

"Just grab it all," Cat answered. "I'll sort it later."

"Right."

Tom appeared a few minutes later, carrying a box filled to overflowing with electronic equipment. He set the box on the floor next to Cat, who still hadn't managed to rise.

"There was a half-empty box on the kitchen table," Tom said. "I just grabbed everything electronic from the closet and put it in with the rest of the stuff." He looked doubtful. "Is that all right?"

"Wonderful, thank you. More than you know." Cat took a deep, steadying breath. She accepted the hand he held out to her, let him help her up. She was still very shaky, but she wanted out of here. *Now.*

Tom used his arm to steady her for a moment. When she could stand on her own, he stepped away, loosening the doorstop, allowing the door to swing closed. He bent down, picking up the box. "I'll carry this to your car for you. You still don't seem too steady."

"Thanks," Cat answered.

"Can you get the door?"

It only took a few minutes to carry the box to the CRX and load it in the hatch. When they were done, he closed the hatch. Cat turned to him and asked, "Are you *sure* you don't want a tip? You've been incredibly nice."

"Nah. Don't worry about it," he assured her, smiling. "But I gotta get back inside. You go home and get to bed." He ordered, pointing a finger to her chest.

"I'll do that," she agreed.

Cat watched his back as he disappeared into the office. Tomorrow she was going to write a complimentary letter to the manager, praising Tom. She could never have done this without his help. He'd been a real sweetheart.

RAPHAEL GRABBED HIS cell phone and dialed Holly's number. Something was wrong with Cat. He just didn't know *what*. The lady in question had slammed down her shields so tight he couldn't get so much as a wisp of stray thought. She was alive, and not in any physical danger. He knew that much. Other than that, trying to read her was like beating his head against a brick wall.

It had started sometime yesterday afternoon or evening. Raphael wasn't sure exactly when. He'd had his hands full and hadn't noticed at first. When it finally had occurred to him, he hadn't minded. He'd had more than enough on his plate. Half of his pack hadn't bothered to show up for the ceremony or the night of his first hunt. Of the ones who had, three different wolves had to be punished for insubordination. He hadn't wanted her to know, and feel responsible, for the trouble he was going through. She had enough problems of her own without that.

But it was morning, and he was getting seriously worried. He felt like hell, his stomach roiling until he was ready to retch. He couldn't reach her mentally and she wouldn't answer her cell.

"Hello?" Holly picked up on the first ring, her voice breathless and raw.

"What in the hell is going on?" Raphael blurted the words out, not bothering with a greeting.

"Oh, thank God!" Holly let out her breath in a sob. "It's so awful!"

"What's happened?" Raphael forced himself not to shout. It wasn't easy. "Where's Cat?"

Raphael stood, listening in horror as Holly told him what Jack had done, and how Cat had been forced to witness it. "Where is she?"

"I don't know! I was cleaning up the mess, and I heard the car take off. I've tried calling her, and thinking at her, but she's completely shut down. Raphael, I'm scared!"

So was he. More than he dared say. Because last night had been the full moon, and while the human in her would be repulsed beyond tolerance, if the cat smelled the blood . . . well, it was the kind of thing that could destroy a person's mind, particularly in light of what Cat had been through with her parents just a few short weeks ago.

Baby, where are you? I need to know you're all right. He closed his eyes and leaned his head against the cold metal roof of his car. He didn't want to force her too hard; after last night she might panic. So instead, he deliberately calmed his mind and searched for the mating link that bound them, sending calm and strength through their bond at the same time that he tried to focus on the connection to see where she was and what she was doing.

He got an image in his mind of a plastic wastebasket, and the feel of cold concrete beneath her. He heard a man's voice call from a distance "Where did you say this stuff was?"

"In the closet of the kitchen," Cat called back.

When she spoke, the connection strengthened, and he knew where she was.

"Raphael? Are you there?" Holly's voice brought him back to himself, standing in a cold parking lot, phone clutched in his hand.

"I'm here. I found her." He started to say, "She's all right," but she wasn't. Not really.

"What should I do?"

"There's nothing you can do, Holly," Raphael said sadly. "You might as well just head back to the apartment. I'm going to talk to her."

"Is she going to be okay?"

"She's tougher than she looks." Raphael spoke the words to

reassure himself as much as Holly, but he knew it was true. Cat was tough, otherwise she'd never have made it this far with her mind and body intact. He just hoped she was strong *enough*.

He hung up without saying good-bye, climbing into the seat of the Mitsubishi.

Weekday morning traffic was ugly. Despite yet another day of clear weather he was stuck in rush hour, his mind divided between the idiot drivers on the road with him and the woman he loved. Even so, he made it to the apartment in Edgewater before she did, parking on the street next to her house and settling in to wait.

It was almost forty-five minutes later when she pulled the CRX into the carport. She met him halfway across the lawn, but she didn't reach out to hug him. Nor did she offer him a kiss. Instead, she stood rigidly still, looking weak, her very scent tainted as she stared at him from haunted eyes.

Raphael stopped short, keeping himself from touching her by sheer force of will. "Talk to me." He knew what had happened from Holly, but he needed to hear it in Cat's own words.

"You know." She accused him, her voice tight with tension. "Holly was bound to talk to you when I left the way I did."

The knot in his stomach tightened. "Cat—"

"He said he'd punish me for choosing you, and he did."

Her shields crumbled, and a tidal wave of pain and memory slammed into him. He physically staggered from the mental blow, and had to steady himself by grabbing onto the fence.

"I can't live with this, Raphael," Cat whispered. "We *have* to stop him. We *have* to! Before he does it again."

She was on the verge of hysteria and he didn't blame her a bit. There were professional law-enforcement agents who had collapsed under less strain than she'd been under. Hell, cops working serial killer cases were routinely rotated every few months. But this wasn't a case. It was her *life*, and there was no stopping point in sight.

He stepped forward, taking her in his arms. She buried her head against his shoulder, her arms tightening around him in a viselike grip.

"We'll get him." He whispered the words into her hair.

"Will we? Really? Or will he just go on, killing more and more innocent people? Brad didn't do *anything* . . . My parents . . . It's my fault. If it weren't for me . . . If I hadn't—"

"Stop it!" Raphael grabbed her by the shoulders, shaking her hard. "Stop it now! This is *not your fault!*" He pulled her close, holding her fiercely, *willing* her to believe him.

She shuddered, her body wracked with the force of her sobs, the moisture from her tears wetting the front of his shirt as he held her close.

Eventually the force of her crying subsided. Raphael reached into his pocket, retrieving a clean cloth handkerchief. He handed it to her, watching as she wiped her eyes and blew her nose noisily. She took a shaky step away from him. "Can you unlock the gate for me? I need to get a box from the car."

"You're the one with the keys. You unlock the gate. I'll get the box."

Raphael strode over to the CRX. He unlatched the hatch, moving aside as it lifted it up. Inside was a white banker's box filled to overflowing with computer equipment. Raphael stopped abruptly, nostrils flaring. The scents rising from the bottom of the box were old, but unmistakable. Jack's scent was there, and the trace of a pair of humans. Over it all, the harsh scent of dried blood.

"Cat, what's in this box?" Raphael tried to keep his voice calm.

She stood on the front porch stoop, her hand on the key she'd slid into the deadbolt. "The computer equipment I needed from the Winnebago, along with some other things. Why?"

"When we get inside, we're going to make some calls."

"Why?"

"Call it a hunch, but I want us to have witnesses here when you unpack this box."

Chapter Forty

"I DON'T ENVY you, Dad. When she wakes up she is going to be seriously pissed."

"Don't remind me." Raphael stifled a yawn. He carried Cat gently into her bedroom and lay her on top of the bed. He pulled off her shoes, dropping them onto the floor. Unfolding the quilt she kept at the end of the bed, he pulled it over her, giving her a quick kiss on the forehead as he did.

He'd hated using his Second Sight magic to put her out, but he'd done it. She was already distraught from last night's horror. The last thing she needed was to relive her parents' attack. He knew she'd be angry. It didn't matter. This was for her own good. Besides, he firmly believed that this was a Wolven matter, and no matter how intimately it might involve Cat, she was not, nor had she ever been, a cop.

Raphael straightened up. Taking a deep, steadying breath he turned to go back into the living room. He heartily wished that either Lucas or Ivan were here. Neither had been able to make it. Lucas had taken the Wolven jet, headed to Chicago on business. He wasn't answering his phone. Ivan was back with Charles. Like Charles and Councilwoman Angelique Calibria, he'd be watching the events unfold via live video feed.

Raphael walked down the narrow hall to Cat's living room, yawning hugely as he went. The bond he shared with her made it damned difficult for him to stay awake and alert.

"What I wouldn't give for a cup of coffee," he muttered.

"Don't even think about it," Charles advised. His voice came through so clearly Raphael would have sworn he was standing in the living room with Raven. "You do *not* want her waking up in the middle of this."

Raphael didn't comment. There was no point arguing, particularly when he agreed completely. Instead, he extended his hand, accepting the box of latex gloves Raven handed him. He pulled on a pair, fighting not to sneeze as the powder tickled his nose.

"I'll unpack the box," Raven suggested. "You take the pictures and bag and tag the evidence."

Raphael nodded his agreement and picked up the camera. A part of him was breathlessly eager to do this. His heart was pounding in his ears. So many years had gone by since he first recognized what Jack had become. So many lives lost.

Raphael said a silent prayer that something in that box would give them the last of what they needed. That *this* would be the last piece of the puzzle so that he could bring Jack down and see justice done.

"This is Agent Raven Ramirez," Raven spoke for the benefit of the voice-activated recorder as well as the video camera that had been set up to record their actions for presentation to the council at their next meeting. He gave the date, and announced the identities of all of the witnesses present both physically and via remote.

Introduction completed, Raven reached inside the box and began pulling items one by one from the box, giving a running commentary as Raphael snapped photographs then bagged and tagged the evidence.

There was a pair of laptops, various cables, a leather case of repair tools. But it was the next pair of items that made Raphael and the others pause. The first was a cast-iron skillet with a long wooden handle, its bottom marred with deep scratches and stains. It smelled of Jack, and blood, and there were four short hairs from his fur caught in the space where the wood met the iron. Raven set the skillet facedown across the box. He walked over to the sofa and opened a black leather case that Raphael had been too preoccupied to notice earlier. Reaching inside, he retrieved tweezers, an evidence bag, and a pair of test tubes. With exquisite care he removed the hairs that had been caught, dropping them into the evidence bag and sealing it shut before giving it to Raphael to tag. Next, he scraped small amounts of the dried blood into each test tube before sealing them and passing them over. He then went back to the case, retrieving fluorescent fingerprint powder with which to dust the pan's handle.

Slowly, meticulously they handled each bit of evidence as professionally as possible. There would be no room for criticism, no legitimate question of authenticity. Raphael knew there would be no helping the unfounded questions. Everyone was well aware of the situation between him and Jack. If Lucas had been available, Raphael would have stepped away from the picture, to avoid even the hint of impropriety.

It took time, but at last they reached the final item in the box. It was a video camera with a cassette still inside.

Raphael took a deep sniff. This was what he had scented most strongly. It smelled of a man and a woman, but most of all, it smelled of blood.

"Someone tried to wipe it clean," Raven observed. "They didn't do a very good job, though. The flap is stuck shut." They processed the evidence on the outside of the camera first. When they'd finished, it was Charles who spoke.

"Open it," he ordered. "We need to see what's on that tape."

"There's nothing here to watch it on," Raphael said.

"I've got a setup next door," Raven said. "It will take a few minutes to bring it over."

"Do it." Charles's voice was curt. The councilwoman and Ivan remained utterly silent. "We'll wait."

Raphael walked down the hall to check on his mate. She was still deeply unconscious. He knew that. But he was not, under any circumstances, going to be alone with the evidence. He lowered himself onto the edge of the bed, reaching one hand out to touch Cat's sleeping form. He was fiercely glad he'd put her under, but he was also proud. He couldn't believe she'd actually hit the cat in the head with a frying pan. It was funny in a sick, pathetic way—an act of desperation straight out of an old movie. Still, the blood and hair on the pan proved it had been more than a little effective. "That's my Cat, all right. You're a fighter. No doubt about it."

He half listened as, in the background, Charles and Angelique, councilwoman for the raptors, argued about what was to be done. It was the first the councilwoman had heard of the plan, and she was clearly unhappy about it. "Zis should have been debated before ze council! It iz *not* ze purview of ze Chief Justice—"

"The council reports to *me,* Angelique. Not the other way around. I will present our evidence to the council, and you may vote as you will. But know this: ultimately, I can override the council's wishes, and I will if I have to."

Raphael heard the slam of the apartment door, heard Raven shuffling around setting up the equipment. Still, he didn't leave Cat's side until Raven called his name and announced they were ready.

The tape was rewinding when Raphael walked into the room. Raven grabbed the remote from on top of the television and took his seat.

The tension was palpable. There was no conversation. Here and in Europe every witness sat on the edge of his seat, attention riveted.

It was a home video of a family vacation. It showed a sunny summer afternoon. Three very happy, affectionate people were teasing each other. He recognized Chris and Janet from the picture Charles had given him to paint the portrait, but seeing them move, watching them speak, he was struck forcibly by how *alive* they'd been. Their resemblance to and affection for their daughter was obvious.

When Cat first came into view Raphael gave a start. It was obviously her, but it was not the Cat he knew. She was acting the part of a put-upon daughter, frustrated and a little angry, but most of all soft. Any sexuality was latent. She wore a baggy pastel T-shirt that hid her figure with (of all things) wolf puppies on it over pink shorts and thongs. When her father said (for the tenth time) that this was their "last family vacation," she groaned audibly.

"Just humor your father, dear," her mother answered, "and wave at the camera." Cat buried her head in her hands in an exaggerated gesture of exasperation.

"I'm going to make myself some lemonade. Do either of you want any?"

"That would be lovely," her mother answered. The camera panned to follow Cat as she went into a very elaborate and expensive motor home. When the door slammed closed behind her the woman spoke. "Put the camera down, Chris."

"Why?"

"Because." It wasn't a reason, but the view from the camera shifted as he set it down. He didn't bother to turn it off. The viewers had a few minutes of picnic-table-height view of the campground and the sound of their quiet conversation.

"You really *are* getting maudlin about this you know." Her voice held a small amount of reproach.

"I know, it's just . . . I wish the two of you would make up."

Janet sighed. "She'll get over it eventually. I can't even blame her. I should have told her."

"Still—"

"Don't push!" she interrupted. "It'll only make her dig in her heels." Her tone turned playful. "Besides, I, for one, am looking forward to reaching our destination and having a little time *alone* with my husband." Her teasing voice got the desired reaction.

"Oh, really?" The husband sounded positively eager. "Just what do you have in mind?"

"Oh, I don't know—" she began and the camera got bumped. The view only changed slightly, but the excellent sound system picked up what sounded like an incredibly passionate kiss.

That went on for a couple of minutes. Then it happened. It was fast—incredibly fast. Neither of the victims had seen it coming. Neither had time to be afraid.

It was gruesome, but it was mercifully quick. In the process of killing the couple Jack hadn't noticed the camera and knocked it to the base of the picnic table. A wet, tearing sound accompanied Jack's evisceration of Chris. Blood, hair, and worse splattered the camera lens.

The camera showed Jack's attentions to Cat's mother, her scream cut off suddenly, replaced by a wet gurgling. In the distance, the slam of the motor home door followed by the crash of glass and the terrified screams.

Jack snarled, and they heard the thump as he leapt to the ground. He was out of camera range now. The viewfinder was focused on a half-eaten arm slowly oozing blood. Still, the sound system picked up every noise.

She fought him. Raphael was so proud. He couldn't see what she was doing, but he could hear. She wasn't giving up without a fight. She managed to get loose, managed to hurt him badly enough to get into a hidey-hole where he couldn't reach her. Raphael knew it because he heard the rage and frustration in Jack's voice. "You can't stay in there forever, you know." Catherine gasped in disbelief. Raphael forced himself to concentrate on the sounds, ignoring the bloody arm.

Jack's suave, rich baritone took on a snarling, toying tone. "Come out, come out, wherever you are."

Raphael heard movement and a cry of pain. There were guttural noises as the cat tried to drag the Cat out of her "hole," followed by the clang of metal hitting a hard surface, a male yelp of pain, and a series of curses. "You little bitch!"

"Atta *girl!*" Raven cheered softly.

"You'll pay for that!" Jack's snarl brought Raphael's attention back to the screen. There was the sound of movement. The arm was dragged out of camera range. There was a gasp, and a feminine sob.

You fucking bastard! Raphael fought not to speak the words aloud. He remembered Cat's words. "He *ate* them in front of me." After seeing this, Raphael wondered how she was even remotely sane.

Jack's voice, smooth and cultured, came from the screen: "Mmm, mmm, fresh meat."

Jack taunted her mercilessly. Each comment, each action was a poisoned barb intended to draw her out—make her angry enough to get careless. It didn't work. But it was the stuff of nightmares and insanity. Raphael didn't know how she'd stood it—how she could stand it even now. He had never in his life wanted to kill someone so badly. That smooth, cultured voice, perfectly reproduced.

Time seemed to stop. Raphael's thoughts cut abruptly away from the film. That was it, the last piece of the puzzle. There was no picture of Jack on the tape—at least not in human form. But it wasn't necessary. That beautiful, perfectly reproduced voice was damning. As a senator involved in water and environmental issues Jack had spoken publicly often enough that anyone, at least anyone from the New Mexico/Colorado area would recognize it. The Sazi Council certainly would.

The tape played on. There were shouts and the sound of gunshots in the background. Cat's screams had brought reinforcements. Jack was forced to flee, leaving behind a live witness and a damning video.

Silence stretched on for long moments. Finally, Raven rose, turning to face the camera phone. "I'll bring the video with me for you to present to the council at the next meeting."

"No." Charles's voice was soft, but there was an energy running beneath the words, a tension that spoke of barely controlled rage. His face on the screen was pale, his hands shaking. "Make me a copy. Keep the original in the safe. We'll need it when the file is complete."

"I don't want Cat seeing this, Charles." Raphael spoke carefully. "I'm not sure what it would do to her after last night."

"What happened last night?" Angelique's voice was a sharp screech that made Raphael wince. Raven turned to his father, his expression questioning. Raphael nodded his permission to tell them.

"Jack murdered a man, and he used a telepathic link to Cat to make her watch it."

Charles absorbed the news as an almost physical blow. "Who? It wouldn't have been random. Who was the victim?"

"Her former fiancé . . . Brad."

"Jenkins." Charles furnished the name. If anything, he paled further, but his eyes were dark, and Raphael could see the alarm on Angelique's face as her nose twitched in response to the scents that were no doubt flowing off of him.

"Lock the original tape in Cat's safe. It *must* stay in Colorado." Raphael didn't say a word. There was no arguing with Charles when he used that tone of voice.

Chapter Forty-one

THE WAITING WAS the hardest part. It was only 6:00 A.M. and Raphael was already sitting at his desk at pack headquarters. He hadn't been able to sleep, so he'd come in to work.

Raven was right. Cat had been more than pissed. She'd been furious. It was the kind of cold, calculating rage that had enabled her to shut him out completely for nearly four days. Her shields were absolutely flawless, and a part of him cursed the very lessons he'd given her. Raphael wasn't pining for her . . . yet. But if this kept up he might well start.

He'd coped thus far by keeping busy, dealing with the towing business, with the collections from Jake's customers. At eleven Holly would be coming by the office to prepare the annual pack Christmas party. He even got around to sending thank-you notes for all of the gifts he was receiving on his promotion. It didn't help. One of the two copies of the replacement file, along with the evidence they'd gathered, was with Raven in Chicago right now being presented by Charles to the full council in an effort to have them vote in favor of issuing a warrant.

Raphael wasn't much of a religious man. He was personally acquainted with Sazi who were old enough to have been worshipped as gods themselves. Still, a part of him wanted to believe in a benevolent creator out there, somewhere. If that deity did exist, surely he'd be in favor of putting an end to Jack's madness.

In the heat of the moment Charles had said he'd proceed with or without the council's blessing, but every hour that passed made Raphael more and more unsure. He wished Raven would call. In fact, it was all he could do to keep from calling himself. But Raphael knew that as soon as the warrant issued, Raphael would be the first person Raven would call.

Of course, *executing* the order would be another trick. Raphael drummed his fingers in a staccato rhythm against the desktop. A sniper, or pair of them, perhaps; maybe a bomb. Whatever they did, it needed to happen *before* Jack caught wind of their plan. Because the fact was, Jack had resources and sources everywhere. Insanity didn't keep him from being ruthless, intelligent, and pragmatic. Given even a hint of their plans he'd take countermeasures, and revenge.

Raphael was sipping his coffee, trying not to dwell on his fears, when he felt Cat's mind slam into his. She didn't bother trying to be gentle. She was too angry. But there was a feeling of triumph to her thoughts as well.

The file is switched.

Cat? My God, what have you done?! Raphael was appalled. Yes, the switch needed to happen, but if the council found out that she'd done it without consent . . .

Charles knows. He approved it. We wanted it switched *before* the council meeting. He didn't trust that the information wouldn't get back to Jack otherwise.

It made perfect sense. But Raphael felt his own anger rising that Cat would've done this without him. It had been damned dangerous. Someone, *anyone* else could have done it.

It was my right to do it. It's *my* plan.

Raphael growled and slammed his hand palm first against the surface of his desk, hard enough to knock over the desk lamp. So I'm just supposed to sit back—

Maybe I wanted to *protect you.*

The bitterness in that thought was palpable. No, she was definitely not over his knocking her out to go through the evidence. He'd explained at the time that he'd wanted to protect her after the shock of Brad's murder. It hadn't calmed her. If anything, it had made her even angrier. But damn it! This was different!

Different *how,* exactly? Because you're *male*?

Oh, no. He was *so* not falling into that trap. Besides, it simply wasn't true. More than half of the agents he'd worked with in Wolven had been female, and they were easily as skilled and as ruthless as their male counterparts. Hell, in jaguar form Cat was bigger, stronger, faster than Raphael, and he knew it. He'd tried to protect Cat because she was his mate, and he always would. He couldn't help himself.

There was a long silence in his head, but he could tell she wasn't gone. He hadn't meant to think that last "out loud," but he knew that she'd heard it. Her next words were quiet and thoughtful.

My flight lands at DIA an hour. When I get back we need to talk.

What airline? I can pick you up at the airport. He didn't say *if you'll let me,* but he couldn't help thinking it.

Southwest.

I'm on my way. Raphael rose from his desk. He hesitated before saying the next words to her. Cat, I'm sorry. I never meant . . .

I know. He heard her mental sigh. It wasn't a happy sound, but he could sense that her anger with him was fading. We'll talk when I get there.

I love you.

I love you, too. She didn't sound particularly happy about it, and she cut the connection cleanly, dropping her shields back in place. But this time he could feel her in the background.

Raphael let out the breath he'd been holding. She'd stopped blocking the mating bond. That *had* to be a good sign. He told himself that they'd work this out.

Unfortunately, he was anything *but* sure of that. He couldn't count the number of relationships he'd screwed up in his life. It was almost a joke among his acquaintances, though it was far from funny. But he loved her, and she loved him. Damn it, they *would* get through this. Once Jack was dead—

Raphael stopped abruptly, his hand on the door handle as the realization hit him. For the first time in decades he had hope, had dared *believe* that there was a life for him *after Jack.* It was the most amazing feeling. He wasn't quite sure how to handle it.

He was still standing there, bemused, when his cell phone rang. He flipped it open to see who was calling. It was Raven. Raphael took a long, shaky breath and hit the button to take the call.

"Ramirez."

Raven kept his voice low, and he sounded more tired than Raphael would've liked, but the words he spoke were just what his father needed to hear. "Dad, it's me. It wasn't easy—things happened here that made the debate a lot closer than we would've liked, but it's done. How's everything at that end?"

"Good," Raphael answered. Like his son, he avoided saying anything specific. "Cat took care of that errand for Charles."

"All right, then. I'll let him know. Be sure to watch the news tonight. It should be interesting."

"Oh, I will."

CAT WAITED FOR Raphael at the edge of the sidewalk in front of the terminal. A pair of inexpensive navy bags sat on the sidewalk beside her. She shivered a little as a cold wind cut through the fabric of the navy blue suit jacket she wore over a white cotton blouse and faded blue jeans. There was no moisture on the breeze coming out of the west, so no snow tonight, despite the heavy clouds that gave the daylight a strange, flat quality.

She'd changed in the bathroom, wanting to meet him as Cat rather than as Cerise. It was silly and vain of her, but she knew he preferred the more clean-cut persona. Cat shook her head. She loved him, arrogance and all. Oh, she'd been truly furious with him over what he'd done. He'd explained himself *afterward*. She even understood. But it didn't change a thing. He should have *talked* to her first. Asked her, instead of using some sort of Sazi equivalent of the Vulcan vise grip or whatever the hell it was called.

But angry as she was, she'd still missed him, more than she would've liked to admit. Hearing his voice today, listening to the apology that was obviously hard for him to give . . . Well, she forgave him. But he'd damn well better promise *never* to do it again!

She turned at the distinct sound of his boots on concrete. He appeared at the parking garage entrance, his hazel eyes scanning the crowded sidewalk at the same time his nose lifted to scent the breeze. That same breeze blew back his hair, giving her a good look at the fine lines of his face. He looked tired, and more than a little worried. But his smile when he caught sight of her was enough to light up the day.

He was wearing a charcoal-gray shirt that looked, and moved, liked silk, over black jeans that were faded from use but showed every muscle to perfect advantage. She sensed more than saw the envious glances of other women up and down the promenade. The fluid quality of his movements as he dashed across the street between traffic made her body ache with pure, undiluted lust.

He stopped just short of touching her, as though he were unsure of himself, of how she would react. Even his scent was uncertain. In that moment she let go of what was left of her anger. She let her purse fall to the ground and stepped into his arms. Even in tennis shoes she was only slightly shorter than he was. She reached up, running her hand lightly over the rough stubble of his beard, relishing the texture and the electricity that sprang to life between them. Slowly, she moved closer, her lips finding his in a slow, almost chaste kiss.

His hands spasmed painfully against her waist and she heard the small, needy noise he made against her lips. He finished the kiss gently, but moved his mouth to the base of her throat finding the pulse point and biting against it hard enough to bruise.

It hurt, but the pain was washed away in a wave of need that overwhelmed her shields and made her body tighten as it stole her breath away. It was good that he held her, because at that moment Cat wasn't positive she'd be able to stand.

"I missed you." Raphael murmured into her hair, and she could hear him drawing in deep breaths as he reveled in her scent.

"Me, too." Her voice was breathy, her pulse racing. "And just as soon as I can walk we're going back to my place and I'll show you just how much."

Raphael gave a low, wicked chuckle. "I can carry you, if it'll help."

"Not and get my bags." Cat teased. She ran her fingers playfully over the thin silk of his shirt, feeling and scenting his body's reaction to her touch.

Raphael sighed happily, but stepped back a pace. "Fine. I'll play bellhop." His eyes twinkled "But I'd better get a *really good* tip."

"I think I can manage that." She gave him a wink, and was rewarded with a grin that flashed those deep dimples she found so irresistible.

Raphael gathered up the bags, leading the way back to the short-term parking section of the covered garage. Cat lagged a step or two behind for the sole purpose of watching the play of muscles as he walked. She couldn't imagine ever getting tired of this man. He could be infuriating and frustrating, but at least he was never, ever dull. The few days she'd spent blocking him out of her mind had felt wrong. She hadn't realized how much she'd come to rely on his solid, comforting presence in the back of her mind.

Raphael stored her bags in the backseat of the Jeep, then walked around the vehicle to open her door. He watched as she climbed inside, even those simple movements making his body tighten with need.

"We'll get there faster if you get in the car and drive." Cat's tone was saucy, her eyes sparkling merrily.

"Yeah. Right." He shut the door with a brisk slam, hurrying around to the other side of the vehicle. He practically jumped inside, slammed the door closed, and started the engine with a roar.

Raphael, you might as well relax. Even hurrying it's going to take at least forty-five minutes to get back to the apartment.

Raphael groaned in frustration.

And it'll take longer if you get stopped for speeding.

Raphael turned, glaring at her balefully, but he did let up on the accelerator. Cat decided it was time to change the subject. She chose the one that was nearly always at the forefront of her mind.

"Any word from Charles or Raven on Jack?"

"The warrant has been issued. Apparently it was a close debate because of something that happened at the Chicago meeting. But it was issued. Since your part's taken care of, they should be able to execute the warrant sometime today."

Cat let out a sigh, her body visibly relaxing into the black leather seat. "Thank God! It's almost over." She closed her eyes as a feeling of utter weariness washed over her.

"Are you sorry it won't be you taking him down?" Raphael's voice was serious.

Cat opened her eyes and stared out the car window at the bare winter fields that lined the road. She searched for a long moment, trying to come up with the right words to express her feelings. "Yes, and no." She turned to him. "I've trained with Raven and Ivan. I'm good, but they're better. *Much,* much better. They just *are.* We can't afford to risk Jack surviving and getting away. Too many lives are at stake. If that means I have to step back and let the professionals finish him off, then so be it. I came up with the idea. I switched the files. That's enough." She took a deep breath, letting it out slowly.

Raphael's scent changed. She drew in a deep breath, reveling in the smells rolling off of him: love, warmth, and *pride.* He was proud of her. That meant a lot. Because letting go of this was *not* easy.

"I love you, Cat Turner."

"I love you, too." She turned giving him a wicked, feral, grin. "Let's go home and celebrate—I've got cable. We can keep CNN on in the background. Just in case there's any *interesting* news."

One minute Cat was laughing in the seat next to him, and the next minute she was staring blankly forward. Raphael pulled the car onto the shoulder and to a stop. As he watched, she slammed forward against the seat belt as though struck.

"Cat?" As soon as he touched her arm he was drawn into the vision with her.

They were in a familiar clearing, the helipad in the distance. Jasmine stood between Holly and Yusef. "You said she was bait for the cat. She wasn't to be harmed!"

Yusef sneered at her down the length of his beakish nose. "I lied." He pulled the trigger, and Jasmine staggered backward, blood blooming from her chest. Holly screamed, and fought with everything she had against the rough hands holding her. But Martin was too strong. She couldn't break free. She could only watch in horror as Yusef stepped calmly forward and placed the gun barrel against her sister's forehead. "And you just became a liability." He pulled the trigger, watching impassively as blood, bone, and worse splattered against the barren ground.

Holly looked up suddenly, as though she could see something. "Help! *Cat, help.* Oh, my God!"

Then, with a burst of adrenaline-fueled strength, Holly broke free—changing forms in midstride, leaping over the nearest boulder in a terrified bid for freedom. There was the crack of a gun firing, and she howled in agony, her hip shattered by a bullet that was meant to injure, not kill. She fell, nose over tail, landing in a graceless heap on the ground, panting and whimpering with pain.

"God you're useless." Yusef snarled as he backhanded Martin to the ground. "You can't even hold a new attack victim? No wonder they won't give you your own pack!" Raphael watched in horror as Charles's most trusted bodyguard stalked toward his niece . . .

He knew that Holly's only hope right now rode on Cat's talent.

"Cat, can you hear me? We have to get there. We're headed to the mountain right now." Cat nodded. Tears were streaming unheeded down her face and her white-knuckled fingers clutched the door handle.

"Can you get in Martin's head? Don't try Yusef. He's too powerful, and too damned likely to catch you. But we need to know what they want with her, and to find out their plans."

As he watched, she closed her eyes. He could tell she'd succeeded when he saw her features harden into harsh lines. When she spoke her voice was cold and had a distant, hollow quality that sounded precisely like Martin Black.

"Jack found out we switched the file. He plans to use Holly as a hostage. He knows Wolven will consider her expendable—but that *I* won't. He's on his way to pick her up. If I don't cooperate they'll force Holly to change on camera and start building a *new* insurance file *before* they kill her."

Raphael's thoughts were dark with rage. He could barely speak through his clenched jaw. "Does Martin know *when* Jack's due?" There was no time to waste. They needed weapons. They had what he wore on his person, and the few things in the car, but not nearly enough.

She shook her head like Martin would. "Not for another three hours. Jasmine was early. They hadn't expected her to bring Holly until after the meeting with you at eleven."

They'd known about his appointment with Holly! Only someone on the office staff would have access to his calendar. Which meant there were more traitors within the pack. Raphael pulled back onto the highway, pressing down on the gas pedal, opening up all eight cylinders in a race to save Holly.

Cat shuddered, her eyes cleared, and she was suddenly back in her own body. "Yusef was getting suspicious. Apparently having me riding along changed Martin's body language or something. I didn't dare stick around. But I did find out that they plan to stay up there. They're loading Holly into the back of a van."

Raphael only half listened to her. His mind was racing. They had three hours. A good half of that time would be taken in the drive up to the helipad. Lucas, Tatya, Raven . . . nearly everyone he truly trusted was clear the hell on the other side of the country. His best weapons were in his office safe—but they didn't have the time to spare to go get them. Reaching into the pocket of his jacket, he grabbed his cell phone and hit the third number on speed dial. If he was wrong . . .

The phone rang, and rang, but there was no answer. Raphael gripped the phone tight enough that the plastic began to crack. He urged the Mitsubishi around a slower-moving car and onto the interstate, headed toward the mountains.

"Cat, can you slide into Betty's thoughts?"

"Betty's?"

"There's a traitor in pack headquarters. I want to make sure it isn't her."

Cat's eyes unfocused. Almost immediately she began swearing under her breath. Raphael watched as her power flared until the hairs on his arms began crawling and the temperature in the car began to rise.

"Cat—"

"She's only semiconscious. Daphne shot her, but she went down fighting. Sally's dead, and she damned near tore Daphne's leg off before she passed out from blood loss.

Raphael grabbed onto Cat's arm, joining his limited gift to hers in an attempt to see and speak with the Second Female while at the same time driving the car. It was tricky, and dangerous. He didn't dare let himself get too distracted by the vision.

Betty was badly hurt. Only the fact that Daphne hadn't *known* to shoot an alpha in both the head and heart had saved her life. As it was, she pulled the power Cat offered into herself using it to augment her own abilities and close the bullet hole in her chest.

Cat, they took Holly. Jasmine was with them. You have to warn Raphael . . .

I'm right here, Raphael told her. I was going to contact you, see if you could bring my weapons from the safe. But—

But nothing, Betty snarled viciously. She reached upward, grabbing the top of the nurse's station and hauled herself upward. She lay gasping on its surface for a long moment afterward, but her thoughts were clear. Give me the combination and pick me up at the bar.

Chapter Forty-two

THE JEEP LURCHED and bucked, its engine whining in protest. Raphael thanked God he'd chosen to drive the Jeep this morning because the tracks were sliced with gullies from the last melt and very nearly vertical. Yellow dust blew into the air in a cloud that marked their passage. Raphael rolled down the window. Tall weeds, bent and bowed from the last snow, slapped at his face as he looked toward the sky. There was no sign of a helicopter yet. The vehicle rocked and slid sideways, its wheels spitting loose gravel in an arc as they sought traction. Finally, they caught and the car lurched forward. It slammed roughly against a half-buried boulder, rocking dangerously onto two wheels before gravity won and the vehicle hit the ground with a solid whump.

Betty swore roundly as her head slammed against the roll bar. She was crammed uncomfortably into the backseat. Cat was bracing herself with her left arm on the dashboard, while her right hand held the handle above the door in a death grip. Her eyes were closed, and Raphael knew she was concentrating, trying to use her gift.

Raphael said a silent prayer of thanks that Betty hadn't been stopped on the way to their meeting point. The arsenal she'd brought with her would've earned her a one-way ticket to prison from the humans, and the graveyard from Wolven. She'd brought *everything:* all the weapons, all the ammo. Since he wasn't sure what they were up against, he hadn't argued when she and Cat had transferred everything from the Volvo to the Jeep.

Raphael slowed slightly. This next section was going to be

difficult, even for the Jeep. He had chosen the most direct route he knew up to the helipad. It was barely more than a trail, and not something he would've dared in any other vehicle. But this route had saved them a good half-hour of time. It was time they'd need because the last part of the route would have to be taken on foot and from upwind if they were to have any hope at all of surprise.

They were probably outnumbered. There were only three of them, after all. Betty hadn't trusted anyone else enough to bring him along as backup. Neither had Raphael.

They were nearly to the point where the trail intersected the two-lane highway. Raphael pulled the vehicle to a skidding stop beneath a small stand of pine. He jumped from the vehicle, and began to strip.

"I'm going to scout ahead while you unload. Cat, if I'm not back in twenty minutes, use your gift to look for me."

Raphael started up the steep incline in wolf form. He tried to use what cover he could. There wasn't much. They were not quite high enough to be above the tree line. The rocky ground was only sparsely dotted with slender pines and dead weeds. Small patches of snow dotted the spots the winter sun couldn't reach. His paws were nearly silent as he moved with practiced ease through familiar territory. Every sense was stretched to its utmost. He circled wide, intending to approach the area from behind and above where Cat had last seen their enemies. He was looking either for scouts, or for signs of electronic surveillance. If he were in charge, he'd use both. He hoped Yusef wasn't as methodical, but he'd be willing to bet otherwise. You didn't rise through the ranks to become one of the Chief Justice's personal bodyguards without being both very good and very thorough.

He stopped, barely daring to breathe. He tilted his head, listening: in the distance, to his left he heard a familiar voice. It was Martin, and he wasn't happy at having been assigned to patrol the perimeter.

"I just *did.* There's no one out here." Raphael heard the click and static from a radio. Yusef's voice coming through the speaker was only slightly distorted.

"The sensors picked up something to your right. It's about the right size for a wolf."

Raphael stepped softly across the rough ground, moving into the deep shadows of a rocky outcropping. He could hear Martin's approach easily. The fool wasn't even *trying* to be quiet.

Raphael.

Not *now*, Cat!

They had someone patrolling in wolf form. I had to kill her. She was getting ready to sound the alarm. Betty and I are moving out. We'll be taking positions on high ground.

Right.

Cat cut the connection just as Martin appeared in the open space opposite the outcropping. He was moving more carefully now, his nostrils flaring as he scented the breeze. He was armed, but it was obvious he wasn't used to carrying a weapon. Still, it didn't take a great deal of skill to kill someone at close range with the right firearm. And it was a perfectly lovely gun, his favorite Ruger, the one that had disappeared at Violet's house. Raphael's eyes narrowed as he recognized his weapon and knew where Martin had to have gotten it.

He waited, tensing every muscle for the perfect instant, when Martin was turned, then leapt with everything he had, claws and teeth rending skin and cloth as his weight carried both of them to the ground with a jarring impact that slammed the breath from Martin's lungs and sent the gun flying from his hand.

It was a quick, dirty fight. Martin was alphic enough to resist most of Raphael's magic, but he'd relied too much on the gun in his hand. With that gone, in human form, he was no match for Raphael's teeth and claws. Still, somehow he managed to get his bent legs beneath the wolf's body straightening them to throw Raphael off of him.

Martin frantically scuttled away on his hands, trying to buy time and space to shift, but Raphael leapt onto his back. Locking his jaws around Martin's spine he jerked his head sideways until he heard the fragile bones snap, felt the spinal cord sever. He shifted then. With a single, brutal kick he rolled Martin's limp body onto its back. He was alive, though paralyzed. His lungs struggled for air, the messages from the brain barely making it through to keep life in his broken body. Given a chance he might heal. But Raphael would make sure there was no chance. Raphael bent down to pick up the Ruger. He put the first bullet in Martin's chest, the second in his skull.

The radio crackled inside the pocket of the dead man's jacket. "Black, *report*."

Raphael retrieved the radio, and pressed the button to transmit. He focused, deliberately mimicking the dead man's voice. "Ramirez is dead." He made his voice triumphant. "I *killed* the bastard!"

"Bring the body down here."

"Why?"

"Just *do it*, Black. Everybody else, report."

Daphne Black was the first to report. "I'm here with the Sanchez woman. She's healing." Raphael counted as three additional voices came over the radio, all wolves, all members of *his* pack. Raphael felt the bile rise, and his eyes bled red as his power rose in reaction to his rage.

"Melissa, report. *Melissa?*" There was no answer. Nor would there be. Raphael cursed under his breath. He should've warned Cat to take the radio, but there was no help for it now, and even with magic augmenting it, he couldn't make his voice a feminine soprano.

"All right people. We have company." Yusef's voice was calm. "Stay alert."

CAT MOVED WITH exquisite care. Avoiding the patches of snow was obvious, but there were other ways of leaving your mark upon the ground, and every one of the Sazi in Yusef's group was bound to be more experienced at hunting and tracking than she was.

She paused, sending out a tendril of thought. Betty was in position and loading her weapons. She had chosen a tall rock formation that would give her an excellent view of the helipad. Of course she'd have to be damned careful *not* to allow herself to be silhouetted against the skyline—but she was smart enough to know it. She was also armed to the teeth, having taken both the Tommy gun and the grenade launcher, and ammunition for both. Her half-healed chest wound might not allow her rapid mobility, or her usual strength, but she was determined to be a part of this fight.

Cat had chosen feline form. Guns were great distance weapons, but they made *noise*. She'd dispatched the female guard with teeth and claws in near silence. It had bought them precious minutes, and Cat wasn't wasting an instant of it.

Holly, are you there?

Cat? Oh, my God, Cat! They killed Jasmine, and I heard them say—

It's all right. That was Raphael pretending to be Martin

But it sounded—

Trust me, I know. But we need information. Do you know where you are, how many of them there are, and how many are guarding you?

I'm in the back of a van. The only one with me is Daphne, but I don't know how many others there are.

Right.

Cat heard the snap of a twig and a metallic click. Her body reacted before her mind could make sense of the sounds, jumping sideways.

The shot was loud. It echoed deafeningly off of the rocks as the bullet sent splinters flying like miniature missiles from the pine she had been standing in front of.

She attacked in a blur of speed, eviscerating the gunman before he could pull the trigger for a second shot. He screamed, a high-pitched, hopeless sound that ended in a wet whistle of air as Cat tore the head from his neck with a single swipe of her massive paw.

Too much was happening at once. There were gunshots, screams, and the howling of injured wolves. Cat felt Raphael's rage and panic. There were too many of them . . . they had him surrounded—

Cat ran with everything she had, the ground a blur beneath her paws. She'd nearly reached him when the explosion from the first grenade hit. It missed by a fair margin, but the noise was deafening and a rain of rock, dirt, and shrapnel flew through the circling wolves.

Though bloodied, the wolves showed no sign of retreating. Growling their defiance, they turned their attention to Cat.

Yusef, meanwhile, stood in a two-handed stance, firing silver bullets at the blur of motion that was Raphael until his gun clicked empty. Cat felt a surge of power, and a huge black bear rose on his back legs where the gunman had stood.

She felt, rather than saw the first wolf's attack. Low and fast, it was a move meant to hamstring an opponent. Cat rolled out of the way, directly into the path of one of the others. He dove onto her, his bared fangs going for the jugular, but she used her momentum and speed to carry her until *she* was on top, her claws digging into the thick meat of his body. She pulled him forcibly away, his jaws snapping at air a fraction from her throat, even as his breathing grew labored from the pressure as she used main strength to try to crush his chest.

There was the thud of impact, and she was thrown off of her opponent by a smaller female wolf. "You killed my son." The animal stalked toward her, its eyes glowing and feral, magic crackling along her body, until each hair stood on end. A second wolf moved to flank her. The injured male had reverted to human form, and was crawling in the direction of a discarded weapon.

Cat positioned herself as best she could, putting a boulder at her back. She crouched, preparing for the attack when the first shot rang out. The injured male went down screaming, blood spraying from the hole in his chest. A second bullet took the female in midleap. It was a clean chest shot, but it did not take her heart. Still, she fell to the ground with a thud, blood spurting from the wound as red bubbles frothed her lips.

Cat glanced over in shock, seeking the source of the gunshots. Holly Sanchez balanced herself against the side of a white van, all her weight on her good leg. Blood oozed from dozens of scratches and bites, but she held a 9 mm Beretta in a classic teacup grip and was firing rounds into their enemies.

There was no time to wonder how her friend had escaped, or where and when she'd learned to shoot with such lethal accuracy. The last wolf was upon her.

Cat took the bulk of the impact of his leap on her shoulder. Turning, she bit at his neck. The coarse fur of his neck ruff filled her mouth as she struggled to reach the vulnerable skin of his throat. His claws raked down the side of her body in long, bloody furrows. She twisted away, emitting a high-pitched yowl of pain and rage as she spit the fur from her mouth.

The wolf darted in, pressing his advantage. Cat spun, lashing out with her claws. She scored along his face, lacerating his eye so that blood and fluid splattered the dusty soil between them. He howled in pain, but continued attacking, keeping his head turned to watch her with his one good eye as he snaked to and fro, looking for an opening.

A shot rang out. Bone and brains sprayed from the wolf's skull. He staggered, and fell to the ground.

Cat looked around the battleground. Holly was hopping on one leg from one to another of the injured wolves, making sure each was dead.

Raphael stood in human form over the corpse of the massive bear. Even as she watched, his terrible wounds began to heal— but too slowly. *Betty. He needs to get to Betty.* That thought brought another, less welcome one. Where *was* Betty? There'd been no fire from her position since the explosion from her firing the grenade launcher.

She was sending her thoughts toward Betty, her ears ringing. Through the other woman's eyes she saw a huge eagle swooping down, yet again for an attack. She was bleeding badly, her injured movements making her too slow. Raphael's thoughts joined Cat's. We have to help her.

Raphael shimmered and changed forms, limping in wolf form toward the cliff where Betty was fighting. Holly did the same.

Cat turned to follow the two of them, but froze when she heard the whine of an engine coming in fast.

I knew you'd come, kitten.

A white helicopter with a navy stripe skimmed the treetops. It started to slow, then banked turning away from the carnage below.

"What are you doing? I told you to land!"

Cat could hear the argument through her link with Jack.

"It's a goddamned war zone down there!" The pilot announced. "I'm not—"

"You will do as your told or you will die."

"You won't shoot me." The pilot's voice was certain. "We'd crash."

Cat heard the sound of gunshots in her head, and the pilot's scream of pain.

"Now," Jack's voice was suave, utterly calm. "Land the helicopter now and I'll heal your wounds. If you don't, you'll die."

The copter turned, its path uneven, as though the pilot were struggling against the controls. He probably was. Cat hadn't gotten a visual along with the conversation, but Jack was definitely cold-blooded enough to do exactly what he said. Particularly since he was absolutely certain in his own mind that *he*, at least, would survive a crash.

I take it Yusef and the others failed? How very annoying. Still, we're here and that's what really matters.

The helicopter was beginning to settle toward the pad. Cat watched as the side door opened. She wanted, *needed* to move, but her muscles simply refused to obey even the simplest commands.

The aircraft was still airborne when an armed guard opened the door. He drew his weapon, aiming it in Cat's direction, only to have Jack swat it away. "She is *mine*."

Cat wanted to scream in frustration, shout for help, but even her vocal cords seemed frozen.

She could see Jack's thoughts clearly now. This wasn't about her. It never had been. It was all an elaborate ruse. He'd chosen to attack her, to kill her parents *so that she would mate to Raphael*. He planned to torture her for days, killing her exquisitely slowly, savoring the pain it would cause her mate. Raphael would die with the knowledge that it was his love that killed his mate.

She watched in horror as Jack shifted forms, preparing to jump. In the distance she heard a deep *whump,* saw a small dark object fly through the open door of the helicopter.

There were male shouts from the chopper. Jack and the guard dived through the open door. They landed badly on the hard ground, but scrambled away with amazing speed, just as an explosion blew the rear portion of the helicopter away, sending shrapnel flying.

She could move! Cat dived behind a boulder as the helicopter seemed to scream in its death knell, the propellers tearing viciously through trees and dirt as it spun in an out-of-control cartwheel before slamming to a stop against unforgiving rock and shattering.

Watching in horror she saw the rear propeller fly loose, beheading the bodyguard. Blood sprayed in an arc from the severed arteries in his neck. It seemed to take forever for his body to crumple to the ground.

She looked frantically for Jack, finding him beneath a chunk of the engine block. He struggled to free himself, but the bottom half of his body wasn't moving

She shifted to human form, staring down at the huge, spotted cat that had haunted her nightmares.

You don't have the balls. Jack's eyes gleamed with malice. It would be cold-blooded murder.

He was stalling. She could see it in his mind. Given a few minutes he would heal. She felt him gathering his strength to try to control her body as he had a few minutes before, but it was still too soon.

She bent down, retrieving the gun from the guard's corpse. She checked to make sure the safety was off, and that it was loaded. By the time she'd taken the few steps back to where she'd left him, Jack was looking stronger, almost able to move. His mind beat against her shields.

"Cat—" She heard Raphael moving behind her. She knew he wanted her to let him be the one to end it. But she couldn't do that, for so very, many reasons.

"No, Raphael. This is mine."

The great cat's eyes followed her as she stepped close to him. She aimed the gun at the center of his massive chest. This, is for my parents, Brad, and the rest. She pulled the trigger. Blood and meat exploded from the animal's chest as the bullet found his heart. She aimed a second time, focusing on a spot between his blazing green eyes. This—she pulled the trigger—is for me.

Chapter Forty-three

THE CROWD GATHERED again in the clearing where the sever-ance and binding ceremonies had been held just a few short days ago. Rumors ran rampant. A number of pack members were missing. Anger flowed and ebbed as humans and wolves millcd nervously around. Raphael had called them, mind-to-mind. They obeyed, but they were not happy about it.

Are you sure you want to do this?

Cat stood, holding hands with Raphael in the deep shadows at the edge of the clearing. Tonight they were dressed alike, in unrelieved black.

I *need* to do this, Raphael corrected her. His expression was grim. The wolves in the clearing weren't the only ones who were angry. Cat just hoped there wouldn't be a fight. She wasn't sure either she or Raphael were up to it right now.

She was just about to ask what they were waiting for when she saw a familiar figure passing through the woods to join them. Ahmad by himself. The power surrounding him was enough to choke on.

You invited *him*?

I needed a witness. Raphael inclined his head in greeting.

Ahmad nodded in response. There was no mockery in his ex-pression. "You survived. Congratulations."

"Yes. We did. Thank you for coming."

"My pleasure." There was a hint of wicked amusement in his eyes then. Raphael ignored it, refusing the bait.

Let's do this.

With a tingle of power the aversion he'd set flared to life. Ahmad flicked his tongue, tasting the air.

In unison Raphael and Cat stepped out of the shadows. They moved across the clearing by the light of the moon and the distant stars. The crowd parted and silenced as they passed. It was a weighted stillness, the breathless tension of an animal poised to attack.

He climbed to the top of the boulder and helped Cat to do the same. Ahmad stood at its base turning sideways to keep both the boulder and the crowd in his line of sight.

All eyes were on Raphael as he released Cat's hand and took a small step to the edge of the huge stone. When he spoke, his voice carried clearly through the cold night air, reaching every last person gathered.

"A healthy pack functions through trust, teamwork, and mutual respect." He turned, looking at familiar faces in the crowd. Cat felt his sadness, anger, and pain at their betrayal. "I have spent decades of my life in Boulder, as a pack member, as Lucas's Second. I would have dedicated my life to doing what I believed was best for the pack—lived, and died, for its members." The silence was complete. Even the wind had stilled.

Raphael couldn't keep the bitterness from his voice. "But I was betrayed. My own people delivered my niece, me, and my mate into the hands of my worst enemy because they *wanted* us dead." Again he looked out at the crowd, many of whom would no longer meet his gaze, their eyes downcast. And yet there were others who stood straight, eyes shining with defiance.

"Those who did the actual deed are no longer with us." Raphael's eyes blazed with his anger. "But what of the others: so many others, who knew of the plan, but chose to do *nothing*?"

He turned and Cat stepped forward, into the curve of his arm. They stood in front of the crowd for a long, silent moment. Only Cat was close enough to see the tears that threatened.

"There are no secrets in a pack. Like it or no, word travels from member to member. I believe that nearly every wolf in this clearing *knew* what was planned for my mate and me and chose not to interfere." Raphael looked down to where Jake stood. His pain was a living, breathing thing. "Only *one* person tried to warn me, came to fight by my side." The crowd murmured at that.

Cat felt Raphael gather his strength. "You say I must choose. I cannot be your leader and be with Cat. I choose Cat. You rejected me. Now I reject you. As of this moment, I am no longer your Alpha. I am no longer of the Boulder pack." With a gesture, Raphael broke the bond which tied him to the pack, then leapt down from the rock and turned to help Cat descend. They passed through the crowd as they came.

Cat could hear bloody fights breaking out in their wake, as various wolves tried to claim the throne. She didn't turn. She didn't want to know.

Chapter Forty-four

RAPHAEL PICKED UP the phone on the third ring. It took him that long to get to the damned thing. Healing ability be damned, he *hurt*. But it was worth it. Oh, hell yeah. Despite the loss of the pack and the myriad of problems facing him, Raphael couldn't keep from grinning.

"Ramirez."

"Raphael, it's Carli, from Albuquerque."

"Hi, Carli. It's been a long time. What can I do for you?"

"Well," she sounded sheepish. "I'm not sure. I got the weirdest call this morning. Some woman who claimed to be Amber Wingate's twin sister called my private cell number and told me to ring you. She said we were the solution to each other's problems."

Raphael's mouth went dry. He managed to choke out the word "Really? *What* problem?"

"Well, that's what's weird. Last night Sam Meade challenged Jordan for the top spot. Neither one of them survived. The pack is in shock, and none of the other males in the pack are even alphic. I know your pack has a lot of strong males, and—"

"It's not my pack anymore," Raphael said softly.

"What?"

"I'm mated to a jaguar. They told me to choose. I chose my mate."

"Oh, my *God*." Carli's voice quivered with excitement. "Raphael, you wouldn't consider . . . I mean, we're really small, and none of us are particularly powerful, but—" She was babbling.

"We'd have no problem with your lady. None. I swear. And the climate's warm, which is great for a jungle cat."

Raphael put his hand over the speaker to the phone and turned to Cat. "Sweetheart, what do you think about moving to Albuquerque?"

CARLI PULLED THE SUV off of the main road into a small subdivision. The houses were spaced far apart, each elegant home sitting on at least a three- or four-acre lot. They followed the curve until the road dead-ended in a circular court, the only house a gorgeous sprawling building of tan stone and weathered timbers, with a peaked cathedral-style roof and huge triple-paned windows to let in light, but minimize the heat.

She parked among a crowd of vehicles. As Raphael climbed from the car he could hear splashing and the sound of children playing. Would he hear children of his own splashing in a pool someday soon? He surely hoped so.

He smiled as he helped Cat out of the SUV, admiring the gold and diamond ring gracing her finger. She would have to return to Denver soon, but she insisted on being here with him today to see the house and meet Carli.

He hated that she would have to leave for a few weeks, but there was a lot to do. Arrangements had to be made for the running of her father's business; then there were the closing for the sales of Violet's house, his own, and the apartment in Denver. Ned had agreed to let Raven buy the mountain residence—just as long as the Boulder pack *never* had any part of it. Raphael had been surprised at how readily his son had agreed. Then again, he'd been appalled when he'd found out their part in the plot against Holly and his father.

Raphael was distracted by the sound of adult voices, too, carrying from behind the building. He raised an eyebrow in inquiry. Carli only laughed, her dark eyes sparkling. "They're here!" she shouted ahead of them. He and Cat looked at each other in surprise.

"About damned time!"

Raphael recognized that voice. *"Ivan?"*

Carli nodded happily. "And Betty, Star and Raven, and Lucas, and Charles and Amber, and—"

"Raphael! Did you know about this?" Cat's voice was filled with excitement.

He shook his head in confusion. "Didn't have a clue."

Their steps quickened as Carli led him along a stone walkway from the driveway to a wide front porch, already furnished with Raphael's own chairs.

A dozen people he didn't know turned as he and Cat stepped through the gate to the back yard. They all, men, women and several children, immediately dropped to one knee and lowered their gaze to the ground. Carli's solemn voice cut through his surprise. "The whole pack asked to be here." She likewise bowed low as Lucas walked through the doorway, a plate overflowing with rare buffalo steak in each hand.

Raphael and Cat looked at each other, neither certain what to say or do.

Lucas's voice was filled with both pride and sorrow as he handed them each a plate. "Welcome to your new pack, Alpha Ramirez. May you and your mate forever rule in peace."